CW01521535

Chapter C

Sinclair Ranch, North Carolina, ____

The present war in Afghanistan began on October 7, 2001when the United States, the United Kingdom, and an Afghan military organisation called the United Front (Northern Alliance), launched Operation Enduring Freedom. With no end to the war in sight, the United States and NATO countries aligned against the Taliban experience increasing pressure from politicians of all stripes to find a lasting solution. Serving to underscore the urgent need for a new initiative is the heart-wrenching spectacle of body bags being unloaded from military aircraft at airports in Europe and the United States. In the intervening time, cries of "Congress, why don't you do your duty and bring our troops home?" is an oft heard plea on the part of disaffected families gathered outside the Capitol in Washington DC.

Meanwhile, in Afghanistan, the so-called "New Taliban" studiously undermines government attempts to bring about a negotiated settlement (even with Taliban participation). They routinely brainwash impressionable Afghan youths to take up an ideological cause which is nothing short of a perversion of Islam that could turn the troubled nation into an Islamic caliphate with support from ISIS foreign fighters.

*

Gazing out of his ground-level study window, Charles Sinclair believes the U.S. government will never allow the New Taliban to establish an enhanced presence in Afghanistan. This is supported by his implicit faith in his son, U.S. Marine Lt. Abdul Sinclair, Commander Tariq Hasan Zahir, and other well-meaning combatants dedicated to finding a peaceful solution.

Yet, at this juncture in life, he's content with the way things are at the ranch. Just a few weeks back, his North Carolina residence was as silent as a grave. Now, his sprawling ranch house and grounds vibrate to the animated chatter of young folk enjoying a period of freedom a world away from the tribulations of a war-weary Afghanistan.

Margaret, Charles's housekeeper, makes a point of chatting amiably with Naoma and Mena discussing their contrasting lifestyles. In fact, everyone present in the ranch house is on a voyage of discovery. Charles Sinclair never dreamt of having so many wonderful people in his life at the same time and all with so much to contribute.

With great pride, he watched as his son Abdul engaged in a rough-and-tumble interlude with daughter Sarah, and adopted son Khalil, now a young teenager; along with Ahktar who is of similar age to Khalil and a ward of the commander's with special skills in grooming horses. Also studying the youngsters at play is the commander's fourteen-year-old daughter Jamila slowly piecing together her life after being sexually assaulted months earlier in Afghanistan at the residence of the governor of Bagram district.

Observing granddaughter Sarah with equal pride, Charles reminisced about the young girl's mother, Syrah, and how proud she would have been to see her beautiful daughter at this impressionable phase of her life. Sarah seemed to have grown more mature since the others arrived at the ranch and looked happier than ever displaying greater confidence in her role at the centre of a great deal of love and attention. And Naoma clearly enjoyed mothering the young girl.

Meanwhile, Madam Mena was making the most of her time with Janan, her long-lost son who today answers to the grand title of Taliban Field Commander Tariq Hasan Zahir. For the commander's mother, it's more than a dream come true, as she

2

had almost given up hope of ever being reunited with him. Finding great joy in her life in place of years of heartache and sorrow had helped her blossom into a handsome woman.

Tariq was equally relaxed, content, and heartened after being reunited with his mother and daughter. And as for his good friend Abdul, the commander saw before him a man he admired and respected even as an enemy of the Taliban. To him he was a brother-in-arms. During their time in Afghanistan, both had grown closer to the point that one would give his life for the other. It was a bond of amity that had grown out of adversity. Though difficult to put into words, it demonstrated that good men, even on opposing sides of a conflict, can find common ground if they can open their hearts and minds.

The shrill ring of a telephone broke the magic of the moment and the ranch owner's bout of daydreaming ended abruptly. Slightly irritated at having his privacy disturbed, he grabbed at the phone, "Charles Sinclair speaking...how can I help you?"

"Hello Charles, Chris Maxwell here. I know you're pretty tied up, but I want to discuss something with you face to face...tomorrow, please, if that's all right with you. Let's say 1200; we can have lunch in the officers' mess."

The general's unexpected call from Fort Bragg brought back the spectre of realism. Intuitively Sinclair felt his son Abdul was about to be recalled for duty. That meant Afghanistan and more goodbyes. It was to be expected but not readily or easily accepted. But orders are orders that must be obeyed.

"Sure, general, I can be at Fort Bragg by noon. Thank you, sir," he added, his voice sounding robotic as the words slipped from his lips.

"Great…one more thing: don't mention this to anyone please. Keep it between ourselves for now and I'll explain more tomorrow."

No stranger to military life, Sinclair knew better than to press a four-star general for details. His entire ranch functioned under armed security. All communications were monitored. But that didn't prevent him from wondering why his presence at Fort Bragg was needed so urgently. It didn't prey on his mind for long. Suddenly, the door of his study burst open to admit two overexcited kids intent on carrying out their boisterous antics in his presence. Sarah and Khalil tumbled in, both laughing fit to burst. Staring at the pair, his heart swelled with a feeling of deep gratitude. Sarah, a bundle of joy, was obviously head over heels in love with her big brother Khalil. They bonded so well together it brought home to Charles that having everyone staying at the ranch together brought happiness all round – and security.

"Grandad," Sarah piped up, "may we have another mule to keep Atuallah company?" His enthusiastic granddaughter was brimming with excitement which Charles found infectious - even compelling. Smiling, he said, "That's a very interesting question young lady. But first, let me ask you a question: what makes you think Atuallah is lonely? She already leads a wonderful life, and the ranch horses keep her company - not to mention her four, devoted, two-legged friends looking after her every need," he teased, a twinkle in his eye.

"Yes, we do understand grandfather," Khalil chipped in, "but it would be nice for her to have a four-legged friend."

Sarah piped up again, "Grandpa the Quarter horses are so much bigger than mules, and they are regularly taken out for exercise. Atuallah is always left behind in the paddock all alone," she added, determined to have her own way. Charles suspected he wasn't going to win the argument, so he changed

4

the subject. "Children, how would you like to have a picnic in the hills tomorrow? You will be able to ride out there together and maybe take Atuallah with you."

It seemed a very good idea and the boisterous duo paused to consider grandfather's tempting invitation.

"May I take Atuallah on a lead reign?" Khalil asked, looking at Sarah for moral support.

Clearly grandfather's idea resonated with both youngsters. Smiling, and heaving a sigh of relief at having solved two problems at one go, Charles left them arguing happily about who would take Atuallah on a lead reign. He figured that with much of the family away on a trip and the children temporarily distracted regarding a permanent friend for Atuallah, he could concentrate on his trip to Fort Bragg.

That same evening, when the children dropped by the stables to bed down Atuallah for the night, and the ladies had retired to the drawing room to chat among themselves, Charles addressed the men seated around the dining room table.

"Tomorrow, I have some urgent business to attend to and will be away from the ranch until mid-afternoon. That being so," he added, turning to Abdul, "I suggest it would be interesting for our guests to explore the ranch's surrounding areas. Earlier, I promised the children they could ride horses into the hills and enjoy a picnic. What do you think son?"

"Dad, I suspect we don't have a great deal of choice in the matter," Abdul responded, a quizzical grin playing around the corners of his mouth. "To be honest with you, neither Tariq nor I have heard nothing other than children arguing about who would be in charge of Atuallah when they head for the hills."

"Exactly! Well, the way I see it, it's either that or we face up to your children's request for a companion mule for Atuallah. That's our choice gentlemen," he added, looking Abdul and Tariq squarely in the eyes.

"We quite understand," Tariq said supportively, "and I am sure we'll find out how that ends soon enough."

Abdul picked up on a previous exchange debating the importance of Mena being appropriately attired. "It seems we must convince Madam Mena to dress for the occasion. Her usual, everyday attire would attract too much attention and could contravene military security requirements. Even the security guards must wear ranchero outfits. By the way, I'll make sure they are made aware of the picnic plans," he added, addressing his father.

The men were only too aware that for the foreseeable future the ranch would be under the tightest security. Each person's arrival must remain a closely guarded secret and that put Fort Bragg and the Sinclair ranch off limits to the media until further notice. From the arrival of Commander Zahir and Lieutenant Sinclair, and until their departure to complete their mission, security must remain a top priority.

"Why don't you leave the question of Mena's leisure attire to me?" Charles smiled, "I can be very persuasive sometimes!" Secretly, he was pleased his diversionary plan had gone down well. That done, he turned his attention to his business meeting with General Maxwell.

*

Charles Sinclair's uneventful drive to Fort Bragg got him there in good time for his noon appointment and General Maxwell was on hand to meet him. Together they walked to the officers' mess for lunch.

"Good to see you Charles, I trust all's well at the ranch?"

"Sure is, general. We're all getting along just fine," he replied. "But I must say I would welcome a break from having to satisfy various demands by my guests." Thereafter, both men engaged in small talk about the ranch and Sinclair's guests.

In his own good time, the general eventually got to the point of the meeting. "With regard to accommodation, are you operating at full capacity at your ranch Charles?"

"Interesting question general which I hadn't anticipated. The short answer is no. I still have one wing of the ranch house unoccupied. Why do you ask?"

"Let me bring you up to speed…not here…in my office," he proposed, as both men got up to leave the mess. Curiosity aroused, Sinclair followed the general into his office. "There's someone I want you to meet and he should be here by now."

On cue, the general's aide opened the door and both men stepped into the office. Sinclair observed a man dressed in military fatigues. He was sitting in a chair with his back to the door. He got up and turned to face Charles Sinclair.

"Hello Charles," the visitor smiled, reaching forward to grasp the ranch owner by the hand.

"I can't believe it!" a totally surprised Sinclair declared. "My dear friend Farez Malikzai as I live and breathe." Taken aback, he stared incredulously at the man across from him -- the renowned *malik* (headman) of the Afghan village of Marwah. Standing before him was someone he liked and respected for many reasons particularly for his dedicated help when his adopted grandson Khalil needed it most.

"Sorry if I surprised you my friend. The last time we met, you will surely recall, I was taking care of Khalil who was waiting to meet his grandfather for the first time," Farez remarked,

7

laughing at the thought. This time, Charles, I'm here for a very different reason," he added as the two men embraced warmly.

"I simply can't believe my eyes. Tell me my dear friend, how are you? How is your health? Have you quite recovered from your ordeal?" Sinclair asked without pausing for breath, at once realising that General Maxwell's talk about accommodation at the ranch may possibly include Farez and his need to regain full health.

Interposing, at what he considered an opportune moment, the general said, "Allow me to cut in if you don't mind and explain what's going on."

Taking a seat, Charles Sinclair listened intently as General Maxwell explained Farez's medical condition following another bout of surgery at the same military hospital where Khalil was treated for his wounds after being injured in an IED blast at Bagram Air Base.

"Advice from the hospital urges Farez to take a long convalescence somewhere safe. As you know, Charles, we have assessed your ranch and found it not only the safest place right now but ideally suited to help the esteemed malik of Marwah village recuperate," he said, smiling at Farez. "Of course, we'd assign increased security personnel disguised as rancheros. Being in the company of Naoma, Ahktar and other people he loves," he added, looking directly at Farez, "would help speed up this special man's recovery would you not agree?"

"Not only do I agree, Chris, I insist Farez stays at my ranch for as long as you, and he, deem it necessary."

"Excellent. One week from now I will inform Commander Zahir and your son of this new arrangement. For now," the general added, as Charles Sinclair got up to leave, "please say nothing of what's been discussed today. We must maintain tight security."

*

Back home, Charles immediately inspected the vacant wing of the ranch house to see what was required to prepare it for a special guest. The picnic party hadn't returned so he had adequate time to prewarn Margaret of what he required. However, his deliberations were cut short by the sound of excited voices and much laughter. Clearly, someone's day had gone well.

*

Charles Sinclair had much on his mind, which did not escape the attention of Abdul and Tariq. Later, after their evening meal, and the children were in bed, blissfully happy but exhausted, Tariq approached his host.

"Charles, I am curious to understand how you managed to persuade my mother to dress like a ranch hand," he asked as Abdul hid his face behind his hands to conceal a broad grin." Nobody would have recognised her under that huge Stetson. She certainly looked – and I dare say felt – like the boss of the prairie or should I say boss of the hills?"

"I can assure you Tariq, and you too Abdul, it wasn't at all humorous or the least bit straightforward. We struck a deal – a very tough deal in my opinion – that she would agree to wear the ranchero outfit at my request -- Stetson and all -- if I agreed to buy a stablemate for Atuallah. Boy, such a hard bargain!"

Clearly, the children had successfully persuaded the formidable Madam Mena to support them in their quest. Before anyone could react, loud laughter from inside the ranch house coincided with a satisfied grunt from a privileged mule in a nearby stable.

*

Two weeks later, Charles Sinclair received a heads-up phone call from General Maxwell explaining that Commander Zahir and Lieutenant Sinclair had been ordered to report to Fort Bragg. They were to be reunited with Farez Malikzai whose relocation to the ranch could go ahead as planned. Naoma and the children were not to be informed until Farez arrived at the ranch so everyone could share a joyous reunion at the same time.

If was time to check with Margaret regarding the guests' accommodation in the empty wing.

"Did you ask me to make up all the beds in the empty wing sir?" Margaret asked, concerned she may have misunderstood her boss's requirements.

"Yes please ...all the beds Margaret. That way we are prepared for any eventuality. And, Margaret, I think it's about time you started addressing me as Charles. Everyone else does and I don't see any reason why you should be the exception to the rule after all the years we've been together."

She blushed but was nonetheless pleased to be recognised. "Very well, sir...I mean Charles," she said shyly which was not in keeping with the Margaret he had come to know over the years.

"Before you leave, Charles...may I ask when we might expect more guests?"

"Fairly soon. I just want to make sure everything is shipshape and in good order," he replied, leaving her to make a final check on arrangements.

*

Lieutenant Abdul Sinclair and Commander Tariq Hasan Zahir were incommunicado during the drive to Fort Bragg. Each had but a single thought after the previous evening's call from General Maxwell. While unsure of what lay ahead, they were quite certain of what they were leaving behind. Both men had taken a welcome break from the pressures of being a part of Afghanistan's unending war yet were only too aware their welcome respite from the conflict had to end sooner or later.

Ushered into the outer officer by the general's aide, they patiently waited to be summoned into the COs presence. They didn't have long to wait. Entering the general's office, they walked slowly towards General Maxwell, stood to attention and saluted. Standing behind his desk, and slightly blocking the view of another uniformed man, the general returned the salute.

"Commander…Lieutenant…at ease. I ordered you here today for one very special reason," he explained, "something that is probably furthest from your thoughts at this time," he added. "I have someone with me you will be pleased to meet. Farez…" the general said, stepping aside to reveal the smiling figure of Farez Malikzai, "I believe you're acquainted with these two gentlemen."

Arms outstretched, Farez walked towards Abdul and Tariq. All three men struggled to find the appropriate words of welcome. Emotions took hold as three brothers-in-arms embraced and, in that poignant moment, unashamedly shed tears of joy.

Tariq, his jubilation tinged with a sense of guilt, let his emotions get the better of him.

"Farez, my dear brother, can you ever forgive me? I was the one who should have borne the brunt of the attack against you. I will never forgive myself for what you have suffered because of my failure to act."

"You must not harbour such dark thoughts brother Tariq. I take responsibility for my actions and for my injuries. I failed to follow your orders for which I give thanks to Allah. Otherwise we would not be standing here today."

General Maxwell excused himself, stepping out of the office to allow three comrades some time alone. Not once, throughout his long and distinguished military service, had he encountered such a strong bond of kinship; it was something he not only admired but knew, in his heart, he would always remember. As a soldier, he could sense the understanding and compassion that bound together this special trio.

Back after his strategic break, the general ordered the men to be seated.

"Gentlemen, there will be time later to reminisce more fully," he cautioned, his tone serious, "but right now we have something quite important to address. First off, you need to know that Charles Sinclair is aware of today's plan to bring the three of you together. We discussed it a couple of weeks ago when I consulted with him about finding a safe place for Farez Malikzai to convalesce. Without hesitation he agreed to offer accommodation at his ranch. Our view is he's safer there than in the hospital which is open to visitors.

"No-one knows the three of you are here and that's how it must stay until we are ready to make our next move. High level talks are taking place and I expect we will have a plan to work on quite soon. Until then, continue with your well-earned break. I intend to hold further discussions to pick-up on other matters we discussed previously such as sourcing suitable educational facilities for Khalil, Ahktar, and Jamila. For the time being they will all have security coverage and we will encourage them to keep a low profile to make everyone's life easier. I hope that clears up any residual concerns you may have. Any questions?"

No one commented so the general pressed on with the meeting.

"Let's take Khalil's case: he is an American citizen by adoption," he stressed, as Abdul nodded. "That was a good move, so others may consider applying for American citizenship in due course.

"In time," he added, turning to Commander Zahir, "I hope your ambition to become an ambassador for your country is realised. Meanwhile, we must protect your mother and daughter on the assumption they may never be able to return to Afghanistan, at least not in the foreseeable future.

"The same goes for you Farez…and Naoma, and Ahktar who could also be targeted. So, give this some serious thought. It is Uncle Sam's intention to protect you all," he added, knowing that later all three would get into a huddle to discuss General Maxwell's advice.

"Finally, I have two surprise packages to deliver then I will bring this meeting to a close," the general announced, pressing a buzzer on his desk. The office door opened to reveal a smiling Noori, Commander Zahir's dedicated follower, and Shanaz, the malik's faithful ward who had given of her time attending to the commander's daughter Jamila as she recovered from being sexually abused at the governor's residence. Shanaz walked towards Commander Zahir. She had eyes for no-one else present, and no-one present was a bit surprised.

"Mister Sinclair has agreed to keep the ladies and children indoors at the ranch tomorrow pending my special delivery," the general stated, clearly feeling quite proud of his plan. "Farez, Noori, and Shanaz will arrive at the ranch in a horsebox in the company of a mule destined to be Atuallah's companion," he said proudly. "The idea came to me when I was informed that Madam Mena would only agree to wearing a ranchero outfit if Charles Sinclair promised the children to buy them a mule to keep Atuallah company. I decide to go along with this form of blackmail and use a horsebox to deliver our other three VIPs," he concluded, to a raft of laughter.

"General, it appears Atuallah is still working her magic," Abdul shouted above the noise of laughter, "and we can all be grateful for that!"

***

Chapter Two

Watching from the ranch's driveway, Charles Sinclair waited until the military staff car was out of sight. It was a moment he'd dreaded ever since Abdul arrived back in the States. He had hoped they would have had a little more time together. But it was inevitable that sooner or later his son would be recalled to duty to address unfinished business waiting for him in Afghanistan. Sarah wanted her father to stay home forever, but at least she was happy to have the company of Khalil, her newly adopted brother.

As for Ahktar and Jamila, both were an added joy in Sarah's life. Their lively interaction confirmed they were a part of each other's lives. Sarah was trying to master a language quite foreign to her, and Ahktar and Jamila were familiarising themselves with American expressions by getting familiar with hotdogs, burgers, cokes, and popcorn.

Marvelling at the adaptability of children, and how they could take everything in their stride, Charles was at least thankful they would be staying at the ranch along with the ladies and Farez Malikzai. A change in their habitat had brought joy to everyone and hope there'd be time to explore newfound freedoms and grow and develop in a place of relative safety as their future was determined.

"Now, now Mr Charles," Margaret chided, as she watched her employer from the open door of his study. Years together told her his mind was bursting with conflicting emotions. Throughout life, he had experienced joy and sorrow including the overwhelming loss of his wife to cancer. He had celebrated the day Abdul married Syrah, the love of his life, only to lose her giving birth to Sarah. Worse, Abdul was on an overseas tour of duty when it happened, and Charles had to shoulder the burden alone.

Margaret was only too delighted to be invited to become his housekeeper with the added duty of caring for Sarah, which began soon after she was born. Since then, Margaret has loved her as if she were her own child. Consequently, she and Sinclair senior shared a close and special relationship. Indeed, Charles relied on her implicitly and Margaret was more than happy to oblige.

"I guess I can see what's on your mind, Margaret," he declared, smiling, "but it will be harder this time because I'm not getting any younger. I'd dearly love to have more time to share with my son," he added, gazing appreciatively at his housekeeper and wondering how on earth he could have coped without this incomparable woman now proudly standing in his den. He marvelled at how she had picked up the broken pieces of his life to become a very dear and valued soul.

"What if something awful should happen to Abdul," he asked, his eyes fixed on the ceiling of his study.

"Nothing's going to happen to Abdul, so stop this nonsense right now!" Margaret proclaimed in the same commanding tone of voice she used when Sarah played up.

Charles knew he was being admonished, but he accepted it – even liked it – coming from his faithful housekeeper.

"Very well Margaret. I will strike a bargain with you. I will stop this nonsense, as you call it, if you drop the 'mister'. Charles will do from now on, is that understood?"

*

Bang on time, Commander Zahir and Lieutenant Sinclair entered General Maxwell's office at Fort Bragg. To their surprise, he was not alone. Standing with his back to them and gazing out of the office window was a tall, broad-shouldered man. As General Maxwell prepared to address his visitors, the tall man turned to face everyone, at the same time revealing an impressive array of decorations and insignia on his dress uniform.

"Good morning…at ease Commander Zahir, Lieutenant Sinclair," ordered General Maxwell by way of welcome. First off, may I present General Austin Miller who is taking over as CO of U.S. and NATO forces in Afghanistan from soon-to-retire General Nicholson. General Miller has extensive experience and outstanding service with Joint Special Operations Command."

"It's a pleasure, gentlemen," the bemedaled general said with great emphasis, "I have been following your exploits with a deal of interest. You are to be congratulated on what you have accomplished through combined efforts. I am aware, as are you, that we have some unfinished business in Afghanistan, and I look forward to working with you to bring that to a close. I came today to assure you of that. For now, you must excuse me," he said, addressing General Maxwell, "as I have a pressing appointment with the Department of Defense." With that, he disappeared without another word. But it was clear to Tariq and Abdul that they had made their mark during their time in Afghanistan and their efforts were appreciated.

"Okay gentlemen…be seated…so now you know General Miller who will be a key player in what comes next. And that's why you are here today," General Maxwell explained, reaching for the phone on his desk. "No further calls sergeant," he ordered before taking his seat.

"So, let's get at it," he proposed, grabbing a notepad from his desk. "I guess you're itching to get back into action. Having that slippery governor of Bagram district evade you must be a huge disappointment – and not just to you guys," he added, smiling at Tariq and Abdul who remained expressionless. It was a sore subject and neither man could find any humour in it.

"Let's be clear; we will bring him to justice," the general said reassuringly, "and your efforts will be fully supported. I asked General Miller to join us today to demonstrate his commitment and you heard what he had to say. But there is something else we must discuss," he stressed, "and that's the big picture which is of prime importance."

Neither man deigned to comment preferring to wait for the general to explain exactly what was considered more important than bringing to book the manipulative and evil governor who had no respect for anyone and who took great pleasure in the suffering of others.

"By big picture I mean we have more than just the governor to track down. But I'll get to that in a moment. General Miller, who takes over from General Nicholson with immediate effect, wanted to size you up," he said, looking first at Commander Zahir and then at Lieutenant Sinclair. "You will find his approach different from that of his predecessor. And there's a good reason for that. Department of Defense officials describe him as a straight shooter who is always approachable. Besides, he has extensive knowledge of the different warring factions in Afghanistan and the geopolitical relationships with the country's neighbours particularly Pakistan, Russia, and Iran. Deteriorating relations with these three countries, so

17

Pentagon thinking goes, will deepen as they intensify their meddling in Afghan's unending war in a drive to punish the U.S.

"To that point, we know Pakistan continues to shelter insurgency leaders and refuses to use its influence to curb recent Taliban momentum. Both Russia and Iran, we believe, are stepping-up aid to the Taliban. This has created a fragile environment and given a new shape to routine life in Afghanistan.

Commander Zahir nodded his agreement; he was beginning to get the picture...the bigger picture. "Also, general, we can include the governor who we think is in Pakistan promoting insurgency on the part of the New Taliban." Tariq found it incredulous that this odious creep, who had affected the commander's life for years, could be successful in commanding the attention of others and inciting them to fight.

"Make no mistake Commander Zahir," the general responded, "he has played a very clever game. I have no doubt he's a coward, but he's also a man crazy for power. And he will do whatever he has to do to become a key figure in Afghanistan's future. Think of the years he spent sanctioning the abuse of women in camps. And as you know from personal experience, he gets what he wants by abducting family members and using them as weapons. And those so-called weekends of entertainment during his tenure as governor of Bagram were to lure targeted guests into compromising situations to blackmail them into doing his bidding.

"Even the juvenile detention centre in Kabul is full of young boys considered national security threats. Most were charged with carrying, planting, or wearing explosive devices as would-be suicide bombers. A dilemma facing Afghanistan's penal services is what will become of these children after they serve their sentences. By the time they reach adulthood they could spread mayhem. Sadly, many will be welcomed by the New Taliban in Pakistan and go back to fighting against the Kabul government."

Getting to his feet, Abdul said, "General, if I may ask, how do you see our role when we return to Afghanistan? Neither the commander nor I can rest until we have brought the governor to justice," he added, looking at Tariq for support.

"I understand how you feel lieutenant and I know it's important for both of you to get back into the fight. But we must do this by the book. The governor is wanted for what amounts to war crimes and the Afghan government agrees with the United States that he must be tried, and justice be seen to be served.

"But as you indicated, general, this governor is very resourceful and knows he's safer if he stays in Pakistan," Abdul mused.

"Precisely gentlemen, and that's why General Miller is today meeting with the Department of Defense. We'll get feedback within twenty-four hours and you will then have your orders," he promised, "so I suggest you make the most of what downtime you have left."

Abdul didn't get a straight answer to his question, but both men knew something big – as in bigger picture – was in the works. Until then, a few more days at the ranch would prove a welcome bonus.

*

The drive back to the ranch was conducted in silence, both men deep in thought. The opportunity to spend more quality time with loved ones was a luxury by any measure. Abdul had bonded with daughter Sarah in the short time they were together. And when the time comes to leave, he will have the comfort of knowing she has the companionship of her new brother Khalil, and the friendship of Jamila and Ahktar.

Moreover, his father will have the amiable companionship of everyone left behind when he and Tariq make their way back to Afghanistan to attend to unfinished business. Tariq's thought process was similar: he was grateful his mother and daughter were now in a safe and secure location leaving him to address the task at hand without having to worry about those he'd be leaving behind.

*

Twenty-four hours later, Commander Zahir and Lieutenant Sinclair were back in General Maxwell's office, this time to embark upon the first stage of their return to Afghanistan, unaware this would be the greatest challenge they had ever faced.

 Expressing goodbyes had been difficult and those remaining at the Sinclair ranch in Hillsborough were consumed with sadness. Khalil had pleaded to join his father and Commander Zahir, but Abdul convinced him he must look after his sister and grandfather.

"Not only that Khalil," Abdul had cautioned, smiling at the boy, "you have to attend school and expand your knowledge. Remember what I said to you in Afghanistan; I want you to fulfil all your dreams for the future. I just know you will make me even prouder than I am at this moment," he added, embracing the boy. "You are the most wonderful son a father could have, and I am relying on you to walk in my footsteps while I'm away," he said, his heart fit to burst. He had meant every word; this brave young boy meant the world to him.

Tariq also had a heavy heart thinking about the lost years without the company of his mother or daughter. Then there was the joy of being reunited. And now, after what seemed just a moment in time, he had yet again to leave them. His only consolation was they were free to console and comfort one another in the relative safety of the United States of America.

When he came to address Farez Malikzai, who would also be left behind, Abdul was thankful his friend would be on hand to support his father. Farez was too polite to refuse, but he was trying hard to hide his disappointment at not being able to join with Tariq and Abdul in what would be their final venture. He had as much right as anyone to secure the downfall of the governor and would dearly love to be part of the team that brings that about. It wasn't easy for him to accept he could no longer stand side-by-side with his two brothers-in-arms.

Commander Zahir sensed the malik's disappointment. "Farez, my dear brother, I fully support the idea that you stay at the ranch, and I insist you return to full fitness. Please also remember that you are a comfort to Abdul and me because we know you will care for our loved ones with help from Charles Sinclair. We rely on you my friend for us to be able to do what we must do," he added, putting his arm around the malik's shoulders. After a brief embrace among the men, Abdul and Tariq boarded the waiting military vehicle. It had begun to rain. Charles Sinclair put a hand on the malik's shoulder. Smiling, he drew him under his umbrella as they watched the car disappear in the pouring rain.

*

When General Maxwell entered the operations room at Fort Bragg Air Base, accompanied by Commander Zahir and Lieutenant Sinclair, General Miller was already there along with a handful of senior officers invited to the briefing. After introductions, instigated by General Maxwell, everyone crowded around the large meeting table to study an array of maps featuring Pakistan.

"Gentlemen, if I may have your full attention," cautioned a serious General Maxwell, "this briefing is to share reliably obtained and substantiated intelligence that the man we know as the governor of Bagram district, has been fraternising with criminal elements for years. Many of these criminals," he stressed, "have particularly unsavoury reputations. This despicable excuse for a human being has deliberately cosied-up to these disreputable characters while running prostitution and human trafficking businesses, using wives and families as pawns to manipulate distraught relatives into serving his needs." The general was angry, and it showed.

"His contacts are international criminals whose names will be withheld for the purpose of this briefing and until mission objectives are drawn-up and sanctioned. However, you all need to consider the governor's contacts in terms of their business enterprises. With help from the CIA we have identified an international arms dealer: he's a man in his early sixties affiliated with Italy's Cosa Nostra. This guy started his criminal life when quite young stealing anything that wasn't nailed down. His speciality for dealing in stolen goods caught the attention of the Sicilian mafia who got him started on selling drugs in Naples and then further afield. His work was praised by the mafia hierarchy which promoted him to section head of their international drug smuggling operations. He focused on production, transportation and cocaine sales," the general added, pausing to let it all sink in.

"Next, we have another hardened criminal, a calculating man in his seventies who would sell his own grandmother just for laughs. This guy is an international arms dealer who honed his business while attached to the Soviet Union's military intelligence unit in the 1980s. His worldwide contacts give him access to all five continents where he has a network of corporate entities. This includes the States and we have a dossier on the man which we'll share at the right time. For now, understand he is clever and sophisticated.

"He has a penchant for beautiful women. usually prostitutes, and is seen with one or more in his company whenever he hits the fleshpots of the world, which is often. This guy is loaded and maintains a jet at Bangkok International Airport for his non-stop hops around the world. Among a few other places, he keeps a condominium home in the sleazy city of Pattaya overlooking the Gulf of Thailand and fraternises with a forty-eight-year old Thai lady who proudly carries the title of The Mamasan of Thailand. Number three on our target list of dangerous, international criminals, this woman keeps him supplied with beautiful girls from her widespread trafficking business in Asia, while he supplies her with clients from his arms dealership. That's what I mean by a cosy relationship. More about her later, but you can see they are a dangerous combination." Again, General Maxwell paused to allow the seriousness of the briefing sink in.

"Gentlemen let's just say the governor's ambitions are supported by all three of these criminal elements. He sells prostitution in high circles in many countries and he can offer drugs and arms to promote himself as a mainstay of the New Taliban while hiding, as we believe he does, in Pakistan sometimes in the borderland but also in one or more cities. We may once have underestimated our wily governor but that won't happen again.

"By now gentlemen it should be clear to you why our mission may take longer than first thought. We want the governor, the drug dealer, the arms dealer, and the trafficker picked up together or as close as circumstances permit. We have enough on the governor to bring him down now but to get all four we must let the governor think all's well and that he's safe carrying on with his nefarious activities. The others are more difficult to pin down because of their high-flying lifestyles mingling with the rich and famous, and partly because they have bought themselves what we might refer to as 'life assurance'. In some cases, national law enforcement officers are in cahoots with these villains and that presents a challenge. But we're up to it," the general said, assuring all present. He then turned to address Commander Zahir and Lieutenant Sinclair.

"For this special operation, we have selected Commander Zahir and Lieutenant Sinclair as the mission's undercover agents. They will receive a separate briefing. At a later stage, we plan to use the special skills of Farez Malikzai after his convalescence. He can bring a unique perspective to the mission," the general added, detecting that both Tariq and Abdul had raised their eyebrows at the suggestion. It was something he'd anticipated; the general knew both men were concerned about Farez being exposed to more danger too soon after being badly wounded in the fight at the governor's residence.

"If I may comment sir," Abdul enquired, clearly bemused by the direction being taken by General Maxwell, "Farez Malikzai is dead as far as most people are concerned."

"Correct lieutenant. But keep in mind the governor has never seen the malik and wouldn't know him if he stood before him in the same room. That plays to our advantage. We plan to give Farez Malikzai a new occupation as a wealthy businessman, with access to a luxurious villa and the good life. A man of the world but with roots in the United States who can mix business with pleasure without questions being asked. Yes, it will require some hard work on our part, but we have someone in mind to help groom the malik. I will come to that. Farez's role will be to get to know and gain the confidence of our three international villains. In support of the mission, staff at the holiday villa will be drawn from elite SAS officers chosen and trained especially for the role.

"There are legitimate security reasons for this subterfuge. Commander Zahir is well-known in Afghanistan and Pakistan…in fact wherever the Taliban is found. So, you, commander," the general said looking directly at Tariq, "could never function undercover in those places unless you agree to a face transplant, and we're not advocating that at this time!" he added, to a bout of muffled sniggering.

"I am greatly relieved to hear that sir," a smiling Tariq responded.

"Commander, while acting undercover, you will interface with Farez Malikzai at his holiday home from time to time, out of reach of the governor and anyone else who might recognise you. That way," the general affirmed, "you, and Lieutenant Sinclair in whatever guise you find him, will be able to liaise with one another."

"The State Department is in close collaboration with the Afghanistan government which has agreed to publicly announce Commander Zahir's appointment as Afghanistan's ambassador to the United States. As his country's ambassador, Commander Zahir will be able to move freely to convey any information he receives from Lieutenant Sinclair. Though the governor will learn of the commander's ambassadorial appointment, we don't think he'll overreact as he'll assume the commander will spend most of his time in Washington," the general explained before turning to Abdul whose hand was raised.

"Sir, we need to be alert to the possibility that the governor may stage an attempt to have Commander Zahir taken out even if he's in Washington."

"Such an attack was discussed with the State Department and Homeland Security and they are working on a solution which includes having an understudy for the commander for some of his diplomatic duties. I don't want to get into the details now, but let's say our contacts in Hollywood are quite talented when it comes to creating facial likenesses and a suitable stand-in has already been identified and will be briefed in due course," the general explained, again to ripples of laughter from those assembled. "How do you see it commander?"

Tariq did not hide his disappointment. "Frankly general, I had anticipated having a more hands-on role though I do agree, sir, that in my case success depends on both keeping a low profile while acting the part. Achieving the right balance will be a challenge. Sir, I wish it to be known here, today, that I stand ready to fulfil my duties as best I can for Afghanistan."

"Well said, commander," the general offered. "And I do understand you have scores to settle with the governor for what your family suffered in the past. Be patient, you will be called upon when the time comes to strike. Before that happens, we must create a false sense of security around those we must bring to justice. Meanwhile, you have my assurance, commander, that you'll have your moment of satisfaction.

"And now we come to you lieutenant and your role," the general continued, turning his attention to Abdul who was still processing the notion that Tariq had to be hugely disappointed at being relegated to what he'd see as a supporting role.

"You have a key role to play and you must prepare accordingly. The arms dealer, whose name will be released in due course, moves in high circles. He has hiding places all around the world that he accesses using his Gulfstream jet based at Bangkok. As his jet has a range of over twelve thousand kilometres, he can meet with clients anywhere without having to put down to refuel at intermediary airports. That makes it difficult to keep a track on his movements. Intelligence suggests he has cultivated corrupt officials supporting his enterprises which means he can go to ground at a moment's notice.

"For this guy, money is no object. He has surrounded himself with handpicked bodyguards but, from what we have been able to establish so far, none have the all-round experience you have lieutenant in terms of military service, particularly in the Middle East and South Asia – not to mention your proven martial arts skills. You have an impeccable background and the necessary skills to present yourself as someone experienced in personnel protection. We will make sure you are in the right places at the right time to sell yourself as his personal bodyguard and aide.

"The Defense Department thinks it's safe to present yourself as Abdul Sinclair. The governor knows you only as Bashir Ahmadi. We may review that. You will study infiltration techniques, probably with the CIA, and your profile will describe you as a former U.S. Marine with a glowing service record which is the case. You will target the arms dealer and convince him of your disillusionment with America's foreign policies – something that has grown over time. The idea is to gain his confidence, get into his inner circle as his personal aide, and build up a case against him. We must have proof of wrongdoing, files, paper trails, recorded conversations and so forth to bring him down. The CIA will tutor you on how to do this.

"We expect our arms dealer to interface with Farez at his holiday home for social occasions and you will accompany him and take that opportunity to pass information to Commander Zahir who will be there at the same time. When the opportunity presents itself, we will stage an undercover operation to support you and Commander Zahir in extracting all the players including the governor and take everyone to Bagram Air Base. From there everyone will be flown to a destination to be decided."

General Maxwell's detailed outline of the complexities of the mission created a hush over proceedings as attendees processed the enormity of the task. Both Abdul and Tariq immediately saw the danger signs but were unfazed. They looked at one another and smiled wryly as if to say that danger was a given whenever the governor was involved. So, nothing new to worry about.

"Well, gentlemen," the general said, addressing Abdul and Tariq, "I am open to any suggestions about the outline plan you are now a part of," he added, not really expecting or wanting a response at this time.

"The key players at this stage of planning," the general continued, quelling any opportunity for a response from attendees, "are the arms dealer and the former governor of Bagram district. We have enough incriminating evidence on the human trafficker and the drugs kingpin to take them down now. But, because the governor is the main link between all of them, we must play this step by step to get them all together and extract them as a package. Got it?"

Again, General Maxwell did not pause long for comments.

"We know a bit about the human trafficker, a mercurial woman referred to as The Mamasan of Thailand. She is smuggling young men into the United States. We suspect they are being trained as suicide bombers who have been indoctrinated by the Taliban. So, if there's a 9-11-style plan in the works, we must know when and where it's likely to happen. If it hadn't struck you before, I guess you now see the potential seriousness of what we're dealing with and why I keep referring to the big picture. To our credit, we have some of these potential suicide bombers under covert surveillance. We know where to find them. But, until we take the core out of the rotten apple, we can't make our move."

There was much to think about. It was becoming clear to both Abdul and Tariq that they would not be leaving the United States for some time. They needed more briefing and training and an opportunity to study the three rogue players thus far unnamed. Tariq must be installed as Afghanistan's new ambassador to the United States; the malik must be groomed in his new role as an international businessman with a sumptuous holiday home, and Abdul must ingratiate himself to become the personal bodyguard and aide to the arms dealer and that pointed to a period of training with the CIA There was much to do.

General Maxwell dismissed everyone from the operations room apart from Commander Zahir and Lieutenant Sinclair.

"Gentlemen, your orders are to return to the ranch until summoned for daily briefings at Fort Bragg. For the next briefing, the malik will accompany you to be updated by me on the essential elements of our plan.

"I don't have to remind you that nothing of this must be discussed with family members – for their sake as much as yours. And to you, commander, when your ambassadorial appointment is announced your family must remain at the ranch. Your daughter could be recognised in a public setting. Same comment goes for Madam Mena and bear in mind the governor believes she is no longer alive.

"I understand general," Tariq acknowledged, "but what about Farez Malikzai? Naoma cannot be seen by his side either," he stated, concerned Naoma would wish to be with her husband after such a long and unhappy separation.

"Correct commander, she must stay behind, and I will impress upon the malik the importance of this. And in your case, Commander Zahir, should you require female presence in the execution of some of your diplomatic duties, we will provide someone to accompany you. These details will form part of future briefings as we develop our plan of action."

"Thank you, general," Tariq responded. "I will resist the temptation to ask if you will be calling upon Hollywood to find a suitable escort," he added, playfully.

General Maxwell smiled, confident that a man of Commander Zahir's stature had regained his customary composure. If anyone could understand the significance of a "bigger picture" it would be Tariq.

"The main point of today's briefing," the general continued, "is to make sure everyone is clear that we can't go after the governor alone. We will make our move when we can bag all four – the governor and the three people we discussed. And keep in mind that each suspect could have a role in any impending attack on the USA in which case we need to prove who's behind it before we make our move."

"The weekend is approaching so return to the ranch and have some quality time with your families. Report back at 1000 hours on Monday for mission training. I intend to invite Farez Malikzai for lunch the same day when he is also due to attend the hospital for a medical check-up. I will explain to him what transpired today.

"You each have very different roles to play, but you must all be convincing. Briefings will go on until we all feel you're ready to roll. Then we will disclose the malik's new role to his family.

"Commander, we will also explain to your mother that after your appointment as ambassador it will not be possible for the family to join you. Too dangerous. For security reasons they must stay at the ranch. I think that's enough for one day. Take it away and think about it over the weekend. If anything gives you pause for thought raise it with me on Monday."

Abdul and Tariq were silent most of the way back to the Sinclair ranch as the enormity of the task sank in. It wasn't quite what they had expected. There were dangers ahead and vastly different to what they'd experienced before, involving arms and drugs smuggling and human trafficking on a scale they could only imagine. It wasn't what they'd anticipated, but it was something to sink their teeth into.

Smiling at Commander Zahir, Abdul said, "Congratulations Mr Ambassador. You finally got your wish."

"Thank you, Lieutenant Sinclair," Tariq responded, with a toothy grin. "I gratefully accept, but it's not quite what I had I mind brother. However, thinking about it all, I guess I'm going to have the best of both worlds in a manner of speaking," he added, inclining his head at an angle.

"In America, the way we characterise your situation," Abdul said, patting his good friend on the shoulder, "is that you get to have your cake and eat it!"

Back at the ranch, family members gathered around the military vehicle as both men disembarked, curious to find out why Abdul and Tariq were laughing aloud when everyone imagined they'd just been given their embarkation orders.

***

Chapter Three

A surprise telephone call to the ranch would forever change the life of Taliban Field Commander Tariq Hasan Zahir. His long-held aspirations, and his hopes and dreams were about to become a reality. Tariq will assume the post of Ambassador to the Embassy of Afghanistan within a matter of days. There was such an air of excitement within the ranch house that Charles Sinclair made no apologies for putting a bottle of Champagne on ice.

"Congratulations Your Excellency," Charles Sinclair announced, pumping his friend's hand. "I am honoured to have you in my home. But, I confess, I do not know how best to address you," he added, with a mischievous grin.

Grinning widely, Tariq gently placed a hand on Sinclair's shoulder. "You are a dear friend Charles and will always be so. I have been called many things in my life and can expect more of the same in the future. But, to you, I shall always be Tariq."

Stepping forward, Abdul embraced his friend. No words were necessary between men who were as close as brothers could ever be.

Smiling proudly, as he observed the expressions of fraternity between his two closest friends, Farez's heart swelled with joy thinking about how far they had all come together. Close by, the ladies wept tears of joy, and the children laughed and joked before running off to inform Atuallah and her new friend Buddy of the breaking news.

The arrival of a military staff car distracted everyone from their ruminations. They watched as General Maxwell alighted and entered the ranch house. After an exchange of greetings, Sinclair led the general, and the other three men into his study. "Thank you, Charles, your den will do nicely to brief everyone...yourself included of course." General Maxwell appeared to be in an upbeat mood as he settled into a comfortable chair indicating the others should do likewise.

"Gentlemen...the game is on! Today, I want to speak to all four of you as a group in this secure environment. Firstly, let me turn to you Charles because you will no doubt be surprised when I say you have an important role to play."

"Indeed, general, tell me more."

"For security reasons you will have to wait a little while longer for full details. Having said that, I can confirm that your son,

Lieutenant Abdul Sinclair, will continue to work undercover with Commander Zahir," he added looking first at Abdul and then Tariq.

"Where we need your help, Charles, is in developing a new persona for Farez Malikzai," he explained, looking at the village headman who sported a worried look on his face. "We are going to give you a new identity Farez, hopefully with Charles Sinclair's assistance."

The industrious ranch owner was also perplexed, but his oft-expressed willingness to play an active part in military proceedings outweighed any misgivings he may harbour. "General Maxwell," he said, looking directly at the senior officer, "I have made it clear that anything I can do to help my country by supporting the military including my son would be my privilege."

At that opportune moment, Margaret, Sinclair's loyal housekeeper, knocked on the door and politely offered everyone refreshments. As she turned to leave the den, the general said, "Charles, there goes a woman after my own heart if I may say so. Before I leave for Fort Bragg I must find out if she has baked any more of those delicious cakes I'm so fond of." No-one was in doubt about the general's cheerful disposition.

"Well, general…as people tend to say.. the way to a man's heart is through his stomach!" Sinclair couldn't resist a moment of levity pretty sure the men's raucous laughter would reach the kitchen and Margaret's burning ears.

Opening up his leather notepad, General Maxwell announced it was time to get back to the briefing: "First off, let's explore the part I want you to play Charles. Farez is still convalescing so we have to bring him in gently," he said, smiling at the malik. "Keep him in the slow lane, so to speak. We need a new identity for Farez as befits a successful and wealthy businessman; a prosperous man who has a luxurious villa in the Afghanistan-Pakistan borderland where he goes to relax from time to time."

Wisely choosing to remain silent, the wily malik monitored the exchange with mounting interest.

"What made you think I was an expert in business practices?" Charles Sinclair asked.

"I, or should I say we, were very impressed with your experience in Afghanistan at the time you worked for a U.S government-sponsored company setting-up a hydroelectric facility. You accomplished a lot -- you said as much yourself. You also mentioned that through your local contacts you met your wife in Afghanistan and I just put two and two together…"

"And arrived at five," Sinclair said, careful to temper his initial irritation because he was keen to assist Farez.

"General, as I have stated on previous occasions, I will help in any way I can. Please allow me to give this some thought and sketch out an outline plan for your approval."

"I'd appreciate that. And now please forgive me Charles if I ask you to step outside your own study for a moment. The briefing I have to give to the others is highly confidential and the less you know the better it is for your own security and others at the ranch."

"I quite understand," Sinclair said shaking the general's hand. "Allow me to say again it will be my pleasure to play even a small part. So, I thank you sir,"

"It is I who should thank you Charles. You are already doing a great service offering safe haven to family members to keep them out of harm's way. For that we are all grateful," he stressed as Sinclair departed.

diplomatic duties within the United States. Meanwhile, you will be living the life of a billionaire businessman. Your villa will be a place where Commander Zahir can seek refuge while waiting for Abdul to feed him intelligence.".

"I understand general," Tariq offered. "And you Farez," he added, turning to the malik, "haven't been seen by the governor. In fact, he believes you're dead."

Nodding his agreement, the general added, "And by the time we finish your makeover Farez you won't even know yourself!"

"I am indebted for your assurances general," Farez responded as the others laughed. "However, I am still anxious to learn more about the Abdul's cover in the overall plan."

"Lieutenant Sinclair's cover will take the guise of a personal bodyguard and close aide. He will find a way to infiltrate the arms dealer's inner sanctum, gain his confidence, and become the man's PA and bodyguard. Wherever the arms dealer goes, so goes Lieutenant Sinclair. He will learn of dates and details of impending deals some of which, we believe, go back to corrupt practices at the Pentagon. You can understand the sensitivities and the lieutenant will have his time cut out to maintain his cover," he added, staring pointedly at Abdul. "You can also understand why this makes him the principal link in the chain. The rest of us form the lieutenant's back-up team. This is something we must get right first time, as we may not get a second bite at the cherry if anyone's cover is blown. So, there you have it gentlemen. And keep in mind that failure is not an option. Any questions?"

If they hadn't realised it before, the trio of friends were now abundantly clear they were about to become involved in a very dangerous game of deception that would play out over an unspecified period of time.

"One question sir," Tariq said, getting to his feet. "When do we get started?"

"We start now gentlemen! Lieutenant Sinclair is to report to a top-secret location for training and to assume a new identity. You will be fully briefed later," he added, again directing his attention to Abdul.

"Commander Zahir...you will fly from Fort Bragg to Washington DC to be installed as the new ambassador to The Embassy of Afghanistan. The event will entail a big splash of PR making it clear you will be predominantly duty-bound in the United States.

"Malik Farez Malikzai," the general said aloud, "you will stay at the ranch and learn from Charles Sinclair how to become an international business magnate! Your villa, which has yet to be sourced, will have all the trappings of a highflying businessman who's frequently known to boast: 'money's no object!' You will undergo a change of identity to support the subterfuge. As you by now realise, Farez, it's time for you to think magnate instead of malik," he added, bringing a wry smile to Farez's wizened face, and muffled laughter from the others.

"One further thing, gentlemen: I trust you don't need reminding that everything discussed between these four walls stays here. You must not discuss today's events with anyone not even your loved ones. The success of this multifaceted plan lives or dies on our joint ability to observe strict security at all times."

"General, what is to become of the children?" asked Abdul, concerned about what would happen during his prolonged absence.

"With the exception of your daughter, all the children will receive private lessons at the ranch with the emphasis on language skills. Isolated from normal classes means other children aren't around to ask awkward questions."

"And what about the womenfolk?" asked Farez.

"Madam Mena and your wife will be safe at the ranch. They know only too well the dangers you are likely to encounter based on your past performance and will understand the need to observe the strictest security at the ranch. And that's how it must be until the job is done," he added, rising from his chair ready to depart.

"Oh...I almost forgot! Charles, where is your wonderful housekeeper? Never mind, I will make my way out via the kitchen and see if I can persuade Margaret to part with some of her wonderful cakes." With that, General Maxwell dashed towards the kitchen leaving the others wondering what really attracts him to Charles Sinclair's incomparable *gouvernante*.

*

Two days later, a military staff car pulled up outside the ranch house. It was ten in the morning and everyone, proud and excited, had gathered to give Afghanistan's ambassador-designate a memorable send-off. And just as they had arrived together, Tariq and Abdul would leave in the same vehicle but to different destinations.

Within the household everyone had mixed feelings. Charles Sinclair was understandably concerned for his son's welfare, as well as for Tariq in his new role as a statesman. For the first time it appeared that two warrior-friends were about to go their different ways – at least for now.

Inside the ranch house, the ladies looked on sadly as the men prepared to leave, especially Mena who was about to lose contact with her beloved son after a reunion she never thought would ever happen. To some extent, Mena was philosophical knowing that whatever the two men had to face they would do so courageously and with honour. She smiled as Naoma squeezed her hand as if saying: "be strong, for you're not alone my dear friend".

For once in their busy lives the four children were sitting quietly, reflecting on events. But Sarah, wise beyond her years, took the initiative to promote an aura of sobriety. She reached for Khalil's hand and squeezed it gently. Looking at his sister, he smiled though his eyes were brimming with tears. Ahktar and Jamila, standing side by side, were consoled by Uncle Farez who had his strong, reassuring arms around both. It was an emotional moment evoking unspoken words of love for one another. Everyone present had been drawn together under desperate circumstances to become a totally united family. Their strength lay in the bonds of friendship so firmly rooted in the sands of time.

With a final wave, Tariq and Abdul clambered aboard the waiting vehicle and were soon on their way leaving a trail of well-wishers waving frantically and shouting their goodbyes. Close-by, two unconcerned mules answering to Atuallah and Buddy raised their heads from grazing and brayed softly.

*

Abdul and Tariq's mission briefings were scheduled to continue at Fort Bragg after a short meeting to introduce representatives from The Embassy of Afghanistan in Washington DC invited to meet with Commander Zahir. Other senior officers from several U.S. agencies were also in attendance.

"Keep in mind gentlemen," the general cautioned, demanding everyone's attention, "that Commander Zahir is ambassador-designate to The Embassy of Afghanistan and therefore strict diplomatic protocol must be observed. Take a seat with the others," he added, motioning to Abdul and Tariq.

39

"As I'm sure you're aware," he announced looking at Tariq, "there is standard protocol to be observed for your inauguration. We have been brushing up on that to make sure we don't screw up," he added, as his aide deposited a tray of refreshments on the table.

Among the other staff present was a senior agent from the CIA who would take Abdul under his wing for the next three months. "Lieutenant Sinclair will receive his briefing later," General Maxwell announced, "but first I want to introduce two gentlemen from The Embassy of Afghanistan in Washington DC who have flown to Fort Bragg to meet with Commander Zahir. They will also ensure the necessary protocol is followed from their standpoint as we go forward with the inauguration. The commander will present his credentials in two days' time," he added as introductions were made.

"We have already set in motion the announcement of your appointment," he confirmed to Tariq, "and details of your arrival date in the States, mode of transport, and port of entry were passed to the Permanent Mission of the USA to the United Nations according to protocol. This means the necessary customs and immigration clearances can be obtained from U.S. authorities and arrangements put in place to extend to you the usual diplomatic courtesies on arrival.

"You have already met with Kevin White our Chief of Protocol for the United States. He has your biographical data in hand and a copy of your Letter of Credence. The other copy," he said, "handing Tariq a buff coloured envelope, "is in this envelope for you to present to the Executive Office of the Secretary-General of the UN on the day of your inauguration. Got it? Good! I now turn to Mr. White to continue this briefing.

"Thank you, General Maxwell. As I am in possession of the necessary documentation, I have already arranged a date and time to present your Letter of Credence to the Executive Office of the Secretary-General of the United Nations. Your inauguration, Commander Zahir, will be in two days' time. Tomorrow will be spent preparing you for the occasion, in conjunction with our friends from The Embassy of Afghanistan who will then fly with you to Washington DC for your inauguration. You will be escorted to the Office of the Secretary-General of the UN to present your credentials. Don't worry, I will be by your side to make sure all goes smoothly. There will be a photographer on hand to take an official photo of you prior to presenting your credentials which will be recorded by the United Nations' visual media folk. Is that clear so far commander?"

"Yes sir, what happens after that?"

"You'll be expected to make a short speech…we'll help you with that. On the same day, a news release with your bio data and announcement of your credentials will come from the UNs Department of Global Communications."

"I understand. What is the protocol regarding dress code for this sort of occasion?"

"They recommend a lounge suit – preferably dark – or national dress."

Noticing a wide grin appearing on Abdul's face, Tariq decided to head off any snide remarks about his national dress. "Please don't be too concerned my friend," he said to Abdul, brandishing an admonishing finger, "I will settle for a dark-coloured lounge suit!

"Thank you, Mr White, for your sound advice. Does that cover everything?"

"Not quite, commander. I should inform you that it's customary for newly appointed ambassadors to call on the UN presidents of the General Assembly, Security Council, and the Economic and Social Council as well as senior officials of the Secretariat. As to the procedure of accreditation for a Permanent Representative of a member observer-state to the offices of the UN in Geneva, Vienna, Nairobi, Addis Ababa, Bangkok, Beirut, and Santiago, a Letter of Credence should be addressed by name to the Secretary-General of the United Nations and presented to his representative at the aforementioned duty stations who will accept them on your behalf. A copy of these credentials should then be forwarded to the Chief of Protocol at the United Nations headquarters in New York," he added, to a stunned gathering, as he paused to draw breath.

"So, no great pressure!" Tariq uttered dejectedly, flopping back in his chair to the sound of laughter.

Nodding, and smiling his approbation, General Maxwell praised the U.S. Chief of Protocol for his comprehensive briefing. "With you to guide us, Mr White, I believe we are in good hands; you are just the man we need to steer us through the next couple of days and I thank you for agreeing to participate."

Turning to Tariq, who was still processing the plethora of data thrown his way, General Maxwell summed up proceedings. "Commander, I think you have your work cut out before you leave here. Quarters have been assigned for you to work on your speech and prepare for your inauguration. Kevin White has agreed to stay on base. He is security cleared and fully briefed about your stand-in. Hmm…I guess you'd like to meet him," the general added, sliding over to his intercom. "Send him in please," he ordered his aide in the outer office.

Tariq got up from his chair and stared at the man walking towards him. The likeness was uncanny. For a second, he went weak at the knees looking at a mirror-image of himself.

"I believe I did inform you commander that we had access to some very creative people who could make you appear in more than one place at the same time," General Maxwell stated, equally pleased with the actor standing before him. No words were exchanged as his double shook hands, bowed slightly, and left as quietly as he had arrived.

"I must confess I'm very impressed sir," Tariq stated enthusiastically, his confidence boosted by his double's convincing appearance. "It was like looking at myself in a mirror."

"This man has been studying you of late, perfecting your mannerisms and general expressions to be as much like you as possible. We don't envisage a speaking part for him, so we have some careful planning to do."

"If you have finished with me general," Kevin White said getting up from his chair, "I request your permission to be excused. Commander Zahir can find me on the base at any time between now and our departure for Washington," he confirmed as he headed for the door followed by the two officials from The Embassy of Afghanistan.

"Thank you, gentlemen, for your input at the meeting today. My sergeant will see you to your quarters," the general added, escorting his visitors to the door.

"Now we should concentrate on Lieutenant Sinclair and his pivotal role in this mission," General Maxwell announced, reaching for another file on his desk.

"Lieutenant, this is a CIA dossier for you to study. You will be assigned to Camp Peary, Virginia for a three-month period and be briefed on the finer points of covert operations. You already have some experience, but the CIA will explain the latest techniques for extracting information and passing it on. I said your role will be pivotal, but you will have support. That said, at times you'll feel like you're swimming in a tank full of dirty water with sharks that are twelve feet long. The best advice I can offer is to assume they aren't friendly.

"Next point: Camp Peary insists you ditch your rank and name and use a false ID with a cover story that our shady arms dealer and his associates with find too good to resist. They are working on that.

"As a battle-tested U.S. Marine, lieutenant," the general continued, eyeing Abdul at close range, "you have proven soldiering abilities, but the Camp Peary course will take you to a higher level in all-round skills in terms of physical and psychological techniques. After training, you and Commander Zahir, a.k.a. His Excellency the Ambassador to The Embassy of Afghanistan, will be briefed about the key players in this mission which should make clearer your individual roles.

"For now, Commander Zahir has to assume his diplomatic role. You, lieutenant, must reach a high level of competency pretty damn quick. And that's an order!"

"No pressure my friend," Tariq commented facetiously. His remark went unnoticed by General Maxwell who was fixated on finishing his briefing. "Did you have something to add commander?" the general queried.

"I was wondering about the role to be played by Farez Malikzai and whether he is up to it given his present physical condition," Tariq offered, drawing attention away for himself and Abdul for a moment."

General Maxwell stiffened. "Do not concern yourselves with the malik. He will be groomed and schooled in the ways of a billionaire playboy and businessman."

"We both understand sir," Abdul acknowledged, "but Farez, though gentle and one of the most honourable of men, is weak from a serious injury. The commander and I have concerns he may not be ready for such a demanding role."

"It's a fair comment lieutenant but Farez Malikzai is keen to play a part in this for reasons I don't need to spell out. We took into consideration his physical condition and we think a successful businessman's profile will largely keep him out of the line of fire. In his diplomatic role, Tariq will spend time at the villa, and he can keep a weather eye on the malik.

"Our intention is to make sure Farez exits the villa before the final extractions take place. I think that's about covered everything. So, gentlemen if there are no further questions we will adjourn and allow Commander Zahir and Lieutenant Sinclair to compare notes as it will be some time before they see one another again."

The next day Tariq flew from Fort Bragg to Washington DC just twenty-four hours before his planned inauguration. On arrival, he was greeted by U.S. officials and representatives from the Embassy of Afghanistan. Reflecting on the past few days, Tariq realised he would finally take up the diplomatic post he dreamt of a thousand times. The time had arrived to serve his country as an international statesman.

*

The day of the inauguration proved to be something Tariq would remember for the rest of his life. Despite assurances given to Abdul that he'd stick to a lounge suit he made his diplomatic debut looking resplendent in a navy-blue field commander dress uniform replete with service medals, contrasted with a majestic turban of dark-green and navy-blue topped with a splendid black plume. White gloves and a ceremonial sword at his right side completed his sartorial appearance. Tall and handsome, he looked every inch a statesman. Everything about him evoked strength and courage.

Accompanied by Kevin White and the representatives from The Embassy of Afghanistan including the defence attaché, Ambassador-designate Zahir boarded his limo to be escorted by a state protocol motorcade that headed straight to the White House where, on arrival, all four men were asked to wait in the Blue Room. Tariq looked confused.

"Please don't be concerned commander," Kevin White said assuringly. "For security reasons, we didn't inform you earlier that we changed your schedule slightly. In recognition of the importance to both the United States and Afghanistan concerning the mission of which you are a part, the presidents of the United States and Afghanistan felt your inauguration should be held here, in the Blue Room. And His Excellency, the secretary-general of the United Nations expressed his interest in attending."

For a second or two Tariq was lost for words, at once wishing his mother and daughter could be present. But there was no time to dwell on what might have been as the President of the United States had arrived at the Blue Room in the company of the Secretary-General of the United Nations. The men stepped inside and waited to be introduced.

"Mister President...Your Excellency," Kevin White announced, "it is my duty and honour to present Field Commander Tariq Hasan Zahir, ambassador-designate to The Embassy of Afghanistan. The ambassador-designate begs your indulgence and asks you to accept his Letter of Credence."

46

"Accepted with pleasure Mister Ambassador," the President said, handing the buff envelope to the Secretary-General for safekeeping before shaking hands with Tariq. Hope we didn't surprise you. We thought it important to endorse your appointment here at the White House, with His Excellency in attendance We want to emphasise to you, and the international media that will be waiting for you in the Rose Garden, the importance we attach to the work you are about to do. Also, it saves a trip to the UN Secretariat Building in New York," he added, with a sidelong glance at the Secretary-General who was smiling broadly.

In a short speech during which he promised to do his utmost to help guide Afghanistan into the international community, Tariq expressed his thanks and intention to work hard to restore peace in his country so that it may prosper. "Also, Mister President…Your Excellency, the obstacles standing in our way I pledge to remove just as soon as humanly possible."

"That's what we want to hear, Mister Ambassador," the President confirmed, "so may I suggest you spend a little time with our State Department officials some of whom are waiting for you in the lobby?"

It had been a full day and Tariq's head was spinning from being a central figure in a day of pomp and pageantry. Retiring to prepare for a new day, it dawned on him that a new chapter had already begun; one that could bring welcome closure to Afghanistan's war without end. There would be no turning back.

***

Chapter Four

Shortly after Abdul and Tariq left the ranch, Charles Sinclair dived into his new role as a business tutor preparing Farez Malikzai for life in the world of international commerce; in short, a wheeler and dealer. Fortuitously, the erstwhile village headman proved himself a willing student eager to learn all he could about doing business on an international scale while immersing himself in the American way of life.

It was never going to be easy, but being offered a key role to play, in association with his two greatest friends, was all the impetus he needed to keep his nose to the grindstone. For him, it was unthinkable he would never again stand side-by-side with Abdul and Tariq when the time came for their nemesis, the evil governor, to be brought to justice.

Forewarned that General Maxwell was on his way from Fort Bragg, Sinclair's indomitable housekeeper pre-prepared a lunch to be served in Charles Sinclair's study. Smiling to himself, Sinclair reflected on the number of occasions General Maxwell had visited the ranch primarily to check on Farez's progress, only to display an equal amount of interest in Margaret. Unable to hide her blushes, Charles Sinclair suspected the interest was mutual.

 On entering the ranch house, General Maxwell's enthusiastic greeting gave emphasis to Sinclair's suspicions.

"A very good morning, gentlemen!" the base CO declared, his nostrils responding to enticing odours coming from the kitchen. "What is that inviting smell I wonder? I confess I've been looking forward to lunch all morning," he added, beaming at Charles and Farez neither of whom deigned to respond.

"Welcome, general," said Sinclair cheerily while offering his hand. "Perhaps we should head straight to my study for lunch before you fade away from starvation!" he suggested, prompting an outburst of laughter from all three.

The general was correct about one thing: Margaret's moules marinière with cream, garlic, and parsley were as good as his sensitive nostrils determined. It was an epicurean moment that generated a most congenial atmosphere which was the intended outcome. Talks got under way soon after the empty plates were cleared away.

Farez's forced convalescence at the ranch – now a secure military zone – offered a convenient opportunity for Charles Sinclair to lecture Farez in business etiquette until such time it was deemed appropriate for the malik to report to Fort Bragg for his final indoctrination.

"Getting to the point of my visit today, Charles, how is your student coming along?"

"I have to say he is one very fast learner general; that much is abundantly clear," Sinclair responded emphatically, at once bringing forth a satisfied smile on the part of the village head.

"If that's the case, my good village headman, let's see how far you have advanced," the general suggested, eager to hear from the student himself.

"Thank you general. Please sit back and I will reveal what I have learned about Charles Sinclair and his business undertakings," the malik declared, getting to his feet to face the senior officer he had come to know and respect.

"First thing I learnt about Charles Sinclair is that he is a qualified geological engineer with vast experience working in Afghanistan. And this goes back to 2002 when the company he represented was awarded a $100 million contract to construct a new building for the U.S. embassy in Kabul. I also learnt about the logistic civil augmentation programme with task orders valued at over $216 million awarded under Operation Enduring Freedom. This included establishing base camps in Kandahar and on Bagram Air Base. How am I doing so far general?"

"I'm listening…carry on."

"Thank you, sir…at that time Charles was a site engineer working under the auspices of the U.S. government, and was obliged to confront angry Afghan farmers who objected to their poppy fields being laid waste by a hydroelectric project. I understand it was a joint venture between the U.S. and Afghan governments. The farmers made their living selling opium using some of their income to pay off the mujahedeen. That happened in Helmand province which, from my own experience, abounds with poppy fields."

"What happened to the project Farez?" the general queried, clearly enthralled and impressed with the malik's progress.

"It collapsed because the mujahedeen banned soil sampling in the poppy fields. Charles had to leave in a hurry because he and others in the team suffered death threats. Again, as I can recall from my own knowledge of events at the time, the mujahedeen traded heroin for arms."

"So, if the project was a failure what do you suppose our friend Charles got out of it?" the general asked, pressing Farez.

"He learnt a lot about the topography of our country and established a valuable list of high-level business and political contacts until the mujahedeen stepped in. He also discovered it wasn't smart to take on the mujahedeen. But it wasn't a total waste of time was it Charles?" Farez probed, turning to Sinclair who had remained silent throughout. "I say this because the Kajaki dam was constructed as one of the two major hydroelectric dams on the Helmand river a hundred miles northwest of Kandahar city."

"My congratulations to you Farez on a very impressive report. I can see you are almost ready for the next phase. But before that, please continue your convalescence here until you're called to report to Fort Bragg for what we might call the finishing touches," General Maxwell instructed before addressing Charles Sinclair.

"You have done well Charles preparing Farez for the next phase which will entail several military personnel visiting the ranch to groom the malik in his new role. So strict privacy is necessary, and I hope this won't inconvenience you further."

"I am always at your disposal General Maxwell," he confirmed, relieved he was not about to lose a good friend in the near term.

"Excellent. I will return tomorrow to discuss with Farez the next phase of his training programme which, as I stated earlier, will be in private."

"Please make use of my study for that purpose. I will be busy entertaining the ladies and children to make sure Farez has complete privacy."

"I guess that's it for today. So, with your permission Charles I will make my way out via the kitchen to see if Margaret has anything to tempt my palate."

Exchanging glances, Sinclair and the malik were of a single thought that it wasn't just Margaret's baking skills that he found tempting.

"Be my guest, general. If, as someone suggested earlier, the way to a man's heart is through his stomach, you do appear to be exhibiting an insatiable appetite!"

*

Bright and early the next day, Charles led the ladies and children out of the ranch for a picnic lunch. Billed as a surprise outing, everyone thrilled to the sight of a large camper van parked outside the ranch. A "Blue Ridge Mountains" decal on the camper's front window caught everyone's attention.

A trip to the Blue Ridge mountains is a must-see spectacle for any visitor to North Carolina. "You will find the area a little different to what you were used to in Afghanistan," Charles Sinclair informed the party as they boarded the van. "The range runs from the state of Georgia to Pennsylvania, but the highest peaks are right here on our doorstep," he stated as he closed the door of the van.

As they entered the national park, and taking charge like a tour guide, Sinclair outlined some of the features of the Blue Ridge Parkway, "Mount Mitchel is the highest peak east of the Mississippi river. The Parkway encourages the growth of rare plants…"

"Grandpa, why are the mountains called blue?" Sarah interrupted, more for the enlightenment of others than for her own edification. She had been there before.

"That's a good question Sarah. If everyone looks closely, you will see the range has a blue tint especially from a distance. It looks that way because of a substance emitted by plants called isoprene," he explained, leaning on his experience as a geological engineer."

Everyone was taken-in by the incredible views, even Mena who was becoming increasingly intrigued by the West -- Mr Charles Sinclair in particular!

The trip proved to be a very good idea and the Parkway perfect for all ages because of its spectacular waterfalls and miles of trails for hikers. They were quite safe in such an environment even though they were accompanied by security officers masquerading as rancheros. Whatever the outcome, it was another smart move on the part of Charles Sinclair.

*

Waiting inside the ranch house, Farez witnessed Margaret rush to the door to greet General Maxwell. She blushed as she announced the general's arrival.

"Good to see you again general," Farez proclaimed. "Please come into the study. I must say I am looking forward to finding out more about the role I will be playing," he added, shaking hands with the base CO. As each selected a chair, Margaret reappeared with a tray of refreshments and newly baked cookies that immediately caught the general's eye.

"Gentlemen, I have prepared a light lunch for you later," she announced. "Would 1 p.m. be convenient?" she asked, turning to make her exit.

"That is kind of you, Margaret; yes, 1 p.m. will be fine," the malik confirmed.

General Maxwell was anxious to get down to business. "Farez, I want to introduce you to your new name -- Kostas Alexopoulos. You are a Greek Cypriot by birth who has lived in America for many years. Your field of business has taken you into computer technology, real estates, and investments in shopping malls. This made you one of the wealthiest people on the planet. That much is up-front and straightforward.

"A few people know you as a man who dabbles in all kinds of businesses using intermediaries to set things up for you to manipulate from a distance allowing you to keep a low profile. That much is not up-front or straightforward!

"A wise Kostas Alexopoulos would claim it's not what you know -- or even who you know -- that's important, but what you know about whom you know! You could deduce his greatest assets -- apart from his obvious business acumen -- to be his international connections, particularly in political circles. He is careful to nurture friendly relations with global decision makers, notably in the States. Many of his deals are dubious to say the least. What I am trying to impart is that he must have friends in high places to ply his trade with the rate of success he enjoys.

"Allegedly in his early seventies, this man has earned a reputation for pursuing a lavish lifestyle including a desire for the company of young, beautiful women. He entertains the world's elite and promotes business from his luxurious villas in the Caribbean, Rome, and Monte Carlo…often between the sheets!" the general added, pausing when the malik's face took on an expression of acute shock.

"Don't be too concerned Farez; all deals brokered are conducted by passing information to the client via one of his front men -- or should I say women – sometimes using a bedroom for such occasions. Look at it this way: if a client becomes difficult, blackmailing becomes a convenient option," the general explained, much to the malik's relief.

"Let me say that the guileful Kostas Alexopoulos strives to portray the image of a playboy unable to resist the good life by which I mean wine, women and song!"

"I think I understand you," Farez said, smiling. "I believe this is where I say something like 'no pressure general!' he added as both men laughed picturing the Marwah village headman basking in the role of an international playboy.

"Farez…again I urge you not to be too concerned. Every aspect of Kostas Alexopoulos is pure fiction. We are creating in him a watertight persona for you to use should anyone decide to investigate your credentials. If asked, you will say you are continuing your convalescence at your villa on the Afghan-Pakistan border, which we hired for the occasion. It is where you will entertain only the principal villains in this escapade.

"Your entire staff will be drawn from special forces operatives posing as hired hands. The story you give to anyone who enquires should portray you as leading a leisurely lifestyle as you recover from a bout of major surgery. If tempted, and if the opportunity arises, you may agree to enter into a bit of wheeling and dealing in arms and/or narcotics."

"Why drugs general? I would expect the New Taliban to be far more interested in acquiring all types of weapons."

"It might strike you that way but consider this: Afghanistan has consistently returned a GDP growth over seven percent in past years despite its instability and the global economic downturn. Take 2010 for example: growth was fifteen percent mainly due to large construction projects financed by the sponsors of international funds and, more importantly, from income generated mainly by the illicit production of opium poppy cultivation which represent ninety percent of global output.

"So, Farez, it's easy to see why drugs and arms purchases go hand in hand and where the Taliban will concentrate its efforts. And those are the two areas of greatest interest to Kostas Alexopoulos. Get the picture?"

"I get it, general. I tie the goat to a tree and wait for the wolves to approach. Once they take the bait, we go in for the kill."

"Right, but you mustn't make it look too easy," cautioned General Maxwell chuckling at Farez's witticism. "Play hard to get so we can spin this out until Abdul is able to gather intel on other shady deals in the offing. After we have assembled all the pieces of the puzzle, we will make our move."

"Where do we – I should say I – go from here? I now have a working knowledge of business deals thanks to Charles Sinclair and I know my part in the play. What's next sir?" Farez queried, clearly enjoying his tutorial and only too happy to have a part in an important mission that could have an enormous effect on the future of Afghanistan.

"Next you will find yourself in the company of highly-trained men who will visit you here at the ranch over the next few weeks to test you on your business profile and teach you a thing or two about name-dropping. I will let them explain what that means in detail, but you must be able to name-drop in high places and be comfortable acting as an American. That means you must have a thorough knowledge of the people you profess to know intimately. Lastly, we need to change your physical appearance."

A pained look of incredulity returned to Farez's face. "Change my appearance! Just how will you do that general?"

"Believe me when I say it can be done; it must be done, and you must not be concerned. When our Hollywood makeup artists are done with you, even your friends won't know you," the general fired back, sparking another bout of nervous laughter particularly on the part of Farez.

"Once that's done, we will bring all three of you together for a final briefing before embarking on this mission. So, that's about it. When you finish your training, you will know more about Kostas Alexopoulos than you do about Farez Malikzai – I can assure you of that."

"Lunch is ready gentlemen," Margaret announced knocking on the door of the study.

"Thank you, Margaret," General Maxwell acknowledged. "We won't keep you waiting long," he added as he and Farez got up to follow Margaret into the dining room for a cold buffet lunch.

Though he felt he'd lost some of his village head persona after the intense sessions with the general, the malik had not lost his appetite. He was drawing closer to working with his two good friends. Together they would engineer the downfall of the governor and his three villainous cohorts. Farez had found a new lease of life and he made a secret promise to play his part to perfection or die in the attempt.

*

Since arriving at Camp Peary, Lieutenant Abdul Sinclair had little time to think about anything other than the 9,000-acre military establishment with which he was gradually becoming acquainted. Located near Williamsburg in Virginia it is officially referred to as an Armed Forces Experimental Training Activity (AFETA) under the authority of the Department of Defense. Camp Peary hosts a covert CIA training facility known as "The Farm", which is used to train officers of the CIA's Directorate of Operations, as well as those of the DIA's Defense Clandestine Service, among other intelligence entities.

Abdul took to the course like a duck to water. He soon discovered that spy craft favours those with enough stamina to stay the course. Despite long stretches without sleep and other creature comforts, intense concentration is essential while battling fatigue, discomfort, and the threat of physical danger. His strengths and weaknesses were put to the test. He discovered his cognitive ability and resilience in stressful situations were more important than raw, physical strength. Techniques were attuned to human psychology and a thorough knowledge of what motivates people.

A crammed training schedule included meetings, networking, studying, and analysing. In addition, he refined his already efficient competency in hand-to-hand combat and weaponry. He had to adjust to acting covertly, as an undercover agent serving in the shadows where rewards are never made public, as opposed to a U.S. Marine. Over time, he developed a knowledge of code-working, lock-picking, and opening packages undetected. He learnt how to evade hostile pursuers -- known as defensive-driving -- and the art of disguise.

This intensive training in spy craft introduced him to a new world of espionage and undercover work that would elevate Abdul into a very select and elite band of unknown operatives. It also marked an important turning point in his life as a U.S. Marine.

Abdul's time at Camp Peary was well spent. He was ready – almost impatient – to get back to Fort Bragg and learn the nature of the role he was to play. His only sadness was that he, and his two closest friends bound by past endeavours, were walking down separate roads -- at least until orders were issued for a final strike. Conversely, his sadness was tempered by the knowledge that his friends would be feeling the same way. Whatever happened, it would never dampen the spirit that united them as brothers and comrades-in-arms. Together they would accomplish everything demanded of them – on a professional and personal level. With that encouraging thought in mind, Abdul looked up to the stars in the night sky and willed Allah to protect all three of them and see them safely through the forthcoming mission and back to their loved ones.

*

In his new surroundings, within the confines of The Embassy of Afghanistan in Washington DC, Ambassador Tariq Hasan Zahir breathed a sigh of relief after contemplating his final engagement in a string of inauguration ceremonies. The speech he would give this day, at a luncheon at the White House, would explain his hopes for the future of his country. It would also set him on a course that would project him as a peacemaker.

As a highly respected Taliban officer, he knew there were some who would judge him to have mixed loyalties and interests. Irrespective of what lay ahead, Tariq was confident that, given time, his true purpose in life to establish peace for his country and gain international respect, would allow others to see his true intent.

When his limo arrived at the White House, he was taken directly to see the President who extended a very warm welcome and an invitation to join the lunch party. Slightly nervous, Tariq ate little, and checked twice to make sure his speech was safely in his pocket. At last invited to deliver his speech, he rose from his chair. At that moment he felt a great weight on his shoulders as the room went quiet.

Mister President, Your Excellencies, Ladies and Gentlemen.

As-salaamu' alaykum. It is a great pleasure to be with you and I thank all our American friends for this wonderful opportunity and your cordial hospitality. I consider it both an honour and a great personal pleasure to be in such dignified surroundings in the company of what I hope are friends and supporters of Afghanistan. I suppose I will find out soon enough!

I am certain everyone present appreciates the direct link between security and development as they are two sides of the same coin. I contend, therefore, that it is essential for the international community to promote an environment of peace and security to bring an end to years of war in my country and facilitate the development of Afghanistan.

Of crucial importance is to ensure that the military option must be aligned with political process and economic development. All people in my country must be offered a sense of hope for the future.

If I may present more concrete details: we are advocating the implementation of an Interim Afghanistan National Development strategy for the next five years. It goes without saying that financial support is crucial. At the same time, an effective strategy needs to be put in place to address multiple challenges stemming from the increased cultivation of opium poppies.

The drug menace is a regional and global challenge. To combat this, I strongly support crop substitution and poppy eradication programmes to eliminate this growing scourge. The drug trade is eroding societies worldwide while providing funds to spread terrorism globally. This means convincing farmers they can make a better living growing peaches than they can growing poppies even if we must establish a means to buy farmers' crops so that the government underwrites the financial risks involved. For this we need international support of course and that's why I am here to address you today. Afghanistan supplies ninety percent of the world's opium so it's in all our interests to tackle this menace.

Mister President, Excellencies, ladies and gentlemen, I would like to assure you today that a new generation of Afghans, both men and women, are alive to the needs of a new Afghanistan where education for all is our promise. We have learned that on the shoulders of each future generation rests the peace and prosperity of the whole world. Thank you and peace be with you.

To some of those present, it was received as an impassioned plea within an enlightened speech that brought silence for a moment or two after Tariq delivered his closing remarks. Then, one by one, attendees got to their feet and applauded the new ambassador. Speaking among themselves, representatives from the UN, NATO, and the U.S. Administration, were able to see in H.E. Tariq Hasan Zahir a man who may just be able to lead Afghanistan out of darkness and into the light of a brave new world, assuming lots of international support, of course.

*

After six weeks, during which all three men were moulded into their new identities, General Maxwell called them to Fort Bragg to outline the plan of action and their individual roles starting with Abdul who would be the first to move out as he would need time to establish himself as an independent player in a changed environment.

All three had looked forward to being reunited. The first to arrive was Commander Zahir to be greeted by the CO. "I guess I should greet you as Your Excellency," he grinned at Tariq who stepped forward to shake hands.

"Tariq will do nicely sir; I see no reason for such formalities within these walls," he replied, curious to know what the general had in store for him.

"Good enough. I guess I'll call you Tariq in private and you can me Chris."

"Fair enough, Chris. So, we'll make it commander and general in front of others and Tariq and Chris in private."

Abdul arrived next and Tariq stepped forward to embrace his good friend.

It was clear to the general that the two men were pleased to be back in one another's company. "While we wait for the malik to arrive, I will rustle up some refreshments," he added, leaving to find his aide.

A knock on the door distracted the men from their deliberations. Abdul opened the door to reveal a clean-shaven, grey-haired gentleman nattily dressed in a dark blue pinstripe

61

"Now, pay attention everyone," General Maxwell ordered, as Tariq, Abdul and Farez resumed their seats. "I would like to be among the first to offer my congratulations to Your Excellency," the general said, to the surprise of Tariq and the others. "No-one, in my humble opinion, is better equipped for a diplomatic role of such international importance," he added.

"Having said that, commander, be mindful you will be working undercover with Lieutenant Sinclair. That means there will be occasions when we'll want you in more than one place at the same time," the CO added, provocatively. "As I explained previously, we will use a stand-in who will never be seen full-face in a public setting. Occasionally you will have to conduct diplomatic duties for the benefit of the world's media. On others, you will be based at Farez's opulent villa where he is dabbling in business enterprises yet to be outlined. So, the villa will double as a safe house for you, commander, when you slip in and out of the country after collecting intelligence from Lieutenant Sinclair. When we have everything needed to bring watertight prosecutions we will apprehend and extract our targets. And, as I outlined at a previous briefing at Fort Bragg, all four abductees will be removed to Bagram Air Base under armed guard to be shipped to a place designated by the Pentagon."

"I fully understand general...but what about Abdul...what is his cover?" He was not the only one who was puzzled: Farez was surprised to learn that Abdul and Tariq would be working independently of one another. It was not what he'd expected.

Sensing Farez's uneasiness, the general moved to put the malik at ease: "I guess I know what you're thinking Farez. You are correct that Commander Zahir and Lieutenant Sinclair will be working independently. I am cognisant of the fact that the commander is known by the governor and the Taliban. So, in his new role as Ambassador to The Embassy of Afghanistan the governor will expect him to be engaged in suit, white shirt, and blue and white-striped tie. A gold *pince nez* was delicately perched on the end of his nose.

"Forgive the intrusion," the man said with a pronounced southern U.S. accent, "but I am looking for General Maxwell," he explained, his smile revealing several gold teeth that seemed to accentuate his *pince nez*.

"Well…sir…this is the general's office," Abdul confirmed, "but he stepped out for a moment. Perhaps you would care to take a seat," he added, indicating a chair beside him. The older man sat down just as the general reappeared. He was followed by an aide carrying a tray of refreshments which were deposited on the general's desk.

The CO beamed, "Good to see our guest has arrived. Gentlemen, may I introduce you to Kostas Alexopoulos?" Abdul and Tariq got up ready to shake hands with the new arrival only to be taken aback when General Maxwell burst out laughing.

"What was it I said to you Farez? Didn't I say even your own friends wouldn't recognise you?"

Abdul and Tariq stared at each other and then at Farez. If the malik needed confirmation that his new persona could fool anyone he only had to ask his two closest friends for an answer. Still, they didn't permit Farez's new identity as a high-flying southern businessman to interfere with their reunion. At least not until the general interrupted.

"Listen up please. I asked you here to apprise you of the plan and how it affects each one of you. Also, I wish to familiarise you with the villains you will encounter. After that, you are free to ask questions.

*

62

"The profiles of two of your would-be adversaries were covered in a previous briefing but you were not given names. Look at the screen," the general instructed. "These are our four villains including the governor who needs no introduction to you guys I believe I can say with confidence. Take a close look and familiarise yourself with their facial features. We will provide written info for you to study so that you know each one inside out and back to front," he added, passing each man a file.

"First up is Angelo Damiano our redoubtable drugs dealer. We covered his story earlier…so I urge you to revise your notes and commit to memory. Then there's Patcha Volcov better known as the Mamasan of Thailand. This lady – using the word in its loosest sense – is a real piece of work. Her pièce de résistance are her wild parties during which she auctions off young girls' virginities to the highest bidder. You will be dealing with an unscrupulous and dangerous woman who stops at nothing to feather her own nest. Be on your toes gentlemen!

"Next up is Adham Volcov our international arms dealer known as 'The Wolf'. He will be a key player so I will not apologise for going into the finer details of his resumé," the general stated, looking directly at Abdul.

"Take a hard look lieutenant. This is one man who requires great study. Your life will depend on being one step ahead of him in terms of mind games. You will also have to deal with the lady Patcha who doesn't trust anyone," he added, as Abdul nodded and glanced at his two friends to make sure they were taking it all in. They were.

"While you worry yourself crazy about her, lieutenant, we will be in the shadows watching your back," the general promised, pulling up a picture of Adham Volcov onto the screen to reveal a man in his early seventies. Heavily built with a bald head and bulbous neck he resembled Nikita Khrushchev. Couldn't miss him, thought Abdul, jotting down a few notes.

"So, gentlemen, this is our dealer-in-arms par excellence. A gifted linguist, Adham honed his craft attached to the Soviet Union's military intelligence unit in the 1980s. During his time in Africa he built a reserve of business contacts while identifying arms dealing opportunities using his knowledge of how the Soviet Union had infiltrated developing countries on the African continent.

"Appearing as a refined and charismatic individual, whose deals arise from flamboyant entertainment soirees in iconic cities around the world where Champagne and caviar characterise the scene, our arms dealer is never without a beautiful lady on his arm. Extravagance defines his lifestyle. He not only sells arms to former client-countries of the Soviet Union, he also services what we might describe as "freedom fighters"; I mean those whom we in the West call terrorists. He is a man who rubs shoulders with dictators and warlords alike in some of the world's most dangerous places.

"With extravagantly furnished homes in Russia, the U.A.E., Hong Kong, and Thailand, Volcov is already a multibillionaire but he won't be satisfied until he holds the mantle of preeminent arms dealer on every continent. And it's a dream fast becoming a reality since entering the orbit of the female human-trafficker of Thailand who styles herself as Patcha "Volcov" though they aren't married. She supplements his arms-dealing with her trafficking expertise. This hard-hitting broad has the audacity to call it "love with a gun!" added the general, clearly contemptuous of the perverted work of this self-styled Mamasan of Thailand.

"She sure sounds darned explosive to me," Abdul remarked, trying to figure out what the general meant by 'love with a gun'.

"Is this what Americans call going off with a bang?" Tariq queried, taking his cue from Abdul.

"Just bear in mind that this man is dangerous and requires careful study," the general continued. "Volcov's activities are known in the States. We know he has a global network with corporate entities and corporations on five continents including America. His clandestine contacts with corrupt officials have so far given him freedom of movement, but the pressure's on. We have identified Volcov as the principal dealer supplying weapons to the New Taliban. We know this from the American markings on the weapons. Other items of weaponry come from Russia, Ukraine, the Czech Republic and..."

Butting in, Tariq asked, "General, are we talking about one of the most dangerous men on the planet?"

"Could be, he's devious too. He comes across as a very likeable man. He has a penchant for beautiful women some being prostitutes, but it would be a big mistake to underestimate his proclivity for vindictiveness. We believe the Mamasan of Thailand, with all her callousness, is becoming jealous of his constant philandering. We are assessing whether we could turn her to betray him to satisfy her own greedy ambitions in this delicate arms-and-love arrangement," the general added.

All three men, concentrating intently, were beginning to understand the magnitude of the deals before them. Not to mention the overarching spectre of danger from several quarters.

Continuing the briefing, General Maxwell said, "Last but not least is Governor Ahmad Hakim Kahir. Someone, I venture to say, who needs no formal introduction to those present. There's little need to spend time on his profile because there's nothing in the file you don't know already.

"Instead, we will concentrate on your individual roles as I see them. Let's start with you Farez. We would all like to hear how much you've learned about your new persona if you don't mind. You have the floor…"

Slowly rising from his chair, the malik walked around the room before standing before General Maxwell. Leaning casually against the general's desk, Farez's speech and mannerisms were transformed much to the astonishment of Abdul and Tariq.

"Permit me to introduce myself," Farez said, in an acquired southern accent. "I am Kostas Alexopoulos, a Greek-Cypriot by birth with many years spent in the United States. You can take it from me that I am one of the wealthiest men in the world having amassed a fortune in computer technology, real estate, building construction, and other less obvious pursuits. Let me put it this way: I have an interest in anything that will make me loads of money. Here…look at my new, golden Rolex," he added, wrapping up his presentation. The malik mesmerised Abdul and Tariq with a show of supreme confidence. They pinched themselves to make sure they weren't dreaming.

Resuming his soliloquy, Farez said, "My preference is to work in the background using my compatriots to front-up deals on my behalf. I move around in high-level circles, particularly those of a political nature. If I do say so myself, I can run with the hare and hunt with the hounds. In my way of thinking business and pleasure go hand in hand. If you ask what I am doing here let's say I am convalescing following major surgery while feeding my appetite for the good things in life."

It was an astonishing performance that brought a smile to the general's face, and polite applause from Abdul and Tariq both immensely impressed with their friend's ability to wrap himself in a new persona as if he were donning a favourite overcoat. The malik's mannerisms and speech inflections had changed him from Farez Malikzai the headman of an Afghan village to a total stranger. What impressed the general most, was the reaction of Malik's two closest friends: they no longer saw him as Marwah village's headman.

Directed by the CO to "…come back to us", the malik relaxed his demeaner and became, once again, his own, unpretentious self.

"Thank you Farez, I guess you've convinced us of your ability to play the part of the billionaire Kostas. Now I wish to discuss your role commander," the general said, changing tack and urging the others to remain seated. "First some background: in theory, the commander will be in Washington DC engaged in ambassadorial duties as befits his position. But he will spend much of his time moving between Bagram Air Base and the villa where he will have quarters. We will install an ops room of sorts. It is there, commander, where you will interface with Lieutenant Sinclair.

"Your main role is to deliver to Bagram Air Base any intelligence picked up by Lieutenant Sinclair. Sealed reports will be flown to Washington – probably to the Pentagon. You will work with the Pentagon to help map out possible incursion plans, as the mission progresses, using your extensive knowledge of Afghanistan, Pakistan and the Taliban organisation. Stationed within the villa you will find highly trained special forces personnel. So, as you can see commander, a great deal of responsibility is attached to the part you must play. On your shoulders rests the success or otherwise of picking up these villains and extracting them to face the music."

Instructing Abdul to stand, General Maxwell read from a prepared brief: "Your assumed name is Sergeant John Dwyer. Using your newly acquired skills, you are to infiltrate Adham

Volcov's inner circle. More on how to do that later. Your duty is to work your way into the heart of this dangerous arms dealer's vast empire and destroy it.

"Volcov is a wily old bird who has developed a rapport between the intelligence community in a number of countries and the near-secret arms trade. It is important for you to understand you will be the subject of suspicion from the get-go from those in Volcov's ranks. Looming large will be Patcha Volcov who will not take lightly to the sudden appearance of a new right-hand man for Volcov, someone she believes she already controls. And as you are not a man of her choosing, you will have to watch your back -- literally.

"We will give you an ironclad profile that will stand up to scrutiny. It will show you quit the U.S. Marine Corps under a bit of a cloud that left you embittered. As a result, and because of your skills, you are offering yourself to the highest bidder as a second-to-none security expert. In that respect you will have a glowing resumé," the general added.

Tariq saw fit to comment: "Forgive the interruption general. Please allow me to sum up to make sure I understand our working arrangements. As I see it, Farez is the front man whose role is to distract and entertain what we might call clients. Lieutenant Sinclair is the conduit of information upon the entire mission is dependant – also the one exposed to the greatest danger. My role is to relay the lieutenant's messages and prepare for a strike and extraction procedure when we get the green light from Washington. Is that it sir?" It was clear that Commander Zahir was beginning to warm to the outline plan realising that though they were working separately, they were very much a team as before.

"Correct commander," the general said, looking at his watch before instructing the trio to read their files and familiarise themselves with all the details.

"One week from today," he continued, "Sergeant John Dwyer will be parachuted into Pakistan engage Volcov as soon as possible. Farez, masquerading as Kostas Alexopoulos, will establish himself at the villa and portray himself as a billionaire playboy. You, commander, will be parachuted in a few days after Kostas Alexopoulos takes up his post.

"All three of you are to remain here for the next twenty-four hours prior to returning to the ranch for a final reunion," General Maxwell instructed, noting that the malik had a strained look on his face. "Don't be concerned Farez, we will restore your appearance to its original manifestation, so you don't cause unnecessary concern to your wife or scare any unsuspecting children!

"Now, if it's all the same to you gentlemen, it's my turn to change my appearance and prepare for an important dinner date."

Still laughing from the general's remark, the malik bravely posed the question that was on everyone's mind: "Are we to understand that Margaret is preparing a special meal for you sir?"

"Negative Farez. I am wining and dining the dear lady in the hope that the way to this woman's heart is through her stomach!"

***

Chapter Five

At 0959 hours, according to the digital clock in General Maxwell's outer-office, Sergeant John Dwyer (alias Bashir Ahmadi, alias Lt. Abdul Sinclair) arrived at the COs door, impatient to gain entry. In fact, he was champing at the bit, much like a thoroughbred racehorse in the starting gate at the Belmont Stakes. As the clock registered 1000 hours Dwyer knew for sure that "D-Day" (D for Dwyer) had arrived as he stepped briskly into the COs office. He had undergone a change in his facial appearance: now cleanshaven; blonde hair instead of dark brown; eyebrows bleached and contact lenses to turn his brown eyes green. Taken altogether, the cosmetic changes were in balance because, fortuitously, he had inherited his Caucasian father's skin colour as opposed to his Afghan American mother's bronzed tones consistent with her origins.

Not even the wily governor of Bagram district would recognise the man he believes to be Bashir Ahmadi should they bump into one another which is bound to happen in the fullness of time.

"Come right in Sergeant Dwyer," the general ordered after acknowledging Abdul's polished salute, "I must admit you looked transformed," he added, motioning the marine to be seated.

"Thank you, sir. I guess I also feel different!" he responded with a straight face.

"That's what I wanted to hear from you. Now, listen up: Commander Zahir and Farez Malikzai will walk through that door in a minute or two and I am anxious to gauge their reaction when they meet Sergeant John Dwyer." As if on cue, the general's aide knocked and ushered the two men into the COs presence.

"Ah, Commander Zahir…Farez…come in and meet Sergeant John Dwyer," the general ordered as both men stepped forward for a closer look, curious to learn why a run-of-the-mill sergeant was commanding the attention of one of the U.S. Army's most illustrious officers.

Though he tried exceedingly hard, Abdul was unable to maintain a straight face. As soon as he smiled it was a dead giveaway.

"I don't believe it sir," Tariq muttered as Farez, disapprovingly, shook his head from side to side.

"Believe it gentlemen," the CO ordered, "and get used to it because you will be seeing a great deal of Sergeant Dwyer. From today, think only of the name Sergeant John Dwyer because neither Abdul Sinclair not Bashir Ahmadi exist.

"Make that a golden rule to follow and never break it because walls have eyes and ears and your safety depends on who you are today…now…this minute. The past is the past so move on."

It was made abundantly clear to all present that the forthcoming mission was going to be different in all facets of a military operation especially as the main combatants involved had to play adopted roles in what could be an action drama movie writing itself.

"You are being brought together for this final pre-op briefing as this will be the last occasion to connect with one another until you regroup in Pakistan. So, listen carefully: Sergeant Dwyer will soon parachute into an area known as the Durand Line near the Pakistan-Afghanistan border. It's a one thousand, five hundred-mile-long mountainous region, named for British India's Sir Mortimer Durand who induced Abdur Rahman Khan, Amir of Afghanistan, to agree to a boundary which, at the time, settled a contentious Indo-Afghan frontier problem.

"In the mid-20th century the area on both sides of the Line became the subject of a movement for Pashtun independence and the establishment of an independent state of Pashtunistan. If you are wondering why I am so well informed," continued the CO, "it's because I am an avid reader of Encyclopaedia Britannica! What you may know, however, is that this area still experiences major conflicts. It also houses some of the world's most dangerous militants. OK, back to Sergeant Dwyer" he said, looking at Abdul.

"You, sergeant, will be met by a contingent of undercover agents – the same special force of U.S. Marines hand-picked to staff the villa for you, Kostas Alexopoulos, "he added turning his attention to Farez.

"Your next move sergeant," the CO stated, turning back to Abdul, "will depend on you selecting an opportune time to make a move on your target – our arms dealer and get the ball rolling.

"The border area between Afghanistan and Pakistan is a bedrock of terrorism and violent extremism. These hot spots have become a hub of terrorist activity where young men are recruited, trained, and used to weaken and destabilise regional governments. Not only local groups but also international terrorist organisations. You could say it has become a H.Q. for global terrorism and al-Qaeda operatives – safe havens for militant groups determined to wage jihad, their idea of a holy war.

"Foremost among these militants is the Taliban with thousands of fighters, plus the masterminds of al-Qaeda all of whom are thought to be hiding in these remote mountainous regions. It is an escalating and volatile situation where well-planned operations are formed. An international counter effort is essential before it all becomes a threat to the future of the world. What I'm getting at is we must bring about the downfall of powerful arms dealers, human traffickers, and drug barons and expose those in high office who give such evildoers freedom of movement. Make no mistake, all of the abovementioned would sell their souls to the devil in a heartbeat!"

Something had been troubling Abdul for the past week since studying operational briefs especially those detailing arms. "Sir, I have a question: do we know where the Taliban source funds for such a wide range of sophisticated weapons?"

"From cross border smuggling, thanks to a largely porous border and transborder tribes with similar ethnic backgrounds. And this is reinforced by transborder networks – political and military – funded and armed by dealers in human trafficking, arms smuggling, and the narcotics trade. We do know that ninety-eight percent of Afghanistan's opium is grown in seven provinces in the southwest where there are Taliban-controlled settlements and where organised crime groups profit from the region's instability."

Even Tariq and Farez who know more than most about Afghanistan's recent history, were stunned by the general's revelations as the enormity of the task before them began to sink in.

"This is how we will proceed," said the general. "Initially, Sergeant Dwyer will head for Islamabad where we know Adham Volcov, our colourful and industrious arms dealer, keeps a large, well-appointed villa on the outskirts of the capital. It boasts several secluded areas, obviously a handpicked location.

"Now, take particular note of this next piece of intel, sergeant, because your life may depend on it," the general cautioned, consulting prepared notes. "Volcov is guarded by at least a dozen bodyguards – guns for hire is how they are characterised. One of these 'guns' sees himself as top gun in the organisation, i.e., the boss's right-hand man. If you are able to impress Volkov, as we expect you to do," the general went on, speaking slowly with emphasis, "and he appoints you as his personal bodyguard, Top Gun will immediately see you as pissing in his private pool. You can bet your bottom dollar he will not like being demoted to second fiddle. So, watch your back at all times, got it?"

"I understand sir. Thank you for the heads-up; I was beginning to think this was all going to be too easy," Abdul responded with more than a hint of sarcasm that was ignored by General Maxwell.

"Be forewarned sergeant; how you respond is up to you. When you are established in Islamabad you will be instructed when and how an attack on Volcov should be staged. Much of this will depend on feedback from you and other intel. As part of the preparations, we have rented a large villa bordering Margalla Hills, a hill range north of Islamabad where Kostas Alexopoulos can pursue his lavish lifestyle during his ongoing convalescence. Commander Zahir…you will make an undercover visit to the villa to check out the facilities before Farez moves in.

"I believe that is all you need to know for the time being. Talk among yourselves until Sergeant Dwyer has to leave," he instructed, leaving the three men mulling over the vitally important intelligence raised by the CO.

"I guess we're close to the moment of truth, "Abdul announced, his voice charged with emotion knowing each one of them was about to journey along his own lonely road.

As the elder statesman of the group, Farez slotted himself between the others. "Remember, dear comrades," he said, his tone heavy with sentiment, "though we walk alone from today we remain as one spiritually. And that will always be so my brothers."

*

General Maxwell accompanied Abdul to the U.S. Army 1st Special Forces C-130 Hercules already lined up at the head of Pope Field runway. The landing zone for Abdul's parachute drop was earmarked ten miles from the Pakistan/Afghanistan border in the mountainous region of the Durand Line where he was to rendezvous with the task force. He was anxious to get started; it had been a long wait and now all he wanted to do was to get on with the job.

"Well, sergeant, it's showtime!" the CO announced cheerfully, "and a successful outcome depends on you exploring the worst and darkest sides of yourself. Cloak yourself in your new identity; remember your training and cultivate your role to become the shadow of Adham Volcov.

"He must believe he can rely upon you totally; more than he's relied on anyone before. Do whatever you have to demonstrate to Volcov and his toadies, cronies and bootlickers, that they would be better off messing with the devil himself than with you. Be ruthless; trust no-one; give no-one the benefit of the doubt. It must all be about you. Whatever it takes – get it done. Go to it, sergeant and good luck," he added, shaking Abdul by the hand after accepting his salute.

After take-off, the C-130 circled once before disappearing into the evening gloom. In a moment of solemnity, General Maxwell uttered a silent prayer for a brave warrior to be successful in his mission and return safely to his family and country. It was an assignment fraught with danger and everything depended on his ability to play the devil at this own game and win.

*

Hours later, Abdul's combat boots struck terra firma a few miles short of the border on the Afghan side near the Kabul-Islamabad road. It was dark when he touched down, which made for a tricky landing by chute deemed essential to avoid the risk of attracting unwanted attention with a daylight drop. After hastily gathering up his parachute silk he activated the miniature radio transmitter on his watch strap.

"Eagle One...this is Eagle Two...activate...over!"

"Roger, Eagle Two...we have punched in your coordinates. Stay low, we'll be with you in ten...out!"

The sound of an approaching vehicle broke the silence. Headlamps pierced the darkness with two short bursts prompting the soldier to respond with three bursts on his flashlight. The sound of a vehicle door slamming preceded footsteps and the appearance of a tall man in native Afghan attire, rifle in hand, walking slowly towards the soldier's position.

"Where are you headed, stranger?" the man asked levelling his rifle.

"As far as you are able to take me," replied Sergeant Dwyer, completing the password exchange according to orders.

Lowering his rifle, the man asked, "Where's your chute?"

Abdul pointed in the approximate direction and another man jumped off the back of a truck and retrieved it by which time the solider had entered the vehicle as directed.

"Turning to face John Dwyer, both men grinned and then shook hands.

"I am Master Sergeant Mike Harper...and this is Sergeant Brian Dickson...U.S. Marine Corps. Welcome to the fight," Harper added, as the truck rolled forward on the next phase of their journey.

"Our orders are to take you to the villa on the outskirts of Islamabad," Dickson said, "You'll get further instructions after you rest up. Try to get some shuteye," he added, though the road was uneven and the chance of falling asleep seemed remote. Nonetheless, after a short while he fell into a deep sleep only to rudely awakened when Sergeant Harper shook his shoulder.

"Shake a leg buddy," he shouted, "we have arrived at the villa. "Try to rest a while longer in your room, you will get to see the rest of the team later," he added.

Shown to his room, Abdul tested the bed after heading for the large window and drawing back the curtain. Eyeing the extra-large moon in a jet-black sky, his thoughts turned to his father, daughter, son and all those left behind at the ranch.

"I love you all to the moon and back," he murmured before tumbling into bed and falling into a deep sleep.

***

Chapter Six

Sergeant John Dwyer spent much of the week exploring the villa and grounds and familiarising himself with other members of the special task force assigned to the villa in support of Kostas Alexopoulos's enforced recuperation.

He also surveyed the surrounding terrain including the imposing property of arms dealer Adham Volcov – all from a safe distance. Drones had been used to survey and produce details of the grounds and layout of Volcov's expansive residence. That way, the Marine had a reasonable understanding of the functions of various rooms and a rough estimate of personnel. He figured a dozen men in the grounds and four or five inside the house.

Master Sgt. Mike Harper was NCO in charge of operations at "Villa Alexopoulos" as the men referred to it. The team identified Lieutenant Abdul Sinclair only as Sgt. John Dwyer and that's all they had to know apart from understanding that this big man in civvies was operating covertly and that his fake service records, however deprecating, did not reflect the true situation. Even Abdul had buried his true identity as much for his own safety and that of his entire family.

"Morning John," declared Sgt. Brian Dickson, peering around Abdul's bedroom door a grin on his face. "Your presence is requested below for a meeting in ten," he added, as Abdul grabbed a wad of paper and a pencil.

"Understood Brian...thanks," Abdul acknowledged heading downstairs directly only to find the entire crew already assembled and waiting for him.

"Take this seat, sergeant," Master Sgt. Harper instructed, indicating the chair next to his own.

Gazing around the room at the sea of faces, Abdul was struck by how much each man resembled an Afghan tribesman: dark-skinned, bearded, and brown-eyed, suggesting they'd been selected for their similarity to native Afghans.

Harper could read Abdul's mind. "Your observations are correct; we have been selected for our good looks and multilingual abilities. Seriously, outsiders will see us as Afghan workers preparing this villa and become curious. Well, that's what we hope. And, to address your next question, we have been briefed on your assignment, but we don't know a whole lot about you, Sgt. John Dwyer, other than the top brass at the Pentagon rate your real estate value highly. So, as a highflyer, you will receive every assistance from us at all times," he added, directing his final remarks at the assembled team.

With a thumbs up, Abdul acknowledged Harper's remarks as the senior NCO got to his feet to read from his notes encapsulating the latest orders: "For the next few days, sergeant, you will be seen helping us to prepare this villa. As

Volcov's goons have been snooping around we can only assume their boss is becoming curious. Unlike us, you will remain in western civilian attire because you are a freelancer and not a native like the rest of us," he added, drawing unflattering guffaws from some members of the team. Your cover is this: we picked you up in Islamabad where you were seeking work. We thought we could help. You were finding it difficult because your aggressive attitude and willingness to fight anyone around you defined you as someone who has a big chip on his shoulder. We decided to give you a chance to show your worth."

Unconcerned his cover story lacked authenticity Abdul had his own ideas on how to advance his assignment. But, before that, he had to know more about the opposition, meaning Volcov and his cronies. "Are you expecting visitors?" he asked, reacting to what sounded like a commotion outside. He hoped it concerned the arms dealer.

"Not that I know of," Harper responded, shrugging his shoulders. "Could be to do with Volcov; I expected curiosity would get the better of him sooner or later," he added. "And that's why we are prepared for any eventuality," he stressed, "looking at each team member in turn, before addressing Abdul. "Sergeant Dwyer, if Volcov comes over here you are going to stick out like a sore thumb in those country slacks and rolled-up shirt sleeves. Surely, that alone would be enough to arouse curiosity."

"I'm inclined to agree and that's okay because it's important for me to establish myself in his camp asap. To that effect, Mike, did you receive an outline strategic plan that I was expecting after my final briefing Stateside?"

"Not yet but should be soon because the Pentagon is putting the final touches to several options. I understand they are anxious to get the ball rolling – same as you sergeant," he added, as increasing sounds of a disturbance came from outside the villa.

"Sounds like we have company men…battle stations!" Harper ordered, noticing that Abdul was already halfway out the door.

*

Outside the villa, a stretched limo with gold-tinted windows had pulled up by the front door. Two men disembarked shouting noisily. One man looked around, the other reached to open the rear door to allow Adham Volcov to alight. He stood for a second or two, looking around until his eyes zeroed-in on Master Sgt. Mike Harper whom Volcov took to be a construction worker.

"You there…are you in charge here? Is this villa being prepared for occupation?" Volcov asked. Harper looked at the man, shuffled his feet, and said nothing.

"What's wrong with you man…are you deaf?" Volcov shouted, beginning to lose his temper and patience in equal measure. It was hot and humid and Volcov yearned for a cooler environment. The aide who opened the door for his boss, stepped forward, fists clenched, and one arm raised to strike Harper. That was when black-belt and former judo champion Abdul made his move: he grabbed the man's raised arm and almost wrenched it from its socket. Engulfed in pain, the aide hit the ground. In that split second, Abdul moved to defend Harper hoping retaliation would follow. He wasn't disappointed. Two more of Volcov's thugs ran forward, reaching under their jackets for their handguns. Dwyer anticipated the move and tackled both before they'd taken two steps. Seconds later they had joined their comrade on the floor.

Without uttering a word, or breaking into a sweat, Abdul emptied the men's revolvers and handed the empty guns to Volcov. "What you need to know is that my friend here does

80

not have your excellent command of the English language," he said referring to Harper. "So, allow me to answer on his behalf: This villa is being readied for a very wealthy man who is renting it to continue his convalescence," he explained, staring straight into Volcov's hard, unrelenting eyes.

"And just who the hell are you?" he fired back, making it clear to Abdul that he felt affronted.

It was just as the soldier intended. "Who I am, and what I'm doing here is entirely my business," he responded dismissively, as a plan began to take shape in his mind. Volcov's eyes revealed a hint of enjoyment on his part from the volatile exchange; perhaps even warming to Abdul's recklessness against the arms dealer's loyal bodyguards. The contrast was obvious: Volcov's men were duty bound to bend over backwards for their boss while Abdul had challenged the man in plain sight. Did Volcov find that appealing?

"Why not indulge my curiosity," Volcov implored, regaining his composure. "I can see you're an American so what are you doing among these Afghan workers?"

Impassively eying the arms dealer, Abdul stood his ground and refused to be drawn. "Like I said, that's my business. Maybe you should explain to me why you are asking questions about something that has nothing to do with you."

The Marine's sassy retort brought forth a smile from Volcov. "Simple curiosity on my part," he explained, "…just acting like a near-neighbour who may wish to offer his hospitality in the fullness of time. I have answered your question, so why don't you answer mine?"

"Nope, I don't think I will. And, if I were you, I'd get going while you can. The natives are getting restless," cautioned Abdul looking around as Harper and several members of the team looked on menacingly as if itching for a fight. They started to inch closer but paused as Abdul spoke to them in Pashto.

Volcov decided further discussion was pointless. "Time to leave…I expect our paths will cross again before too long, young man," he added, as he sought refuge in the back seat of the limo which Abdul expected to be reinforced with bullet-proof material. Two very sore and disgruntled apes from Volcov's back-up team glared at Abdul with undisguised hostility before joining their boss in the car. The thug with the dislocated shoulder shuffled painfully to the front passenger door and flashed Abdul an icy stare that told him he had just made an enemy for life.

As the gleaming black limo disappeared from view, Master Sgt. Harper and the entire team burst out laughing mostly because their disguises had passed the test. Each man waited his turn to shake Abdul by the hand impressed by the way he'd handled Volcov and his thugs.

"I guess you made your presence felt in no uncertain way Sergeant John Dwyer," Harper remarked, unable to keep a straight face. "I assume that was the play today, am I right?" he asked amused and impressed by what had taken place.

"An opportunity presented itself and I acted on it. Maybe I made a few enemies, but I also suspect Volcov will want to know more about me and that's the plan. Curiosity got the better of him as you predicted," he added, wondering if the Pentagon could come up with a better plan to get closer to Volcov. He must get the arms dealer on side to keep the dogs at bay, meaning Volcov's bodyguards. "And my congratulations to the team; they sure passed the test today."

Harper again read Dwyer's thoughts. "Thanks. I must bring Washington up-to-speed with what happened today," he announced. "The sooner we get you into the lion's den the better it will be for all of us."

After three days familiarising himself with the city of Islamabad, Abdul headed back to the villa. He had purposely used his time away for a bit of personal shopping providing an excellent excuse for being absent from the estate.

Rounding a bend in the road in his borrowed Toyota Highlander SUV he chanced upon a truck parked by a stony verge. Two men were eyeing the engine engrossed in a heated debate.

"What's the problem?" Abdul asked walking to within a couple of feet of the vehicle. One of the men looked up and beckoned him to move closer, pointing to something in the engine. Obligingly Abdul approached but not cautious enough to prevent someone sticking something hard into his back. Instantly, he knew he had a gun pressed against his ribs.

"Get into the truck...now!" the man said. Abdul complied believing and hoping the men were from Volcov's contingent thus suggesting no reason to resist. Inside the truck his suspicions were confirmed when he came face to face with one of the men he had disarmed earlier. The man sneered at him as his comrade got into the front seat and started the engine. No words were exchanged all the way to Adham Volcov's estate where Abdul was invited to disembark at the point of a gun. So far, so good, thought Abdul as a plan took on more shape.

Standing atop the steps at the villa's main entrance was the man himself, exhibiting a wide smile of satisfaction on his face. Pushed from behind by the man with the gun, Dwyer stood at the base of the steps looking up at Volcov. He wasn't alone. Beside him stood another unfortunate thug with one arm in a sling. A quick glance to his rear revealed more men – possibly six not counting the two that waylaid him on the road.

"I predicted we would meet again, and here we are," Volcov said, lighting up a large cigar. "This time it's on my terms. So, let's start again: who are you and what are you doing here?"

"Like I said before, who I am and what I'm doing here is my business," he responded glibly, prompting the arms dealer's trigger-happy coterie to stiffen-up ready for action. But the boss didn't follow-up as anticipated; in fact, Volcov appeared unconcerned which induced the men to relax their guard.

It was all Abdul needed to make his move. In a split second, he had lined up his shoulder with the man to his left targeting an unguarded area of the man's chest. Left foot forward he brought his right foot around as he leapt high into the air. His adversary's hands went up leaving his upper body undefended. All Abdul had to do was rotate again, so his other side faced his opponent, wait for gravity to pull him down, and then shoot his right leg out in a straight line and into his opponent's chest. Dead centre. Wind knocked out of him the man flew backwards taking four men with him, guns flying in all directions. Abdul rolled on the ground, grabbed a gun and fired first at the man to his right. He counter rolled and fired at the man to his left, winging both men as intended causing them to drop their weapons.

Leaping to his feet, Abdul surveyed the scene, gun in hand. Four men were out of action; two more were writhing in pain with bullets in their shoulders. More men poured out of the villa, guns in hand, but Volcov raised his hand and stopped them in their tracks. To the men's profound surprise (and Abdul's), Volcov, slowly clapping his hands, walked down the steps to stand face to face with the enemy. "Bravo! I am most impressed," he smiled, before addressing the men who had just come out of the villa.

"Clean up this mess," he ordered, pointing to the men on the ground. While this took place, the Marine and Volcov eyeballed one another attempting to gauge one another's strength.

"At the risk of repeating myself," said the arms dealer, "I am most impressed. Now, will you please come into the house because I would like to discuss something with you that I think will be to our mutual benefit," he added, waving an arm towards the house by way of endorsing his invitation.

"No need to be concerned; no-one will try anything on with you – not after that. At this rate I won't have any men left," he said smiling as they entered the house together followed by a scowling man with one arm in a sling whom Abdul recognised as Mike Harper's attacker some three days earlier.

"Darius, you can leave us now. Find someone to position this gentleman's vehicle to the front drive ready to leave after we finish our discussion." Darius was apoplectic at being dismissed in such an embarrassing manner but did not dare object in front of his lord and master.

Turning to Abdul, Volcov invited him to take a seat. "May I offer some refreshments?" he asked politely, making it clear that the arms dealer had some kind of deal in mind. A little more pressure wouldn't go amiss.

"Just what is it that you want with me," Abdul queried feigning impatience. "You know nothing about me so why don't we just leave it like that and go our separate ways," he added, feeling confident that he was about to get his feet under this man's table without any help from Washington."

"Not so fast young man; I am interested in knowing more about you such as your name, why you are at the villa, and most of all, whether you would come to work for me," he explained, before lighting up another cigar.

Abdul allowed a few minutes to slip by, and for the smoke to clear, before responding. "And what makes you think I'd want to work for you?" he asked chuckling aloud.

"Because you are very efficient at protecting yourself and I would like you to do the same for me."

"Thanks, but I already have a job," Abdul replied, feigning disinterest.

"I don't know what you earn now, but I'll wager it's nickels and dimes compared with what I can offer. I am looking for a skilled bodyguard, someone who would double as my right-hand man. A man I can trust in every way. I believe you have the qualities I seek and could be that man," he said.

"From your accent I place you as an American," Volcov observed. "Judging by your fighting prowess you are a trained soldier, possibly special forces. What I don't know is what the hell you are doing in the Islamabad neighbourhood. Further, I see you as an angry man, a very angry man. How am I doing? Am I on the right track?"

Abdul leaned back on his chair, stared at the ceiling for seconds before addressing Volcov.

"OK, I'll give you the ten-dollar version. My name is John Dwyer. Until recently U.S. Marine Corps. No longer; now I'm as free as the wind. I go where I please; I do as I choose, and I answer to no-one," he said nonchalantly to the older man's continued amusement and apparent admiration. Abdul had his full interest; it was time to seal the deal. Taking a deep breath, he said, "I killed a civilian when I was on patrol; a young, heavily pregnant woman. It was a deliberate act on my part."

"A man like you must have had good reason. Tell me about it," Volcov said, warming to his guest.

"Not much to tell I guess. I was out on patrol and entered a village where we knew insurgents were hiding. We were watching a house. Moments after we arrived a woman ran out screaming at the top of her voice. She saw us and stopped in her tracks… she was standing on a land mine. I wanted to help but couldn't make a move because Taliban fighters were in the house. Of the two options of a clear shot at the woman or watching her and her unborn child blown to pieces I took the shot. I killed her," he explained, false emotion replacing the bitterness in his voice liked an experienced actor.

"Seems you acted out of compassion so I can't see what's to regret."

"Tell that to the marines as the saying goes. I was court-marshalled, faced a murder rap, and spent five years in the brig before being dishonourably discharged."

"Why didn't you return to the States?"

"Like I said: I answer to no-one. Here, in the borders, I can please myself where I go and what I do. I get by…"

Taking a card from the inner pocket of his safari jacket, Volcov passed it to Abdul. "This is my telephone number. Come and work for me as my personal bodyguard and assistant. With you I would feel safe. You would get to live with me in the big house and go wherever I go. I can guarantee a financial package that you'd find very generous. Give it some thought and call me with your answer."

Pocketing the card after looking at it closely, Abdul got up leave. "What about your men. Somehow, I don't think I made a great impression on them if you see what I mean," he said grinning at Volcov.

"Perhaps not, but they take orders from me and what I say goes. Apart from that, I don't think they'd be in a great hurry to mess with you again," he answered shaking Abdul's hand.

Driving back to Villa Alexopoulos, the Marine was aware that he'd given the arms dealer enough background data to check on him and that's what he wanted.

Master Sergeant Mike Harper met Abdul on arrival. "How did it go?"

Contact Washington and tell them the cuckoo is in the nest.

*

Back in Fort Bragg General Maxwell's phone was ringing off the hook. Washington acknowledged the coded message from Islamabad without admitting surprise that Lieutenant Sinclair had established firm contact with Adham Volcov without their help. If nothing else, the Pentagon was assured they had the right man for the mission. Next it was imperative for Farez Malikzai and Ambassador Tariq Hasan Zahir to take up their new positions without delay. Sinclair would need their support as soon as possible and the arrival of Kostas Alexopoulos would surely capture Volcov's attention. For sure, he'd be sorely tempted to learn more about his wealthy neighbour.

At noon, as arranged, Farez and Tariq strode into General Maxwell's office.

"Good to see you both. Take a seat please. I have news that Lieutenant Sinclair has impregnated the arms dealer's den without our help. How he managed to do so was not communicated but it does mean we can move faster than anticipated. That means both of you will soon be leaving for Pakistan. How do you feel about that, especially you Farez? Are you up to it?"

"Thank you for the good news general. And please do not be concerned about me. My physical condition has improved well enough to do something positive. I am bored and need to be active."

"I am also ready and willing General Maxwell," confirmed Tariq reassuringly.

"That's what I hoped to hear...so we can discuss the next move. Farez, we have a Gulfstream laid on to take you to Pakistan. It will look like your own private jet, but crew members are U.S. military personnel posing as personal staff. Take note Farez that they will stay at the villa along with a small retinue of staff already there. All are highly trained special forces personnel. Among them is a private secretary who will arrange all social and business arrangements for you. A doctor and nurse – also military – will accompany you with knowledge of your injuries and ongoing convalescence. This is the truth and your reason for being in Pakistan. We can all feel satisfied that you have skilled medical support at all times. Traveling with you will be three security personnel – your bodyguards. Where you go, they go.

"You leave tonight for Benazir Bhutto International Airport from where you will travel in grand style to your villa on the outskirts of Islamabad with enough hype to ensure Adham Volcov swallows the bait. Any questions so far?"

Neither Farez nor Tariq had anything in mind other than to get started. They had trained and been briefed and now it was time to act. Turning to Tariq, General Maxwell had more to convey.

"You will resume your identity as Commander Zahir before being parachuted into the drop zone. And, similar to Lieutenant Sinclair, you will be driven to the villa to familiarise yourself with the operations room and general layout. You will stay there on standby until you contact

Lieutenant Sinclair and together formulate a plan for receiving and transmitting intelligence data.

"Your other duty, commander, is to remain in situ until Farez contacts his neighbour. Your exit strategy, when needed, is by crossing the border into Afghanistan and then on to Bagram Air Base. From there you will be flown to Fort Bragg. That will be necessary when you are required to conduct your ambassadorial duties – otherwise you stay at the villa as the focal point for intel transfers. Is that clear? Do you have any questions, either of you?"

"That's clear general, thank you," Tariq responded. "However, there is something I wish to bring to your notice. I have requested my aide Noori to accompany me. He is used to working alongside me and I really need assistance."

"Already taken care of. I'm glad you reminded me as Noori will be one of Farez's security guards I spoke of earlier. So, he can be a go-between."

"That covers it very well general. Like me, he'll be happy to keep an eye on Farez."

"In that case, there's nothing left but for me to wish you good hunting. It goes without saying that what you are about to do is of great importance to both the United States and Afghanistan and we recognise your willingness and courage in putting your lives on the line, yet again in the quest for peace and to bring closure to this unending war. If I may be so bold as to quote from Islam, with your approval of course…may Allah the Merciful keep you safe and guide you on your journey?"

It was the moment of truth. Both men had worked hard to prepare for this assignment. It was a dangerous road they were about to walk down in the interest of freedom, justice and peace. It was time to act.

"As they say in America general," Tariq said, a wide grin on his face, "let's get this show on the road!"

***

Chapter Seven

Relaxing in Villa Magnolia and deep in thought, Abdul suddenly became aware that he was no longer alone. A smiling Master Sgt. Mike Harper was at his side with some timely reminders.

"Well, today is the day my friend when you enter the lion's den. It is also the day that the self-made billionaire Kostas Alexopoulos arrives at the villa, which means we're all on red alert. So how do you feel?

Grinning, Abdul looked at Harper happy to have him as his new friend. "I feel great. I also feel the sooner we get started the sooner it will be over."

The men had become firm friends in a relatively short space of time and if Abdul had any regrets at all it was that he would miss the company of his buddy when the mission ended, and everyone left for the States.

"Mike, there is something I must ask you to do for me. Mister Alexopoulos is a close friend – more like family – and I would like you to keep an eye on him. He's had his ups and downs and he's not as strong as he makes out. I would hate for anything to happen to him. To give you a bit of background, some while back he saved my life. He means a lot to me and my family and I want to make sure he stays safe.

Serious for a second, Mike, who was fully briefed on the history of both men, sought to reassure Abdul. "You can relax knowing I will look out for him day and night. He will be in safe hands, you have my word," he added as they shook hands as if to seal the deal.

"So, come for a ride now Sergeant John Dwyer and I'll drop you off at the gates of hell!" Harper said, hoping to inject some levity into the proceedings. Leaving the villa together, they jumped into a pickup truck and drove in silence until they reached the gates of Volcov's villa -- the "Gates of Hell" – where the truck slowed to a stop.

"Good luck John Dwyer and don't forget to duck!" Harper chuckled, reminding Abdul of his new identity while fist-bumping his friend as he disembarked. Abdul walked up to the iron gates as the truck drove on in the direction of Islamabad. Seconds later a car from the villa pulled up on the other side of the gates already half-open to admit Abdul. The front passenger door of the vehicle was thrust open and Abdul stooped down to see who was in the car, coming face to face with Volcov's so-called right-hand man who eyeballed the man he knew as John Dwyer with undisguised hostility.

"Get in!" he snarled. The two men drove to the villa in silence. "Get out!" the driver growled like a mad dog that had just had his bone stolen, convincing Abdul he had made an enemy for life. As a parting gesture, Abdul slammed shut the car door. That said it all.

The entrance door to the villa opened to reveal the same four men who had a set-to with Abdul, seemingly recovered from their ordeal. They formed a welcoming party at the entrance as Volcov came into view.

"Welcome John Dwyer; I am delighted you decided to accept my offer. Follow me please," Volcov said smiling as he turned and led the way into his office followed by Abdul and Volcov's goons. They all flinched slightly when Abdul turned and stared at them. The Marine grinned with undisguised satisfaction.

*

The long-range Gulfstream jet touched down at Benazir Bhutto International Airport and taxied straight to a predetermined parking area beside a cavalcade of black limos. As the jet's integral stairs were lowered, Kostas Alexopoulos (a.k.a. Farez Malikzai) stood at the aircraft door looking a picture of sartorial elegance in a brand new, pure white $2,000 suit. He paused for a moment to survey the scene before slowly descending and being swallowed up by an entourage of local officials. Media outlets were thick on the ground, some training TV cameras on Farez which served to stir interest among folk watching from inside the terminal building anxious to see more of this celebrity.

Intent on playing his role like an Oscar winner, following a spell of rehearsals and too much waiting around, the billionaire shook hands with just about everybody. He was anxious to create the right impression before fighting his way into the backseat of the front limo, where he was briskly followed by a female secretary and two men in black suits. Other staff poured into three trailing vehicles and all four cars drove away in convoy.

Sixteen kilometres from the airport the cavalcade kicked up clouds of dust as they deftly navigated the narrow dirt road leading to Villa Magnolia, passing by Volcov's villa in the process where there were signs of activity within the gates. Several men were on watch for the arrival of Adham Volcov's much anticipated neighbour and the billionaire didn't disappoint; he smiled at the assembled men, at the same time realising the game had begun.

Meanwhile, Master Sgt. Mike Harper waited patiently outside the villa to welcome Kostas Alexopoulos. Following orders, Harper was dressed in traditional Afghan attire, this time white, loose, baggy trousers and a long overshirt (also white) and a dark brown, buttonless waistcoat. Ten more staff were

93

similarly dressed as befits servants of a wealthy and influential man; but they wore grey.

Observing cultural etiquette, and established customs, Farez shook each man's hand before putting his right hand to his heart while uttering a polite "as-salaamu alaykum". It was done for effect in the sure knowledge that Adham Volcov's goons had eyes on "Villa Alexopoulos" and were taking notes for the boss.

Inside the villa, the prominent arms dealer was able to relax his pose and become Farez Malikzai if only for a while, as Mike Harper stepped forward to give his new boss a tour of the villa.

"Sir, this is your private study with a view over the gardens at the rear with maximum security from any peeping toms. To spy on anyone here or in the garden would require someone to sneak into the estate and bypass our security system. We will ensure you have low-profile protection wherever you are and wherever you wish to go at all times, and I do mean day or night," Harper added, at pains to reassure the older man. What Harper didn't get into was how much General Maxwell (and Lt. Abdul Sinclair) had impressed on him the importance of ensuring Farez Malikzai was protected at all times.

"Yes sir," Harper went on enthusiastically, "I believe our security is tighter than a fish's armpit." The curious remark seemed to fly right over Farez's head, but it brought a measure of comfort and relief to the proceedings and drew a wry smile from the celebrated arms dealer.

"Thank you. Now, tell me how I should address you young man?" Farez asked, shrugging his shoulders as though apologising for not being able to afford Harper the courtesy he had earned.

"While I'm undercover sir my name is Asad Jaheel. Call me Asad in the company of strangers. You should know sir that all staff her are special service operatives; handpicked because they speak Pashto and are able to pass for Afghans. They report to me and I am responsible for your safety so please get used to me shadowing you. Look upon me as your right-hand man in this villa."

A knock on the study door curbed their tête-à-tête and the tour of the villa when Commander Zahir made his entrance. Farez's face lit up with joy. Both men embraced as brothers as Mike Harper courteously slipped out of the room to allow them a moment of private reflection.

"Tariq, my dear brother, I rejoice at seeing a familiar face in unfamiliar surroundings. It's good to establish contact with someone I can address by his real name in this world of pretence which I can only describe as the lap of luxury," he added, looking around at his opulent environs. "I must confess, my dear friend, that my head spins with everything going on around me."

Commander Zahir knew full well that Farez would do his duty though he was acutely aware how difficult it would be for a man as modest and self-effacing as Farez Malikzai to easily assimilate with his luxurious surroundings. But he would succeed because of his sense of duty and love of country. Not to mention he had been well-tutored for the role.

"My dear Farez," Tariq smiled, "I am quite sure you will soon adjust to life as a billionaire and I shall enjoy watching you make that adjustment. Every morning, while I'm here with you, we will meet, along with Asad Jaheel, and those here to support your business activities and social engagements, to discuss what may have happened and what is likely to happen going forward," Tariq added, concerned for his friend whom he still found difficult to identify as the malik he'd first encountered. That said, he was full of admiration for Farez's contribution to the cause though concerned it could all prove too much for this brave and determined village headman.

The wily malik, as always, could read his friend's mind. "You must stop worrying about me. I am in control of myself and very happy to be here and playing a part in this important assignment."

They exchanged smiles with a depth of understanding afforded only to those with deep-rooted bonds of affection. They had come a long way, and each man was determined to continue down the same path irrespective of the risks.

*

Inside Villa Margalla, Adham Volcov led John Dwyer into a large and beautifully appointed room adorned with thick-pile rugs from Lahore and fine tapestries from India. From behind a rosewood desk, with its a panoramic view of the Margalla Hills that contributed to the villa's name, Abdul could see that money was no object as he watched this bald-headed, heavily-built man – not with features similar to Nikita Khrushchev -- slip into a large, leather chair behind an oversized desk.

"From today you are my bodyguard and right-hand man," Volcov announced at the same time directing Abdul to sit opposite him. The Marine took his time as Volcov continued with his welcome speech. "That means you go where I go. I have many business contacts and have managed to make just about the same number of friends as enemies. I trust no-one but you need to know that doesn't apply to you. You and I must be able to trust each other. And whatever you see or hear you keep to yourself. Got it?"

Silence.

"I will take your silence as affirmation. Remember, John Dwyer, you will be well taken care of as my shadow. At all times you answer only to me. I know you can look after yourself which is just as well because you have managed to amass a few enemies along the way by demonstrating your fighting skills. I guess I'm stating the obvious, but you will find Darius, my former right-hand man, is not your biggest fan but I don't suppose that will bother you much," Volcov said, smiling at the man opposite. "So, John Dwyer, do we have a deal?"

Abdul pretended to go into deep thought for a minute or two before confirming his willingness to work for the arms dealer. "We have a deal. What do I call you?"

"Sir will do fine. Now, I want your passport," Volcov said holding out his hand.

Our bold warrior had not figured on being asked to hand over his passport, fake though it may be, and he hesitated for a moment. It didn't resonate with the trust Volcov had spoken of and Abdul was irked by the suggestion.

"Is there some problem?" Volcov enquired, hand still outstretched.

"If curiosity ranks as a problem then, yes, I have a problem with that."

"Curiosity, John Dwyer, killed the cat so I'm told. Let's start over again because I like you. Let me explain; anyone who works for me has to hand in his passport. I call it insurance – my insurance against quitters. You won't get far without it and that's how I like it. Understand now?"

Abdul withdrew his passport and handed it over, smiling inwardly at the thought the document was worthless. Outwardly, he remained impassive, probing Volcov for weaknesses. Clearly trust was not his strongest attribute and that was good to know. So far, the feeling was mutual.

Any residual tension between the pair subsided as the door was flung open to reveal a woman on an urgent mission. In her haste, she failed to see Volcov's new, right-hand man, concealed from view by his high-backed chair. Her voice was harsh, lacking any hint of sophistication. Approaching Volcov's desk, she began spouting off about a "...new shipment of cargo ready to go..." but stopped midstream when she spotted the man in the high-backed chair.

"Who the hell is this? I wasn't informed you had company," she bellowed, staring harshly at Abdul who immediately guessed he was being stared down by the infamous Patcha Volcov. The briefing he'd received about this woman appeared disturbingly accurate, he mused, as he looked on and listened to her sound off like a factory siren. She came across as a bitter and hard-faced, forty-something-year old woman heavily made-up which served to define her tough nature. She projected a great sense of her own importance with lots of attitude backed by ambition. All that from a couple of sentences, thought Abdul, as Volcov slowly rose from behind his desk.

"Patcha, meet John Dwyer, my new bodyguard and right-hand man. He has replaced Darius."

She stared at Volcov in total disbelief. "Are you mad? Why wasn't I consulted?" she demanded furious about the sudden, unannounced change to their working relationship.

Primed for resistance, Volcov countered, "I will never consult you on matters that concern me only. I decide who works for me and who doesn't, so get used to it Patcha!" he stated forcefully. Directing a hateful stare at Volcov, she walked over to Abdul and stood defiantly behind his chair. Sensing an imminent problem in his immediate vicinity Abdul took the initiative. "Is there a problem madam?"

"None I can't resolve." Unsure of her meaning, Abdul withheld further comment half-expecting to be tested in one way or another.

"I repeat, no problem that can't be resolved," this time her words were hissed out like a snake as she withdrew a knife from within her clothing. Gripping it in her right hand she lunged at Abdul who, alert, was up in a flash. Stepping smartly to his left he dropped in behind her, grabbed her hair with one hand and put a choke hold on her neck with his other arm. She was blindsided by his fast moves and unable to respond effectively.

"Drop it now," the new bodyguard ordered, watching her face turn blue as she choked. Her choice, he thought to himself. She had no good way out and knew it. If this man pulled her back, she could wind up on the floor possibly unconscious. If she fell forward, she would also wind up on the floor, probably on her face. Neither option appealed to her strong sense of survival. Defences neutralised she dropped the knife. Volcov picked it up and Abdul released his grip at which point Patcha spun round and slapped his face. Turning on her heel she swept out of the room slamming the door behind her for good effect.

"A real nice lady," Abdul remarked as if it were all part of a normal day's work.

"I guess just another example of your inability to win friends and influence people John Dwyer," Volcov grinned, having enjoyed the exchange and secretly delighted to see his right-hand man rise to the occasion and wipe the arrogant look off the bitch's face. He was also aware that Patcha was not the forgiving type, so he'd have to be extra careful when she was around particularly if John Dwyer wasn't there to cover his back. In truth, Volcov was tiring of Patcha but, for now, he needed her for business.

"As I see it, and please correct me if I'm wrong sir, I'm not here to win friends or influence people. I am her to shadow you. And for that I don't need friends," Abdul declared, his face a picture of seriousness.

Impressed, Volcov smiled, "Sooner or later," he said his voice heavy with emotion, "everyone needs a friend. One day you'll agree with me." In that moment of incongruity, Abdul felt some empathy for the man. It was an irrational sentiment and he knew it, but there was something wistful in Volcov's tone and the words he spoke.

The study door opened, and a grim-faced Darius entered. "Did you call me sir?" he asked, in a voice heavy with resentment.

"Yes, I did, come in Darius. As I mentioned before, John Dwyer has taken over your position. I have other plans for you my friend," he explained, eager to keep his former personal assistant on side. "As I see it, Dwyer is better-suited for the cut-and-thrust protection role; I want you to spend more time organising events for me. I hope you can be big enough to accept these changes and come to terms with Dwyer. You guys have to work together. Let bygone be bygones. So, shake hands, and that's an order," Volcov instructed in a commanding tone.

Grudgingly Darius obeyed, offering his hand to Abdul. But his eyes told a different story.

But Volcov appeared satisfied. "Good, that's out of the way. Now you can show Dwyer to his quarters."

The arms dealer, clearly in constant need of reassurance as far as his safety and security was concerned, had assigned Abdul a room next to his. "And as for you, Dwyer, take the rest of the day and familiarise yourself with the house and grounds. Make a thorough study because tomorrow, at nine sharp, you will report to me for further instructions," he added, turning his back to signal the meeting was over.

Abdul left with Darius and headed up the staircase. Halfway up, Darius got something off his mind "Don't think for one minute this is the end of the matter Dwyer," he said threateningly. "I've got your number pal. You may think you're playing a winning hand but nobody…repeat nobody makes a fool of Darius Forsetti and gets away with it."

"You don't say. Well as you can see, Darius Forsetti, I'm quaking in my boots!"

"Just watch yourself, Dwyer. You may be watching the boss but make no mistake I am watching you," a livid Forsetti threatened, gripping Abdul's arm and leaving no doubt he was deeply upset about his sudden and dramatic fall from grace.

"I'll keep that in mind," Abdul said, fending him off. "So, if you don't have any more helpful advice suppose you show me to my room and get out of my face!"

*

A refreshed Abdul woke early. He had made good use of his time the day before thoroughly exploring the villa and grounds without raising suspicion. Knowing he would be spied upon from the side-lines by numerous folk – some curious, some carrying a grudge – he resigned himself to experiencing a spell of anecdotal intrigue in the coming days. At least life promised to be anything but dull, he thought to himself, as he gazed out of his bedroom window overlooking the grounds to the rear of the villa.

And there she was a young woman walking in the garden. Slim, fair-haired and strikingly beautiful. He followed her every movement. Obviously Caucasian he wondered just who she was and why she was walking around alone and in full view. She hadn't been mentioned in his briefing and he hadn't reckoned for a female presence, expecting all villa personnel to be males. She looked to be in her mid-twenties, dressed in a way that foretold a refined taste in clothes. He found the diversion entertaining and, curiosity on the rise, he decided to establish contact with her as soon as an opportunity arose. Checking his watch, he set off to report to Volcov. It was almost nine and he sensed punctuality would be an important factor in Volcov's busy life.

"Good morning Dwyer...or may I call you John?" Volcov queried as Abdul arrived on the stroke of nine.

"Good, then that's settled John," he declared without waiting for a response. "And I'm pleased to see you respect punctuality as I do. Punctuality is the politeness of kings so sayeth Louis XVIII – as it should be with all men and women says I," he pronounced reaching for a jug of coffee already set up on a tray on his desk. There were two cups which made Abdul suspect his boss was expecting a third party. So, it came as somewhat of a surprise when Volcov offered him a cup of coffee.

"Let's get down to business John. As I said yesterday, I want you to accompany me everywhere I go whether for official functions or business meetings. If I deem it inappropriate for you to be in the same room as myself, which will happen on occasions, you will stand by until I signal you to return. Anything you witness or hear must be treated as strictly confidential and not to be discussed with anyone at any time. Is that clear?"

"Loud and clear boss!"

Aware that his new bodyguard was economical with words, of which Volcov approved, the arms dealer smiled recollecting their initial encounters during which he had said on more than one occasion, "…getting a response from you is like pulling teeth!" But there was something about Abdul that fascinated him. It also brought out the more compassionate side of Volcov's nature. Maybe in the fullness of time they would understand one another better. Indeed, Volcov hoped this would be the case. He had never married and harboured regrets. His line of business was undeniably high-risk in every way and left little time for personal pursuits even making friends.

Both men were startled when the doors to the garden swung open. Abdul was on his feet in a flash. In strode the same young lady he had spotted earlier from his bedroom.

"My darling girl…please come in," Volcov said smiling, his face a picture of pure joy and devotion.

"Sorry…bad timing I guess Uncle Adham. Should I come back later?" she added, turning to leave. Volcov got to his feet and steered her into the room, clearly thrilled to have her present, if for no other reason than to introduce her to his new personal assistant.

"John, I'd like you to meet my niece, Miss Laura Brody; a more delightful young lady I find it difficult to imagine," he added proudly. Fortunately, she is staying here with me indefinitely," Volcov added, his tone of voice full of warmth that amazed Abdul as he reached out to shake Laura's hand. Volcov seemed transformed by her presence making it clear that this little lady was an important part of the old man's life.

"My dear," he said, putting an arm around her shoulders, "your timing is perfect, you arrived at precisely the right moment. I have a favour to ask of you my dear. John Dwyer is my new bodyguard and personal assistant – you might say my man for all seasons. As you have probably noticed, he needs a new wardrobe that befits his position as he will be accompanying me everywhere. It would please me if you would take him into Islamabad and have my tailor kit him out appropriately. I mean in a style that meets with your insightful approbation," he added, a twinkle in his eye as he looked from one to the other. Abdul was beginning to think Volcov was something of an enigma; but it was early days.

"Of course, Uncle Adham if that's what you want. I will do as you say because your wish is my command!" she said playfully, at the same time eyeing up the new bodyguard. "When shall we go?" she added with undisguised enthusiasm.

It was Volcov who answered for his PA. "Now would be a good time. I will not require John's services until later this afternoon. So, away you go and enjoy yourselves. Darius will stand in for you John. Have lunch somewhere nice and expensive!" he emphasised, clearly pleased with developments.

Though slightly perplexed at the fast pace, Abdul decided it would be imprudent to ask too many questions, at least right now. "I guess I just go with the flow," he muttered under his breath.

"Off with you," shouted Volcov as Abdul, suitably confused, tried to rationalise his own thoughts on the relationship between the scheming Volcov and his charming niece. Being surprised and delighted at one and the same time was a new sensation for Abdul. He was curious to learn more.

"On your way out, John," Volcov called after him, "ask Darius to come in here please."

Acknowledging the boss's instruction with a nod and a smile Abdul pictured Darius being more than irritated to receive such an order from the man who'd just taken over his job. All things considered, it had been a successful and rewarding morning at Villa Margalla – at least for bodyguard and PA Sergeant John Dwyer.

*

Abdul was still trying to process the morning's events. Not only had he found himself in good stead with his new boss who insisted he was given a new wardrobe, he had been encouraged to accompany the boss's drop-dead gorgeous niece.

Without doubt, it had been a successful encounter topped off by an excellent lunch they were in the midst of enjoying. It was enough to make a man feel guilty, Abdul thought to himself. But he was too smart and experienced to let down his guard over one meal even though Volcov had revealed an unexpected softer side to his nature It was something important missing from the dossier and it belied his vicious reputation as the "Wolf".

Studying Laura's behaviour, he was inclined to believe she idolised her uncle. "How long have you been staying at Villa Margalla?" he asked. She smiled, at the same time weighing up her rugged, good-looking lunch partner. This is someone she would like to know better, she told herself as she tried to concentrate on her meal.   "Three weeks or so. Uncle Adham insisted I stay with him. I think he wants to keep a close eye on me -- unfortunately," she said, a twinkle in her eye.

"That isn't difficult to understand; I'd do the same in your uncle's shoes," he responded, the words tumbling forth extemporaneously. Immediately he felt and looked awkward.

"In that case, John Dwyer, thank goodness you're not my uncle!" she fired back, looking into his eyes in a manner that left her meaning in no doubt. "You ask so many questions," she said, "so I assume you are curious about my situation and

105

why I'm in Pakistan. Okay, John, I'll explain: my mother died quite recently in an automobile accident in the States. That left me alone and Uncle Adham came to my rescue," she added, feeling dejected recalling the unfortunate incident.

Without a second thought, Abdul reached across the table and took her hand in his demonstrating a willingness to share her distress. "What about your father and other family members?"

"I never knew my father. He died before I was born," she lamented, recovering her composure though in no hurry to withdraw her hand. "Uncle Adham has always been a father figure to me. So, when he asked me to join him here, I was more than happy to keep him company."

It was impossible for Abdul not to admire Laura for her apparent sincerity. However, he decided it would be wise to hold back from asking more personal questions for the time being. Besides, he didn't want to spoil the magic of a wonderful couple of hours in her company. His feelings towards the lady were growing and his professionalism told him life could become difficult if he let his feelings cloud his judgement. He had an assignment to fulfil and personal feelings for this lovely young lady must not get in the way of duty. After all, Volcov is a wanted villain who must answer for his crimes come what may. A passing glimpse of the man's softer side changes nothing even though Abdul had to admit to being caught off guard. Yet, it will become difficult, even contentious, when Laura discovers that her uncle's bodyguard sitting across from her is playing a leading role in bringing her uncle to justice. No doubt she'll hate him for it and that incongruous thought was already playing on his mind.

"We had better get going young lady before I get fired for keeping you to myself for too long," Abdul said, smiling. Laura rose from the table, deliberately positioning her body too close to Abdul for comfort. Placing a hand on his shoulder, she looked into his eyes, leant forward and kissed him gently on the lips before he knew what was happening.

"That's just to say thank you John Dwyer for a lovely morning and delicious meal. I am sure this is the first of many more," she added walking towards the car. The drive to Villa Margalla was conducted in silence. Two people had much to think about.

*

Pulling up at the villa, Abdul spotted two unfamiliar cars on the driveway suggesting Volcov had visitors. Laura preceded him into the house and headed for the study door where she knocked and waited. It opened to reveal Darius who announced her arrival.

"Excellent," responded Volcov. "Please ask her to come in and bring John Dwyer."

Grudgingly, Darius stepped aside to allow both to enter. Desperately he tried to contain his resentment watching a man in the role he assumed was his. His impassioned expression spoke volumes. He had not only suffered the humiliation of losing his top dog position he had to endure the indignation of having salt rubbed into his wounds.

Inside the study, two men were sitting across from Volcov, their backs to Abdul.

"Laura, my dear girl, I hope you enjoyed your morning in town," Volcov beamed.

"Much more than you'll ever know uncle," she said a wide grin on her face. "And your bodyguard has a new wardrobe that will arrive tomorrow. I think you'll approve of the choices we made."

Forsetti grimaced like a wounded animal.

Ignoring Forsetti's discomfort, Volcov teased his niece, "…choices *we* made, you say," he said with eyebrows raised. "I wonder who got their way in the end?" he quizzed. Blushing, Laura laughed aloud.

Volcov turned to his visitors who had arrived at the villa moments before Abdul and Laura. "Gentlemen, I believe you already know my niece. But you haven't met my new right-hand man John Dwyer," he stated, bidding Abdul step forward to come face to face with both men, one of whom he knew only too well.

"John, this is my distinguished guest Governor Ahmad Hakim Kahir," he announced with more than a hint of pride. "He is the driving force behind the New Taliban in Pakistan. And my other guest," he announced proudly, "is my business colleague Angelo Damiano."

Volcov's guests remained seated each man eyeing the arms dealer's bodyguard at close quarters. Abdul held his breath as he stared disapprovingly at the governor in a resurgence of hate for the man. He fought to disguise his feelings as he surveyed the man before him now morbidly obese. His bloated face and ample neck gave him a clownlike appearance. For sure he would be the same ill-mannered mountain of jello that Abdul recalled so well. Meanwhile, the portly governor, wheezing like a rusty set of bellows stared ahead, his enormous stomach under pressure like a python that had swallowed a goat. Abdul was close enough to touch the governor but there was no sign he recognised the man he knew as Bashir Ahmadi who had served him during his tenure as governor of Bagram district in Afghanistan's Parwan province. With some relief Abdul had to believe his "Hollywood makeover" was holding up.

He turned his attention to Angelo Damiano. By contrast, this well-dressed man was physically well proportioned compared with the amorphous blob sitting alongside him. Damiano's carefully manicured hands spoke volumes, but his documented reputation, which read like a horror-novel, suggested he was highly dangerous when provoked. Now in his early sixties, the man known as The Angel of Death was suspected of maintaining close links with Italy's Cosa Nostra. Eyeing him up and down, Abdul recalled that Damiano in Italian means "to tame and subdue", so Angelo was a man to approach with extreme care.

Neither man chose to speak to Abdul they simply stared at Volcov's bodyguard with little interest.

Volcov broke the silence, "I detected from the animated expression on Laura's face that she enjoyed her morning's outing. So, you can take a break John; I don't need you here. Keep an eye on Laura for me. You'll probably find her by the pool," he ordered, making it clear he did not want Abdul present.

"But, sir, I thought…" Abdul started to voice his concern but Volcov held up his hand.

"Hold it right there. If I need you, I'll have Darius fetch you. Now go!" he insisted as if Volcov did not want Abdul to be any part of what was to follow. It was obvious that it was going to take time to gain Volcov's full confidence. Meanwhile, Abdul had to tease out the reason for the tripartite meeting of international villains and whether it tied-in with the conversation that ended abruptly a few days ago when Patcha realised she and Volcov were not alone. He was perturbed, but not surprised, when Governor Kahir was introduced as a leading light in the New Taliban of Pakistan. It wasn't fresh news, but it was confirmation of previous intel on the subject. Following Volcov's orders, Abdul headed for his room.

Seated on the side of his bed, Abdul mulled over the day's events. Something big was going down and Volcov's guests were involved. He had to learn the what, when and where of it even though the boss was keeping him at arm's length. Perhaps he hadn't yet earned the privilege of being wholly welcome at Volcov's meetings and that had to change.

He was distracted from his ruminations by the sound of laughter coming from the garden below. Laura was playing with a small dog. Though he didn't relish the thought that Laura could be involved in her uncle's corrupt business practices, he had to find out if she knew anything that could aid or advance his assignment. He also knew he had to exercise care as he felt attracted to her in a way that could spell big trouble. Grabbing his swimming trunks, he headed for the pool.

*

Finding himself alone, he jumped in and swam a few lengths. Heaving himself onto the side of the pool he sat dangling his feet in the water letting his thoughts wander freely like a butterfly frantically exploring a tree of frangipani blossoms. He had a lot on his mind.

His privacy was interrupted by the sound of scampering paws belonging to a small terrier-type dog that launched itself at him with supreme joy. Looking down at Abdul, Laura laughed aloud at the wild antics of her canine companion. By now her uncle's burly bodyguard had the dog firmly in his hands forced to join in the laughter as the animal furiously beat its tail against his chest.

"Is he a friend of yours?" Abdul enquired.

"Meet Sykes; yes, he's my happy little friend," Laura responded. "When I came here to stay with Uncle Adham I brought Sykes with me. He seems to like you John," she added, picking him up to allow uncle's bodyguard to recover from a very boisterous introduction.

Scrambling to his feet, Abdul wrapped a towel around his torso like a sarong and joined Laura who had positioned herself on a sun lounger in a shaded part of the garden.

"I enjoyed my time with you today, John," she whispered, "and I'd like to thank you for making it special."

Surprised, Abdul said, "I think I should be thanking you. After all, I benefited not only from a new wardrobe but also from the company of a beautiful young lady," he said, watching her face turn crimson.

"Will we be able to do it again? I would like to get to know you better."

"Whoa...now steady on little lady. Let's not lose sight of my reason for being here. My job is to look out for your uncle, and I can hardly be in two places at the same time, can I? Not to mention your uncle may have other ideas." He said cheerily and they laughed together. Abdul had not felt so relaxed and carefree for years. As much as he tried, he couldn't ignore his feelings.

He changed tack, "Tell me about yourself Laura," he suggested, eager to learn more but dreading the thought of discovering something about her that would pop his balloon in mid-air.

"There isn't that much to tell, John. I grew up with my mother. She was a doctor...actually a cardiac specialist who seemed to me to be always at work. So, I had a series of nannies who filled in for my mother's many absences. I never knew my father. He died before I was born. Uncle Adham was very good to me. Time spent with him was pure magic. I guess he was the father figure in my life. As a result, my childhood was filled with laugher and happiness."

"Your mother…surely, she wasn't always at work," Abdul pressed, sensing there was more to the story than appeared from Laura's account of her childhood.

"I should have said my adopted mother. I never knew my real mother who died in childbirth. Margaret, my adopted mother, was a medical consultant in the hospital where I was born. She attended my mother and helped bring me into the world. Mother died from a massive haemorrhage. Margaret fell in love with me I suppose. Her husband was killed in Vietnam and it left a great void in her life. Uncle Adham pulled a few strings so Margaret could adopt me. You can see why my uncle is the father I never had. I owe him everything," she said, speaking quietly her eyes tearing up. It was plain she adored Volcov.

"I guess I understand now, Laura, and I apologise for bringing back sad memories by prying. So, changing the subject, what do you want to do with your life? Sorry, another question! But you must have goals or ambitions," he added anxious to learn as much as he could without causing her further emotional pain.

He was not prepared for her response. "I followed my mother and qualified as a doctor. So far, I haven't specialised, but I may take up cardiology. For now, I just want to chill out as they say. It is only six weeks since my mother died, and I feel I need to take time to find myself again. In this place, with Uncle Adham, I can do that. And I have a strong feeling he needs me as much as I need him," she added with a smile.

Her last remark got Abdul's attention. "What makes you think he needs you?"

"It's difficult to put into words…more a case of intuition on my part. He used to be a strong and colourful personality; these days, he seems quiet and at times very tired. As I said, it's hard to explain. He won't discuss how he feels so I really can't do much to help. I do worry however, so I'm relieved to be here where I can keep an eye on him," she answered, revealing a niece's heartfelt concern.

"Are you suggesting he may be suffering some kind of illness?"

"I'm not suggesting anything John. All I can say is he's a changed man. His mind seems more preoccupied these days."

A sudden movement in the vicinity of the pathway leading to the residence caught their attention. Sykes growled softly as Patcha Volcov strode into view. Immediately, she noticed Abdul and Laura engaged in what appeared to be an intimate exchange and broke her stride. Eyes ablaze, The Mamasan of Thailand stared at both with a look of pure hatred.

Patcha challenged Abdul. "Dwyer, what the hell do you think you're doing? Put some clothes on and get back to your duties," she ordered, before turning to Laura. "Take that creature out of here," she yelled looking at Sykes, "and find something better to do than chatting with the hired help," she spluttered.

Neither Laura nor Abdul responded or moved an inch.

"Didn't you hear me?" Patcha screamed, beside herself with anger.

A calming voice from the rear joined the conversation. It was Adham Volcov himself. "I have no doubt they heard you Patcha. Everyone in the villa heard you," he said, his voice soft but his eyes steely with rage. "Maybe they heard you in Islamabad!"

113

"I thought I'd made it clear to you that John Dwyer answers to no-one but me at any time and for any reason. My niece is free to please herself what she does, where she goes, and with whom she keeps company. Stop treating her as a guest -- she is family! My family! This is her home for as long a she wants it to be. It is you, Patcha, who's a guest in this house and don't ever forget it."

Patcha was livid and bit through her tongue. Until Laura arrived on the scene, she had had things very much her own way. But now it was different, and she didn't like it one bit. Volcov was a changed man, so it seemed to her, and with this new man John Dwyer watching out for him she considered her life would become much more difficult. In short, she would no longer rule the roost. For the time being, and until things became clearer where Laura and Dwyer were concerned, she resolved to tread more carefully. But in time she would find a way to turn the tables on all of them. Nobody insults The Mamasan of Thailand and gets away with it. Turning on her heels, she disappeared at warp speed leaving a wake of obscenities.

"I apologise for that minor disturbance," Volcov said, his tone still calm. "Get dressed John and meet me in the study. I have to prepare for tomorrow, and you will be involved."

As Abdul left the garden, Volcov turned to his niece who hadn't toned-down her stance throughout the entire altercation. "Laura my dear, I can see you enjoyed your day and the company of my new PA. That pleases me," he said, not referring to the Patcha interlude. "So, tell me, what you think of John Dwyer. What sort of man is he in your opinion?"

Uncle Adham's loaded question caught her off-guard but she kept her cool. "I like him very much uncle. His is quiet, polite, but strong-willed and, I'd say, considerate. I detected an aura of sadness about him at times as though he'd been hurt badly at some point in his life," she speculated, desperate to not openly reveal the true depth of her interest in uncle's new bodyguard. For a student of cardiology, she exhibited a shrewd understanding of psychology after just one meeting with the man.

Volcov did not respond. He just put his arms around her shoulders and squeezed her gently. "Did anyone ever tell you how lovely you are my darling girl?" he asked, kissing the top of her head. "Now, please forgive me. I must get back before John arrives in the study," he added, walking away briskly.

Gazing after him, Laura knew in her heart something was terribly wrong.

*

The next morning, Abdul presented himself at Volcov's study. He knocked and waited for permission to enter. "Come in, if that's you John...almost ready," the arms dealer said from behind his desk as he fiddled with a sheaf of papers. "Grab a chair; I'll be right with you," he instructed stuffing papers into a box file which he transferred to a filing cabinet. Abdul could see he kept it locked but made a note to try to find out more about it later.

"So, as we discussed yesterday, we are heading for Islamabad this morning. There are one or two stops to make along the way. I was informed we have a new neighbour at the Villa Magnolia down the road. When we're through in Islamabad you can bring me home and then deliver a welcome note to the occupier of the villa. Find out what you can about the new owner," he added. Abdul could hardly believe his luck. Here was an opportunity to contact the team with his boss's blessing.

*

In addition to visiting the same tailor as the day before, this time for Volcov's benefit, Abdul's morning was largely uneventful. They stopped by a large and imposing office building. Volcov disappeared inside and Abdul followed at an appropriate interval to take stock of the occupied offices, noting that most of them were allocated to solicitors or accountants. Not having any idea which office his boss had entered, Abdul returned to the car to wait. The next stop was Kulsum International Hospital at Kulsum Plaza. Abdul was told to remain with the car; he was beginning to feel he was nothing but a glorified driver.

There was nothing to suggest his boss was ill, but Laura's previous comments played on his mind. Maybe he was arranging meetings with the right people for his niece; after all she's a doctor looking to specialise. After what seemed a long wait, Volcov emerged in the company of a distinguished looking gentleman wearing dark glasses and a neatly trimmed beard. Probably a physician of some importance, thought Abdul. Following a brief goodbye, Volcov got into the car. "Job done; let's go home John."

They travelled home in silence. It seemed to Abdul that Volcov had a lot on his mind. Disembarking at Villa Margalla, Volcov handed Abdul an envelope. "Take that to Villa Magnolia, hand it to the new occupant, and wait for a reply please."

*

Nobody in Villa Magnolia had anticipated seeing Abdul so soon, though his unexpected appearance inspired a mixture of surprise and pleasure on Mike Harper's face. Greeting his buddy, Mike said, "Well this is an unexpected pleasure Sergeant Dwyer. I didn't expect to see you back for days," he beamed, applying a firm grip on Abdul's outstretched hand.

"No more surprised than I am," Abdul responded. "I never expected to find it this easy to organise a return visit," he added, going on to explain how the boss had urged him to extend a welcome to his new neighbour.

"How darned lucky is that?" Harper asked, believing that sometimes you get a good break when you're least expecting one. Grinning at one another, the two men went to the main reception room and came upon Farez Malikzai relaxing on a huge settee. Seeing Abdul, the old man got to his feet and, arms outstretched, embraced his friend. Leaving them to get reacquainted, Harper went off in search of Commander Zahir.

Elated at being reunited with Farez, Abdul was relieved to be among friends again and able to relax if just for a short while. "It is so good to see you brother," he declared. "Come, sit with me. Let's take tea together and talk."

The "newly-minted" billionaire Kostas Alexopoulos could hardly contain himself at seeing Abdul standing before him. But before he had an opportunity to express his joy, Commander Zahir strode into the reception room prompting a round of greetings that Mike Harper might have equated to a schoolboy reunion had he not been briefed otherwise. The arrival of a tray of sweet tea, carried by Harper, helped restore normal service. The four men sat down to talk, share thoughts and experiences. Everyone watched with interest as Kostas Alexopoulos opened the envelope from Adham Volcov.

Smiling, Farez said, "Well, my friends, it appears our neighbour can't contain his curiosity. Adham Volcov requests my company for lunchtime drinks at Villa Margalla. That's a good start."

"What is the date, Farez?" Abdul asked not being privy to the content of his boss's invitation.

"The day after tomorrow."

Commander Zahir was less sure; his main concern being for Farez's safety. "I think the meeting should be here in this villa on home ground as Abdul would say. Perhaps Farez could respond by saying he has just arrived and is continuing his convalescence and it would be more convenient for Volcov to come to Villa Magnolia. What does everyone else think?" he asked. "If we do it that way, we can all see the man for ourselves," he added, sensing that others saw the wisdom of his idea.

Turning to Abdul, Farez asked for his opinion. "What would you advise me to do brother? I am prepared for either course of action."

"I agree with Tariq. It will be easier to host the event here then everyone will have access to Adham Volcov to make his own assessment of the man. And as I will be driving Volcov to Villa Magnolia I expect to be the only one accompanying him. At least that's what I will suggest to Volcov if he asks. With none of Volcov's goons in tow Kostas will be in a better position to respond should anything untoward occur.

"There is one small matter I must raise," Abdul cautioned, as the others pricked up their ears. "Volcov has his niece staying with him. She is a charming young lady and I would suggest inviting her along to bolster the impression you are hosting a relaxed, social occasion. Incidentally, she is a qualified doctor," Abdul added, carefully trying to downplay any personal interest in Laura. But Tariq and Farez were way too astute and familiar with the marine not to realise that Abdul had more than a passing interest in the lady.

"If it's as you say," responded Farez, "we must include this young lady. Mike, or should I say Asad, please ask my secretary to prepare a response to Volcov including an invitation to his niece. And come back and join us as we discuss recent events."

During Mike Harper's brief absence, Abdul reported on Volcov's movements including his visit to a solicitor's office and a hospital in Islamabad. "So, you see, there's little to tell regarding the arms dealer's activities. More on that in a moment or two. But I have managed to make a few enemies among Volcov's goons. In particular Darius Forsetti, formerly his right-hand man, who is dangerous and would give anything to see me gone – permanently.

"Another thing: I had a contentious few moments with The Mamasan of Thailand an absolute bitch of a woman. But Volcov put her in her place," he added, explaining how she was humiliated to everyone's amusement.

"My first encounter with Patcha was in Volcov's study. She burst in uninvited and began sounding off about…and I quote another shipment of cargo ready to go unquote. Volcov shut her up. I assumed at the time -- and I'm still of the view -- she was referring to human cargo; the basic commodity she deals in. But here's the kicker: I was introduced to our old friend Governor Ahmad Hakim Kahir. Volcov described him as the driving force behind the New Taliban in Pakistan. It was difficult to keep a straight face. By the way, the portly governor failed to recognise me." Abdul's last remark stunned all present, including Mike Harper who had re-joined the meeting in time to hear the final few minutes.

"My assessment from all of this," Abdul stated, "is that there's a high probability that Governor Kahir is active in sourcing and training young men and women as suicide bombers using Patcha's far-reaching network. I propose we report this," he said, turning to Harper, "because there may be plans to utilise these young suicide bombers to carry out terrorist act in the United States."

Mike Harper, already briefed on the vile acts conducted by the former Governor of Bagram district, understood the importance. "I agree. This intel has to be relayed to the Pentagon to alert them of the possibility of terrorist acts Stateside. Obviously, we need sounder intel as a follow-up," he added, looking at Abdul. "Meanwhile, I will beef up the security detail at the airport and have them watch out for what you describe as human cargo and whoever fits the profile. Of course, trafficked women could always travel on forged passports and that will make it more difficult," he added, jotting down notes for his team briefing.

"Agreed Mike," Abdul responded, "and I suggest putting a tail on Patcha. That could save us a lot of legwork later. But, don't go in too hard; we can't make a move until we are ready and for that we need more intel. We don't want to spook anyone unnecessarily, so maximum caution all round."

"Roger that," Mike acknowledged, "I will brief the team."

"I agree this is important information," Tariq added, "and I must say I am very impressed with the progress you have made in the short time you've been here," he added, addressing Abdul who had a flair for understating his accomplishments.

"Thank you, Mr Ambassador," Abdul responded cordially, "but there is something bugging me which I will raise now. I can't figure out why Volcov visited the hospital in Islamabad. Best I can come up with is that it's to do with his niece who's a doctor. She lost her mother recently in an automobile accident so she's not in the right frame of mind to take up work at this time. Later she may consider starting a practice in Islamabad. But that's all conjecture on my part."

Abdul's reckoning only added to Farez's curiosity. "What sort of a man is Volcov?" he wondered, showing empathy for Abdul's speculation concerning Laura.

"I don't have a definitive answer; too early. I can see that he's in control in every way imaginable and he appears to be single-minded when it comes to business. But he's shown me a softer side that I hadn't expected after studying his mind-blowing crime sheet. I put this down to having his niece around. She seems to bring out the best in him and he is totally devoted to her. Another point: he keeps a locked filing cabinet in his study. I plan to investigate as soon as I can. No doubt the old man is being careful. As for me, he hasn't taken me fully into his confidence. I have to earn my place as his PA and confidante. I think he likes me, if so I should have more to report at a later date," he added, signalling they should disband the meeting to allow him to get back to Villa Margalla before Volcov questions his prolonged absence.

Watching from the steps of the villa as Abdul left, Tariq and Farez praised their good fortune to be able to share time with their friend, regretting it hadn't been longer. "But it was an excellent reunion and a useful meeting. We learned quite a lot," Tariq remarked, "with plenty to follow-up on."

"Let us not forget that during Soviet Union days," Farez interjected, "Volcov was known as 'The Wolf' because of his mysterious and sometimes shadowy behaviour that some men and women may find attractive under certain circumstances."

"You make an interesting point my good friend. Perhaps you should inform Abdul," Tariq suggested as they turned to go back into the residence.

"I have enough faith in Abdul to believe he has already recognised this."

What wasn't discussed, but occupied the minds of both men, was the developing situation between Abdul and Volcov's niece. Abdul's attraction to Laura could put them all in great danger but, for now, it was a case of wait and see how things played out. They trusted their good friend to do the right thing to keep ahead of the game.

***

Chapter Eight

When Abdul got back to Villa Margalla, Volcov was waiting for him.

"You have been gone a while John; any problems?" he asked displaying some concern.

"No problems sir. I delivered the envelope as instructed and waited while Mr Alexopoulos dealt with it," Abdul reported impassively as he handed over the reply from Farez. Tearing it open, Volcov skimmed through the message. He looked surprised.

"Mister Kostas Alexopoulos says he's convalescing and suggests we go to his villa. He includes Laura in the invitation. How could he know about her I wonder?" Volcov queried looking at Abdul.

"That's down to me sir. I was asked if you had any family members with you as Mr Alexopoulos said he wanted to include them. I explained you have your niece residing with you. Did I do wrong sir?"

"By no means John," Volcov smiled. "And as you will be coming along it will no doubt please both you and Laura to have each other for company."

Volcov's quirky remark came right out of the blue and troubled Abdul. The old man had discerned a spark of interest between his precious niece and his newly appointed bodyguard. Extreme care would be needed, he thought, going forward.

"Well young man, I suggest you head for your quarters and attend to the boxes that where delivered today. I guess you have a complete new wardrobe thanks to my niece who I might add has a very expensive taste judging by the invoice!" Again, Volcov appeared to Abdul to be quite relaxed so it came as some relief that the boss seemed satisfied with his explanation of what occurred earlier at Villa Magnolia.

Leaving the room to inspect his new wardrobe, Abdul found Laura waiting for him outside his room. "John, I dropped by to help you unpack the boxes and hang up your new clothes. Are you okay with that?"

Together they entered Abdul's room, quietly closing the door behind them. Neither of them had noticed that Darius, an unapproving scowl on his face, had crept halfway up the stairs in time to see them disappear into the bedroom.

But Darius was similarly unaware that Patcha was behind him and she too had seen the pair disappear into Abdul's room. Seeing the resentful expression on Darius's face, she smiled mischievously, making a mental note to capitalise on the man's festering anger. Also, she had an axe to grind herself. No-one made a fool of The Mamasan of Thailand and lived to boast about it. A devious idea began to form in her mind. She would sweet-talk Darius into believing that she was sympathetic to his cause, and that together they could turn the tables on John Dwyer. Patcha slinked away as quickly as she had appeared, leaving Darius unaware of her presence.

From Abdul's room the sound of laughter was infectious as Abdul and Laura sorted out the new clothes before hanging them up in the wardrobe. All except for a dark navy linen suit, pink shirt and a dark blue tie that Laura suggested Abdul should wear the next day for the visit to Kostas Alexopoulos' villa. She was delighted to learn she'd been invited to join her uncle.

"There you are John," she said, laying the clothes on his bed, "this will make you the centre of attention when we visit Villa Magnolia tomorrow."

"So, you are not only choosing my wardrobe but also dictating what I should wear tomorrow evening," he said jokingly, eyes twinkling as he gazed into her face. There was no denying he felt relaxed in her company. It was a long time since a woman had made him feel special and he liked it.

"I admit I enjoy helping you John. In any case, I think Uncle Adham would approve of my choice in clothes for you," she said laughing as she left the room.

*

Later that evening, Abdul entered the garden enjoying the cool air. But his intention to switch off and relax was short-lived, shattered by the sound of raised voices. It came from an open window in Volcov's study. "You are such a fool Adham. And you're getting soft in your old age. Since your niece arrived nothing has been the same. The sooner she leaves the better." Abdul realised he was listening to the jarring tones of The Mamasan of Thailand. She was on the warpath and out to give Adham Volcov a hard time.

The arms dealer was incensed by her coarseness. "Never speak to me like that again," he said firmly. "You are a guest in this house – my house!" he stressed, "and you are within an inch of being thrown out on your butt. My niece is family, something you'll never be even if you associate yourself with my name," he added firmly but without raising his voice.

Patcha fought back like a cornered cobra. "I warn you, do not let this cosy family feeling get in the way of business – our business – or you will regret it. Nothing, not even your niece, is more important than the master plan. We failed once but we won't this time," she fired back defiantly. Abdul moved closer to the window but stayed in the shadows.

"Failed, you say!" Volcov gasped, this time with emphasis. "What the hell are you bitching about Patcha? All I can think about are those cruel and heartless terrorist attacks, probably the most outrageous undertaking by a sub-state group in the history of the world!" he yelled, becoming increasingly furious with the stubborn woman standing before him. "Had I known the intended targets I would have had no part in it!"

Riveted by the heated exchange, it suddenly struck Abdul that they were talking about the hijackings and suicide attacks of 9/11 in the United States.

"Let's get this straight," Patcha said, fighting back angrily, "your only contribution to the mission was to supply weapons – and that's all! What we used them for was never your concern!" she said screaming at Volcov.

Patcha had gone too far. "Stop right there," Volcov ordered, beginning to calm down. "Yes, I am an arms dealer. Yes, I sell to whoever can meet my price. I ask no questions. That said, I'm the one with great contacts in the right places. Without that vital element in the supply chain you would hit a brick wall in a day. Your cohorts would struggle to find safe havens for the people you're trafficking into the States. Chew on that Patcha! Without my goodwill your life would become extremely uncomfortable. Now go…get the hell out of my sight before I throw you out."

At the sound of a door slamming Abdul dashed from the garden into his room, his mind in overdrive. What had just transpired was the most vital intel they could ever hope to have to support the next phase of the mission. And it must be immediately passed on. Suddenly tomorrow's visit to Villa Magnolia was as crucial as it was convenient.

*

Up early the next morning, Abdul found himself alone in the arms dealer's study. His boss's instructions were to monitor phone calls, check documents – mostly bills – and a few other trivial duties that could be handled by a junior clerk. A call to deal with the heavier stuff, such as beating up people, served to break the monotony.

Relaxing in the garden with his niece, Volcov was on hand if Abdul needed any advice. By chance, Abdul noticed the usually locked filing cabinet was open. It crossed his mind the boss could be testing him, so he decided to play it safe and leave well alone. There could be a camera concealed somewhere, he thought, and now was not a good time to rock the boat after being gifted such a wealth of information from the heated exchange with Madam Patcha.

Instead, he spent an hour or so examining filing material. Apart from the name on a headed invoice from his solicitor's office in Islamabad, for services rendered including a codicil of the old man's will, there was nothing to explain the motive yesterday's visit.

The telephone rang. It was Volcov's direct line.

"Good morning. Mr Volcov's residence. Can I be of assistance?" Abdul announced cheerily.

"Oh…is Mr Volcov engaged at the moment? When he's available, I'd appreciate a word with him," said the woman at other end.

"He isn't in his study at the moment," Abdul responded, "and I'm not certain where he is in the grounds. Can I perhaps take a message or ask him to return your call? My name is John Dwyer, Mr Volcov's personal assistant."

"I understand. Thank you. I am happy to leave a message with you Mr Dwyer. Please inform him we have made an appointment for him with Mr Khan, the day after tomorrow at 3 p.m. If this is not convenient, let us know and we will rearrange it."

"I see, may I have your name please?"

"I am Miss Jumo, Mr Khan's private secretary."

"I'll inform Mr Volcov the moment I see him, Miss Jumo. Thank you and goodbye."

As Abdul jotted down the message on a small notepad the French doors opened and Laura and Volcov came in from the garden.

"Relax John...Laura insisted we have coffee indoors so that you can join us. I insisted you had work to do, but my words fell on deaf ears! You have a lot to answer for young man," Volcov said smiling first at his niece and then at Abdul.

"Sir, I have a message for you phoned in a few minutes ago. It's regarding an appointment with a Mr Khan," Abdul said, handing his boss the note. Volcov glanced at it, sat down and waited for Laura to pour the coffee. "Thank you, John. I will take care of that later. Right now, let's relax and enjoy our coffee." He was smiling but from the look in his eyes Abdul suspected the message carried some ominous meaning.

The welcome coffee break made a pleasant interlude to the morning's work and Abdul relaxed grateful to be in Laura's company. However, he wished the situation were otherwise; that he was not labouring under false pretences. It was becoming increasingly difficult to ignore the feelings that stirred in his breast. He also sensed his boss was not entirely unaware of developments and that troubled him. But not as troubling as the fact that Volcov appeared comfortable with their growing relationship. It would become more and more bewildering for Abdul as days went by because he was finding it more and more difficult to dislike the man.

The tranquillity of the moment was broken when Sykes made a grand appearance after a swim in the pool, generously shaking water over all three of them as a greeting.

"Oh, Sykes! You wretched creature!" Laura exclaimed, brushing down her dress. "Now we are all as wet as you are you naughty dog!" she said laughing as she jumped to her feet to gather a wet and wriggling Sykes in her arms before heading for her room.

"Maybe you need a change of clothes also John," Volcov offered. "Me too, I guess," he added, eyeing his shoes and trousers. At the door, he turned to speak to Abdul. "There's a middle drawer in my desk containing my diary John. Fish it out please and jot down the appointment. Call Miss Jumo to confirm. Naturally you will accompany me."

As instructed Abdul walked to the desk and withdrew the diary. As he did, he noticed a small red notebook towards the back of the drawer. Removing it, he glanced through it quickly. It contained a number of men's names but nothing else. He memorised each and every one, just as he'd been taught to do by his counterintelligence tutors at Camp Pear.. Then he filled in his boss's appointment in the diary and saw there had been several appointments in quick succession all associated with the hospital in Islamabad. Curious, he thought, that Volcov was spending so much time at the hospital. There didn't appear to be too much wrong with him, but Laura had remarked on how he had slowed down from his usual self. Perhaps it had nothing to do with Volcov's health but was associated with his niece and any plans she may have for the future in connection with a consultancy in cardiology. It wasn't something he could ask his new boss or share with Laura. Sitting tight to see what transpired was all he could do.

*

Volcov's stretched limo, Abdul at the wheel, drew up at the outer gates of Magnolia Villa at 6.30 p.m. Laura sat in the back with her father. Darius rode alongside Abdul. The gates opened and the car moved forward along the long drive coming to a standstill outside the front door of the villa. Before Darius could leap out to open the door for Volcov and Laura, Master Sgt. Mike Harper, a.k.a. Asad Jaleel, stepped forward to assist the old man. As to be expected, Darius scowled menacingly at Harper for trespassing on his responsibilities.

"Greetings Excellency, I am Asad Jaleel. Kindly follow me into the villa. Mr Alexopoulos is waiting to welcome you sir." Abdul was standing beside Volcov and as Harper had spoken in Pashto, he translated the message for his boss. Volcov was suitably impressed. Darius seethed.

Moving towards the villa, Volcov turned to Forsetti. "Not you. I want you to stay with the car Darius." Abdul smiled imagining his nemesis trying to contain his fury at being humiliated twice in the matter of a couple of minutes. Leading the way into the villa, Volcov was followed by Laura and Abdul. As they entered, Kostas Alexopoulos moved forward his hand outstretched and a broad, welcoming smile on his face.

"So happy you could come. Welcome to Villa Magnolia," Farez said slipping into his billionaire roll with gusto. The two men shook hands, each looking deeply into the other's eyes as if for a hint of affability in one another.

"Mr Volcov, I assume this beautiful lady is your niece," Farez smiled, bowing slightly, hand on heart. Taking her hand, he kissed it gently, an abnormal and frowned upon act for any practising Moslem. But this particular Moslem was playing the role of an eccentric billionaire with a fortune accumulated from illicit arms sales. And he was determined live up to his international reputation as a playboy and connoisseur of wine, women, and song, while not forgetting of course, that he was at Villa Magnolia to convalesce.

"Yes, Mr Alexopoulos, may I introduce my niece, Miss Laura Brody. And please call me Adham. I think you are already acquainted with my personal assistant John Dwyer."

"Indeed, I met your man briefly," Farez confirmed, looking at Abdul, "when he delivered your kind invitation. And please call me Kostas. I apologise for insisting you come here but I am still convalescing, and my personal medical team is very strict regarding my social and business activities."

"I quite understand," Volcov confirmed, "and I'm sure my niece, who is a doctor, would concur with the advice given by your medical team."

Within the reception room, everyone observed the courtesies of the occasion by chatting politely while enjoying a variety of Pakistani canapes. Abdul declined an alcoholic drink explaining he was on duty, but Volcov suggested he should take the opportunity to relax and enjoy the evening. Abdul was bowled over by Farez's convincing performance as an international playboy who appeared to be revelling his centre-stage, billionaire moment.

"Adham, allow me to show you and Laura around the house and gardens – that's if you're interested of course," Farez offered. "You may wish to remain here Dwyer," Farez suggested, "but if you want to take a turn round the grounds, my personal secretary is at your service," he added, skilfully fabricating an opportunity for Abdul to split from his boss and Laura. It was the opportunity Abdul was hoping for to pass on important intel he'd gathered during the heated exchange between Volcov and Patcha. But would Volcov oblige by taking up Farez's offer?

"Excellent idea, Kostas...thank you. We'd love to see around the villa if you are up to it. John can decide what he wants to do, though I guess I must not keep Laura away too long," he said with a wink and a smile. Yet again there was a hint of mischief in his tone, and Abdul felt a similar level of discomfort when Volcov had previously implied there was something going on.

"Come with me please Mister Dwyer, Farez's secretary said, picking up on her boss's skilful manoeuvre to separate Abdul from the others. He followed her along a corridor, through a side door, and into another area of the house altogether. They stopped outside a heavy-duty door that opened to reveal Commander Zahir standing inside a fully provisioned operations room with videos and comms equipment.

"Welcome brother," Tariq said, pleased to see Abdul. "You have come upon some interesting information I believe," he added as they sat at the large ops table in the centre of the room.

"Yes, I have, and by pure chance. I overheard Volcov arguing with Patcha and picked up some vital intel," Abdul responded, before launching into a detailed explanation of the entire episode.

"And the most crucial remark I heard," continued Abdul, "was when Patcha said they could not afford to fail for a second time.

"Clearly this relates to the 9/11 attacks," offered Irene Ryan, Farez's private secretary, who was taking notes at the bidding of Commander Zahir. "Volcov was the supplier of arms, and Patcha was the end user, I would conclude based upon our knowledge of events at the time."

Irene Ryan was not part of the deceptive plan to portray Farez as an arms billionaire because she was just a pretty face. A daughter of Irish immigrants, and now living alone in Boston, Irene was seconded from the CIA by Defense Secretary Wright to assist Farez, Tariq, and Abdul interpret intel. Her background as a counterintelligence officer specialising in terrorism makes her eminently suitable for the task. Moreover, she was a member of the post-9/11 committee set up to analyse and report on the attacks by Al-Qaeda. Consequently, she knows as much about those events as anyone alive today.

"Just as you say Irene, or there was an intermediary supporting the teams involved in the assault on the Twin Towers and other targets eighteen years ago. In that case, the hijackers were the end-users I suppose," Tariq added, allowing the significance of Abdul's report to sink in.

"I think that's right," responded Abdul, "but I also detected from Volcov's reaction that he had no idea of the identity of the end-user. He was very angry and made that clear to Patcha," he added, to some extent defending Volcov despite the fact the arms dealer was clearly implicated in the terrorist acts of 9/11.

Commander Zahir was less forgiving. "What Volcov did enabled others to carry out the evil acts that followed and for that he must be held responsible my friend."

It was stated in a matter-of-fact manner by Tariq as he stared deeply into Abdul's eyes leaving no doubt that Volcov was as much an enemy as others involved at the time. Abdul knew as much but it gave him no pleasure because of his feelings for Laura. He was walking a thin line between reality and wishful thinking. That said, as a highly trained professional soldier he would fulfil his duties despite his emotions.

"Do not worry my brother," Abdul reassured the commander, "I am focused on the job ahead and I will not fail to carry out my sworn duty no matter what happens and irrespective of who's involved."

Smiling, and reassured by his friend's commitment, Tariq said, "Let's discuss this for a little longer and before Farez returns with Volcov."

"Perhaps a review of 9/11 would be helpful," Irene Ryan suggested. "The attacks involved four aircraft: Flight 11 travelling north from Boston to Los Angeles struck the North Tower of the World Trade Centre; flight 175 from Boston to Los Angeles struck the South Tower. Then flight 77 from Dulles International to Los Angeles struck the Pentagon building in Washington…" Interrupting, Abdul said, "And that left flight 93 from Newark to San Francisco."

"Correct, and because it was late departing Newark passengers already seated on the aircraft were alerted of the other three incidents, probably via their cell phones and airphone calls after take-off," Irene added, recollecting the 9/11 washup meetings. "As a result, some brave passengers conspired to overpower the hijackers and their aircraft crashed in a rural area near Shanksville, Pennsylvania."

Abdul and Tariq looked at one another without speaking for a moment, realising – not for the first time perhaps -- that the fourth aircraft's target was never established. "The fourth aircraft could have been heading for the Capitol Building, Camp David, or any one of a number of high-profile targets such as nuclear power plants," Farez's secretary speculated.

"That's right," Abdul agreed, "and Patcha said they failed the last time and so it seems likely something is being planned to compensate for what the perpetrators of the 9/11 attacks consider a failure. We know that trained suicide bombers are being smuggled into the States which makes it highly likely that a plan is being formulated as we speak."

"From that we must conclude there is a high probability that America may be facing another terrorist attack," Tariq said, "maybe even worse that 9/11 though I shudder to think what could be worse. We have some vital intel here, Abdul, and it must be relayed to the Pentagon without delay. Though we have some idea of why a further attack is being planned, we don't know when and we don't know where," he said, quantifying the situation. "So, Abdul, we are relying on you to answer the 'when' and 'where' questions. Somewhere in Villa Margalla, perhaps, lies the answers we seek."

In the silence of the ops room everyone paused to consider Irene Ryan's review and the implications of Commander Zahir's startling and significant summation.

***

Chapter Nine

Back in Washington, Commander Tariq Hasan Zahir headed straight to the Pentagon armed with the game-changing intel gathered by Abdul. He was picked up from Andrews Airforce Base and driven downtown. General Maxwell, visiting DC from Fort Bragg, was on hand to greet Tariq and usher him into a Pentagon meeting room.

"Your Excellency, I trust your journey from Pakistan was uneventful," the general said, maintaining accepted protocol in front of assembled military staffers who had been busy preparing the meeting room. After they departed, the commander put the general straight: "General Maxwell I hope you can still remember that my name is Tariq where you and I are concerned," he joked, "though I do appreciate the need to observe protocol under official circumstances."

"Of course, Tariq. Now, let me say right off the bat the intel from our lieutenant on the scene is pure gold and amounts to a significant breakthrough. A meeting has been set up in the

Department of State later this morning to dissect the report you submitted. Hopefully we will be able to form an opinion concerning the bigger picture. Before we drive over to C Street, I wanted to get you on your own," he added. "Without doubt Lieutenant Sinclair has excelled himself – and done so in a very short space of time. I don't think anyone would disagree we have the right man for the job."

"I agree, but, if you understand Abdul as well as I do, general, he will say he just happened to be in the right place at the right time," Tariq responded drolly.

"Quite so, Tariq. But in our world, it's always about being in the right place at the right time and that's why people like Lieutenant Sinclair get these plum jobs!" he countered, pumping the commander's hand and underscoring his delight at seeing him back in DC.

"However, I do agree with you general that Lieutenant Sinclair did not waste time ingratiating himself – getting into the cuckoo's nest as he put it – by taking an unusual approach to maximise the benefits of any situation. I think it will be only a matter of time before he takes another step closer to securing more evidence. Of course, he is involved in a high-risk gamble and has already made a number of pugnacious enemies – chief among them being the notorious Madam Patcha also known as The Mamasan of Thailand."

"Is she as dangerous a bitch as she's painted in intel reports?"

"Maybe worse, general. She would like nothing more than to see Abdul dead and buried, seeing him as a serious threat," Tariq explained.

"What about Sinclair and Adham Volcov? How is that relationship working out? I ask because I foresee difficulties when our man is acting alone. Sometimes the last chick in the cuckoo's nest get booted out if you get my drift," the general said, concerned that Abdul did not have too many opportunities to touch base with Tariq or Farez and had to make the best of such occasions when they did arise.

"You raise an interesting point, general. My observation is that Abdul has found some light relief in Volcov's attractive niece who is staying with her uncle. And it seems Volcov encourages what we might describe as a growing friendship," he added.

"Be candid, Tariq, could this growing friendship lead to complications and threaten the mission?"

"I carefully considered and discounted that," Tariq said, "for a couple of reasons that I will explain more fully: firstly, from Abdul's first-hand account we have no reason to believe that Laura Brody knows anything about her uncle's business activities. Her mother died recently leaving her on her own. Uncle Adham stepped in and insisted she stay with him for the foreseeable future.

"Secondly, she is a qualified medical doctor taking time out to mourn her mother's passing. For her to be seen around Volcov's villa makes Lieutenant Sinclair's work easier because her uncle feels she has found a companion in a remote part of the world. And if Volcov feels he can trust his new PA with his beloved niece, he can feel more relaxed with Sinclair.

"If I may, I will give you my assessment general. The lieutenant knows what he's doing, and nothing will divert him from the task in hand," Tariq said, labouring his explanation with great conviction. Commander Zahir did not inform the general he was keeping a close watch on Abdul to ensure the heart did not rule the head. Fortunately, General Maxwell did not press him for more details.

"Okay, I've got faith in both of you enough to fill the pool at Volcov's villa. That said, I will run a check on his niece even if just for her own protection as the mission develops. If, as you suspect, the little lady knows absolutely nothing of her uncle's criminal undertakings, she may one day need our protection.

"That's about all I wanted to discuss with you before the main meeting," he said, checking his watch. "Mister Ambassador it's time we left for the U.S. Department of State."

*

The U.S. Department of State is located in the Harry S Truman Building in DCs Foggy Bottom neighbourhood at 2201 C Street in DC. General Maxwell and Ambassador Tariq Hasan Zahir entered and were greeted by Secretary of State Ray Hollingworth and General John Wright Secretary of Defense. Also present was General Austin Miller the recently appointed CO of U.S. and NATO Forces in Afghanistan, along with other officials from the both state departments, the Department of Homeland Security, and the Pentagon.

"Ambassador Zahir!" Secretary Hollingworth declared enthusiastically, "welcome back to Washington. We missed you!" he added picking out a chair for Tariq. "Please be seated everyone," he said, preparing to make a few introductory remarks.

"Gentlemen, the intel collected by our point man in Pakistan constitutes a vital insight into the relationship between the arms dealer we are watching closely and any visitors he receives. The intel takes us back to 9/11 days. Having set the scene, I will hand over to General Wright to present an overview with a bit more meat on the bone. If you would please, John."

"Thank you, Mister Secretary. Gentlemen, I refer to the confidential report you received on this subject that you have probably read by now. According to our team on the ground we know that weapons for the attackers up to and during 9/11 were provided by Adham Volcov. An intuitive presumption on the part of our lieutenant in the field is that Volcov was probably unaware of the end users for these weapons; therefore, he was not aware they would be used in connection with the 9/11 attacks. If he were asked, for example under interrogation, we would expect Volcov to admit he is an arms dealer who never asks questions about their end use. This does not excuse him, of course, nor does it remove him from continued scrutiny," he stressed, addressing the last remark towards Secretary Hollingworth.

"Point noted, general, and I subscribe to your view that not knowing the end user of his weapons does not absolve him at all," Hollingworth agreed, "but, using the same criteria, proving he had operational knowledge other than the sale of arms would be difficult...please continue."

"With that said, gentlemen," General Wright continued, "intel points to bigger fish to fry than Volcov. I am referring to someone who stands out as a prime mover in planning terrorist attacks. Her name is Madam Patcha Volcov a.k.a. The Mamasan of Thailand. She associates herself with the man's surname though she's not related to Adham Volcov. However, she is a madam in every other sense of the word especially in the context of human trafficking on a massive scale.

"Our interpretation of the latest batch of intel places her at Villa Margalla to monitor Volcov and ingratiate herself with his influential contacts in the States and elsewhere. There have been signs of such activity right under our noses, but we have not picked up on them. We need to be more proactive and fix the weak links in our intelligence gathering. We must stop being reactive and get on top of this situation. Who is it in this country, I want to know, who is prepared to hunt with the hounds and run with the hare? We need to hop to it – no pun intended -- and find who it is who sells themselves to the highest bidder against the interests of America, and still regard themselves Americans…" the general added, disgusted with the concept of the picture he'd just painted.

"The intelligence community has harboured suspicions for some time but fingering these individuals, some of whom are well connected, has so far proved elusive. They maintain a close-knit circle that enables them to operate within the United States with impunity. They sponsor safe houses for wannabe terrorists smuggled into the country. Then they arrange for them to move around unhindered. We learned from the 9/11 attacks that some of the hijackers received pilot training in the States. We must be more proactive, to repeat myself," the general added, pausing to take a sip of water.

"So, that's what I wanted to share with you for openers," General Wright stressed, deadly serious in his presentation because he was under constant pressure from the President of the United States to come up with answers.

"Now, stay focused gentlemen while I recap the 9/11 attacks which I think is important at this juncture. We know the Islamic terrorist organisation al-Qaeda carried out four coordinated attacks on September 11, 2001 – almost twenty years ago. Of the nineteen hijackers involved, fifteen were Saudi nationals including the mastermind Osama bin Laden. There is no need to go into chapter and verse but, as we all recall the terrible loss of life, I want you to concentrate on one aircraft -- the one operating Flight 93. This flight experienced a late departure. On board, the crew and passengers were able to get updated on what had happened to the other three aircraft. The mind-blowing news they received prompted a brave band of passengers on Flight 93 to tackle the four hijackers on their aircraft to prevent them from reaching their target. Their actions caused havoc on the flight deck and the aircraft crashed in a field in Somerset County, Pennsylvania. There were no survivors and the intended target remains unknown. We have plenty of theories such as The White House, Capitol Building...maybe nuclear power plants along the Eastern Seaboard but no clues.

"I submit we will never know. But what we do know is the attackers were Islamist terrorists financed and trained by al-Qaeda allegedly acting in retaliation for America's support for Israel and America's involvement in the Gulf wars and an ongoing military presence in the Middle East.

"Some of the 9/11 hijackers lived in the States for over a year before the attacks. They even took flying lessons at commercial flying schools. Others slipped into the country unchallenged in the months prior to September 11, 2001 and acted as muscle for the operation.

"As everyone here knows, the Department of Homeland Security coordinated a comprehensive national strategy to safeguard the country against terrorism and to respond to future attacks. Operation Enduring Freedom is the official name used by the U.S. government for the war in Afghanistan, together with a number of smaller military actions, under the umbrella of the Global 'War on Terror'. This combined effort began on October 5, 2001 and while we can claim the Taliban was weakened, the war continued, and Osama bin Laden remained at large for nearly a decade. Again, as you all know, but I wanted to revisit the period as it's now a decade ago, U.S. special forces SEAL Team Six attacked Bin Laden's fortified position in Abbottabad and took him out. Everything I have put before you today are all facts," General Wright stressed, looking around the table for comments.

Continuing, the general said, "The latest intel from our man on the ground points to the possibility of another attack, in all probability on American soil. The heated conversation between Volcov and Madam Patcha supports that probability. She regards Flight 93 as a failed mission to be corrected by staging another deadly assault, perhaps against one or more targets. Another fact supporting this is her efforts to smuggle young men into the States – suicide bombers to be accurate. It stands to reason she is not working alone.

"Also referenced in the intel report is updated activity on former Bagram district governor Ahmad Hakim Kahir, now the appointed leader of the New Taliban. He is supporting training camps and drug distribution.

"To summarise, gentlemen, we must accept and prepare for the possibility of the U.S. coming under attack by terrorists in one or more locations in the States. And it could happen at any time. Any comments?"

"General Wright, I wish to make a comment if I may," Tariq proposed, getting to his feet.

"Go ahead Mr Ambassador."

"First, I totally agree with your summation. Based on what we know today, I have been thinking of the next steps we need to take to guard against another attack on the United States of America. It is just a suggestion for the meeting to consider," Tariq added.

"Let's hear what you have to say, Mister Ambassador, your local knowledge is essential to any decision-making," General Wright responded.

"Well, general, I would propose that Farez Malikzai, in his role as international arms dealer Kostas Alexopoulos, should again engage with Volcov and try to draw him out with regard to his business contacts in America. It would be a similar approach to that being tried by Patcha Volcov.

"Any success in that direction would enable us to check on any suspects and establish if networking is taking place particularly in connection with safe houses. I don't know this country as well as everyone sitting around this table, but it is clear to me that people in privileged positions are involved in this massive underground conspiracy. Those who run with the hare, and hunt with the hounds, as General Wright puts it, can be flushed out if Lieutenant Sinclair or Farez Malikzai are able to trick Volcov into identifying some of his associates in America. It would open an opportunity for Farez," Tariq added, noting that Secretary Hollingworth wished to intervene.

"If I understand your proposal correctly, Mister Ambassador, you are suggesting that Farez, in his guise as an international arms dealer, could offer to do business with Volcov and through that identify some of his contacts Stateside. Do I have that correct?"

"That's exactly what I'm suggesting Mister Secretary."

"Do you believe Volcov would accept Kostas Alexopoulos to have the necessary credentials to work alongside him. What I'm getting at is that Kostas the arms dealer is an invention of ours. Do you get my point?"

"I do sir. The underground arms dealing world, Mr Secretary, operates in its own twilight zone. Volcov's clients know who Volcov is and what he stands for," explained Tariq. "In the same way he keeps his clients' names and contact details to himself, he would expect Kostas Alexopoulos to do the same. The fact he may not have heard of him would not stop him from talking to the man – it has already happened – and so long as they are honest with one another, I see no reason why they can't work together."

"How do you judge it General Wright?" Secretary Hollingworth queried.

"I see it as a possible way forward Mister Secretary and suggest this be taken back to Villa Magnolia and discussed with Farez Malikzai and Lieutenant Sinclair with a view to implementation. Would you please coordinate this plan Mister Ambassador on your return to Islamabad?" General Wright requested, "and take with you our thanks for tabling a possible way forward.

"Meanwhile, with your agreement Secretary Hollingworth, we need to set up a task force to identify high-risk and vulnerable targets Stateside so we can take the necessary precautions," General Wright said addressing everyone at the meeting.

"Everyone should take that on board," Secretary Hollingworth instructed, addressing the representatives from the Department of Homeland Security, "and I don't need to remind you of the need to keep this under wraps. That said, my thanks to General Wright and Ambassador Zahir for setting up a plan to take us forward, and my thanks to you all for contributing today. This meeting is now officially closed."

General Maxwell escorted Tariq from the building to his car. "I think it's fair to say Tariq that this is moving along faster than anticipated, thanks to Lieutenant Sinclair, Farez and yourself. Your suggestion was roundly accepted today, and I hope you find that your compatriots agree with the plan when you meet with them at the villa. I would ask you to convey my thanks to both along with my support for everything they are doing.

"I wish you a safe journey and may your god protect you," the general added, as Tariq's car pulled away. Mindful of the dangers that lay ahead, the general mouthed a quiet prayer for three brave men whose commitment to duty and their success or failure will never be known to the world at large.

*

More than satisfied with the outcome of the meeting, Tariq could report to Abdul that his intel had provided a breakthrough acknowledged by both the Secretary of Defense and Secretary of State. That much was clear, and it had inspired a plan to move forward.

What was less clear, in Tariq's mind, was how Farez would cope with the additional pressure about to be placed on him. Would he be physically able, and sufficiently astute to take on Volcov over his U.S. contacts? It was a course of action that would find Farez playing the devil at his own game.

Another, less serious concern but nevertheless important, was the growing relationship between Abdul and Laura. To some extent it strengthened Abdul's position in earning Volcov's trust, but it also made him more vulnerable. Should it transpire that Laura is completely unaware and therefore uninvolved in her uncle's nefarious activities, and she discovered the real purpose of Abdul's presence at the villa, any trust she held in him would evaporate like dry ice on a hot summer's day.

They were all engaged in a high-wire act trying hard to find the right balance. Tariq and Abdul were brothers-in-arms and the last thing Tariq wanted to face was a broken-hearted Abdul. That must not be allowed to happen and, going forward, protecting his friend from heartbreak would be Tariq's cause célèbre.

***

Chapter Ten

Eager to learn what had transpired in Washington DC, Farez Malikzai was front and centre to welcome home Ambassador Zahir as he walked into Villa Magnolia. The team was assembled in the operations room each member as anxious as Farez to hear first-hand from Tariq.

"It's good to see you again gentlemen…and lady," Tariq said, bowing his head in deference to Irene Ryan as the only female present. She smiled at his mid-sentence correction, as did Master Sgt Mike Harper (alias Asad Jaheel) and other members of the villa's handpicked security team.

"Forgive me, Miss Irene," Tariq said humbly, "it was not my intention to ignore your presence," he announced apologetically, causing her to blush. "In truth, my first task today is to offer you congratulations," he added, moving to stand alongside her chair. "Everyone attending the State Department strategy meeting agreed with your post-9/11 assessment. May I say Irene that we are indeed fortunate to have you on our team. Well done and thank you."

"Thank you, sir; I am here to be of service."

"For those who are unfamiliar with Irene Ryan's outstanding work, kindly be informed you are in the presence of an expert counterintelligence officer courtesy of the CIA. She is here in a dual capacity," Tariq continued, "to help protect our billionaire benefactor Kostas Alexopoulos as well as to decipher sensitive intelligence as required.

"There was general agreement in Washington that a breakthrough occurred when John Dwyer overheard enough of a conversation pointing to the possibility of another 9/11-style attack in the United States – perhaps involving more than one target. Where, when, and how remain unknown at this stage but are a major focus of this assignment within the Pentagon.

"As always, time is not on our side and to some extent we are in John Dwyer's hands as he builds on the information from the Volcov-Patcha quarrel. Just a reminder to everyone that everything discussed in this operations room stays within these four walls. Beyond the walls of this room your focus must be on ensuring the safety and security of Kostas

Alexopoulos, as he steps up his efforts to gain Adham Volcov's full confidence. Any comments?"

"Sir are you suggesting Adham Volcov is the mastermind behind all this?" questioned Master Sgt Harper.

"That is not what I'm suggesting. My assessment from what John Dwyer overheard indicates Volcov is not our greatest problem. He is an arms dealer for certain, but one who may have been unwittingly misled or excluded. He sells to anyone in the market seeking black-market weapons and that's enough of a crime in itself. But he was unaware, we are informed, that weapons he sold to The Mamasan of Thailand were destined to be used in the 9/11 attacks As I already indicated our big breakthrough came when the Volcov-Patcha argument was overheard by John Dwyer," he added, noticing that Harper had his hand raised again.

"Sir, do you consider Patcha Volcov to be the driving force behind all of this?"

"Everything points to that. We must not underestimate this devious madam who will not be put off from achieving her objectives. She thrives on money and power -- her favourite currencies -- and she is dedicated to her cause.

"It appears you are not entirely convinced," Tariq commented, observing the deep frown on Mike Harper's face, "so I will give you an insight into the background of this unscrupulous and manipulative woman. Widely known as The Mamasan of Thailand – a dubious title she earned form the Royal Thai Police – she is forty-eight years old. Her notoriety dates from human trafficking activities that began when she recruited girls and young women from among poor families in Thailand's rural northeast – also from Laos and Cambodia. At first, she received little more than a light fine and a slap on the wrist for her crimes, probably because of her guile in bribing senior police officials. Today she operates a supply network in Thailand, Myanmar, and Indochina that ensures a steady flow of Asian girls for the sex industry. Everyone involved in the chain is taken care of by Patcha. She smooths the way, you could say, with kickbacks. It seems her ambition knows no bounds, and she is prepared to fight for what she wants – even against Volcov.

"This ambitious madam had at least one romantic association with a man called Mohammed Tenku a senior associate of BRN -- that's the Barisan Revolusi Nasional. This is a militant group working to turn Thailand's southernmost provinces into an Islamic state similar to the Sultanate of Pattani that existed as a part of northern Malay today known as Malaysia. Patcha intended to marry Tenku and, to that end, did everything he asked of her. She even converted to Islam and, like Tenku, became radicalised.

"Their relationship ended when Tenku died in a firefight with Thai security forces. That was about ten years ago. It left Patcha incensed at being cheated out of marriage which would have projected her status within the BRN that supports Sharia law as does she.

"Since then she has concentrated on expanding her procurement business which the intelligence community refers to as a worldwide human trafficking franchise. She added narcotics to her stock-in-trade using contacts introduced by Angelo Damiano the international drug dealer with Mafia connections. She uses the drugs on children – boys and girls – selected to be brainwashed by the former governor of Bagram province Ahmad Hakim Kahir now the self-styled leader of the so-called New Taliban here in Pakistan. These once-innocent children are being schooled as suicide bombers and we know many have already been smuggled into the States by The Mamasan of Thailand."

It was a lot of detail for anyone to take in and Tariq's briefing inspired a flood of questions, none the least from Mike Harper who found the length and breadth of Patcha's industriousness quite depressing. "How the hell does she manage all that and get away with it?" he asked Tariq, trying hard to figure out how she was able to avoid being caught.

"She is smart, cunning, and well connected," Tariq explained, "and she knows how to handle law enforcement especially in the case of the Royal Thai Police who fine her then let her go each time she's arrested. Bear in mind," Tariq continued, "that the top echelon of some Asian countries' police commanders are among her best and most appreciative customers benefiting financially and sometimes in kind from her generosity.

"Patcha is so well entrenched with the Royal Thai Police she can operate her own 'meet and greet' service at Thailand's international airports, with support from airport authorities and Immigration.

"And that brings us to her connection with Adham Volcov and how it all started. To generate more income from the sex industry she teamed up with Volcov and began by introducing him to wealthy men who were interest in purchasing weapons. They first met in Thailand's Pattaya City – often referred to as Sin City – when Volcov dropped by one of Patcha's many massage parlours in search of underage female company to satisfy his fondness for young girls. Over time, Volcov introduced Patcha to some of his clients that travel from place to place in his private jet based in Thailand. These trips are referred to as vacations but are a cover for discussing arms sales usually consummated between bed sheets I might add. Patcha sends in beautiful girls to soften-up clients to then step in to seal the deal. That way she has come to be personally acquainted with a large number of Volcov's most important and politically well-placed contacts. We believe that later she blackmails them into doing her bidding."

Mike Harper interrupted, "Sir, she certainly is a busy madam, but why does she call herself Patcha Volcov?"

Smiling at the question, Tariq said, "That is because she provides Volcov with beautiful girls, mostly Thailand-based, to accompany him on his overseas jaunts. By styling herself as Patcha Volcov she is able to demonstrate her importance to, say, eastern European women who socialise with Adham in the course of his arms negotiations. She's clinging onto her hard-earned assets, Master Sergeant."

"It brings to mind a 'keep off the grass warning' But we can be sure they are not married to one another, is that correct, sir?" Harper asked a wide grin on his face.

"Correct. Patcha is not what you'd describe as attractive and has no marital claims on Volcov. But, to grow her business, she needs to keep close to him to ensure she keeps in touch with his contacts. She is particularly jealous and that can be lethal as demonstrated when Adham Volcov's niece joined him in his villa. We know he dotes on his niece.

"Patcha acted like a woman scorned after Volcov made it clear to her that Laura is part of his family whereas Patcha is a house guest. That points to trouble ahead as she's been given an ultimatum from Volcov to accept his terms or pack her bags and leave."

"Fall in line, or find the door," Harper interjected causing everyone to laugh aloud.

"Is Volcov's niece aware of her uncle's notorious background?" asked Irene Ryan.

"John Dwyer's latest feedback suggests Laura Brody may not be aware of her uncle's illegal business activities. She considers him a wonderful man with above-board business interests. After her mother passed away – that's Volcov's sister – he invited Laura to stay at his villa indefinitely.

"She is a qualified medical doctor and could re-join the medical profession when she considers her mourning period over. That was a good point you raised Irene and, going forward, we have to be very careful how we view this young lady. We just don't know enough about her. John Dwyer is adamant she knows nothing about Volcov's life, but he is monitoring the situation carefully and I suggest we all keep an open mind for the time being.

"Any further questions…Irene…gentlemen? No, then let me repeat what I said earlier: everything discussed here today remains in this room. If you wish to raise anything with me at any time, please feel free to do so. Otherwise, it's back to your normal duties.

"Up until now, many of you would not have known much about this assignment. But with the new information, it is important we keep everybody abreast of the state of play. Our villa host, Kostas Alexopoulos, is about to become more involved and it remains the duty of all of us to make sure he comes to no harm. We are dealing with very dangerous people who behave as though they have nothing to lose. Lives are at stake particularly if we fail the mission," he added, closing the meeting. Everyone left the ops room apart from Tariq and Farez.

*

Farez Malikzai, notably silent throughout the briefing, looked at Tariq with a glint in his eye. At last he could speak freely, "Brother Tariq, watching you today I sensed you have something on your mind – a problem perhaps. Remember, a problem shared is a problem halved, I believe you once told me."

With a wry smile, Tariq responded, "I must always keep in mind that there's no way to fool you Farez. You are correct that several things give me cause for concern. For example, the possibility of a closer relationship developing between Laura and Abdul could complicate matters going forward. What do you think?"

"I can understand how you feel, brother, but why would you think that Abdul would allow his judgement to be influenced by any affection he might hold for Laura? Remember, he is a highly trained professional soldier and discipline is his guiding trait. Emotional recollections of losing his wife in childbirth and not having contact with his daughter haven't influenced previous missions according to everything we know about Abdul."

"I don't question his commitment to see this through, Farez," Tariq responded, "I am concerned that later he may have to pay a high price for it. If he becomes emotionally entangled there will come a point when he will have to make a choice. My fear is he'll end up with a broken heart," Tariq pointed out, despondent at the thought of that happening.

Farez's response was more to the point. "You should not be concerned about something that may never happen. Whatever transpires will be Abdul's destiny and he will deal with it as he does everything else. If he learns, over time, that Laura is ignorant of her uncle's shady businesses, it seems logical he would want to protect her from the truth because knowledge of these deeds could place her in danger. Not from her uncle, because I think he truly loves her, but from his associates who could try to use her as a pawn," he added, introducing a mixture of wisdom and common sense to their exchange.

"I am sure you are correct as usual my good friend. I suppose we must watch and wait and see what happens with the passage of time."

"Tariq, I believe you have another concern. What else is troubling you?" Farez asked, himself quite curious because he suspected he was part of Tariq's other problem.

"The Washington talks touched on the sensitivities and urgency of the latest intelligence. It was my suggestion that we would have to involve you…I mean Kostas Alexopoulos of course…to a greater degree than first planned. Moreover, it would not be without risk," Tariq said, laying it out as clearly as he could without causing undue alarm. He looked at Farez for any signs of heightened apprehension, but Farez seemed unconcerned.

"So, that's what's making you depressed. Please understand I am very pleased to learn I am not about to die of boredom sitting here doing little or nothing all day," Farez responded a broad smile on his face at the thought of becoming more actively involved and at a practical level.

Responding to his good friend's positive remarks, Tariq smiled, "We must find a way to play Volcov at his own game. We must not forget that you are a billionaire, sir, who has been everywhere and done everything," he added tongue in cheek. "I assume you'll feel increasingly bored as your health improves, which makes you crave for a bit of excitement in your life once again.

"If that sounds like a fair summation, Farez, then my idea is to persuade Volcov to take you into his inner circle, assuming it exists, where you can convince him to introduce you to some of his highly-placed contacts. That could lead us to discover who in the political arena is double-dealing.

"This idea was tabled and discussed in Washington. It was agreed, in general, that this approach could uncover the network in the States that is harbouring and grooming an army of suicide bombers. We may even get some idea where the next targets are," Tariq added, unsure of how Farez would react.

"My good friend," Farez responded taking in a deep breath, "this is an interesting idea that I won't dismiss out of hand. But I have no expertise in Volcov's business world of shady deals. And, if Adham Volcov is as smart as everyone thinks, he may doubt my motives, even distrust me. I have a slightly different approach and I'd appreciate your views," Farez offered, keen to build upon the possibility of expanding his role.

"Befriending Volcov is essential, so we can agree on that Tariq. But to gain this man's confidence I suggest it's better to allow him to lead me into his business world as and when he feels comfortable having me around -- perhaps in his close circle of associates as you put it," Farez suggested, after considering how best to use his exceptional interpersonal skills.

"If we accept, for now, that Laura is unaware of Volcov's corrupt behaviour, he will not want that to change. If, as we believe, he is remorseful after discovering the weapons he supplied to Patcha were used in the 9/11 attacks we are beginning to see a different, softer side to his character since Laura entered his life. My conclusion is that there is a better angel in this man that might benefit from the friendship and wisdom of Kostas Alexopoulos," he added, a twinkle in his eye. After all, social, interactive communication was Farez's stock in trade. It is what he does best – offering advice and guidance and words of wisdom. Farez was approaching this as a challenge he could not refuse.

Sceptical, but unwilling to go against his friend, Tariq delved into the wisdom of Farez's approach "My concern is that there is danger ahead and I am not sure if your idea won't place you in far greater danger than necessary," he questioned as tactfully as he could.

"I don't see how the danger could be greater, my brother. Perhaps you can explain," the older man suggested with a clear challenge in the tone of his voice.

"Using my approach, you would not be totally alone. Your secretary and right-hand man could accompany you wherever you go even to meetings with Volcov," Tariq responded, knowing as he said it that his argument would not resonate with Farez. In truth, Tariq preferred Farez's idea but it gave him a great sense of foreboding in terms of his friend's safety.

"That is not how I see it. If Volcov sees me as his friend and then as a confidante he will not consider me as a threat. John Dwyer is always with Volcov and he could be my back-up, and I could also have a right-hand man lurking in the shadows. Maybe Noori would be suited to that role with Asad Jaheel, as my driver. I would have three men in the lion's den all watching out for me -- Abdul, Noori, and Mike Harper."

It was clear to Commander Zahir that Farez as billionaire Kostas Alexopoulos was becoming quite animated in his theatrical role and utterly determined to rise to any challenge.

"You seem to have it all worked out brother," he said, smiling but still concerned. "Your idea has merit and it's clever but carries greater risk than my idea in my opinion. On the positive side, you would have three trusty supporters close by you in the enemy's camp and that is important. Knowing you the way I do, Farez, if you've set your mind on doing something you are unlikely to be dissuaded," Tariq added, mulling over Farez's plan.

"Time for you to decide…do you agree with my plan?" the older man asked scrutinising Tariq closely, well aware of the fears his friend had for him. It was a moot question, because the commander knew in his heart that Farez would not be deterred. In truth, Tariq considered Farez's idea to be a novel approach that could prove rewarding, but he foresaw a path strewn with danger. His greatest concern was not being able to help the old man because he wouldn't be with him in his hour of need. Tariq could see that what started as his idea, with some safeguards, had morphed into a much riskier plan thanks to Farez.

Whatever argument Tariq presented he knew it would be shot down in flames because Farez had set his heart on doing what he was most able to do in exercising his skills at befriending, counselling and supporting people. Nobody could deny his past accomplishments dealing with people. Ingratiating himself to Volcov and his inner circle, to put it bluntly, was the malik's forte. He had addressed and overcome monumental problems in his life, and he saw the Volcov saga as nothing more than one more mountain to climb.

Tariq did not quite see it that way, but he decided not to push-back. "I agree with your plan, Farez, but I want to make something very clear: Your safety is of paramount importance. At the first sign of real danger you must promise me to find a way to drop out of the fight or I'll drag you out! Is that clear? Are you comfortable with that?"

"Crystal clear my brother; I hear what you say," Farez acknowledged, a mischievous expression on his face.

***

Chapter Eleven

Back at Villa Margalla, Adham Volcov had entered his study earlier than usual.

"Good morning sir," Abdul declared, surprised yet intrigued to find the old man studying files presumably from the usually locked cabinet.

Noticing the surprise on his assistant's face, Volcov smiled, "Good morning John. I see you are shocked to find me busy at work so early in the day. I guess there's no need to remind you that we have an appointment with Mr Khan at the hospital in Islamabad this afternoon. That's why I am trying to get to grips with a few outstanding matters."

"I see. Sir, is there anything I can help you with? Abdul offered. "Perhaps I can assist you with your task in hand," he suggested prompting Volcov to abruptly close the file. Was he working on something too sensitive to share?

"You can start by sorting out this pile of mail and prioritise it. We will go through it later," Volcov instructed, pointing to a mountain of unopened envelopes of all shapes and sizes on his capacious desktop.

Seated at their respective workstations, each man concentrated on the task at hand. After thirty minutes or so, Volcov pushed back his chair, walked to the filing cabinet, replaced the file, and then locked the drawer. "Young man I believe it's time for me to meet with members of the staff, so I will leave you to your duties. We will leave the residence at 2.30 p.m. which gives us ample time to get to the hospital for the appointment," he added, leaving the study and Abdul to himself.

Seconds after Volcov's departure, the telephone rang on Volcov's desk. Abdul fielded the call, "Good morning, this is Villa Margalla. John Dwyer speaking; how can I help you?"

"Good morning Mr Dwyer. This is Kostas Alexopoulos. I wish to speak to Mr Volcov," Farez Malikzai stated in a business-like manner.

Smiling at his friend's formal approach, Abdul kept up the pretence. "Good morning sir. Unfortunately, Mr Volcov is not here at the moment. Is there anything I can help you with Mr Alexopoulos?"

"Please let him know I called to invite him and his charming niece to join me for lunch at Villa Magnolia tomorrow. I would like to…what should I say…get to know your boss more intimately," he said, leaving Abdul with the feeling that the wily old fox was trying to tell him something.

"Happy to oblige, Mr Alexopoulos. I am sure Mr Volcov will get back to you later," Abdul confirmed, cradling the phone. What is Farez up to, he asked himself, contemplating the older man's out-of-the-blue invite? His attention was diverted when he heard Adham Volcov chatting to Laura somewhere close at hand. Peering out of the French doors he spotted them in the rose garden deep in conversation.

"I am sorry darling, but I won't change my mind," Volcov was explaining to Laura. "You can't come with me today; my meeting is of a private nature and that's all there is to it," he added. She could see he was resolute so, turning away from her uncle, Laura returned to the house leaving him looking after her in despair.

The sound of approaching footsteps caught Volcov's attention. It was Abdul.

"Sir, Mr Alexopoulos called a little while ago. He invites you and Laura to join him for lunch tomorrow at Villa Magnolia. I said you'd confirm as soon as you could."

"Indeed…thank you John. I didn't expect that so soon after our first meeting. However, it should help bring some cheer to Laura. She is annoyed because I refused to let her come with us to Islamabad. I will write accepting Mr Alexopoulos' invitation and you can drive to Villa Magnolia and hand it to him in person. I think that's more personal. Let's see if this lunch invitation brings a smile to Laura's face. And I will want you to come with us tomorrow, John," he added, stepping inside the house with Abdul in tow. It was just the timely opportunity Abdul wanted to find out what Farez was up to.

*

Arriving at Villa Magnolia at midday, Abdul was met by Mike Harper who ushered him into the expansive lounge where Farez was relaxing. The older man looked up and smiled with delight as Abdul entered. Immediately the two men embraced.

"This is for you Mr Alexopoulos," Abdul said, handing over an envelope to Farez. "And now tell me what you are up to my friend? he asked, a quizzical expression on his face. "I sense you are up to something," he added, grinning at the older man just as Commander Zahir joined them.

"You may well ask, brother," Tariq commented in response to Abdul's question. "Take a seat Abdul, there's something we must all discuss together."

After Tariq had recalled his previous discussions with Farez and the older man's insistence on doing things his way, Abdul voiced concern, "What are you thinking about Farez? Cosying up to Volcov could expose you to danger," he said firmly, his concern clearly aligned with that already expressed by Tariq who was still shrugging his shoulders and shaking his head reproachfully.

"I have been through this already," Tariq confirmed, "and probably everything else I expect you to say to dissuade Farez from going through with this crazy idea. I lost the argument," he added, disconsolately, "and I think you will too."

The younger men looked despairingly at their good friend who appeared undaunted by their concern.

"Tariq is right," Farez said firmly. "I do have a plan that I believe will succeed in getting to the heart of Adham Volcov. And that, my good friends, is the only way we can breach his defences.

"We all accept Volcov is a master of his profession. But what I have heard from both of you leads me to believe there is some good in him and we must not be in a rush to judge. People change. You will recall, Abdul, the words I said to you and Khalil when you arrived in Marwah village. I reminded you of an Afghan proverb that says, 'The first day you meet, you are friends; the next day you meet you are brothers.'

"Yes, I do recall that Farez. And yes, we are brothers," Abdul conceded, "but…"

He was unable to finish because Farez interrupted him in mid-sentence. "What I'm trying to say can be best said in another Afghan proverb: 'There is a way from heart to heart', and that's why my idea is more subtle and more likely to succeed in my humble opinion," the older man stated emphatically to two friends he had grown to admire above all others. Their very presence made him realise how lucky he was to have them in his life. All three men were travellers on a difficult journey, but their bonds of friendship had never been stronger.

Still not convinced, and because of his concern for Farez's safety, Abdul suggested they talk more about the plan. Farez was still quite frail and the marine was conscious of the edict from the highest authorities that the old man should not come to any harm. "Humour me, brother, by telling me what you have in mind."

"Very well. You have mentioned on two separate occasions that you saw a softer side to Volcov. That is clear from the way he treats his beloved niece. The man does not lack the ability to love; nor is he blind to his obligations to Laura. Such feelings have been shown on more than one occasion.

159

"He has expressed genuine remorse for supplying arms that supported the 9/11 attacks. He would like to turn back the clock. That can't be done of course but such an expression of remorse goes to the heart of the man. I believe he now accepts the horrific mistakes of his past actions. And this, I think, is connected to his new and immediate responsibilities towards his niece.

"Both of you detected a softer side to the man. Volcov, I believe, has also discovered his gentler side and his morals and dubious business ethics may be under siege as his mind and heart fight it out. If this observation holds true, he may be seeking changes to his lifestyle before it's too late. That's where I believe I can get into his heart, gain his confidence as a friend, and let him open up about his hopes and dreams. I suspect he is a very lonely man born of such clandestine business undertakings. The key to all of this my brothers is Laura. Her devotion and love are something he likes; she is the change he needs. For my part I can only encourage him to see the wisdom of changing his ways and embracing a new way of life in the company of his niece.

"That said, I know nothing about arms sales. I do not have all the connections he would expect me to have for a man with an arsenal of weapons as his prime business interest. I know we previously agreed to my acting role with that in mind but, don't you see, it would be a massive gamble for me with my inadequate credentials to try to enter his world of darkness. I would get caught out. I want to try to bring him out of the darkness and into the light. And I think with the help of Allah the Merciful and Compassionate it is possible."

Both Abdul and Tariq were stunned trying to process everything Farez had articulated. They knew he was right; wasn't he always when it came to understanding people and their aspirations? Both Abdul and Tariq had undergone similar scrutiny from the old sage, and that made it difficult to argue with the man.

Abdul was warming to Farez's idea, but his concern for mission safety remained strong. "My honest assessment of your plan is that it makes good sense. And I cannot fault your argument or wisdom in wanting to find a more acceptable way forward. But I am still concerned about your safety.

"My contact with Volcov," Farez stated, "is likely to be at either of the villas as I see it. In both cases I have protection. At Villa Margalla I will have support from Master Sgt Mike Harper, in the guise of Asad Jaheel, and I will have Noori to..." Abdul jumped in, "Hold it right there my friend. You can't take Noori because if you are in Volcov's villa when Ahmad Hakim Kahir is present Noori will be exposed. Don't forget he was a manservant to the governor," Abdul stated forcefully, beginning to wonder if he'd spoken too soon in support of Farez's plan.

"I haven't forgotten brother. Let me talk about being exposed for a moment. Did either of you recognise me after my Hollywood makeover? Did the governor recognise you Abdul when you came face to face with him at Volcov's villa?"

Before Abdul could answer, there was a knock on the door and a servant entered carrying refreshments for the three men.

"Thank you, Saeed," Farez said, as the manservant served drinks before bowing politely to all three men. Turning to Farez, the manservant asked, "Sir, will that be all for now?" before bowing again and turning to leave the room after Farez shook his head. Before he reached the door Farez stopped him in his tracks.

"My friends, you have just been served refreshments by Saeed, better known to you as Noori!" Abdul and Tariq looked deflated but only for a second or two before bursting into laughter to be joined by Farez and Noori.

"You are a cunning old fox!" Abdul declared. "I think you have made your case Farez and you have our support for your plan," he added looking at Tariq who was in total agreement.

"Somehow, I thought I could convince both of you given enough time," Farez said, a smug expression on his face.

"I have just one further suggestion," Tariq said. "Take Asad Jaheel as your right-hand man and Saeed as your chauffer. That way the governor will not come in contact with Saeed, or should I say Noori. And don't forget," Tariq continued, "Harper in the guise of Asad Jaheel, does not understand English."

"I do agree, my brothers," he said as both Abdul and Tariq let out sighs of relief.

*

Arriving back at Villa Margalla in good time to drive Volcov to Islamabad, Abdul's mind was still processing the pros and cons of Farez's plan though he realised there was little he or Tariq could do other than go along with it. Abdul knew the old man was correct; it was a subtle tactic to get to the heart of the man. He was as convinced as Farez that there were two sides to Volcov: on one hand, we have the infamous arms dealer; on the other hand, the doting uncle suddenly revealed by the arrival of Laura. In pleasing his niece, everything else in Volcov's world now took second place.

He acted as though he had to make up for lost time. But why? He had been around her since her childhood years and kept in touch throughout. Laura devoted every moment of her time to him which was expressed in the very strong bond holding them together. It was a relationship Abdul would watch carefully by spending as many hours as possible with Laura believing that, in time, something would come to light that more clearly explained their relationship.

Back in Volcov's study, Abdul settled down to peruse some documents but was disturbed by raised voices outdoors. Quickly and quietly walking towards the open doors he positioned himself to be able to hear what was being said.

"How dare you speak to me in that way Volcov; I could cut you down where you stand!" threatened a furious Patcha. "That damned dog must go and hopefully your niece with it," she fumed. "I have been here for a long time and you and I are at a critical moment in our business relationship as you well know. I cannot have you going weak on me now because of that worthless piece of American trash!" she added, her voice louder and more menacing than in previous exchanges.

Volcov boiled over. "How dare you speak so cruelly of my niece? The only trash around here is you, Patcha, and your welcome in this house just expired. Pack your bags, you vile creature, and don't come back. You are no longer welcome," he blurted out, his face contorted in anger.

But Patcha was not to be put off. "Don't threaten me you old fool. If you think for one minute, I will allow you to jeopardise this mission, you don't know me. This craziness you show over a silly, spoilt bitch is unacceptable. I will slit your throat first," she bellowed hoping to browbeat Volcov into changing his mind.

"It won't work Patcha. You can't get far without my contacts. And one word from me and you'll be cut off and find yourself high and dry. Try cutting my throat if you don't believe me," he added, calling her bluff. "Just as I thought," he said, as she failed to make her move, "you would not get far without my connections. So, don't just stand there, get your things together and hit the road. When I get back, I don't want to see any sign of you. Do you understand?"

"This is not the end of it, you stupid old fool. You have a role to play in the next mission, and you will play it. I will leave for now, but this is not the last you'll hear from me. No-one treats the Mamasan of Thailand this way and gets away with it, take it from me Volcov!"

"Don't threaten me Patcha. What do you think you can do to hurt me?

"You will find out. I will have my revenge," she said menacingly.

Suspecting the heated exchange had run its course, Abdul slipped out of the office and crept upstairs to his room so as not to be caught when Volcov returned to his study.

Reflecting on the bitter argument Abdul saw trouble ahead. From what he'd overheard he sensed Patcha would seek revenge. Clearly, she was capable of just about anything. Presumably protecting the mission, and the role Volcov had to play, would keep her from doing anything proactive. It also raised the question of whether a "mission" was imminent.

Of equal concern to Abdul was Laura's safety. Patcha had not exactly spoken of Laura in glowing terms and this made him more certain she was an innocent bystander. He had to find a way to protect her. But how? And from what? With Patcha persona non grata at Villa Margalla that would help to some extent, but he was still uneasy. A quick glance at his watch told him it was time to take his boss to Islamabad for his hospital appointment.

*

Several miles of the drive to Islamabad were conducted in silence. Volcov was still fuming from the assault by Patcha which registered in his rising blood pressure. And Abdul was still mulling over Patcha's options for retaliation and her physical threats against Laura.

Arriving with five minutes to spare, Volcov disembarked from the car and addressed Abdul "Stay with the car John; this meeting won't take long." There was tension in the old man's voice that Abdul attributed to the earlier squabble. Clearly, Abdul wasn't the only one considering the implications of Patcha's threats.

As predicted, the meeting with Mr Kahn lasted just twenty minutes though Volcov returned to the vehicle looking somewhat grey. Again, Abdul attributed it to the morning argument.

On the way back to Villa Margalla Volcov revisited his exchange with Patcha. "That bitch should be long gone by now. I threw her out of the house today John after she had the audacity to threaten me and also my niece. That's something I will not accept. I am explaining this because she's a dangerous woman who bears watching carefully particularly when she can't get her own way. What I want you to do is to keep a close eye on Laura. Can you do that for me John?"

"Of course, sir, willingly. I will do what I can to protect both you and Laura," he promised before he had time to check himself.

Volcov looked at Abdul, a smile playing around his mouth. "If I'm not mistaken, I do believe you have a soft spot for my niece."

For once in his life Abdul was unable to formulate a credible response.

"Pull over John. We need to talk," Volcov ordered realising Abdul was someone who cared for Laura. As instructed Abdul parked, wound down the windows, and turned off the engine. After a short pause, Volcov said, "Bear with me, John, because what I have to say isn't easy. You must know by now that I love my niece dearly. She is everything and more to me – my whole life you might say. She knows nothing of my business undertakings. To her I am her beloved uncle; a wealthy businessman who has been in and out of her life for as long a she can remember. And my love for her is unconditional.

"Until recently, she had her mother – my sister – as company but since her death I am all Laura has. The day will come when she'll be totally alone. And no amount of money can make up for the loss of anyone dear to you.

"I worry about that day and I need to know there will be someone who will care for her out of love and not just for gain. I need to know she will escape being implicated in my business undertakings. That's a cross she shouldn't have to carry. Do you understand what I'm saying John?"

"Do you know what you are saying sir?" Abdul cross-questioned, anxiety in his voice. "Laura's love for you is also unconditional. You can see it in every fibre of her being. Whatever happened in your past could never destroy such a love. And she's stronger than you think. And one more thing, if I may," ventured Abdul, "her love for you deserves the truth in return."

Had the marine gone too far this time? Perhaps not. The old man smiled at Abdul, a man he had come to respect. Shaking his head from side to side Volcov said, "So much truth has been left untold over the years John. My fear is it may be too late to do much about it now. Time is running out. I need to know there's someone who will care for Laura and look after her when I'm gone. When I see you together, I suspect there's more than just a spark. You could be the man to care for her. Tell me, are you that man John?

As the words left Volcov's lips, Abdul recoiled. He could not deny he had feelings for Laura but as Volcov's employee it was impossible to admit so.

"I regard Laura as a beautiful, warm, and wonderful young woman. A man's heart cannot help but beat a little faster in her presence," he conceded. "I can't deny that, sir. But my job is to protect you and assist you. If I may say so, you know nothing about me – the real me. You only know what I've become during my time in your employment," Abdul explained, involuntarily reaching out to the man with a response that had not been thought through; it just came out.

"Please credit me with something," Volcov fired back. "I know I am right about you. I trust you. True, you're a man of few words, as I have discovered, but nothing you say, or don't say, will change my opinion of you. All I'm asking, right now, is for you to protect Laura by being her good friend. One day, when I am no longer able to protect her, she will need you in her life. Promise me, John, that you'll look after her," Volcov added evidently distraught.

"Yes sir. I promise I will protect Laura to the best of my ability. You have my word. And in return, sir, I must ask you why we're having this conversation, right now, at the side of a dusty road outside of Islamabad?"

"Because I am dying. I have Hodgkin's lymphoma. With luck I might live another six months according to Mr Khan. But you must understand John that I have no concern for my mortality; you could say I earned everything that's coming to me and I deserve all I get after the life I have lived. God help me. Laura is my only concern; all I want is to see her safe and happy.

"Today, Patcha made vile threats against us. I am concerned only for Laura's safety and will sleep better knowing you are looking out for her."

Volcov's point was well made and as a witness to the heated exchange Abdul shared his concern. "Would you like me to deal with Patcha, sir," he asked, relishing the thought of putting her in her place. He had done so once and would willingly deal with her a second time.

"No, let's hope she was just making an empty threat. For now, just keep a watchful eye on Laura because I could never forgive myself if anything happened to her," Volcov added, his former depressed state surfacing again.

"Try putting such thoughts out of your mind, sir," Abdul suggested, "and try to stay calm for your own sake. You must think more about your health right now," he added, gunning the engine into life for the drive back to the villa. Silence fell again, each man immersed in his own thoughts.

*

The roadside conversation brought some relief to Abdul and strengthened his view that Volcov was not all bad - he did have a kinder side. That also made Abdul feel more confident about Farez playing his acting part according to his own rules. And the evolving circumstances seemed to favour the redoubtable Mr Kostas Alexopoulos getting closer to Volcov to gain his confidence, and even persuade him to cooperate in preventing another act of terrorism. There was much at stake and Farez's role suddenly took on greater significance than when it was first discussed in Washington, DC.

"Thank you, John," Volcov said smiling as Abdul pulled up outside of the front door of the villa to allow his boss to disembark. "The matters we discussed back there are between the two of us. Laura must not know about my medical condition. Understand? I meant it, John. Now I will tell you something else that I have not told Laura. I think this will dispel any lingering doubts you may have about me. Laura is not my niece," he said, bringing a look of incredulity to Abdul's face. "She is my daughter!" he announced emphatically before disappearing inside the villa.

***

Chapter Twelve

Never in a million years would Abdul and anyone else on the team have guessed that Laura was Volcov's daughter and not his niece as widely announced. And, by anyone, that included Laura herself who was ignorant of the fact. This staggering revelation, coupled with Volcov's assertion he may have only six months to live, all added up to Abdul's first sleepless night at Villa Margalla. Yet, being wide awake and wide-eyed did grant him time and space to revisit previously held suspicions surrounding Volcov and try to figure out the true situation with a clearer mind.

Volcov's open display of devotion towards Laura was the first indication the old man possessed a temperate side to his character. Moreover, he even encouraged Abdul to spend more time with Lara when his personal assistant might otherwise be anchored in the study immersed in paperwork.

Abdul's thought process was interrupted by subdued knocking on his bedroom door.

"It's me...Laura," she whispered. "Are you decently attired John to receive a visitor?" she asked, light-heartedly.

Abdul's heartrate quickened not entirely due to the close proximity of a beautiful woman. He dug his nails into the palms of his hands. A feeling of guilt sent his heart racing at top speed. His heart and mind struggled to come to grips with the newly acquired information about her father that had served to heighten the game of deception he was dutybound to play. He did not want to respond to Laura, preferring to wait and hope she would assume he was asleep. Deceitfulness did not sit well with him, but he was right to wait. After a minute or two he detected footsteps receding from his bedroom door. Relieved he sank back on the bed ashamed of his mendacious behaviour.

*

The next morning, Abdul sat alone in the study with time to compose himself before Volcov arrived on the scene which he did just as his PA was opening the day's mail.

"Good morning John," Volcov said cheerily. "I trust you are well."

It was an unusual greeting that wrongfooted Abdul. "I am quite well, sir," he responded coyly. "Why would you think otherwise if I may ask?"

"Laura said you did not respond when she knocked on your door. My niece," he said deliberately emphasising her status, "took your silence to imply there was a problem."

Abdul smiled, suspicious of Volcov's carefully crafted explanation. "Apart from suffering a disturbed night with little sleep there's nothing sinister to report sir. But I thank you for your concern," he added, as Adham Volcov walked to the French doors and closed them.

"I see. I suppose I should not be surprised. What I revealed yesterday shocked you. You must understand, John, that I told you the truth because I am putting my faith in you to protect Laura when the time comes. I turned to you because I sensed something between you and Laura. I know it to be true where Laura is concerned and I believe, young man, I am right in terms of your feelings towards her," he stated, drawing up a chair next to Abdul.

"I have done things in my life for which I am not particularly proud. But Laura is the one good thing that came out of my life. She is the best daughter any father could wish for. Now, faced with the reality of my own mortality, I must ensure her safety and do what I can for her future happiness. I see you as the key to that," Volcov added, looking into Abdul's eyes for some sign his plea was resonating with his assistant.

Abdul was haunted by guilt and mounting remorse. While he would readily admit to having strong feelings for Laura, he would not deny he was also finding it harder to dislike Adham Volcov. But he was back in South Asia to do a job, and nothing would prevent him from achieving mission objectives. Yet he sensed and feared there would be a high price to pay at some point along the way.

"Sir, you already have my promise to do all I can to protect Laura. If I may ask, I would like to know if you intend revealing the truth to her. You must know she is going to find out one day."

"And how would it help her to learn that Uncle Adham was an unruly businessman who made a fortune from the blood of innocent people and that he'd lied to her about their true relationship?" Volcov asked sarcastically.

"As I see it, sir, it's one thing to say she'll never find out in your lifetime, but for her to find out after you're gone is something else. And there's no guarantee, you must agree, that she will never find out. If I'm not speaking out of turn, I think she should learn the truth – all of it – and hear it from you sir while there's time and opportunity to make your peace," Abdul declared, forthright but with sincere concern.

Volcov appeared pensive for a moment or two. "Oh…John…you paint me into a difficult corner. It will be tough enough to lose her when I die, but if I'm honest with her now I may lose her while I'm alive and that would be unbearable," he added, his weathered brow sporting a deep frown.

Before anything more was said on the matter, the telephone rang in the study and Volcov turned to field the call. "Adham Volcov speaking, who's calling please?"

Whoever called wished to speak in private. Placing a hand over the receiver Volcov asked Abdul to take a break. "John, please catch up with Laura; join her for a coffee and perhaps apologise for any earlier misunderstanding."

Leaving by the French windows, Abdul was grateful for a break in what had become a very sensitive conversation, but he realised deep down that it was by no means over.

*

As Abdul approached the swimming pool, Laura's terrier, Sykes, jumped off a sunbed and threw himself into his arms drenching the marine in the process.

Startled, but able to see the funny side, Abdul cheerfully chastised Sykes. "Look what you've done you crazy, soaking-wet pooch." The bundle of wet fur squirmed with delight licking Abdul's face enthusiastically. The scuffle caused Laura to lower her sunglasses and watch quietly from her sunbed. She opened her mouth to speak but Abdul got in first.

"Good morning Laura; sorry about what happened earlier," he apologised, still holding Sykes.

"Oh…so you are still speaking to me, are you?" Laura queried, unable to resist the jibe.

"Do me a favour Laura and rescue me from your savage hound!"

Smiling, she called the dog and Sykes responded by doubling down on his task of washing Abdul's face. Laura stepped into the fray and removed one very reluctant Sykes from Abdul's arms and deposited him on the ground. Relieved and able to wring some water out of his shirt, Abdul followed Laura to the sunbeds.

"I called on you earlier, John, to let you know that Madam Patcha was no longer resident in Villa Margalla. She was given her marching orders by Uncle Adham and told never to come back," she said, clearly pleased with the decision. It seemed Patcha's dismissal had taken the edge off any pent-up anger Laura may have had for Abdul. Even so, he decided it would be wise to say as little as possible on the subject.

"So, I was given to understand," Abdul said. "I am sure Villa Margalla will be a better place without her," he ventured, feeling strangely uncomfortable. He sought to temper his strong feelings for her against yesterday's revelations and today's earlier, unfinished conversation with Volcov.

Shaking her head slowly, Laura said, "Uncle Adham was very angry at her for bullying me. What I can't understand, and maybe you can help me John, is why he would want her in the villa in the first place."

"Beats me! Your guess is as good as mine Laura. Maybe she was a business partner or associate," he postulated, nimbly tiptoeing the conversation forward anxious to see if Laura knew anything at all about Volcov's dubious business activities.

"I simply can't imagine why uncle would have any association with a vile woman like Patcha – businesswise or otherwise," she stated with great certainly. "I am certain he did not like her at all," she added, a puzzled look on her face.

"Do you know much about your uncle's business?" he asked, moving the conversation a step further at the same time wandering whether he was pushing the boundaries.

"Nothing at all John. All I can say is that he has always been there for me. We have laughed and played together, and he's been like a father to me. He looked after my mother and me even though his business took him away for long periods. Somehow, he managed to be in our lives when it mattered. I never knew my father. He died when I was a baby. But Uncle Adham always made up for that and I couldn't love him more if he'd been my father," she declared, eyes shining with love as she spoke of the seasoned arms dealer oblivious to the fact she's his daughter.

More than ever convinced she knows nothing of Volcov's shady business ventures, or their true real relationship, Abdul reasoned that learning the truth would not remove or even diminish the love she had for him. He was even more convinced than he was just a few hours ago that Volcov must find the courage to tell Laura the truth – all of it – before it was too late.

The emotional aspects of his relationship with Laura and Volcov were weighing heavily on Abdul's mind – and heart. He wanted to manage everyone's expectations through patience and understanding, but time was of the essence.

His private ruminations ended when Volcov walked towards the pair. "I hope I don't have to remind you guys that we have a lunch invitation at Villa Magnolia. So, Laura, I suggest you take Sykes and get ready while I speak to John," he said, smiling indulgently at Laura who gave him a light kiss on the cheek before departing with her dog.

Turning to Abdul, Volcov motioned him to return to the study where he asked if he'd made his peace with Laura. "Yes, sir, I have. But it's an uneasy peace knowing what I know about your relationship. Again, I would ask you to reconsider informing her of your real self whi.e you still have the opportunity for a face-to-face discussion.

"John, my young friend, can't you see what you're asking me to do?"

"Perhaps I can. But then again you may be underestimating the depth of my understanding. Sir, with your permission I will freshen up before we leave for Villa Magnolia," Abdul added, eager to disengage from further discussion for the time being.

The old man nodded towards Abdul who left the room quietly closing the door behind him. Adham Volcov continued to stare at the closed door and, under his breath uttered one short sentence. "Just who are you, John Dwyer?"

*

"Welcome back to Villa Magnolia," Farez exclaimed graciously as he slid into his cameo role as Kostas Alexopoulos renowned international weapons dealer and billionaire villa owner.

"You look as lovely as ever," he beamed planting a gentle kiss on Laura's hand - an act of familiarly that Farez the village malik would never condone - before addressing Volcov. "Adham, welcome once again to my humble home," he proclaimed leading his guests into the lounge. Following close behind, Abdul strived to attract the attention of either Farez or Mike Harper. Alas to no avail.

"As the weather is less humid today, I requested lunch be served in the gazebo. Allow me to show you the way," Farez said, looking in Abdul's direction. "And that includes you John Dwyer."

Arriving at the villa's Pakistani-style gazebo, with its circular, ornate white railings and multicoloured drapes, Laura's eyes almost popped out of her head when she saw the large, round table laden with food fit for a prince. Two punka wallahs, squatting either side of the gazebo, were studiously pulling on ropes back and forth to stimulate a breeze and protect the tempting dishes from unwelcome insects.

For the next two hours, Farez and his guests tackled the spread before them, engaging in small talk until Laura took centre stage to talk about her medical career and future aspirations. Farez had skilfully guided the conversation to put Volcov at ease, knowing that nothing would please him more than Laura being the centre of attention.

"Laura, may I ask how you spend your time at the villa?" Farez enquired, a twinkle in his eye. "I hear most young ladies enjoy shopping, but you can only shop for so long. Is that not so, Adham?"

"I am inclined to agree, Kostas, at least each time I get the bills!" Volcov said, to polite laughter from the others including Laura.

"Please, gentlemen, don't believe all you hear about women shopping till they drop. I am not addicted to spending money, I can assure you," she retorted, her face a picture of mock pain.

"Please forgive us young lady for teasing you so unsportingly," Farez pleaded. "Tell me, Laura, are you interested in horses?" he asked, changing gear. The remark drew looks of incredulity from those around the table. What was the wise old seer up to now?

"I love horses. Why do you ask?"

"Would you like to inspect my stables? All of you of course," Farez suggested, allowing his eyes to rest on Abdul who, by now, was more than curious.

Leaving the punka wallahs fanning the gazebo, the lunch party walked to the stables at the rear of the villa. Approaching the half-open stable doors, Laura gasped at the sight of two magnificent black stallions that looked at her before inspecting Farez and Volcov. Unexpectedly, one horse fixed his gaze on Abdul and whinnied, bowing his head up and down excitedly. Abdul could only stare at the splendid horses he instantly recognised as Commander Zahir's pride and joy, as well as worthy stable companions for Atuallah his son Khalil's mule. So, this is where they had ended up. But how?

"One of those magnificent beasts seems to have taken a shine to you, John," Volcov declared as Farez brought forward a smartly dressed young man who had been standing by the stable door.

"Mister Volcov, this gentleman is Saeed my faithful guardian. He has been by my side for many a year. I am indebted to him for his untiring support. I suppose you could look upon him as my PA, similar to John Dwyer," Farez said, clearly enjoying his theatrical virtuoso at centre stage.

Bowing respectfully towards Adham Volcov, Saeed's presence was acknowledged by Volcov. Abdul smiled at the scene, inwardly admiring the artistic creativity of the folk in the cosmetics department who had crafted a new Noori his own mother wouldn't know.

By now, Laura had approached the stallions, caressing them while speaking in gentle tones.

Farez saw it as an opportunity to exercise some control over events. "Adham, with your approval, I would like to suggest that Saeed takes Laura for a ride into the Margalla hills. The stallions could use some exercise. She will be perfectly safe with him I can assure you. And it would give you and I time to become better acquainted."

"If that's what Laura wishes to do, then I would not object my friend?" Volcov responded, smiling at Laura who looked as happy as he'd seen her since she joined him at the villa.

"That is such a good idea, Kostas. I would very much like to go for a ride into the hills," Laura responded, delighted at the offer.

"I will set that up for tomorrow," Farez said, "if that is alright with you," he added, as Laura nodded enthusiastically. "Adham, I suggest John drives Laura over to the villa early tomorrow morning. Then he can return and bring you over later so you and I can continue talking until it's time for all of you to go back to Villa Margalla. How does that sound?"

It also pleased Abdul as he desperately wanted to brief Tariq and Farez about the latest information regarding Volcov and Laura that could impact the mission going forward. Once again, Farez, had skilfully controlled proceedings and done so quite brilliantly.

***

Keeping to Farez's timetable, Abdul drove Laura to Villa Margalla at 8.30 am where Saeed, her chaperone and riding companion, was waiting with two saddled horses all set for their morning ride into the hills. As soon as they left, Abdul dropped by the operations room where Commander Zahir and Farez were waiting along with Mike Harper and Irene Ryan.

"At last an opportunity to get together," Abdul said, grateful to Farez for his initiative in creating time and space to catch up on important developments. "I must congratulate you Farez on yesterday's excellent lunch," he added, stepping forward to embrace his friend and Tariq in turn.

"I thought from your body language that you had an urgent need to make contact. I only hope that whatever you're trying to report did not lose any importance as a result of an overnight delay," Farez said smiling at his younger friend. I am still smiling from the expression on your face yesterday when you confronted the horses. I will tell you what happened," Farez continued, settling into a chair around the ops table, "Tariq and Noori got in touch with General Gardiner at Bagram Air Base and, through a combined effort with my villagers who had taken good care of the animals, he had them picked up from Marwah village to be reunited with Tariq."

"But how did they come to be here?" Abdul questioned, assuming there was more to the story.

"The U. S. Army made it clear that Afghanistan's new ambassador to the United States had requested his horses be shipped to America. From Bagram they were flown to Benazir Bhutto international airport and from there by road to the villa," Farez said, proud of his part in reuniting Tariq with his horses.

"Your acting skills never cease to amaze me my talented friend," Tariq said, patting Farez on the shoulder.

"You are welcome, Mister Ambassador" Farez responded cheerily.

"We must now get down to business," Tariq urged, "because Volcov's PA John Dwyer must return to Villa Margalla later to bring his boss here, and we don't want Volcov thinking his assistant is taking a long time to drop off his niece.

Slowly, but in great detail, Abdul relayed recent events in Villa Margalla.

"So, as you can see," Abdul concluded, "Adham Volcov finds himself in a Catch-22 situation: He is dying of cancer with maybe six months to live, and he doesn't know whether or not to be truthful to Laura about his past transgressions." It was stunning news, quite unanticipated by those present, and it took a few moments to sink in.

"Now we can understand your need for an urgent meeting said Farez. "It is sad news my friend and does present a predicament for Volcov. My first reaction is that he is struggling with a huge emotional problem and I don't mean his imminent demise. We all die one day but he must be suffering great agony of mind in terms of ruining the one good thing that truly matters in his life," the old sage offered, as the others listened intently.

"In one way, he wants to bare his soul and tell the truth to honour the great love he holds for his daughter," Farez reasoned. "But he is fearful of investing her with his dark deeds all of which have been kept from her up till now. At this moment, that is still a step too far for Volcov," he added, to stunned silence.

"Yet he felt able to explain his predicament to his PA, didn't he?" Mike Harper postulated. "Surely that was a huge risk for Volcov to take."

"Not as I see it Mike," Farez said refuting the notion. "Volcov had to confide in someone and it was natural for him to choose the one individual he trusts with the safety of his beloved daughter. It is obvious that when he dies, he wants John Dwyer to remain in Laura's life. Try to see it as a measure of a father's love for his child," Farez added, looking at Abdul.

"It is also a measure of the trust Volcov has in his right-hand man," Tariq suggested. "What do you think, you are closer to this than any of us," he added addressing Abdul.

"Volcov would not have confided in me if he had any doubts. Yet, I have a gut feeling he suspects there is more he can discover about me. It's hard to put into words; as I say it's just a feeling," Abdul explained but not to anyone's complete understanding.

"Do you suspect Volcov is suspicious about your identity?" Mike Harper questioned, concerned and looking uneasy.

"No, I think it goes deeper than that," Abdul responded, failing again to satisfactorily explain his gut feeling. He was unable to put into words a rational explanation that would serve as an appropriate answer to the doubts he was experiencing.

The wise Farez Malikzai could see Abdul struggling with his own quandary and while he could not conjure up a solution, he would never let his young brother fight alone. "My dear friend, I have no doubt you will never allow anything to distract you from your sworn duty. You have demonstrated as much on many occasions. And from what you reported today, I also believe Laura has no knowledge of the underhand dealings of the man she knows as her uncle. Adham Volcov is facing his mortality, the final moment of truth in his life. Because of his infinite love for his beloved daughter, he is searching for an acceptable path forward. He has to trust someone not only with the truth but also someone who cares for Laura. You are that someone. His latest diagnosis added urgency to his quest. He sees what you mean to her, and he senses a similar spark in you. So, tell me, John Dwyer," Farez urged, "do you care for her?"

"I would by lying to you if I said I didn't. But I will never allow my emotions to rule my head. I have made a promise to

Volcov to protect his daughter when he can no longer take care of her. That said I will never lose sight of the importance of the mission. You all have my word," Abdul said, making it clear to everyone at the meeting.

"That's all we need to know," Tariq stated, patting Abdul on his back.

Farez was becoming concerned that Abdul had been away from Villa Margalla for too long. "I agree, that's all we need to know. So now, John Dwyer, I suggest you get back to your boss while we continue to consider the news you reported today. We can't have him questioning your absence. We don't want a suspicious Volcov on our hands, not at this stage," he added as Mike got to his feet to accompany Abdul to the car.

"Would I be correct in saying you have found yourself between a rock and a hard place?" the Sgt Major asked wryly.

"It sure looks like that Mike. To be honest, I have experienced a few twists and turns not part of the plan nor anticipated. Things may still work out in our favour. But for me, buddy, it's back to Villa Margalla and business as usual. Be seeing you pal," Abdul announced cheerily as he gunned the car's engine. It was important to remain positive.

*

On his return to the ops room, Mike Harper found Tariq, Farez and Irene deep in conversation. Tariq was speaking of being bemused by Abdul's report on Volcov and Laura. "It took me completely by surprise," he said, looking to the others for input.

Equally puzzled, and not just by the revelations but by Commander Zahir's comment, Irene asked, "Do you think it weakened Volcov's position and strengthened ours?"

"Not exactly Irene. There is a crack in his armour that may work in our favour. But we can't move on anything we learned until Volcov's trusty assistant John Dwyer makes his next move. For us, it's a waiting game," he added.

Joining in the exchange between Tariq and Irene, Farez cautioned against moving too quickly. "I think we must pause to review the situation. It is clear that Volcov trusts his PA. Why? Two reasons: he likes what he sees in John Dwyer and feels he can trust him with his daughter's safety and welfare when he's no longer around. It's a decision based on his calculation of two people being fond of one another – he certainly knows how Laura feels.

"It seems Volcov has had a wakeup call, but in three different ways. It started with the accidental death of his sister resulting in Laura living with him. That meant he could live the dream of caring for her in every way. Then he discovered that through his association with Patcha he was indirectly responsible for the deaths of innocent people in the 9/11 terrorist attacks. That struck a personal note because it could have been his sister and daughter in America at that time. So, for the first time in his business life he realised his indirect involvement carried tragic consequences.

"He responded to this wakeup call by getting rid of Patcha from his home, and out of his life, to protect his daughter from repercussions by the feared Mamasan of Thailand. No-one knew better than he the lengths she was willing to go to get her own way," he added, as the others listened intently.

"Thirdly, he was diagnosed with a terminal illness and the prognosis is not good. Immediately, his priority became Laura and the need to protect her from the truth because he fears he'll lose her if he bares his soul to her. John Dwyer, as he sees it, is his only hope and that's why he reached out for help," Farez added, watching the others as they absorbed his brilliant analysis.

"Where is this leading brother?" Tariq asked, suspecting Farez to have more on his mind.

"I am suggesting we have a very different Volcov to deal with than when we began the mission. We started with intel that Volcov was a dangerous international criminal. This is no longer the case from what we now know. He is an emotionally changed person and this transformation could work in our favour over time. That's why we must give our inside man, John Dwyer, the space and time he needs to make his own moves. We must take our lead from him my friends, that's how I see it.

"Meanwhile," Farez continued", I can build up a relationship of trust with Volcov. Remember we live each and every day of our lives, but we face the reality of death only once. Volcov is at that stage; facing his mortality and hoping for a good death, if I can put it that way, so his soul can rest in peace. In mountaineering terms, he has to find the courage to climb some emotional peaks. Perhaps, given time, I can help him with his climb."

Farez's ability to express a complex situation in simple terms - anticipated to some extent by Tariq - was considered compelling by Irene and inspiring by Mike Harper. But Farez had one more pearl of wisdom to share: "My greatest concern right now is for Laura's health. Patcha, a proud woman disparaged and expelled by Volcov, may see her as a target. She will seek revenge. And the way her mind works, she will view Laura as a bargaining tool. We should be alert to this possibility," he stressed before taking a sip of cool water.

Mike Harper saw it as a real possibility. "Should we warn our man on the inside?" he asked.

Farez was opposed to the idea. "This doesn't change my advice to wait until our man makes his move and/or raises any red flags where Patcha is concerned."

"So, we are waiting to see which way the wind will blow," Tariq said, stating the obvious.

But none of them could possibly know just how soon the wind's direction would change in their favour.

***

Chapter Thirteen

On his return to Villa Margalla, Abdul noticed an unfamiliar vehicle in the driveway – a shiny black, 4WD Land Rover. "Must be someone important," Abdul mumbled to himself, curious as to whom it could be. As far as he was aware Volcov was not expecting visitors. Then he noticed the driver was dressed in *khet partug*, the same style worn by Taliban fighters. Curious to learn more, he approached the study door only to find his way blocked by someone stepping out of the shadows. It was Darius Forsetti and he was wearing his trademark smirk.

"Sorry pal, no entry!" Forsetti declared tetchily, his hostile stance of legs akimbo and arms raised suggesting he was itching for a fight. Always happy to oblige Forsetti, Abdul viciously kicked the man's splayed legs from under him sending his adversary crashing to the floor in some pain. Before poor Darius could recover his composure, the study door opened and Volcov peered out. Observing, but not commenting on the altercation, Abdul's boss invited him into the study.

"Ah, I see you're back, John. Good, come in please we have a visitor," he stated as Darius scrambled to his feet to follow but was stopped when Volcov shut the door in his face. Once again, Forsetti was left licking his wounds.

Striding boldly into the study, Abdul's heart began to pound fiercely the moment he came face to face with an old foe -- former Governor Ahmad Hakim Kahir. Morbidly obese and attired in military-style *khet partug* consistent with a Taliban commander, Kahir was firmly wedged in his armchair. It was clear he had not shed an ounce of weight since Abdul last saw the odious excuse for a human being.

"I believe you have already met my esteemed guest Commander Ahmad Hakim Kahir" Volcov said, with signs of strain on his face that made Abdul feel uncomfortable.

"Yes, of course sir," Abdul acknowledged, noting his boss addressed the former governor as "commander", an approbation of the man's importance in the New Taliban. Abdul moved close enough to the toady ex-governor to inspect him at arm's length. Abdul found it amusing that the portly ex-governor did not recognise him. Smiling at the thought he credited his skilful makeup artists.

"Ah...yes, I know you," Kahir spluttered, "you're John Dwyer, the mystery man. You must tell me all about yourself Dwyer. Let's start with what brought you to this part of the world," he challenged, staring at Abdul with his beady eyes.

"As you wish sir. I am working for Mister Volcov who knows all there is to know about me. Beyond that, I don't have anything to add," Abdul replied, fixing Kahir with a steely gaze that tempted the Taliban leader to retaliate. Volcov decided to intervene by distracting his guest and save him from what could become a difficult situation.

"My man Dwyer returned a short while ago from visiting our new neighbour in Villa Magnolia where my niece has been invited to ride one of Mr. Alexopoulos's magnificent horses," Volcov explained as Abdul melted into the background

"I see, and just when am I going to meet Mister Alexopoulos? You appear to be reluctant to introduce your new friend," Commander Kahir stated with more than a hint of sarcasm.

"There is no reluctance on my part commander. Kostas Alexopoulos is convalescing at this time and that's why we have spent more time at his villa than at mine. Let me assure you I will arrange for you to be introduced just as soon as his medical team allows him to be out and about. I think you'll find him quite interesting."

Abdul stifled a laugh both at what his boss had said and at the Taliban supremo's half-hearted attempt to extricate himself from his chair. He was stuck fast but after a short bout of puffing and panting he broke free, found his feet. He turned to leave, his face turning purple from his labours.

"Remember my words Adham," the commander nagged before turning on his heel to leave. Volcov was by his side, impatient to see the back of his boring guest.

Abdul was back at his desk when the old man, pale and flustered, returned to the study. Sweating profusely, he sat down and closed his eyes.

"Are you unwell, sir?" Abdul asked, concerned because Volcov appeared unsettled by Commander Kahir's visit.

Waving away any concern on the part of his assistant, Volcov said, "There's nothing to worry about, John, I will be fine in a moment or two. I must confess that Commander Kahir is not to my liking. Patcha is cosying up to him, complaining about how I threw her out of the villa. I have a feeling she's up to no good, so please keep an eye on my daughter. I sense trouble ahead," he said, mopping his brow with a handkerchief.

Abdul did not comment though his thoughts were aligned with his boss's fears.

*

Abdul was already seated at his desk when Volcov appeared the next morning. He was later than usual and looked as though he'd endured a sleepless night. "Good morning sir," Abdul said cheerily ignoring his boss's unkempt appearance.

"Ah…good morning John. I can't find Laura. Do you have any idea where she is?" Volcov's asked, due concern transmitted in the tone of his voice.

"Not so far, sir. I had assumed you would both be in the garden," Abdul replied.

"Maybe she's taken Sykes for a walk," Volcov said hopefully as he sat at his desk to tackle a stack of newly opened mail. Abdul returned to his tasks also, but neither man seemed able to concentrate.

The recent unpleasant occurrences at the villa involving Patcha still troubled both men inviting apprehension where Laura's absence was concerned. Patcha's threatening behaviour had to be taken seriously. Possible scenarios for Laura's absence – none of them pleasant -- began to marinate in the marine's mind.

A dog's frenzied barking broke the uneasy silence, quickly followed by the appearance of a wet but happy Sykes. The feisty dog generously and vigorously rubbed his soaking wet body against Volcov and Abdul, all to joyful laughter on Laura's part. She had magically appeared in the doorway of the study. It was becoming a habit, Abdul thought, determined to make light of the moment. At least Laura was safe, and that's all that mattered.

Relieved, Volcov moved to embrace Laura. He held her tightly as if she'd been lost and then found again. "My darling girl, where have you been? I was so worried," the old man said, beginning to tear up.

"Please don't upset yourself uncle," she pleaded. "I am perfectly alright. As it is a fine day, I went for a morning walk with Sykes and enjoyed every minute of it," she added, giving him a peck on the cheek.

"When you failed to join me this morning for our coffee date by the pool, I thought something had happened to you," he said, the words bursting forth before he could check himself. Laura was taken aback, herself concerned that the old man looked the worse for wear. She glanced towards Abdul who shook his head. He placed a finger to his lips as if to say, "Don't go there!".

Soldiering on, she said, "Well, uncle, here I am and, as you can see, I'm perfectly safe and dying for a coffee. Let's all sit by the pool," she suggested, leading the old man into the garden followed by Abdul anxious to learn where she'd been for her morning walk. Sykes lay down at Laura's feet, exhausted after his morning run. Volcov appeared to recover to become his usual self after being reunited with his daughter and downing a double espresso.

Abdul realised just how vulnerable Volcov had become after Laura moved into the villa. When she was living safely in the United States, he could pursue his business interests without having to look left or right for someone else's benefit. Now it was different. On a number of occasions, he had longed to be a father in her life but settled on securing her safety and happiness. This meant admiring her from afar and allowing her to believe he was her loving Uncle Adham. The sudden death of his sister, while a very sad and unfortunate occurrence, had also given him an opportunity to live his dream. But how could he risk telling her about his business dealings? She was the one precious thing in his life he wished to preserve.

Recent revelations regarding 9/11 had forced him to face the reality of his actions. He was ashamed and woeful for his part in the loss of life. Parents, sons, daughters lost forever leaving a wake of torment for those left behind with nothing but grief and an acute sense of loss. Now he could understand their pain through his love for his own daughter. He was not only afraid of losing Laura's love if he revealed the whole truth, he balked at becoming an accessory in a dangerous game involving bad actors primed to carry out their vile plans. Surely, under such circumstances, Laura would also become a pawn in a high-stakes chess game especially if Volcov interfered with their plans.

Abdul knew little about the lives of Volcov and his daughter. That made it extremely difficult to scrutinise two people so obviously drawn to one another. Laura was not an intended part of this mission but that's how it had turned out. Nor could Abdul ignore his feelings for her which were not going away.

The possibility that Laura would go for a walk all alone causing her father to become distressed and very concerned had not occurred to Abdul. But he now felt similar concern. Patcha, if nothing else, was a cruel bitch of a woman with evil intent. And the visit from self-appointed Commander Kahir, an unprincipled man of questionable morals, only served to convince Abdul that Laura could be in danger. Today, such concern was unfounded. But what about tomorrow, the next day, or next week?

Lost in his own ruminations, Abdul suddenly became aware that Volcov was speaking to him. "You do agree with me, don't you John?"

"Absolutely sir!" Abdul said a broad smile on his face. He hadn't the vaguest idea what Volcov had said but going along with one's boss was not only smart but necessary. Laura smiled at him mischievously.

"Good," Volcov said as he left the pair in the study. "I will let you have five minutes with Laura and then expect you to get back to work young man."

Laura chuckled, "John your mind was somewhere in the Margalla Hills I think. You haven't the slightest idea what you agreed to, am I right?"

Abdul sighed, slightly peeved but resigned to not knowing what he'd agreed to. "Alright Laura, so if you won't tell me now, I won't ask again. My five minutes are up, and I must get back to work. Before I go, I must point out that your uncle was very worried this morning when he couldn't find you. For his sake, you should tell one of us where you are going before wandering off on your own. He is an old man and can do without the stress of worrying about you. Now, if you'll excuse me, I have work to do," he added, immediately hating himself for speaking to her so harshly. But it was out before he could check himself.

"Just one moment John...tell me please...is my uncle unwell?"

Her question threw him off balance, "You are the doctor, Laura, why don't you ask him yourself?" he said peevishly, leaving her alone to ponder her next move.

*

The next few days passed without Volcov or Abdul seeking to rekindle their previous discussions concerning Laura and her true relationship with the man she calls uncle. It was Abdul's view that giving Volcov time for reflection may cause him to change his mind. Meanwhile, it was business as usual at Villa Margalla. Laura took her morning walks with Sykes inside the villa grounds but today would be different. As Volcov and Abdul poured over the morning mail, Laura burst into the study. It was obvious she was not her usual self.

"What is it Laura, my dear, you seem so upset," Volcov asked always concerned for her wellbeing.

"It's about Sykes. Have either of you seen him this morning? I can't find him uncle," she responded nervously.

"Oh, I expect he's gone off for a walk on his own. Please don't let it upset you my dear," Volcov pleaded trying to calm her nerves.

But she wouldn't be put off. "He never goes far from me Uncle Adham. I am sure there's something wrong," she added, looking towards Abdul for support.

Getting up from his desk, Abdul walked to her and placed his hands on her shoulders. "Laura, I am certain there's nothing wrong. Sykes is a dog after all, and dogs always like to chase things. He probably decided to go after something in the grounds. I will be finished here in thirty minutes and then I will help you find him. Meanwhile, why don't you sit by the pool where Sykes can find you?

Saddened by Abdul's apparent lack of interest, she shrugged her shoulders and headed for the garden. "I will retrace my steps along the route I take each day and see if I can find him. He could be hurt or, worse still, stuck in a hole! When you feel up to it, you can follow me but I'm going now," she said emphatically, leaving Volcov and Abdul staring after her.

"Laura seems quite anxious about her dog, John," Volcov said watching Laura leave. "But I tend to think Sykes will show up in due course," he added smiling at Abdul who saw his boss's remark as a faintly disguised plea for help.

"With your permission, sir, I will join Laura as promised when I finish this task. I am sure there's no cause for concern as you say and that Laura is worrying unnecessarily," he offered, trying to put Volcov at ease though, inside, he felt anything but calm. Something was making him feel uneasy and the remaining twenty-five minutes passed slowly.

Volcov felt the same, "John, I can't concentrate; go after her please. I will question the staff to see if anyone saw the dog this morning. If not, I'll have them organise a search."

*

Laura was both worried and upset when she left the study: worried about Sykes and upset with her uncle and Abdul for what she viewed as their indifference to her predicament. But she knew better; Sykes never went off on his own. She feared for his safety.

"Sykes, Sykes, where are you?" she called out several times as she got deeper into the house surrounds. But she heard nothing other than a rustling of the wind in the trees. After a few more steps, she spun round when she heard a movement behind her and came face to face with Darius Forsetti. Standing with arms folded, he sported a cheeky a grin that made Laura feel most uncomfortable. She found him an irritating individual at the best of times and braced herself for what he had to say.

"Do you have a problem missy?" he asked in his usual irritating manner. "Were you calling for someone?"

"Yes, Darius I was calling for my dog. Sykes is missing and I am worried something may have happened to him." She spoke plainly wishing it was anybody other than Darius standing before her. He was the last man she wanted to see at the moment.

"Oh, you're looking for your dog," he repeated sarcastically. "Well, let's see…he can't have gone very far. I will search with you and maybe together we'll get lucky," Darius suggested in a way that invited Laura to turn down his offer to help. But Sykes was her one concern and extra hands were welcome. After all, she thought, John Dwyer did not rush to her assistance as she'd expected.

"Well, I would appreciate some help Darius," she conceded, as they continued the search calling out Sykes' name frequently.

Suddenly, Darius stopped and reached out for Laura's arm. "Did you hear that, Miss Laura?" he queried.

"Hear what?" she asked looking at him in desperation.

"I thought I heard a bark. We should go this way," he said insistently. "Your dog may have deviated from his usual route and got stuck somewhere," he added, guiding Laura off the main track, out of the villa grounds, and into a wooded area. There was a building in the distance beyond the trees. They stopped and called out again. This time Laura did hear something – muffled barking that seemed to be coming from inside the building.

As they drew closer the barking became louder and more frenzied. "That is definitely Sykes…I know his bark," Laura screamed. "Don't worry Sykes, I'm coming to get you," she yelled quickening her pace until she was way ahead of Darius who seemed to have slowed down. Opening the door of the barn-like building she went inside. It was dark and her eyes had to adjust from being in strong sunlight. It was then she saw him.

"Sykes...there you are! You are a very naughty boy," she screamed. "But why are you tied up, what happened to you?" The dog was covered in mud but reacted with a mixture of joy and relief as Laura approached. Bending down to release him she was taken aback when Sykes bared his teeth. He was growling at something behind her. It was Darius wearing his trademark smirk. He leant forward to grab her by the arm.

"What in God's name are you doing Darius. Take your filthy hands off me," she screamed wrenching her arm free. It was then she took a blow to the side of her head. Her knees buckled and she crashed to the floor alongside Sykes. Stunned, she struggled against the pain in her head and tried to understand what was happening. She was vaguely aware of cries and yelps from Sykes. Then silence.

Darius yanked her to her feet, slung her semiconscious frame over his shoulder and strode out of the building. Forcefully, he threw her face down in the back of a van. Dazed, she was unable to resist or help herself. She felt her hands being tied behind her back. It was then she realised she was being abducted. Before she could react, she felt a sudden shooting pain in her arm as Darius plunged a hypodermic syringe into the flesh, and then oblivion.

*

With little success, Abdul combed an area where he figured Laura was a regular visitor. He was worried and had a gut feeling that something was very wrong. After a few minutes his ears picked up a faint whimpering. He moved in the direction of the cry and arrived at what appeared to be a deserted building. Sykes, tied up, was bleeding from a wound in his side. The dog was badly injured. There was no sign of Laura. His worst fears were coming true. Two sets of footprints on the dust-covered floor led outdoors to a set of tyre marks. It wasn't difficult to conclude that Laura had been abducted after being lured by a decoy in the shape of Sykes. Taking off his shirt, he scooped up the dog in his arms, wrapped it in his shirt, and doubled back to the villa as fast as his legs could carry him.

Volcov was uncontrollably distressed by Abdul's news. But the seasoned marine didn't have time to discuss what might have happened. Thinking on his feet he bundled Volcov and the injured animal into the car. Men in the villa were briefed on what had occurred and given instructions to keep the outer gates closed and refuse entry to anyone until Abdul returned. Jumping in the car he put his foot down and took off for the short drive to Villa Magnolia.

His first priority was to seek medical assistance for his injured charges from the resident doctor at Villa Magnolia. What happened subsequently would depend on both man and beast being stabilised. Abdul figured that wise owl Farez would know how to handle the situation. Circumstances had changed beyond anything they had rehearsed. Was it time to review their entire approach?

It was abundantly clear to Abdul that Patcha had made her move. "If it's war she wants, it's war she'll get," Abdul muttered clenching his fists.

***

Chapter Fourteen

Hurtling into the driveway at high speed, Abdul pumped the car horn inviting a flurry of activity inside and outside Villa Magnolia. As the car screeched to a halt, he lowered a window and yelled at Mike Harper to find and fetch the team doctor, taking care to speak in Pashto. "I have two casualties in need of medical assistance asap," he urged as willing hands helped extricate an unsteady Volcov and guide him into the villa. Abdul followed cradling Sykes in his bloodstained arms.

"What happened here?" a confused Farez asked as he followed Abdul to where the doctor was already treating Adham Volcov.

"This way doc," Abdul shouted, ignoring Farez's question. "I guess my little friend is in more urgent need of assistance. He's been stabbed and is in bad shape. Do what you can for him doc; we don't want to lose him!" Abdul pleaded, as the doctor lifted a frightened, whimpering terrier from Abdul's arms and laid him on a hastily cleared tabletop.

"Mister Alexopoulos, I wish to request your assistance sir," Abdul declared, respectfully addressing the owner of Villa Magnolia. "Mister Volcov is in extreme shock and I think he should stay here at least for tonight if you don't mind."

"Of course, John," Farez acknowledged, cautiously using Abdul's nom de guerre as previously agreed when in the company of anyone outside their close circle of confidants. "Be assured he will be well cared for by the medical team supporting my convalescence," Farez added, noticing that Abdul was not only bloodied but shirtless. "Why don't you take a break and clean yourself up. I will have someone find a fresh shirt for you."

"I apologise for my appearance; I'll see to it right away. And thank you, sir." Abdul replied, grateful for the opportunity to take time out. It was essential to make sense of recent events.

"Asad, take John Dwyer to my room and see to his needs if you please. When you're feeling refreshed, we will talk some more," he assured Abdul, before sitting alongside Adham Volcov who was as white as a sheet and sweating and trembling uncontrollably.

"Thank you for your help Miss Irene," Farez said praising Irene Ryan for sitting with Volcov, holding his hand and speaking to him in gentle tones. "I will take over until the doctor comes back," he confirmed placing a hand on Volcov's trembling hands. This wasn't the right time for talking as the old man was far too distressed to listen or speak. Farez, forever compassionate, knew the right thing to do was just to be there in Volcov's hour of need.

*

Feeling refreshed after a shower, Abdul began to unwind and address recent events. Having enlisted help from the team in Villa Magnolia he figured he could attend to explanations later on. The important thing, he mused, had been to safely deliver Volcov into capable hands, along with Sykes who had come to mean as much to Abdul as he did to Laura.

As he was trying on one of the many colourful silk shirts from billionaire Kostas Alexopoulos's well-stocked wardrobe, a tense-looking Commander Zahir entered the bedroom. "What happened today?" he asked, shaking his head from side to side. "When you arrived earlier, I thought it best to stay out of sight from Volcov and wait to speak to you in private," he added, looking towards Mike Harper who was half-in and half-out of the giant wardrobe.

"Would you rather I left you alone?" Harper asked not wishing his presence to inhibit their conversation.

Smiling, Abdul said, "Stay Mike; what I have to say concerns all of us. The breaking news is Laura has been abducted and Volcov is overcome with grief," he declared candidly, before bidding the others to be seated as he recounted the entire episode. Dumbfounded by Abdul's account of Laura's abduction, Commander Zahir and Mike Harper just stared ahead struggling to find words.

"As I see it," Abdul went on, "whoever carried out this kidnapping used the dog as a decoy to lure Laura into the building. It is clear from Sykes' injuries the poor mutt was left to die a slow and painful death. Looking around I noticed the floor was thick with dust and picked out two sets of footprints. There were vehicle tyre tracks at one side of the building. I figure she was taken away in a vehicle and that's about all I know," he added, sounding disconnected from the incident. In fact, he was battling to keep his emotions under control.

Command Zahir, with thoughts of his own daughter, was incensed at what had happened. "This is outrageous and totally unacceptable. Any idea who might be behind it?"

"That's a no-brainer Tariq," Abdul said forcefully. "That darned woman Patcha is behind this for sure. She's getting back at Volcov for throwing her out of the villa. Did I ever mention that she's a vindictive bitch?" he asked sarcastically. "Her plan is to ensure Volcov upholds his end of whatever bargain was struck and she's discovered a failsafe means of persuasion," he added, his sharp retort fuelled by anger.

"Do you mean she's using Laura as a bargaining tool?" Harper asked, a tortured look on his face.

"That sums it up Mike: a means to an end; a pawn in a very dirty game of human chess!" Abdul fired back, raising his voice and then checking himself as the bedroom door opened. Farez entered, squinting at the bright blue silk shirt Abdul had picked out for himself. "I have a situation update on Volcov," he announced, pulling up a chair and joining the others. "The doctor has examined him and placed him under heavy sedation. He is in a guest suite and there's nothing more we can do tonight. We will have someone stay with him overnight and tomorrow we can review our options. That said, would someone please tell me what's going on?" he insisted, looking from one man to the other.

"Of course, Farez," Abdul responded. "But first, what news of Sykes? Is he out of danger?"

"Everything that can be done is being done. The doctor will fill you in shortly. I would say the dog is holding his own."

"He's one plucky animal," Abdul remarked approvingly, "to bravely fight his corner. Now, Farez, let me update you on today's events," he offered, changing the subject before carefully repeating everything he'd explained to Commander Zahir and Mike Harper moments earlier.

"I had a feeling you were the bearer of bad news," Farez remarked to Abdul. "I think suggest we take this discussion into the operations room so you can put everyone in the picture."

"We must place everyone in the villa on full alert," Mike Harper commented. I will see to that when everyone is assembled."

"We also need a plan of action including how we deal with Volcov when he's strong enough to face facts," Farez suggested, stamping his authority on proceedings. "My brothers, what happened today could be a turning point in our entire mission."

*

"I think that about covers everything," Abdul declared to everyone assembled in the ops room. "I never doubted for a minute that scheming bitch Madam Patcha would seek revenge on Adham Volcov to have him commit to whatever they are planning. She must avoid any weak links in the chain. And she can't move without Volcov's contacts some of whom are probably already in play in the States as organisers of safe houses and training schedules. If there is a plan similar to the magnitude of 9/11, they will have to establish a number safe havens in the United States. This is where Volcov comes in. That's my summation based on events to date. Anybody got any questions or comments?"

As usual, Mike Harper had something to contribute. "Going forward, John, do you have a new plan for handling this unforeseen development?" He didn't phrase it as such, but he was concerned how much Laura's disappearance would impinge on the mission and Abdul's involvement.

Abdul knew what he was getting at. "If you are concerned that I might allow my emotions get in the way of the mission my response is: don't worry! I know what has to be done. We may be singing from a different hymn sheet, but our overall objective is unchanged. We must arrest and bring them all to justice. The way we go about it may have to be modified to answer your question.

"Looking at the big picture, and for what it's worth, I believe no harm will come to Laura if Volcov plays along with Patcha and her cohorts. There is nothing to be gained from her death so long as Volcov cooperates," he said, looking at the assembled team and expecting some pushback. Deliberately he did not address what might happen if Volcov failed to cooperate for one reason or another.

"How do you rate Volcov's ability to perform given his present condition?" Harper asked. "Clearly, he's in deep shock now, but how is he going to react when he comes around?"

"I have no idea how he will react. Mike, you raise some good points and I think it is time to bring everyone assembled up to speed. So, let's start by considering that Adham Volcov may have only six months to live. Of course, he must never know that we are all aware of that. Equally obvious, is that the abduction of Laura will not help his terminal condition.

"Our best move concerning Volcov, is to play a waiting game and try to turn the situation to our advantage. How we do that I can't say while we are groping our way through a minefield of difficulties. For now, it's vitally important we gain

Volcov's complete trust because it may be the only way we can pull off a successful mission."

"I would call that a fair assessment," Commander Zahir offered. "But what are your immediate plans?"

"I must speak to the staff at Villa Margalla and see what is in the office files. I will leave Volcov in your capable hands," Abdul said to no-one in particular, "and come back in the morning."

The doctor had a point to raise. "What about Volcov's own medical consultant? Should we inform him of Volcov's present condition?"

"Let's keep it all in the villa doc," Abdul answered. "Tomorrow I'll hand over Volcov's prescribed medication to you. We'll keep Volcov here until you think he's well enough to go to his own villa. If we brief his medical consultant, he may question the circumstances that led to his condition and no-one must know of Laura's abduction.

"Okay, I think that wraps things up for now. I will get back to Villa Margalla and see what's happened in my absence," Abdul added, as he headed for the door, and the car, followed by Tariq and Farez.

"Before you leave my friend," Farez said, placing his hands on the shoulders of both Abdul and Tariq. "We know you'll do the right thing brother."

Both Tariq and Farez were confident that Abdul would not let his heart rule his head. "You don't have to explain anything to us, my friend," Tariq assured him. "The way you have reacted to recent events is more than enough proof of your determination to finish the task in hand," he added as all three embraced one another.

Smiling at Abdul, Farez suggested they talk again in the morning. "I will take care of Volcov until he feels better. We will have to see how he reacts when anger takes over from shock – two emotions I am sure he will experience in short order. For now, my friends, I suggest we sleep on it and review our options in the cold light of day," he added, looking up at the rising moon. It promised to be a night full of bright stars.

Taking a final look at his two compatriots as he boarded the car, Abdul left Villa Magnolia feeling strangely alone though he knew the bond he shared with Tariq and Farez would withstand any challenge. At that poignant moment an unexpected wave of emotion swept through his body. He pulled over and switched off the engine. Staring into the darkness he shuddered slightly, and his eyes welled up with tears. "Laura, my darling, stay strong for I will find you! No matter where you are, always believe that I love you to the moon and back!"

***

Chapter Fifteen

Drifting in and out of consciousness, Laura was vaguely aware of being in a vehicle but had no sense of what was happening to her. Trussed up like a chicken, her hands and feet bound, and her head covered by a blanket, she was unable to identify her surroundings. She had the strangest feeling of being spaced out and unable to move though she called out for John Dwyer and Uncle Adham, and she thought she could hear Sykes bark from somewhere in the back of her confused mind. Why was she in this vehicle? To where was she being taken? Nothing made sense.

After a while, the vehicle slowed then came to a halt. A door opened. There were voices but in her befuddled state Laura could not make sense of anything. Someone grabbed at her and pulled her from the vehicle. Resisting was pointless as she was bodily carried some distance before being unceremoniously dumped onto a bed. More chatting…a man's voice then a woman's voice. Footsteps receding into the distance and then the sound of steady breathing in close proximity. Suddenly, the blanket was removed from her head and she found herself staring at a woman - the wicked madam Patcha replete with wild eyes and a cruel, insensitive grin.

"Welcome to my world Laura," she hissed. "It's time for you to sample Patcha's unique form of hospitality; you may find it different from your pampered lifestyle at Villa Margalla," she added, clearly enjoying the moment.

"Why are you doing this? And where is Sykes?" Laura pleaded recalling his cries of pain from being tied up. If she was expecting Patcha to show compassion it seemed an unlikely prospect given the foul mood she was in.

"Fortunately, none of us have to worry anymore about that wretched dog," Patcha said with menacing conviction, the venom in her voice reverberating in Laura's ears. Seconds later, everything went black as she sank into a state of oblivion.

*

Arriving at Villa Margalla, exhausted, puzzled, and worried, Abdul tried to make sense of Laura's abduction. Undoubtedly, it was a powerful way to keep Volcov on message – Patcha's message. That said, nobody knew that the old man was living on borrowed time, which added a new dimension. What seemed safe to assume, however, was that Laura would be unharmed if Volcov cooperated with the kidnappers. But that boiled down to discovering who was behind the kidnapping and, more importantly, where she'd been taken.

Abdul had already pinned the dastardly deed on Patcha aided and abetted by the incorrigible Ahmad Hakim Kahir who would delight in such an abduction. Nevertheless, the duo had to have help from within Villa Margalla to carry out their plan and that's where Abdul would start.

Inside Villa Margalla everyone had assembled eager to hear John Dwyer's explanation, following which each man was asked to wait outside Volcov's study to be interviewed individually. The same question was put to everyone: where were you at the time Laura disappeared?

Each man's movements were accounted for save for Darius Forsetti. "Hold up one moment," Abdul yelled at the last man – Jack Cummings -- as he left the study. "Do you have any idea where Darius Forsetti is Jack?"

"No, Mr Dwyer, I haven't seen him all day."

"In that case, get everyone back in here. And I will ask each man the same question."

Minutes later everyone gathered in the hallway. "Does anyone know where Darius Forsetti is?" Abdul asked, eyeing each man with guarded suspicion. Silence. "You are close to the stairs, Jack, run up to his room and report back. We'll wait."

After an uncomfortable two-minute silence, with most men staring at their shoes to avoid eye contact with Abdul, Jack Cummings returned. "His room is empty, and it doesn't look to have been used today."

"Understood. Now, listen up gentlemen: until Mr Volcov returns everyone in the villa will report to me. Carry on with your assigned duties as usual and be extra vigilant. I intend to flush out whoever is responsible for recent events whatever it takes and punish them accordingly. You can bet the farm on that," he added as an uncomfortable silence enveloped the lobby area. Each man knew what PA John Dwyer meant.

Some had already been on the receiving end of harsh treatment meted out by the vastly experienced marine.

After being dismissed, every man dispersed apart from Jack Cummings who had something on his mind.

"Yes, Jack, what can I do for you?" Abdul asked wearily. All he wanted to do was take a break and think through events. He knew sleep would not come easy with all he had on his mind.

"It is more a case of what I can do for you Mister Dwyer. May I call you John?" he stated without waiting for a response. "As I see it, you need eyes and ears in the villa that you can trust. This is where I can help. Most of the guys here were either attached to Forsetti or are wary of you, particularly those who received a lesson in martial arts and are still nursing their bruises and injured pride."

Jack Cummings's openness appealed to Abdul, and he was compelled to smile at the thought of how several of Volcov's men had been sent flying during earlier skirmishes. And he could use a man on the inside. But can he be trusted?

"You make a valid observation Jack. By the way call me John. I do need someone I can rely on and I'm inclined to give you a try. I hope my trust will not be unfounded," he added, intending Cummings to earn his trust.

"Thank you, John, I won't let you down," Cummings promised, as both men shook hands and parted ways.

Draining a well-earned Jack Daniels, Abdul sank into a comfortable armchair. He was dog-tired but unable to relax because the game just became much more dangerous with Laura's abduction. It troubled both heart and mind: he could no longer refute, or disregard, the love he felt for her. At the same time, he was resolute in his determination to finish the job whatever the cost. The mental effort required to address such conflicting emotions led him into a troubled sleep.

Jack Cummings was determined to prove his worth to John Dwyer. He had his own reasons for offering to assist Volcov's PA. Cummings was neither a fan of Volcov nor a keen member of the security team. After studying John Dwyer, he decided he liked what he saw. Here was a man who could be trusted. So, he would grasp the metal and prove he was worth the trust being place in him.

Darius Forsetti was unpopular with everyone and Cummings never felt at ease when the man was around. Nor did he have any doubt that Forsetti had played a part in Laura's disappearance figuring he was just getting back at John Dwyer for unseating him as Volcov's right-hand man. And it hadn't escaped Cummings' notice that Patcha was cosying up to Darius in a very friendly manner. He may not even be aware she is just playing him to get him to do her dirty work. After careful analysis, Cummings decided to reveal all in the morning. Meanwhile he headed for Forsetti's bedroom to see if he could find anything to corroborate his suspicions. "Don't worry John Dwyer," Cummings muttered to himself, "you have one more man in Villa Margalla playing on your team."

*

Back at Villa Magnolia, Tariq and Farez had talked into the early hours assessing recent developments. Both men were able to empathise with Volcov because each had suffered the loss of loved ones. In some instances, there had been a happy outcome. But would that follow in Laura's case?

"I am willing to bet my ambassadorship that the notorious Kahir and treacherous Madam Patcha are behind this abduction," Commander Tariq stated, harbouring bitter memories in particular where the former governor was concerned. "When Volcov threw Patcha out of the villa she knew she could no longer compete against Laura," he added, as if thinking allowed and testing his own theory.

Farez Malikzai was one step ahead of his friend. "You are correct brother," Farez said smiling. "A woman scorned can become a very dangerous enemy. Patcha wants to ensure Volcov does not interfere with plans to stage another terrorist attack that we believe is in the planning stage; she also stands as a woman summarily rejected and greatly humiliated. That has inspired her to cut deep into Volcov's heart by taking away the great love of his life," the old sage added, a sardonic smile on his face. Laura had won his heart also. He admired this delightful young woman and he knew Volcov worshipped the ground she walked on.

Nodding his approval, Tariq asked, "But what of Abdul? His heart must be breaking. That said, we both know he will do his duty but at what cost to himself I wonder," he added, looking strained as his concern for Abdul's emotional status filled his mind.

"As always, and as brothers in arms, we stand side by side with Abdul. If my plan is successful, the tide will turn in our favour. And, by the Grace of Allah, Laura will be returned unharmed," Farez replied reassuringly.

"Just what is it you are planning that will persuade Adham Volcov to cooperate?"

"My friend, all will be revealed in due course. For now, I will leave you with something I learned from my father: 'When you go fishing my son,' he said to me, 'keep in mind that the spicier the bait the more successful the catch.'"

*

Abdul suffered a fitful night and was grateful to see dawn break. Determined to make progress, he showered and dressed, impatient to get over to Villa Magnolia to see how Volcov was progressing while wondering if Sykes had made it through the night. Something told him that if Sykes survived so would Laura. It was an illogical notion, but it spurred him on.

He arrived at the study door to be greeted by a cheerful Jack Cummings. "Good morning John, I trust you enjoyed a restful night."

"Jack, good morning to you. I am pleased you are up and about I want to brief you on my plans for today," Abdul said, bidding Cummings to follow him into the study. Seated in Volcov's chair he motioned Cummings to sit across from him.

"I want you to collect all the mail this morning and bring it to me at Villa Magnolia. Before I go there to check on Volcov, I want to make your new role clear to the men. So, let's get them together," Abdul instructed, eyeing the man closely hoping that he'd made the right decision to put his trust in Cummings.

"Before I assemble the men," Cummings said, "I wish to report that I went through Forsetti's bedroom last night and can confirm all of his belongings are missing. There was no indication when he left or where he might be. But I have a gut feeling he is very much involved with what happened. It was no secret he resented losing his position to you. And I noticed that he became friendly with Patcha. It does seem to add up don't you think?"

"I tend to agree he had a finger in the pie and his disappearance confirms as much. Good work, but don't discuss with anyone else because Forsetti may not have been working alone. And you will have to watch your back after the team learns you are my right-hand man. I guess I don't have to remind you not to trust anyone."

After briefing the team, Abdul drove over to Villa Magnolia anxious to touch base with Tariq, Farez, and Mike Harper. Progress was being made, he thought as he drove along, fairly sure he had made the right decision concerning Jack Cummings.

*

On arrival at Villa Magnolia, Mike Harper ushered Abdul indoors where Farez and Tariq were already assembled. "Did the little dog make it through the night?" was Abdul's first question to no-one in particular. The others smiled, as Tariq praised Almighty Allah that the dog was somewhat smaller than Atuallah the mule!

"Let us check with the doctor," Farez suggested grasping Abdul's elbow to steer him along a corridor to the doctor's office. There, situated in one corner of the room, was one large basket containing one small canine. A sorry-looking Sykes raised his head and wagged his tail - weakly - at the sight of Abdul. Seeing man and dog reunited offered a sense of joy and profound relief. The big man was close to tears as he gently cradled Sykes's head in his hands. His prayers had been answered and he felt assured that no matter how long it would take he'd find Laura and bring her home.

The doctor reassured Abdul that although the dog's wounds were deep with a serious loss of blood, no vital organs had been damaged. "Given time," the doctor said, grinning, "Sykes will live to bark a tale of his experience. For now, he needs a bit of tender loving care," he added knowing full well the animal would get that from everyone in the villa.

"Thanks, doc, for taking care of a good friend," Abdul said, considering where Sykes might find time to recover. "I think he should stay at Villa Magnolia to be safe from any further attempts on his life," Abdul proposed, looking to the others for support. "In any case, whoever attacked Sykes would assume they had killed him, so let's keep the dog here and out of view from everyone."

Moving into the operations room, Abdul briefed Tariq, Farez and Mike Harper about Jack Cummings coming aboard as his inside man at Villa Margalla.

Commander Tariq arched his eyebrows. "Are you sure you can trust him?"

"I will put it this way: I don't trust anyone at Villa Margalla, but I do need some eyes and ears on the inside. Cummings came to me offering his assistance and I decided to go along with him for the time being. It is not my intention to brief him on anything of importance, but I want to give him a chance to prove himself. He has made a good start.

"There is no doubt Forsetti had a hand in Laura's disappearance. Cummings searched the man's room and found he'd removed all of his belongings and has since disappeared. To me that smacks of collusion. What I don't know is if anyone else at Villa Margalla is implicated. Until I do, it has to be business as usual. I have briefed the team in the villa accordingly. And, as far as Jack Cummings is concerned, you can meet him later when he brings the mail over. Meanwhile, I suggest someone runs a background check on him."

Mike Harper got to his feet. "Excellent idea, I will ask Irene Ryan to get onto it right away."

"Good man. Now, let's see how Volcov is getting along. We need to talk about everything that's happened. With the doctor's approval, we should suggest to Volcov that he continues to stay here," Abdul said, looking at Farez.

"Agreed, and that will give us more time to gain his confidence."

"Meanwhile, I will oversee the running of Villa Margalla and meet with you here on a daily basis to update Volcov," Abdul explained.

"Farez, I hope you and Tariq can persuade Volcov to cooperate if for no other reason than to find out what happened to Laura. Surely that should be the man's main concern at this time."

*

Looking up from his armchair, Volcov stared despondently as Abdul entered the bedroom. The old man's eyes betrayed extreme anxiety on his part. "John, John…come closer…put me out of my agony. What news of Laura?" he asked his voice weak. Clearly, he was still in shock evidenced by his ghostlike appearance and vacant gaze.

Pulling up a chair, Abdul got closer. "Good morning sir, I hope you're feeling better today," he said as cheerily as he dared though it was obvious Volcov had been hit hard. "I don't have any update but it's early days, sir, and I expect to hear soon from whoever is responsible. There are bound to be demands," he added, trying not to sound too dramatic, "and I'm ready for that." Abdul was desperate to offer some words of comfort to the old man, but it was obvious that nothing he could say at this particular time would make matters any easier.

"My suggestion sir is for you to accept Mr Alexopoulos's invitation to stay at Villa Magnolia until the doctor clears you to go home. Meanwhile, I have arranged to oversee day-to-day business matters at Villa Margalla according to your wishes. I suggest we meet here on a daily basis if that's okay with you."

Leaning forward, Volcov admitted his inability to function efficiently. "I confess, John, that I cannot cope at the moment.

My mind is consumed with the thought of Laura coming home, unharmed. Whatever it takes to achieve that, you must understand I will do it. But I must know that Laura is safe. I know you understand, just as I know that you love my daughter. I trust you John. Please find her before it is too late for me. You know what I'm saying. I promise before God that I will make my peace with her. I will tell her the truth John – all of it. Just find her please!" he implored, reaching to touch Abdul's hands.

Cupping Volcov's hands in his, Abdul pledged support. "I give you my solemn word sir to find Laura and return her to you. And I give you my word to look after her not only because she's your daughter whom you love beyond life itself, but because you are right about my feelings for her. I love her too!"

*

Volcov was resting when Farez knocked on the old man's bedroom door. There wasn't any response, so he entered quietly. Volcov was seated in a chair, by the window. "How are you my friend? Farez enquired keeping his voice low. "It's such a beautiful day I thought you might like to spend some time outdoors. I have arranged for us to have a quiet lunch in the gazebo," he added as he approached Volcov who was slowly shaking his head from side to side.

"I owe you a debt of gratitude Kostas for your kindness and hospitality," Volcov declared, his voice a mere whisper, "But I have neither the strength nor the will to get out of this chair.

"That is not a good enough excuse Adham," Farez said, as if he were gently scolding a child. "You have experienced a shock, my friend, but sitting here alone will not help. It's time to share your problems with those of us who wish to help you. Until Laura is found, and I'm sure that's just a matter of time, you must hold yourself together and be strong for her sake.

Please trust me and come downstairs where we can sit and talk. A problem shared is a problem halved, after all," Farez added, doing his level best to pull Volcov out of his depressing mood.

Extending his hand to Volcov, Farez succeeded in persuading Volcov to get to his feet. Holding onto Farez's arm he walked slowly to the stairs where Mike Harper -- alias Asad Jaheel -- was on hand to safely guide the old man down the staircase.

Seated in the gazebo, Farez insisted on Volcov taking a bite of food hoping it would raise his spirits. "Do you feel like talking?" Farez asked, figuring that the arms dealer looked slightly more relaxed now he was in the fresh air. "Allow me to ask you if you have any idea who took Laura and why?"

"My dear friend," Volcov responded, nodding his head and sighing heavily, "I believe I have the answer to your question. But for you to fully understand you need to know something about me that may surprise you. It may seem obvious to you that I have been a successful businessman for many years. Many of my dealings were quite legitimate, but there is a darker side to my affairs," he added, sheepishly. Farez did not respond.

"Speaking honestly, I am consumed by a great sense of guilt from some of the things I've done. That has all changed; I didn't give a second thought at the time, but right now I feel very responsible for my deceitful past," Volcov added, sitting upright and staring into Farez's expressionless face. The wise owl sensed Volcov was about to unload his life of misdeeds and was disinclined to interrupt.

"I have been an arms dealer in my time, supplying whatever anyone wanted with no questions asked," he blurted out uncontrollably before looking to Farez for some reaction. Wisely, Farez maintained his impartial position though he could see Volcov's relief at getting things off his chest.

"I never asked for details of their businesses, or what the arms were intended for. The people I dealt with had money and I met their needs. It was that simple. I accumulated many business contacts along the way, some in high positions including a few dubious characters. By the time I realised what I had got myself into it was too late to make a break. And these people won't let you go until they have finished with you.

"Recently, I managed to upset someone by saying they were no longer welcome in my home. I took this action because Laura was being constantly harassed by this person who had made it clear she wanted Laura out of the villa and preferably back in the States. I guess you can imagine how I felt. Offering a home to Laura brought me great joy and I never want her to leave.

"Laura doesn't know anything about my work. To her I am a loving uncle who has always been there for her in every way possible. I could not take the risk of her finding out that Uncle Adham is not her knight in shining armour after all," he added, showing signs of stress and fatigue from his efforts. Reaching over, Farez poured a glass of water for Volcov.

"Drink this Adham and catch your breath. If I understand what you are saying this person is responsible for Laura's disappearance. What puzzles me," Farez continued, pushing his luck as far as he dared, "is why anyone would revert to such drastic action simply because they were no longer welcome in your home. Could it be this person still has a grudge with you? If that's the case, let me help you," he added, feeling he'd gone as far as he dared to go at least for now.

Volcov reacted strongly, "Kostas, my friend, you don't understand. We are dealing with highly dangerous people who will stop at nothing to achieve their objectives."

"I am trying hard to understand Adham. And I do want to help you. Why are you afraid of these people you speak of? What do they want?" Farez asked after which both men fell silent for what seemed like an age. Hoping that Volcov would open his heart it was becoming clear to Farez that the poor man was terrified of the consequences of being truthful.

Maybe there is another way, thought Farez, concerned about Volcov's frail appearance. Clearly the shock of what had happened to Laura, coupled with his diminished life expectancy, was taking its toll. But Farez felt he had to seize the opportunity and press him further.

"I can understand your great concern that Laura could be harmed, even killed. You may find this difficult to accept, but there are worse fates than death itself," Farez said, choosing his words with care. "And I am acquainted with some friends who would agree with me."

Volcov stared at Farez unbelievingly. "What are you saying Kostas? What could be worse than death?" he asked, angrily.

Touching Volcov's arm gently, Farez said, "I am referring to the slave and sex market: human trafficking involving innocent women and children who are spirited away and never seen again…families torn apart forever!"

It was too much for Volcov. "Stop Kostas, I can't listen to this…you don't know what you are talking about!"

"But I do know what I'm talking about my friend. Two men I know as brothers have personal experiences: one man I know as well as I know myself lost a wife and young child; another man I also love as a brother lost a mother, father, brother, and then had to endure his daughter being violated in the cruellest of ways. Yes, my friend, there are fates worse than death," Farez stated bluntly. It was immediately clear that he had made his point and sown the seeds of doubt in Volcov's mind.

"I will leave you to think over what I have said. Now we will get you back to your room to rest. Remember Adham, I want to help but I can only do so with your approval and cooperation. For that to happen we need complete honesty between us," Farez stated, helping Volcov to his feet.

"Kostas…Kostas…you are asking me to choose between the devil and the deep blue sea for goodness sake!"

Farez smiled. "I have learned in my life that nothing is quite what it seems to be my friend. In your case, I suggest that what you fear most is fear itself. But fear not while you are in this villa, I will make sure you're safe. You can trust me; you have my word."

*

Later that same afternoon Abdul, Tariq and Farez met to discuss the outcome of Farez's lunch meeting with Volcov. Both Abdul and Tariq felt uneasy about Farez confiding in the old man about people he knew whose lives had been affected by human trafficking. It was a concern that Farez was able to placate, "I was very careful not to mention any names. I would never disclose anything without approval," he added.

Commander Tariq, less concerned after receiving Farez's assurances, was anxious to find out if Volcov had agreed to help. "Did he take the bait my brother. Was it sufficiently tempting do you think?"

"I would sum it up this way," Farez said, smiling, "with an English expression: I baited a sprat to catch a mackerel. Now we wait."

It was a moment of light relief that got all three men laughing, but only for a moment. Mike Harper, looking serious, joined the others. "Irene ran a security check on Jack Cummings and the feedback may surprise you," he said handing a single sheet of paper to Tariq.

"So, don't keep us waiting, what does it say?" Farez asked.

"Cummings' real name is Allan Kemp and he's a field operative for MI6 currently conducting covert undercover duties in Pakistan."

"I wasn't expecting that," Abdul confessed, struggling to process the new information.

"It is very surprising," Tariq agreed. "I find it confusing, and amusing to some extent, finding that MI6 has a presence in Volcov's household!"

Mike Harper was more able to accept the surprising news. "Great, at least he's on our side," he said grinning at the others, "and he's a Brit!"

Coincidently, Irene Ryan knocked on the door and walked in holding a bundle of papers. "I see the Cummings announcement surprised everyone," she said. "I guess that's the nature of covert work. I double-checked with Washington and they contacted Britain's Secret Intelligence Service – better known as MI6 – for confirmation.

"An hour from now we will have a link in the ops room with the Brits and our own top brass and we'll be fully briefed. Until then we should keep this under wraps to observe standard security protocol. And when Cummings arrives with the mail," she said, looking at Abdul, "please have him hang around and wait for you. After everyone has been briefed, he will be invited to attend the ops room from where he can address his superiors. I think that's all I have to relate," she added, leaving the others to mull over events.

*

An hour later, everyone had gathered in the ops room anxious to be updated. First up on the video screen was General John Wright, America's defense secretary along with the chiefs of MI5 and MI6 who were not introduced by name.

"Good morning gentlemen," General Wright greeted everyone assembled, unaware there was a lady in the audience. "Like me, I guess you were also surprised to discover a covert British operative on your patch! Well, the good news going forward is that he is one less person to worry about," he whispered to a mixture of applause and laughter from the ops room. "That said, the chief of MI5 has a few words to say," he added nodding to the man to his left.

"Much obliged general, and good morning everyone. Bear with me please while I recap events following the 9/11 terrorist attacks on the United States. Following the attacks, our foreign secretary approved deploying MI6 officers to Afghanistan and the South Asia region in general. We assigned officers familiar with the mujahedeen in the '80s with language skills and the necessary expertise. A handful of MI6 operatives landed in northeast Afghanistan and met up with General Mohammed Fahin of the Northern Alliance. From there they worked with contacts in the north and south to build alliances, secure support, and bribe as many Taliban commanders as they could to change sides or leave the fight."

Pausing for a sip of water, the MI5 chief continued his summing up: "By 2016, MI6 had opened new stations overseas with Islamabad being the largest; the goal was to maintain intel coverage of suspects, particularly in Pakistan. Agent Cummings's brief was to supply the SAS and other British forces with intel as part of a multinational special forces operation concerning British jihadists and kill or capture them before any attempted to return to the UK to conduct terrorist activities."

Checking his notes, the MI5 chief adopted a more serious tone, "Now this next bit is particularly pertinent, so listen carefully please. Both in the UK and the United States we were dismayed to discover that a former CIA contractor, who shall remain nameless, stole a wealth of highly secret data and fled to Russia. Many of the stolen files contained intel that played a vital role in preventing a number of terrorist incidents during the past ten years.

"Today things have changed considerably. Terrorists have tens of thousands of means of communication whether via email, IP telephone, in-game communications, social networking, chat room, anonymising services, and a myriad of mobile apps. Thus, it became vital for MI5 to be able to access such information to protect the country.

"It cannot be overstressed that threats to the UK are growing more diverse and diffuse. It's a fact that there are several thousand Islamic extremists in Britain who regard the British public as a legitimate target. Now, I will ask MI6 to take it from here."

"Good day, again, and I ask you all to lend your attention for a while longer," the MI6 chief requested. "Al-Qaeda and its affiliates in Southeast Asia and the Arabian Peninsula pose the most direct and immediate threats to the UK. In Pakistan, al-Qaeda has succeeded on three occasions in four years to smuggle explosives through security and onto aircraft. Our intel suggests British-based jihadists will return from the killing fields and use their new-found skills on the great British public. So far, quite a few have been stopped at airports and arrested on the suspicion of planning acts of terrorism," he added, pausing for effect.

"Now listen to me very carefully," he said, "we believe there could be a plan in the works for a 7/7-style attack experienced in London, this time using rucksack bombs. As my colleague from MI5 explained terrorism today is more diffuse, more complicated and less predictable," he added, addressing an ops room that had suddenly gone silent. "In case you have forgotten," he continued, "London experienced a series of coordinated Islamic terrorist attacks on July 7, 2005."

Commander Zahir, who had been listening with heightened interest, was the first to pose a question. "Thank you, gentlemen, for offering a very clear briefing. In trying to align this with our mission, I would like to ask exactly what Jack Cummings's connection is to this? Surely Adham Volcov is not his prime interest?

"You are quite right, commander. Cummings is interested in a lady – and I use that word purely symbolically – who goes by the name of Patcha Volcov. When it was discovered she was residing in Villa Margalla we arranged for Cummings to gain a place on Volcov's security detail. He has the credentials; you can take it from me. Cummings monitored her movements against the background of her involvement in human trafficking and arms and people smuggling. She is our prime interest coupled with Commander Ahmad Hakim Kahir the self-styled leader of the so-called new Taliban. We are aware of Kahir's involvement in training boys and youths as suicide bombers and we know of his connections with sex trafficking. These two villains are of great interest to us," the MI6 chief added. "As I see it," he continued, "we are all working to a common cause and that is to be applauded. So, if there are no further questions, I suggest Jack Cummings joins us for the rest of the briefing."

As he entered the ops room, Jack Cummings was smiling, appreciating that the raison d'etre for him being in Villa Margalla was the main subject of the briefing.

"Why don't you take a seat Mister Cummings," General Wright proposed as he took charge of the briefing.

"The issue I wish to raise, initially with you John Dwyer," the general said, taking care to address Abdul by his nom de guerre, "concerns the unfortunate disappearance of Adham Volcov's niece. Please report; we need to gauge if and how this may affect plans going forward."

"Volcov has taken her abduction badly sir; he is in extreme shock. With your permission sir I wish to clarify the situation regarding Volcov and Laura. She is his daughter; a fact he has hidden from her for fear she discovers the unsavoury parts of his background. I am convinced she knows nothing of his nefarious activities. To her he is plain old Uncle Adham. Apart from this, Volcov's health is failing sir. He has Hodgkin's lymphoma and the prognosis is that he has less than six months to live. Outside of this room, general, and whomever is tuned into this video link, nobody is aware of the intel I have just reported on."

"Did you learn this directly from Volcov?"

"Yes sir. He made me promise to take care of his daughter in the event of his death."

"Why you?" asked the general clearly weighing up the pros and cons.

Abdul could see where this was heading, but he knew he had no option but to be truthful as Laura's life was at stake. He came right out with it, "Volcov said he had noticed how Laura was attracted to me. That convinced him he could trust me to honour his wish to take care of her. I want to make it clear, sir, that I would never allow personal feelings to compromise this mission. That's not who I am sir."

"Your military record, which I have before me, supports your assertions Dwyer," the general stated, obviously convinced and relieved that Abdul's first-rate service record spoke volumes of the man's impeccable credentials. "I guess we can trust you with this one," he added to the relief of Tariq and Farez who were holding their breath.

"Permission to ask a question sir...concerning Adham Volcov." Abdul figured this was the best opportunity he had to explain Volcov's relationship with his daughter, the man's failing health and his intention to pay amends for past wrongdoings which were troubling his conscience. "There is no getting away from Volcov's past indiscretions sir, but circumstances have changed and Volcov is unlikely to live long enough to face trial. I am convinced he bitterly regrets his past life and wishes to make amends. Is there a way he can be given a chance to do so sir?"

"Well, that would depend on what he's prepared to offer us as quid pro quo. No-one would want to cause further pain to a dying man, but we can't ignore that he was indirectly culpable in the massive loss of life as an arms dealer and I have in mind 9/11," the general said disinclined to give Abdul a straight answer.

Farez detected reluctance on the part of General Wright but decided to add his support for Abdul anyway. "I agree with Dwyer sir, having had the opportunity to know and understand Volcov these past months. And there is a way he can help in my view."

"How so?"

"I believe we can get his cooperation to disclose everything he knows about Patcha...what she and others are planning. And if this leads to preventing another terrorist attack would that not stand in the man's favour?"

"I can't make any promises," General Wright declared, "but I find the idea appealing. Of course, there are those who must be consulted, so I'll inform you of our decision in due course.

I will say one thing, however: I will do my level best," he added at which point the screen went dead.

Jack Cummings, who had been watching the exchange with fascination, grinned at Abdul and offered his hand. Looking the man squarely in the eyes, Abdul grasped Jack's hand and uttered five words: "Welcome to the firm buddy!"

***

Chapter Sixteen

Abdul impressed upon Jack Cummings the need to keep their true identities concealed whenever they were together in Villa Margalla. If a meeting became necessary, it would be held at Villa Magnolia to maintain tight security. While Volcov remained at Villa Magnolia, Abdul would visit him on a daily basis leaving Cummings at Villa Margalla to keep an eye on the house staff. Otherwise it would be business as usual with Cummings reporting to Abdul – a.k.a. John Dwyer. Since Darius Forsetti's unannounced disappearance, nobody among the Villa Margalla staff displayed resentment at Jack Cummings' promotion.

Back at Villa Magnolia, Adham Volcov was in no hurry to leave. He couldn't focus on anything other than his missing daughter not knowing where she was or what he could do about it. He had no doubt in his mind that the scheming Madam Patcha was directly responsible for the girl's abduction, aided and abetted by the New Taliban Commander Kahir. There were no leads as to her whereabouts so all anyone could do was wait until they received some form of ransom demand. Important questions required answers: Was Laura's abduction an act of sheer spite by the evil-minded Patcha because she'd been humiliated by Volcov? Or, was someone applying pressure on him to ensure his full cooperation in whatever plans were in the works? The wait went on and the abductors appeared in no particular hurry to make their next move.

*

Picking his way through various files in the study in Villa Margalla, Abdul searched for clues relating to Volcov's contacts or dealings in arms sales. Nothing of importance was found indicating Volcov kept that sort of information in a very safe place.

A commotion in the reception area caught Abdul's attention. It was followed by a knock on the study door and Jack Cummings's announcement that Taliban Commander Ahmad Hakim Kahir had arrived at the villa. Seconds later, the morbidly obese military leader unceremoniously pushed Cummings aside as he headed for the study. He was drooling from both sides of his mouth which indicated a recent snack. Sweating profusely and wheezing from the effort to walk from the driveway to the house he staggered into the study and threw himself down in the nearest chair with such force he was winded by his own efforts.

"Where is Adham Volcov?" he demanded, gasping for breath, his beady eyes settling on Abdul that suggested he was spoiling for a fight.

Relishing the prospect, Abdul pushed back: "My boss is indisposed and not receiving any visitors…sir!"

"He'll see me Dwyer, and I demand as much. Get him immediately," he ordered, spluttering profusely, saliva dripping from his mouth and onto his shirt front.

"Sir, Mister Volcov will not be seeing anyone because he isn't here."

"Not here! So, where in the name of Allah the Merciful is he?" Commander Kahir demanded with mounting frustration, his face as red as a chili pepper.

"He is at Villa Magnolia as the guest of Kostas Alexopoulos," Abdul responded, "and will remain there until he's well enough to come back. I am in charge here, during his absence, so how can I help you commander?" he asked, enjoying the opportunity to boost the blood pressure of the rude, overweight bore stuck fast in his chair.

"I can see that talking to you Dwyer is a waste of my valuable time so I will depart immediately," Commander Kahir declared, vainly trying to extricate his bulky frame from the chair. He was wedged in firmly and no amount of puffing and panting proved successful. Stifling the urge to laugh out loud, Abdul walked slowly to the stricken man and, placing his hands on the arms of the chair, looked directly into the commander's pudgy face.

"Allow me to help you sir," Abdul said, signalling Cummings to step forward. He had been standing in the doorway trying to maintain a straight face and finding it a huge challenge. As Jack pushed down on the chair, Abdul grabbed hold of the commander's arms and pulled hard. After much puffing and blowing on everyone's part, Kahir became unstuck and flew out of the chair like a high-pressure cork popping out of a Champagne bottle. Cursing under his breath, the commander gathered himself. Then, brushing aside Abdul, he stormed out of the study to his waiting vehicle leaving the two men laughing fit to burst.

*

Recent revelations from Britain's MI5 and MI6 kept everyone in Villa Magnolia on their toes. A great deal of research and discussion ensued to make sure everyone was fully conversant with the roles to be played by each section. To some extent, the entire scenario had become a much wider issue with each aspect of the operation taking on a new meaning both in the United States and the UK. Going forward, it was clear that enhanced cooperation was the order of the day

Relatively unchanged in the new scenario, however, was the link between Patcha, Commander Kahir and, to a lesser degree, Adham Volcov. The trio remained the prime suspects ultimately responsible for any acts of terrorism being planned. Updated intelligence from the British meant that any attack could no longer be solely considered in the light of the partially failed 9/11 attacks. Rather, recent intel strongly suggested that future terrorism acts could well involve the United Kingdom as well as the United States.

*

The telephone rang in Kostas Alexopoulos's study and was answered by Mike Harper who recognised Abdul's voice: "Good day John," he said cheerily, "what can I do for you today?"

"I would say it's more a case of what I can do for you Mike," Abdul responded. "We are just picking ourselves up from an unannounced visit by Commander Kahir. He demanded to see Adham Volcov, so I explained he was unwell and staying at Villa Magnolia as a guest. He left here in a hurry, so just a heads-up buddy; he may suddenly appear outside your front door."

"Understood John, and thanks for the advanced warning. I will inform Mister Alexopoulos immediately. Over and out..." he said, rushing to brief Farez and Tariq accordingly.

"I will let Volcov know about this right away," Farez said, heading straight for the old man's room where he found him staring mournfully into space.

"Adham, my friend, I have news for you. John Dwyer called to let you know that Commander Kahir turned up at Villa Margalla demanding to see you. The situation was explained to him and he was most unhappy. He left in a hurry, possibly to come here. How do you feel about that? If you don't want to see him," Farez continued, "I can inform him you are indisposed."

Farez could see from Volcov's reaction that the mere mention of the commander's name put him on edge. "I must be courteous and receive him Kostas, in case he has news of Laura. I would prefer not to have to meet him, but I don't have a choice. You do understand don't you?" he pleaded almost naïvely as if looking to Farez for approbation. In turn, Farez felt compassionate towards Volcov knowing he really didn't have a choice. Perhaps an encounter with Commander Kahir, Farez mused, could convince the arms dealer it was time to stand up and be counted.

"Would you like me to accompany you?"

"No, no...I must speak with Kahir alone," Volcov replied, annoyed at the thought of accepting any offer of support. "Kostas, I don't think you quite understand," he added, tersely without elaborating.

"Try not to upset yourself Adham. Perhaps you'd prefer to have John Dwyer with you. After all, he's your right-hand man," Farez suggested, placing a hand on the old man's arm.

Volcov hesitated at first. "No, I must speak to him alone," he answered, shaking his head vigorously. Perhaps you would ask Dwyer to remain downstairs in case I need him later." Clearly, Volcov was concerned about doing anything that could endanger his daughter.

"Do not to worry Adham, I will see to it that John Dwyer is standing by if you need him. Remember you are quite safe here and you have me ready to help at all times. You can count on me; my word is my bond. Remember there is always a solution for whatever problem you face; keep that in mind and let me help you," Farez said almost pleading with Volcov as he pictured the anguish he was suffering.

Whatever the man's faults, he was approaching his own salvation. If he could be persuaded to show enough courage to make amends it would give him peace of mind and the confidence to reveal his true identity to his daughter while there was time.

Leaving Volcov to prepare for Kahir's visit, Farez went downstairs to look for Tariq.

*

"Farez, how is Mister Volcov today?" Tariq asked noticing his good friend's tense facial expression.

"Sadly, not much change brother. The poor man is dying; his daughter is missing almost certainly kidnapped by villains who intend using her as a weapon to influence her father. Little wonder he is so dejected," Farez added, looking forlornly at Tariq.

"I see it that way too, my friend. Volcov faces an unenviable decision. It seems there are two people pressuring Volcov to play a role they intend him to play to keep his important business contacts in the United States and the UK as a part of their plan. Without that support," Tariq continued, "any terrorists already smuggled into those countries, and who need safe houses, will find it difficult to carry out their business."

"We are talking about Commander Kahir and Madam Patcha correct?" Farez asked.

Tariq nodded his agreement but, before anyone spoke again, Mike Harper interrupted to announce the arrival of John Dwyer from Villa Margalla.

"So, what do you have to say John," Tariq asked after he and Farez brought Abdul up to speed with the rationale of their thinking.

"I agree with your assessment: for sure Commander Kahir and that bitch Patcha are behind this. I am also convinced Darius Forsetti played a part also based on his own disappearance from Villa Margalla at the time Laura was abducted; too much of a coincidence in my opinion.

"The sixty-four-thousand-dollar question, gentlemen, is what have they done with Laura?" Abdul observed, while noting that Mike Harper was still present requiring him to be circumspect with details. "I doubt she's been taken to any of the Taliban encampments because that would be too easy. Right now, we don't even know on which side of the border she is on. That aside, I need your expert advice Mister Ambassador," he added smiling in an effort to lighten up the atmosphere which was deeply gloomy.

"Let's see if you agree with this bit of reasoning," Abdul said, settling into a comfortable armchair. "We know that the former governor of Bagram is now a field commander within the New Taliban. That said, can we assume a new governor of Bagram has been appointed to replace him?" he asked, looking to Tariq for a reasoned response.

"From my knowledge, an early appointment would follow because the former governor fled the residence to hide in the borderlands. The importance of the governorship would dictate Kahir should be replaced as a matter of urgency. In fact, I understand that Arman Ahmadzai, the governor of Parwan province which oversees Bagram district, was ordered by the central government in Kabul to find a suitable replacement for Kahir. The bad news is Arman Ahmadzai, like Kahir, is sympathetic to Taliban causes and is likely to be playing a double game and the Kabul government is aware of this.

"It occurred to me at the time that the governor of Parwan had two choices: appoint either his deputy, Abusin Yousufzai, whose family have Pashtun tribal origins that would qualify him for the post. And, in my view, he's an honest man and would be a good choice.

"His other option would be Aazar Yousufzai who is Abusin's younger brother though entirely different in every way and certainly not known for his honesty. Aazar was a junior officer in the New Taliban until Kahir took command and conferred on him a senior command position. Later, Kahir cashed in on a past favour owed to him by Abusin and requested that Aazar be appointed governor of Bagram.

"That is very interesting and if that is what transpired," Abdul stated, with growing interest, "it means our illustrious Commander Kahir retains access to the powers of the governor's office via the younger brother who also owes him a big favour. It seems reasonable to assume if you consider the commander's corrupt practices," he continued, "that Kahir is pulling strings in the background. Is that a fair assessment?" he asked to no-one in particular.

"It is an interesting theory John," Farez commented. "I don't quite see where you are going with this however," he added, puzzled to some extent by the entire exchange.

But Tariq wasn't confused and was following Abdul's logic. "I can see your point: You suspect that Commander Kahir has arranged for Laura to be taken to Bagram. I suspect you have in mind that hidden room in the governor's residence that would be a perfect place to hold someone. Nobody would think of searching for her there and Patcha would also have freedom of movement. I would expect Commander Kahir to make periodic visits to the residence where the new governor would be little more than a puppet with former governor Kahir as the master puppeteer," he added, a large grin on his face as he warmed to his own scenario.

"I think you are onto something brother," Farez said, recollecting the scheming Kahir of old. Mike Harper, meanwhile, hadn't a clue what everyone was talking about. Sensibly, he remained quiet.

"My suggestion, John," Farez continued, "is to despatch Noori to Bagram to find evidence to support this scenario. At Bagram Air Base, the CO, General Gardiner, may be able to help. If we can establish Laura is being held there then we can put a plan together. I would suggest, however, John, that if you are correct it would not be wise to try to launch an immediate rescue plan. We need to keep an eye on the situation and that's where General Gardiner could be useful. If we rush to rescue her we could jeopardise any chances of picking up important leads and other information that might help stop any terrorist attacks."

"I agree, that does make good sense," acknowledged Abdul.

"My other thought on this scenario," Farez said, continuing his theme, "concerns Volcov and how we could get him to switch sides if we can convince him we know where Laura is being held and that she is safe. So, the sooner we get the full picture and any other intelligence," Farez suggested, "the sooner we can get Laura released."

Further exchanges on the subject were curtailed when someone tapped on the door. Mike Harper went to check and came back within seconds. "Commander Kahir is in the reception area," he said, "and he demands to speak with Volcov immediately."

Farez, accompanied by Harper in the guise of Asad Jaheel aide to Kostas Alexopoulos, moved swiftly to greet the portly man. "Commander Kahir!" announced the startled villa owner, "what a nice surprise. Welcome to my humble home," he added, steering the overweight Taliban chief into a small reception room. I have heard so much about you," Farez continued, speaking through gritted teeth, "and I am honoured to be able to offer you my hospitality," he said, stepping aside as the commander wheezed and spluttered his way past Farez and Mike Harper to hurl himself into a very large chair this time spacious enough to accommodate his unstructured frame.

"So, you are Kostas Alexopoulos! I was beginning to wonder if you actually existed," Kahir muttered, leering at Farez through his small beady eyes.

"I am indeed, and I am at your service commander," Farez offered, encouraging his aide to fetch refreshments. "I heard much about you from my friend Adham Volcov. Being able to meet you is something I have anticipated for quite a while," he added, clearly savouring the uniqueness of the moment.

"I will come straight to the point," Kahir spluttered, obviously disinterested in the social graces, "I am not here to see you. I wish to see Adham Volcov so where is he?" he asked in his characteristically rude manner his piercing gaze fixated on the room and beyond.

"Ah…Adham Volcov…of course," Farez repeated slowly, "but I must inform you commander that the poor man is in a serious state of shock. You may not be aware that Volcov's niece is missing and the poor man is out of his mind with worry. So much so I persuaded him to stay here until he's able to return to his own villa. Here we have an experienced medical team supporting my own convalescence and I wanted him to have the best medical attention available."

Perspiration pouring down his face, Kahir said, "I want to see for myself. Take me to Volcov immediately," the bloated commander ordered gruffly while struggling to extricate himself from his chair and this time succeeding without help. He headed for the door as Farez ordered his aide to accompany him.

"My aide will take you to his room and wait until you leave," Farez stated. "Please do not stay for too long otherwise the doctor will ask you to go," he cautioned turning on his heal while leaving Mike Harper to escort the big man upstairs. Farez's obvious snub enraged Kahir who turned purple with frustration and rage, but he followed instructions.

Re-joining Abdul and Tariq, Farez scrutinised each man in turn before sitting down to gather his thoughts. Meeting Commander Kahir, for the first time, had proved a nauseating experience. All he could think of was his wife Naomi and the years they had spent apart thanks to the evil actions of former Governor Ahmad Hakim Kahir. Imagining what Naomi was forced to endure, while he was in the presence of this obese oaf, proved unnerving and sickening. Fortunately, he was able to take solace from the fact the commander did not know the true identity of Kostas Alexopoulos. At that moment, sitting alongside his two close friends, Farez vowed that the day would come when Kahir would face his wrath.

The door of the reception room opened suddenly revealing a worried looking Mike Harper. "Mister Alexopoulos," he shouted, "better get over here quickly. Mister Volcov is beside himself with grief and I have asked the doctor to attend to him."

"What about Commander Kahir, is he still there?" Farez asked.

"No sir, he left moments ago."

Accompanied by Abdul, Farez raced upstairs where an anxious doctor was waiting. "Today's visit by Commander Kahir has greatly upset Mister Volcov," the doctor said. "I am concerned because he is in extreme pain from his diagnosed ailment. Added stress could have a severe effect; he could even have a stroke," the doctor added laying out the seriousness of Volcov's condition.

"I understand doctor, we are all concerned," said Farez, moving closer to Volcov's room. "I would like to talk to him and reassure him. Also, we need to find out what was said that caused his added distress. John, you should come with me; maybe together we can put the poor man at ease," Farez added as Abdul joined him in Volcov's room.

Volcov was sweating profusely and breathing heavily. From his ashen face it was obvious that added pressure was taking a serious toll on Volcov's deteriorating health resulting from Hodgkinson's lymphoma.

"Adham, my friend, you must not distress yourself. The medical team wants you to remain as calm as possible. And we all want to help you. I was informed that Commander Kahir left in a hurry; did he say something to upset you?" Farez asked, speaking in soothing tones to try to relax Volcov.

"John Dwyer is here also; we thought we could try and work things out together," Farez stated as Abdul sat next to Volcov and gripped his hand.

"Please try to relax sir," Abdul pleaded. "You will recall I made certain promises to you that I intend honouring. I am asking you to put your trust in me and Mister Alexopoulos. We can help you if you permit us to do so. It requires a huge leap of faith on your part but, for your sake, and Laura's, we feel now is the time for you to act."

Both men waited anxiously as Volcov, slowly shaking his head from side to side, wrestled with his innermost feelings, visibly trying to cope with pain and fear. After a few minutes, his breathing regulated, and he relaxed. Slowly he looked from one man to the other his gaze finally settling on Abdul.

"Tell me John Dwyer…just who are you?" Volcov uttered weakly, the words dying on his lips as his mind drifted into sleep.

Abdul looked at Farez and then Volcov not knowing how to respond. Fortuitously, Doctor James stepped up to check Volcov's pulse. "The sedative I gave him has kicked in, so you won't get much from him for a few hours. Meanwhile, gentlemen, I will have someone sit with him and alert you when he wakes up," he added as Abdul and Farez got up to leave.

"We must find out what Kahir said to Volcov," Abdul impressed upon Farez as they left Volcov sleeping. "Somehow, we need to turn the tide in our favour," he added putting a hand on his friend's shoulder.

*

Brought up to speed by Abdul and Farez, Tariq had no doubt that Commander Kahir's visit had placed Volcov under greater pressure. "We are still somewhere between a rock and a hard place," the commander noted. "Kahir must have leant heavily on Volcov probably threatening to injure the poor man's daughter. My friends, we must find a way to persuade Volcov, to come over to our side and time is of the essence."

Though Farez agreed in principle he suggested Volcov needed some inducement to act. "This is a nut we must crack, my brother. But first, we have to find a way to impress upon him that changing sides is better than remaining silent. And that,"

Farez added, "means making sure his daughter is safe. Do you agree?"

"You are quite right Farez," Tariq concurred, "ensuring his daughter's safety is key. For such peace of mind, he would sell his soul to the devil for sure," Tariq added, a wry smile on his face.

"While I also support the rationale," Abdul chimed in, "we must also convince Volcov we can deliver any assurances we give him. Promises are not enough; unless we can convince him we can deliver he won't trust us. We must be seen to be men of our word," Abdul added.

"So, just what do you have in mind?" Tariq asked, suspecting he knew where Abdul was heading, but required confirmation.

"I believe the moment has arrived for truth and openness. To gain Volcov's confidence he must have peace of mind and his daughter is the catalyst for that. This man is living on borrowed time and is desperate to find a way to reveal the truth about his life and accept her forgiveness. Nothing less will give him peace of mind. He is ready to do what has to be done if we can give him the assurances he needs. Then he'll come over to us. That's what I have in mind," Abdul added.

"That means revealing our true identities," Tariq fired back, a worried expression on his face. "And then we still have to convince Volcov we can deliver. I have to say that seems a very dangerous game with so much at stake," he added not wholly convinced he could go along with Abdul's suggestion.

Farez was more sanguine about Abdul's plan. "I disagree with you Tariq. I think Abdul is right. Trust is paramount: Volcov's trust in us; our trust in him. If we can produce a scenario in which we find Laura, ensure her security, but impress upon him he may have to wait a while before he sees her again, we may gain his trust.

"This man still has to answer for his part in supplying arms for the 9/11 attacks. He is also aligned with contacts in the United States that allow terrorists to live there undetected just waiting to pounce. We may conclude his crimes are, to some extent, less serious than those of Commander Kahir and Patcha. If he accepts to reveal all he knows about future terrorism activities in the works; and if he accepts to reveal his contacts in America; and if he swears allegiance to work with us from now on then surely all that can be taken into consideration especially as he is dying.

"There is more to be gained by having Volcov on our side working under cover. It will be possible for him to serve a greater cause, maybe save lives. Of course, he will never go to prison because he won't live long enough to be tried in court. But this way we can give Adham Volcov the opportunity to make reparations for his crimes and straighten out matters with his daughter before it's too late," Farez concluded, once again demonstrating his unparalleled sagaciousness for disentangling complex situations.

It was difficult to refute his erudite analysis, but Tariq had a proposal to air: "If all three of us are like-minded, and it seems we are, I will contact the Pentagon, update them about recent developments, and put to them our justification for cracking a big nut! How does that sound?" he asked as the three friends joined hands in a spirit of kinship. With luck, and cooperation from Adham Volcov, their mission might well reach a successful conclusion sooner than expected.

*

A day later, Abdul and Jack Cummings were asked to attend a meeting at Villa Magnolia scheduled for 1400 hours local time. Anticipating it would include a response from the Pentagon to Tariq's report, both men arrived early. They were taken to the ops room by Mike Harper where the entire team was assembled.

Commander Zahir took charge of proceedings. "Everyone attending the Pentagon meeting was apprised of developments and our recommendations. From what I know, there was some pushback initially; some attendees were reluctant to countenance full disclosure of our identities unless we could be absolutely certain Volcov could be trusted to uphold his side of the bargain. It's not just a case of securing his daughter's release but getting the necessary assurances from him. The Pentagon insists the scales need to be balanced at all times.

"We will have the support we need if Volcov is persuaded to change allegiances and that we come up with an acceptable strategy to locate and secure the woman in a stealth operation. If the other side feels it no longer has persuasive powers over Volcov nobody stands to gain anything. And we need to be absolutely certain Volcov has the strength to play a constructive part in the rescue. I don't need to state that there is no margin for error. And the Pentagon reminded me of such.

"I called this important meeting today so that we all know the state of play. Also, to work out a way of securing the daughter's release without Commander Kahir or Madam Patcha being aware. I realise that sounds improbable but that's our objective. We have twenty-four hours to give the Pentagon the assurances they ask for in respect of Volcov changing sides and then we'll get their decision," Tariq said, gazing around the room.

"Go away, think and plan; we will not discuss it any further today," Tariq concluded before turning to Abdul who wanted a word in private. Everyone left the ops room save for Abdul, Farez, Jack Cummings and Mike Harper.

"My immediate concern," Abdul said to Tariq, "is to make sure Noori was despatched to Bagram Air Base as we agreed."

"He left yesterday and should now be in position," confirmed Tariq.

"In that case," Abdul continued, "we should keep him at the air base until we establish our plan of action. I have some ideas, but I'm concerned about the tight timescale laid down by the Pentagon."

"I am interested in getting your thoughts John," Farez commented, "because I also have something to say about this," he added, wondering if their ideas might work together.

"Let me run this before you…" Abdul said, almost thinking aloud as he often did. "If Laura is being held at the governor's residence in Bagram district I would expect few people to be guarding her – probably only Forsetti and Patcha I would guess. I doubt the newly appointed governor knows much about it; he may not even know Laura is being held there. I believe that Patcha, a scheming bitch if ever I saw one, will exploit her position as a guest of the new governor and use her unique powers of persuasion to woo him into a false sense of security.

"If Patcha feels there's anything to be gained she will dangle the governor on the end of her little finger for as long as it suits her. And he will go along with her out of a sense of flattery and self-aggrandisement, bearing in mind he gets his orders from our portly friend Commander Kahir. One word from the Taliban chief and everyone will be referring to the new governor in the past tense…replaced by his older brother no doubt. So, that said, it is my belief no one wants that to happen – least of all the new governor himself," Abdul concluded, before gazing around the room which showed an audience of rapidly growing interest in his erudite summation.

Unsurprisingly, Mike Harper had a question, "I get your drift John. But how could you figure a minimum of guards if Laura is being held where you say."

Before Abdul could explain, Commander Zahir intervened.

"Because it's a reasonable assumption that no-one here in this part of the world would consider looking for her as far away as the residence of the governor of Bagram district. Commander Kahir and his collaborators would assume there is no-one here who would know much about Bagram. And why should they?" he added, smiling at both Abdul and Farez who were nodding in agreement.

"So, are they wrong?" Harper questioned, not understanding the degree of interaction being shown between Abdul, Farez and Tariq.

"They are wrong," Farez said, picking up Harper's question. But before he could elaborate, Commander Zahir jumped in to explain.

"For the time being, Mike, some things must be taken on trust. There are three people in this room with first-hand knowledge of the governor's residence in Bagram – John Dwyer, Kostas Alexopoulos and me. Let me put it this way: it all happened in a former life and you should accept it at face value – and then forget it! That includes you too Jack," Tariq added, gesturing towards Jack Cummings who, more than anyone present, got the message as a tried and tested practitioner of counterintelligence work. He smiled and nodded politely.

But Commander Zahir was anxious to learn where Abdul was leading with his summation. "John, I for one would like to know what you have in mind."

"My assumption concerning Laura's whereabouts requires confirmation. So, what I have in mind, Tariq, to answer your question," Abdul said, raising his arms aloft as if seeking divine intervention, "is to have Noori access the residence and find out for sure. I suspect the new governor is supported by new staff. Therefore, it is reasonable to assume that only Commander Kahir would recognise Noori but as Noori's appearance has changed beyond recognition that assumption is indeterminate. Even I didn't recognise Noori at first!

"It is essential to find a way for Noori to get into the residence and access the secret room that leads off the governor's study. If Laura is being held there, she won't be able to see anyone looking at her because it's a one-way mirror. But, if Noori can take a photograph of Laura we can show it to Volcov as evidence that we know where she is and prove that we can control the situation," he added.

Tariq and Farez nodded their understanding while Cummings and Harper exhibited bemused expressions from all the talk about one-way mirrors in secret rooms.

"So, how can we get Noori into the residence and the governor's study without anyone becoming alarmed or suspicious?" Commander Zahir queried.

Before Abdul could respond, Farez said, "I think a visit from the Republic of Afghanistan's ambassador to the United States of America could be one way of going about this."

"Are you serious?" questioned Tariq, gazing at his friend in total amazement. "What possible reason could an ambassador have for visiting the governor of Bagram's residence?" he asked, his mind spinning at what he perceived to be an off-the-cuff remark on the part of Farez.

"Ah, my friend, you must learn to think like a seasoned statesman," Farez counselled. "I imagine Afghanistan's newly-appointed ambassador to the United States would wish to fit in a trip to Bagram Air Base and visit the base CO in charge of U.S. and NATO forces. It could happen as part of his visit to the Afghan government in Kabul concerning upcoming peace talks. It would not raise any suspicions if the ambassador flew into and out of Bagram with a military escort approved by the Pentagon. It may even be expected as a matter of courtesy for the ambassador to pay a courtesy call on the new governor at his residence if just to offer his congratulations.

"If the new governor is aware of such a visit he would be duty bound to invite the ambassador for lunch at the residence along with General Gardiner the CO of Bagram Air Base," Farez added, his mind working overtime. "That being the case," he continued, "I would expect Madam Patcha to use her proven guile to be a guest at the same lunch. That would keep her busy. Darius Forsetti would also have to be distracted."

Abdul added to the scenario: "There would also be a large military presence for the ambassador that would provide a distraction to allow Noori to get in and out of the residence. We don't have to worry about Forsetti," looking at Tariq who seemed to be buying into the idea.

"Both of you have taken my breath away with this outlandish plan. But, it may just work!" he added. "That said, I am sure the Pentagon will have something to say," he countered while warming to the strategy outlined by Abdul and Farez.

Tariq said, "You are correct to point out that establishing Laura's whereabouts would be a huge step forward. But how can we persuade Volcov to accept that his daughter will remain safe? Again, I am sure the Pentagon will want an answer to that before they approve the plan." Tariq's observation was left hanging as someone knocked on the door. It was one of Harper's guards announcing that Adham Volcov

unexpectedly found herself on her own I was able, at long last, to enjoy so much more of her life than before.

"Now I have lost her, and God alone knows where she is. I confess I am beside myself with guilt and worry. I feel helpless because I cannot do anything to help her. And now I am dying and too weak to be of much use to myself let alone anyone else. Everything seems hopeless. The only saving grace I have, John, is knowing that you love her and will take care of her for me," he said, laying bare his soul and falling back into his former listless state.

"Sir," Abdul said, drawing closer to Volcov, "I need you to remain calm and listen carefully to what I'm about to say. "We believe we know where Laura is. But before we make a move, we need to know where you stand," Abdul explained, immediately feeling guilty for putting the old man on the spot. But it had to be done.

"I don't think I understand…what are you saying John?" Volcov asked, a puzzled look on his face. The very mention of knowing Laura's whereabouts acted like an electric shock pulling him out of his malaise and encouraging him to take notice.

Farez stepped into the conversation. "John is trying to explain to you, Adham, that trust is a two-way process. He has a plan to find your daughter, but you must understand that he has to negotiate a dangerous path to help you. The time has arrived for you to say what you're prepared to do in return. You have a window of opportunity to put things right with your daughter in the time you have left and share precious moments as father and daughter. Please put and an end to this charade; seize this unique opportunity and face the truth. Your daughter loves you unconditionally, we can all see that," Farez added, speaking gently but firmly looking directly into the old man's eyes.

Perplexed, Volcov turned to Abdul. "John, I have asked this of you twice and I ask you again: who are you?"

Taking Volcov's hand in his, Abdul said, "I cannot answer that question sir. You know me as John Dwyer and, for your safety as well as my own, that's how it must remain. I can assure you that we can offer you the help you require if you permit us to do so," Abdul said reassuringly, preparing the ground to delve into Volcov's past.

"Over the years you have traded in arms, sometimes dishonestly. Your reputation is well documented particularly in the United States. More recently you became involved with something being masterminded by Madam Patcha aided and abetted by Commander Kahir the self-appointed leader of the New Taliban. By now you know that both of these unsavoury characters would sell their souls to the devil in a heartbeat. They are credited with being the instigators of the 9/11 atrocities in the United States and they are using you now to provide arms for another terrorist attack in America.

"From what you told us previously it is clear you feel remorse for the part you played in the 9/11 terrorist acts. Another similar attack is in the planning phase and we – that is Kostas, me, and a few others – are determined to prevent it from happening. But we need your help sir which would go a long way towards exonerating you for your past mistakes. And, think of this: in your daughter's eyes you would be a very brave man," Abdul said, pausing for a reaction.

It was out in the open now and there was no going back. Volcov was aware that others knew of his past. Although unaware of Abdul's true identity, Volcov is sufficiently astute to know he is being presented with facts. But was he being offered a quid pro quo arrangement?

"Are you suggesting I change sides to secure the release of my daughter. Is that what you are saying John?"

"That's not what I am suggesting sir. I was as concerned and upset as you were when Laura disappeared. But, I can say with absolute certainty that this was the handiwork of Patcha, Commander Kahir, and Darius Forsetti. They want to force your hand to support their plans for another terrorist attack. And that is about all I am able to say at this stage," Abdul offered.

"John is giving you the facts, Adham." Farez said. "We are not the enemy; far from it. Your daughter was abducted to ensure you continue working for the kidnappers… by providing them with arms. It is fair to conclude, therefore," Farez continued, "that your daughter will be safe as long as they believe you are still on their side willing to provide the arms they require." The agony in Volcov's face was clear to see as he struggled with his conscience.

Abdul could see that Volcov was not entirely reassured. "Mister Volcov," he said, "allow me to repeat what I said before: I love your daughter and I will always look after her. I gave you my word and I meant it. I will move heaven and earth to keep her safe. I believe I know where she is being held, and her safety depends on her remaining there until we are ready to rescue her.

"I am sorry if this all sounds mysterious, but if I am right you will be shown a photograph that proves she is in good health. We have men posted around the place we believe she's being held to ensure her safety while she remains there. I can't say much more about the details; I may have said too much already but I want to assure you, sir, she will remain safe. You have my word of honour as someone who loves your daughter," he added, squeezing the old man's hand.

It was clear to Farez and Abdul that their exchange of facts had given Volcov much to think about with the added hope he would not betray their trust. They were taking an enormous risk.

"Rest now old friend," Farez said. "You have much to consider. We will talk again after you have had time to mull things over."

As the pair got up to leave, Volcov lifted his arm and motioned for them to hold back. "I must tell you something before you leave here," he said, propping himself up with a pillow. "After the visit from that loathsome Commander Kahir I made up my mind I could not go along with the new plan. He revealed to me a situation they were finalising of which I had no prior knowledge. I swear," he added. "They want me to work in a very different capacity than before and that's why I may appear to you to be so distressed. In fact, I still have difficulty reconciling their request which weighs heavily on my conscience.

Looking at Abdul he smiled faintly. "I always felt there was something different about you John Dwyer. And now I thank God for that. You and Kostas have offered me a lifeline with your honesty. And I will put my trust in you where my darling daughter is concerned. I feel I can do so because I know in my heart that you love her too and that you will bring her safely back to me before it is too late. I am depending on you John and I am ready to work with you. It is time to bring an end to all of this madness. I won't live long enough to enjoy being exonerated but at least I will have peace of mind knowing that I can speak honestly with my daughter if only to hear her call me father just once before I die. From what you have said today, I know I must do everything in my power to prevent what would be an even bigger disaster than 9/11."

Abdul's ears pricked up. He sensed there was something troubling Volcov that was even more serious than Laura's abduction. "What are you trying to say sir?"

"What I have to tell you is far more sinister than the 9/11 terrorist attacks. This time they intend to affect not only the United States but also the United Kingdom," Volcov said, thinking back to the visit by Commander Kahir that had caused him so much distress.

Farez gripped Volcov by the hand. "Please stay calm Adham. And tell us what it is that's upsetting you so much," he added holding onto the old man's hand.

"You don't understand Kostas. This time they are planning a nuclear attack and they demand I help them to obtain nuclear weapons on the black market."

***

Chapter Seventeen

Heightened concern was apparent within Villa Magnolia's operations room after Adham Volcov delivered the crushing news that Commander Kahir, Madam Patcha and their terrorist collaborators were actively seeking nuclear weapons.

The undeniable seriousness of the situation was assessed by Commander Zahir. "The significance of this latest information," he impressed upon Abdul and Farez, "simply cannot be underestimated. I must immediately inform the Pentagon of developments and seek advice according to our brief," he added. "In the light of what we have learned from Adham Volcov, the entire mission takes on a new depth of meaning. We are facing a different kind of terrorism and we don't have a minute to lose. I hope you'll agree that until we hear back from the Pentagon we should not discuss this with anyone other than Mike Harper and Jack Cummings. Jack will wish to contact the UK security network to coordinate with US authorities. Then I would expect a roundtable conference to decide the next move," Tariq added, not waiting for Abdul or Farez to comment as he raced out the door to the comms centre.

Both Farez and Abdul were still recovering from the shocked announcement by Volcov. Never, in their wildest dreams, had they imagined such a development.

"We are confronting a new face of terrorism," Abdul pronounced dryly, "and if these villains succeed with their nuclear plans many thousands of people will be affected and not just those in the immediate vicinity. Think of the aftereffects of such a catastrophe! Think Chernobyl!" he exclaimed, as the severity of the situation began to sink in.

Typically, Farez was deep in thought weighing up the consequences while predisposed to withhold his response for the time being allowing Abdul to suggest a way forward.

"We have to put a stop to this, Farez. The situation could spiral out of control. Let's face it, Volcov is our only hope," he added, acknowledging that Volcov had made an informed choice not entirely based on Laura's plight but also out of a sense of horror of past events for which he could be held partially responsible.

But is Volcov strong enough to see it through? The question is important as it will take a great deal of daring and determination on the part of the old man. Measured against his current state of health it has to be a big ask. Abdul would have to shadow his boss as never before but not because he can't trust him; Volcov will keep his word because now he has more to live for than to die for.

*

The following day at 1000 hours everyone assembled in Villa Magnolia's operations room amid a low buzz of conversation as they waited for Commander Zahir to open the briefing. At one end of the room a large video screen had been erected to live-stream the planned meeting between senior officials of the Pentagon, MI5 and MI6.

"Good morning everyone," Tariq said cheerfully as he entered the ops room followed by Abdul, Farez and Mike Harper who turned to close the door before taking a seat alongside Jack Cummings.

"Thank you for your patience," the commander said, checking his notes. "New developments in our area of influence prompted us to contact the Pentagon for mission guidance. An hour from now we will receive a briefing from the secretary of defense. Before that, I want to bring everyone up to speed with where we are to date.

"If I may have your attention everyone…circumstances have changed; the stakes are much higher than we first thought. Our original strategy to manoeuvre the villains into a corner, arrest them, and take them to the United States to stand trial for acts of terrorism, including the 9/11 attacks, has changed. Since our work began, we now know that Madam Patcha, aided and abetted by Commander Kahir of the New Taliban, is the prime organiser. Adham Volcov is also implicated as an international arms dealer known for his business dealings over the years including supplying arms for the 9/11 attacks.

"I should add, in fairness, that Adham Volcov is also a man who has moved in high circles in many countries not the least the United States which is his home of choice. He is well liked by many - some may say admired not only for his business ventures but for himself. People say that no-one is wholly bad and from what I have learned since arriving here, I believe this to be true in Volcov's case.

"Everyone present here today is aware that Volcov is staying at Villa Magnolia to recover from the shock of Laura's abduction. She was thought to be his niece – not so. I can inform you today that she is his daughter though she is unaware of that and that's how it must remain for the time being. Mister Volcov is dying from Hodgkin's lymphoma - a form of cancer of the blood for those not aware. That, and his recent understanding that weapons he once brokered on behalf of Patcha were used in the 9/11 attacks, is testing his resolve. In America I believe you would characterise it as a wake-up call!

"You may be aware that Commander Kahir of the New Taliban paid a visit to Volcov recently during which he laid down new demands coupled with threats against Laura if Volcov failed to comply. Keep in mind that the commander, Madam Patcha, and Darius Forsetti, all believe that Laura is Volcov's niece. We believe they are also unaware that Volcov is a dying man.

"Because of these changed circumstances, Adham Volcov has agreed to work with us to bring down the others. He is seeking reparation for his past deeds before it's too late. To prove he's sincere in this endeavour he revealed to us the nature of the business discussed with Commander Kahir. And that's not all," Commander Tariq said, his audience hanging onto his every word. We were informed that the next terrorist attacks could affect the United Kingdom as well as the USA. Volcov says we could experience nuclear attacks and he believes his daughter is being used as a pawn in a game of nuclear chess to pressure him to facilitate the purchase of illicit nuclear components to make several of these dirty bombs," the commander revealed to a stunned gathering.

"That brings all present up to date with what we know. General Wright will address us shortly after which we will discover exactly what lays ahead. Keep any questions you have until after the Pentagon briefing if you please," Tariq added, before resuming his seat.

Seconds later, the lights in the ops room dimmed as the huge monitor screen burst into life focusing on Secretary Ray Hollingworth. "Good day to you Commander Zahir and everyone in the operations room. "I understand our friend Jack Cummings from MI6 is present along with some other familiar faces. I think you know most of the faces at my end so I will not waste any time in handing over to Defense Secretary General John Wright," he added, turning over the briefing.

"Good day and listen up please. Facing facts, we are now wrestling with an increasingly difficult set of circumstances. Illicit trafficking in useable nuclear material poses more questions than answers. In any potential scenario concerning terrorism, there is nothing worse than the detonation of a nuclear weapon. The short- and long-term consequences are devastating. That said, we believe the chance of terrorists obtaining ready-to-use nuclear weapons is still remote but there is great concern that some groups could construct crude nuclear devices from weapons-grade, weapon-useable nuclear material such as highly enriched uranium or plutonium.

"Any buyers interested in weapon-usable nuclear material give us concern, particularly if they are from volatile regions of the world that supports terrorist organisations. We have information where intermediate buyers, or re-sellers, have shown interest in investing in nuclear or radiological materials expecting to enjoy substantial re-sale profits. Though multi-sales chains are rare, ultimate buyers – or end users of nuclear materials, especially fissile materials – do exist. We are aware, for example, that Al Qaeda showed an interest in acquiring a nuclear weapons capability. Therefore, any intelligence concerning the existence of buyers interested in fissile material is cause for great concern. This brings us to our meeting today. Adham Volcov gave us enough information to view this matter seriously. For that we have a reason to be grateful to Volcov for his cooperation and to the team in Villa Magnolia for being on the ball.

"Since the terrorist attacks of September 11, 2001, Americans have been lucky not to have experienced additional atrocities on American soil. Yet the enemy, while weakened, is far from being destroyed and we forget that at our peril.

"If terrorist organisations are to find a trusted criminal group in possession of – or capable of providing – enriched uranium or plutonium of a quality and in sufficient quantities to produce a crude nuclear explosive device, we could be facing a nuclear 9/11! And if that doesn't frighten the crap out of everyone present you aren't paying attention. Osama bin Laden described the use of weapons of mass destruction against the United States as a 'religious duty'. He neither confirmed nor denied chasing after WMDs but there's a body of evidence that he did actively seek them. Even though he is no longer alive his legacy survives, and his work continues. Back in 2005, America's director of central intelligence, a gentleman called Porter Goss, testified that Al-Qaeda might be in possession of radioactive material of Russian or even Soviet origins. So, listen and learn everyone.

"As you all know, Al-Qaeda is religiously and ideologically committed to the destruction of the United States and Israel, subjugation of the West, and the overthrow of existing Muslim and Arab regimes throughout the greater Middle East and even beyond from Nigeria to Saudi Arabia to Indonesia. The group's proclaimed goal is to establish a caliphate as a militarised dictatorship based on sharia or holy law and dedicated to the conquest of the non-Muslim world…what we call dar al-harb - literally 'land of war'.

"Other radical Islamist organisations share these far-reaching goals and anti-American agendas including Lebanon's Shi'a Hezbollah and Pakistan's Lashkar-e-Taiba both with links to

Al-Qaeda and technological sophistication and personnel and international connections reaching into the United States that could help them acquire nuclear capabilities.

"All of these organisations attract a number of highly-qualified engineers and technicians who could facilitate their own homegrown nuclear weapons programmes. With considerable resources at their disposal, they can also recruit engineers and scientists who have received education in related fields in Russia, the West and the Islamic world.

"Organised crime in Russia could well be a conduit through which terrorists acquire and ship nuclear components or weapons to final destinations. And it is more than a theoretical possibility that terrorists could buy a working warhead and deliver it to the United States in one of the millions of shipping containers that enter the country without examination by U.S. Customs. Terrorists could also smuggle such a weapon through a porous land border or maritime border or smuggle component parts and assemble the weapons in-country. As I said before, we must listen and learn.

"So, who is capable of executing such an attack? The answer is Al-Qaeda, Hezbollah, or Lashkar-e-Taiba – take your pick! Each may have the technical expertise and motivation. By now you should have concluded that ignoring these possibilities could prove deadly," the Secretary added, pausing to look at the sea of faces staring back at him. The ensuing silence spoke volumes.

"Any questions so far?"

The silence was broken when Mike Harper got to his feet. Harper always had a question.

"Thank you for the briefing sir. My question is this: If a small, nuclear-orientated device was assembled and used by suicide bombers what level of devastation could it cause? I presume a small device is more easily kept in check than a larger nuclear weapon."

"Good question which I will pass over to Major Clive Davis one of our consultant surgeons who has studied the medical effects of nuclear fallout," General Wright stated, regaining his seat.

"Good morning…very good question," Major Davis stated, "which I will address by explaining that there are two significant and fatal impacts to consider in the event of a nuclear accident. The first impact concerns the number of direct deaths at the time of the incident and days following impact. The second effect comes from the long-term chronic effects from radiation exposure with known links to several forms of cancer.

"Take Chernobyl as a working example: the city was evacuated nine days after the accident at the nearby nuclear power plant. There were significant doses released from short-lived isotope radiation which has a half-life of about eight days.

"The World Health Organisation estimated in its 2005 study that four thousand people died due to the long-term effects of radiation and the Ukraine stated that long-term deaths are closer to 845,000. Even today it is illegal to live inside the exclusion zone. So, we can see that even explosions of lesser proportions like Chernobyl produce serious risks of radiation. Given enough of these small but very dirty bombs, the long-term effects of radiation would do a great deal of damage not solely to the population but also to agricultural land and water supplies."

"Thank you Major," General Wright said, once again getting to his feet. "I think from that overview you can appreciate the seriousness of this turn of events. I guess we owe a debt of gratitude to Adham Volcov for exposing this threat. He has was awake and wished to speak to Kostas Alexopoulos and John Dwyer.

Farez and Abdul rushed upstairs. "Come in," Volcov shouted as they knocked on the door. "Sit, please, I have something to say."

Volcov was propped up on pillows and looked much better after a restful night's sleep.

"Kostas, I owe you an apology for my impolite outburst," he said, grasping Farez by the hand before leaning to his side to offer his other hand to the man he knows and trusts as John Dwyer his faithful PA.

Noticing the deep concern on Volcov's face, Farez attempted to calm the man. "Adham, I can see you are upset, and I would like to help you get through this difficult period in your life. I am sure I can be of service to you, but I am bound to say it will require a great leap of faith on your part," he pronounced smiling reassuringly at the old man who gazed back through grief-stricken eyes.

"Sir, I would like you to listen to Mister Alexopoulos. He is a good friend and you can trust him as you trust me," Abdul said, reinforcing Farez's attempt to bring some calm to Volcov's turbulent existence.

"I must inform you John that I have never been able to afford the luxury of trusting people. I have walked a solitary road because I saw it as the safest to walk. So, trust does not come easily after years of walking in the shadows," he added looking at both men through saddened eyes.

"Suddenly, in the twilight of my life, I have discovered the love of a daughter; something I longed for over many years. It has not been easy playing a false role with Laura, loving her as her father but accepting her as my niece. When she expressed a wish to come over to our side and work undercover to fight the threat of a nuclear attack that could affect the UK as well as the United States. The man is seriously ill, anxious to make amends, and we are inclined to take him at his word when he says he wants to help. Together we can prevent what would be devastating attacks," the general added, ready to wrap up the initial briefing.

"Apart from Commander Zahir, Mister Alexopoulos and John Dwyer, with whom I intend discussing matters further, this briefing is now at an end. Thank you for your attention and keep up the good work," General Wright added as the screen went blank, room lights came up, and everyone began talking excitedly. It had been an eye-popping revelation of what could be in store and it highlighted the importance of getting a grip on the situation.

Everyone apart from Farez and Abdul was dismissed by Commander Zahir. "All of you please carry on as usual until we give you a further update on proceedings. Thank you for your excellent work," the commander added, turning to Farez and Abdul.

"The general has made it very clear, my brothers, that Adham Volcov is changing sides. My first thought is this will require some careful planning. I fear the brave man may not prove strong enough to cope with the pressure. We need to decide how to handle his involvement and give him whatever support we can."

Farez was likeminded, "Abdul will support him at all times as before and I think Jack Cummings will be able to offer added strength."

"I am sure you're right about that, brother," Tariq conceded, "but there are some difficult negotiations ahead. Also bear in mind that Volcov's compatriots do not know he is a dying man. Surely they would take advantage of that fact were they to find out," he added, a worried expression on his face.

"I have a plan, my friends," Farez announced, "though I fear it may not meet with your approval. But, as I see it, is the only way forward. I feel strongly about it and will not be put off no matter how hard you try," he added to the astonishment of Abdul and Tariq who looked at one another with alarm. They knew that when Farez wore his trademark look of intransigence, now in full view, there was no way to change his mind.

Unable to decide whether to be amused or alarmed, Abdul had to prevent a tense standoff from developing. "I think we should sit down and hear your plan Brother Farez," he said, knowing from experience that the malik usually got his own way and this occasion would be no different.

"Overnight I gave a great deal of thought to how we move forward, and I ask you to please listen to what I have to say. Then you can decide whether or not I have lost control of my senses. I believe the time has arrived for us to put our personal feelings to one side. We face a difficult task that will take a mountain of ingenuity to dupe the enemy into believing that Adham Volcov is going to comply with their demands. He is dying and I question if his health will deteriorate further because of the emotional strain he will encounter when he's in close contact with Patcha and former governor Kahir. These people needle him and that will affect him physically and mentally. What I am trying to say is he will try to fulfil his commitment, but he can't do this all alone.

"Consider this," Farez went on, "Volcov must convince Patcha and Kahir that he can not only do what they require but is happy to do it! He has to convince them he's one of them: that he's with them all the way but knowing all the time that they are holding his daughter yet hoping they will release her in exchange for his cooperation. Think of what we are asking of the man," Farez counselled, wise as ever, while Tariq and Abdul looked on perplexed.

"I accept what you say brother," Tariq stated, "but I can't see Patcha or Kahir releasing Laura at any stage unless they have another trump card in hand. They would not trust him to finish the job if they let his daughter go. That just wouldn't work at all," Tariq added, shaking his head while Abdul appeared to be warming to Farez's reasoning.

"Farez, are you thinking of substituting Laura for someone else? Someone they would regard as an even better hostage than Laura…someone like Kostas Alexopoulos?"

Smiling, the village headman stood erect, drew himself to his full height and, pointing to his own chest said, "Yes, me because I am Kostas Alexopoulos famous billionaire, playboy of the Western world with hundreds of contacts. I have influential friends who could be persuaded to help Patcha and Kahir. Maybe the pair can be persuaded that Kostas Alexopoulos has better connections than Volcov, particularly concerning nuclear components, making me more useful to them…"

Interrupting Farez in full flow, Tariq was adamant in his response. "…absolutely no way will I allow you to do this. It is a crazy idea fraught with great danger. I would remind you, brother, you are part of this mission on the basis you will not be put at risk. So, no way my friend!"

"Be easy Brother Tariq, "Farez said admonishingly. "Think carefully. Along with Abdul I will look after Volcov. And Abdul and Jack Cummings will be watching my back. We should make the terms of the agreement conditional upon the release of Laura in exchange for what I'm able to offer. That takes the pressure off Adham because his daughter will be safe. This could work. The way I look at it my brothers is that we would be four against two. I see a deal to provide weapons as requested but as an arranged set-up with security backup. As the weapons are handed over we would arrest the ringleaders - 'red-handed' as Americans say -with no excuses and no way out."

Abdul could see the merit in Farez's plan, with the proposed sting. But Tariq, always fearful for Farez's safety, remained unconvinced and Abdul sensed that.

"We know how you feel Farez," Abdul said, "it is a sound plan. But Tariq and I could never forgive ourselves if anything happened to you. I must be honest; we only agreed to you being part of this mission because you would be in a secure environment. Now you suggest moving into an insecure environment that would place you at great risk."

"Thank you for your concern, but you miss the point. I have been schooled for this moment – you might say groomed. I have listened and learned from my tutors and trainers and I know I can carry it off. As far as risks are concerned that is my decision and mine alone. I have every reason to return to America after being reunited with my beloved Naoma. And I know in my heart that Ahktar is my son. So, both of you must see – and agree with me – that I need to do this for myself."

Respected for his wisdom, and dogged determination to succeed, Tariq and Abdul lapsed into a moment of silence not wishing to oppose Farez head-on knowing he would never change his mind. They had got the message and their reluctance was tempered only by the thought that his plan just might work despite the inherent risks.

"We hear what you say my friend," said Tariq, looking to Abdul for support, "and I think we should communicate your idea to Washington. If they agree I will go along with it."

"That goes for me too. If the Pentagon greenlights your idea, I won't object," Abdul added. "But no unnecessary heroics on your part if you don't mind. Neither of us could bear losing such a dear friend and brother. Do we have your word?"

Standing before the two most important friends in his life, Farez put a hand to his heart. "I give you my solemn oath I will undertake my duties faithfully and as safely as possible. I would not wish anything to come between us that could affect our long-held sacred pledge to be brothers all for one and one for all."

**

Chapter Eighteen

The video link with the Pentagon, streamed live to an engrossed audience in Villa Magnolia's ops room had hammered home the seriousness of the task ahead. Adham Volcov's startling revelation that dangerous terrorists were blackmailing him to obtain nuclear weapons had changed the calculus of the entire undertaking.

On the plus side, Abdul, Farez, and Tariq noticed that Volcov was slowly regaining strength after agreeing to switch allegiance to work on the right side of history. Volcov admitted to feeling calmer though he was still quite weak and would become weaker as Hodgkin's lymphoma took hold. The shock of Laura's abduction and the subsequent visit by Commander Kahir had not helped his disposition. But, for the first time in months, he no longer had to stand alone. He found that comforting and it helped him decide to do all he could to atone for past transgressions and hope his daughter would find it in her heart to forgive him when the time came.

Abdul and Farez decided to continue spending time with the old man but Tariq, as agreed beforehand, would adapt a low profile as the only one among the three friends not to have had a physical makeover and, as such, would be immediately recognisable to Commander Zahir. With the ex-governor of Bagram district becoming a regular visitor to Villa Magnolia it was far too risky for Tariq to be seen anywhere near the man.

*

Arriving early at Villa Magnolia, Abdul leapt upstairs to check on Adham Volcov. Today they planned to discuss how to strategically inject Farez into the proceedings as an internationally accredited arms dealer in weapons of mass destruction in this case nuclear. The sooner the better.

As Abdul entered Volcov's bedroom he noticed the old man was sitting in his chair, fully dressed and looking a great deal stronger than of late.

Smiling, Volcov said, "Good morning John! I see you are surprised to see me looking more like my old self. I must confess I feel a huge weight has been lifted from my shoulders. I dare to think I can face each new day with renewed hope," he added, much to Abdul's relief. There was much to do and Volcov had to be up to the task – physically and mentally.

"That is very good news sir," Abdul responded. "I can see you look much better and I would put some of that down to your changed environment and excellent medical care provided by Mister Alexopoulos's medical team."

"I am sure that has a lot to do with it. John. You know, I always felt there was something different about you…I mean different from what you would have me believe. That said, I always felt I could trust you. I still do and that has helped me to relax," he added.

Abdul couldn't help being touched by the man's concern. "Sir, you must try to think positively. The past can't be changed but the future can make a great difference to your life. None of us know how long we will be on this earth, but to live each moment well is what counts and you must see that," Abdul said pointedly, while cognisant of the need to focus Volcov on the difficult work ahead. "You have taken a great leap of faith by agreeing to help the American authorities and that has made a difference in the way you feel about life. I can only say, sir, all will end well if you continue to be positive," he added, offering a hand to the old man who sat back in his chair to contemplate his aide's prophetic advice.

But not for very long. Farez peered around the bedroom door. "Good morning Adham, I see you are looking much better today," he said, walking towards Volcov to grasp his hand. "Today, my friend, we must progress to the next phase by taking the fight to Madam Patcha and Commander Kahir. It is time to remove the sting from the scorpion's tale. I take the view that Kahir believes he has the upper hand. We must let him believe that but work to turn the tables by ensuring the game is played according to our rules not his," Farez added, noticing how Volcov appeared confused by his statement.

"I am not sure I am following you Kostas. Just how can we convince him that the rules of the game have changed. Surely, as long as he has Laura he has the upper hand. She is a pawn in the game, and I cannot play games when it comes to my daughter's safety," he shot back. Volcov became agitated.

Concerned, Farez said, "Be easy Adham. We have developed a strategy that will work. John, please sit with us and help explain to Mister Volcov how we plan to gain the upper hand in this high stakes game of chess."

Dutifully, the old man sat back and listened intently as Farez explained in great detail his willingness to confront their adversaries head-on. "Therefore, our overall view Adham,"

Farez concluded, "is to take the pressure off you and transfer it to us," he added looking at Abdul.

"I am lost for words Kostas. I am amazed you would risk so much for me. I don't deserve it and I don't think I can allow you to do this…" he spluttered, unable to finish his point before Abdul interjected.

"Please listen to Mister Alexopoulos, sir," he pleaded. "He knows what he's talking about and he is quite determined to see this through. And with all due respect to you sir, you lack the physical strength to carry the burden on your own. Also, I believe I am correct in saying you have never dabbled in the black market for nuclear weapons. Our strategy pitches Mister Alexopoulos as someone with the necessary contacts to facilitate the purchase and sale of such weapons. This is an important assurance he can offer Patcha and Kahir, and one that you are unable to support, sir," Abdul stressed, watching as Volcov took it all on board.

"Furthermore," Abdul went on, "our undercover team will provide backup for all of us. We will convince the buyers we have the material they need but we will drive a hard bargain. Allow me to spell this out for you sir: if they want to do business with Mr Alexopoulos they must release Laura beforehand. Once she's released we will agree a time and place for the exchange. Once in place, we will make our move and arrest everyone involved," Abdul added, pausing to give Volcov time to take it all in.

"John, I hardly deserve such support," Volcov responded, close to tears. "When I recall how I exploited my business undertakings and the damage I have done I feel ashamed with myself," he confessed, looking first at Abdul and then Farez both of whom sensed the old man was ready to atone for his past. The time for exploitation was long gone; it was time to turn over a new leaf. There was no denying his past indiscretions, but it was clear this man not only regretted his past but was willing to make amends. It will take an intense amount of courage to make the switch and many people are pinning their hopes on him succeeding for more than one reason.

It was time to take a break. The morning's bout of strategising had taken its toll. "We have reached the point where we must now invite Commander Kahir to meet with us," Farez announced. "We will present him with an offer on the lines we have discussed. He can spend time thinking about it and discuss it with Madam Patcha. "I suggest the next meeting is held here in Villa Magnolia because you, Adham, are still under doctor's orders," Farez added, pleased with the way the plan was developing. Concerned about Laura's fate, he was anxious to move things along as quickly as possible.

Volcov did not protest about the venue for the next meeting. He knew he was not strong enough to cope unassisted and he valued the protection afforded by Villa Magnolia and Farez's sturdy companionship. "May I ask you something Kostas? Do you really believe Commander Kahir will go along with the plan?"

"I suppose we'll find out soon enough. Meanwhile, you should stay here until Laura is released. .as I am sure she will be my friend. Jack Cummings and John Dwyer will keep an eye on Villa Margalla and make sure no uninvited guests are admitted."

Volcov had to concede that everything that could be done had been done.

"As I see it," Farez said to the others, "we now dangle the bait and wait for the fish to bite!"

*

265

Commander Kahir accepted the invitation to meet at Villa Magnolia instantly sparking a great deal of activity particularly in the kitchen. Working to Abdul's instructions, cooks were preparing a special lunch known as one of the commander's favourites. On many occasions, back in Bagram, Abdul – at that time under deep cover as the governor's assistant - had watched amazed as his portly boss tucked into Baluchi-style chicken sajji. It's a favourite dish of nomadic goatherders and shepherds in Baluchistan - sometimes using lamb, stuffed with rice and papaya paste, slow-roasted over an open fire - or the more common sajji popular in urban Pakistan, and relished by Commander Kahir that features whole chickens stuffed with a mixture of cumin seeds, coriander seeds, cardamom seeds, dried pomegranate seeds, fennel seeds and more. From those days, Abdul became convinced that the way to a certain Taliban commander's heart was via his distended stomach! A sumptuous meal of chicken sajji would be totally irresistible to the avaricious, overweight bore and likely to place him in a reasonable mood for striking a deal. That was the theory and, if Abdul had it right, negotiations should become much easier.

Adham Volcov was nervous, realising he had to put his entire trust in Kostas Alexopoulos and John Dwyer to ensure the commander would be in no doubt about the terms of the deal.

Working to a suggestion by Commander Zahir, arrangements were made to record salient points of the negotiation as it took place to make sure that U.S. government departments including the Pentagon were aware of everything that was agreed. Nothing would be left to chance.

*

Promptly at noon, Commander Kahir's staff car turned into the driveway of Villa Magnolia. Abdul escorted him into the visitors' room where Volcov and Farez were already seated.

Sweeping aside Abdul in his usual brusque manner, the stony-faced, overweight commander walked over to the two men. He was wheezing loudly, vainly attempting to catch his breath. The exertion required to disembark from the vehicle and enter the villa had tested his physical ability and found him wanting. It prompted Abdul to reflect on how such a man would fare on the field of battle.

Getting to his feet, Farez offered his hand, "Greetings Commander, please be seated." He pointed to a large armchair into which Kahir carefully lowered his outsized frame.

Mopping his brow, the commander sneered at Volcov. "I see you have managed to make it downstairs Mr Volcov. Does that mean you are well enough to return to you own villa?"

"Adham is much better but far from well enough to return to Villa Margalla," Farez answered on Volcov's behalf. "Our medical team insists he stays here for further treatment. The disappearance of his niece has proven to be a huge shock," he added, in a tone lacking any warmth. Farez nodded towards Abdul signalling lunch should be served in the dining room. Kahir's sensitive nostrils had already detected the unmistakeable, spicy odours of a Baluchi-style meal and was licking his lips in anticipation.

"Mr Alexopoulos…is that chicken sajji I smell?" he asked as the party entered the capacious dining room.

"Yes, commander you are quite correct. My cooks have prepared their own marinade of yogurt and spices, but I'm sure you will recognise the Baluchi origins of the stuffing. I suggest we all enjoy lunch and talk later," Farez proposed, as six whole chickens, fresh from the ovens, were temptingly arranged on the dining table.

Reaching over, the commander grabbed a whole chicken and began tearing the flesh with great relish. Stuffing his mouth to excess it was abundantly clear he was a man who lived to eat, rather than one who ate to live! Abdul's eleventh-hour idea to serve chicken sajji was proving to be a stroke of genius.

"With such an excellent spread before us, I can't think of anything we have to discuss that can't wait," the commander lamented.

The others watched as a happy Taliban commander gleefully licked his lips and fingers after every mouthful until he polished off the entire chicken in short order. Wiping his mouth on a napkin, he reached over for a second chicken and gave it similar short shrift. Finally, he accepted a bowl of rose-scented water and cleaned his mouth and hands before settling back in his chair. "Well, gentlemen, what shall we talk about?"

Standing, Volcov began by referring to Commander Kahir's previous visit. "During your last visit, commander, you made it clear to me that you required my cooperation to source specific weapons. You also made it clear, if I am not mistaken, that my failure to cooperate would result in unspecified threats against me. Am I correct thus far?" he asked looking intently at Commander Kahir who was clearly taken aback by what seemed an impromptu and clumsy attack after such a satisfying lunch offered so gracefully.

"Are you suggesting this should be discussed here and now?" the commander questioned, still slightly confused.

Farez intervened. "I would say this is the perfect moment to discuss your requirement for weapons of mass destruction. And, before you respond, please understand that I am Mr Volcov's prime contact for such weapons," he added, smiling.

Hammering home the point, Volcov said. "I am a weapons dealer commander, but I don't stock what you want. That's why I approached Kostas Alexopoulos for such weaponry.

And that's why you were invited here today – as well as to enjoy a sajji meal. I suggest you communicate your requirements directly to Mr Alexopoulos if you wish to take this further," he added, quite pleased with himself for finding the strength and moral fibre to stand up to Commander Kahir. For one brief moment he felt he was controlling the exchange which was providing cathartic relief.

"I must say, gentlemen, that you have taken me by surprise," the commander admitted, frowning deeply. "And how am I to judge Mr Alexopoulos's credentials? Such discussions are of a sensitive nature and must be based on more than a chicken lunch and goodwill," he added, looking decidedly uncomfortable.

"You will find my credentials stand up to scrutiny, commander" Farez announced reassuringly. I suggest you look me up – the American government keeps a large dossier on me I am reliably informed. Why don't you start there? Please come back when you're satisfied we can do business together - here at Villa Magnolia.

"I should also inform you that I hold Adham Volcov in high esteem which is why I am prepared to work alongside him. Unless you have anything further to add, commander, it seems this meeting has run its course. My servant will show you to your vehicle. Please let us know if and when you wish to continue this discussion," Farez added, clapping his hands to bring his aide, Mike Harper, running into the room.

Commander Kahir was inwardly furious at being summarily dismissed with thoughts of delicious chicken sajji occupying his mind. But he swallowed his pride not wishing to act pre-emptively before discussing the situation with his compatriots particularly Patcha. Acquiring nuclear weapons was pivotal to their plans. Leaving the visitors room, he approached his

assurances they sought but only after Laura's release. He was sure the terrorists' check of his credentials would prove successful; the profiling and fake postings on the internet would confirm his bona fides projecting Kostas Alexopoulos as the real deal. America's counterintelligence experts were already onto that. Madam Patcha and Commander Kahir would inevitably conclude that the billionaire dealer was the man to do business with because he was one of a small handful of people with access to weapons of mass destruction. And Kostas Alexopoulos had to believe that their adversaries' burning desire for such weapons would outweigh their intent to use Laura as a pawn.

Considering his past exposure to dangerous missions, Abdul was unusually nervous this time around. So much hinged on the outcome of the day's negotiations and that meant Laura was permanently on his mind. Rapidly developing circumstances steeped in danger, only served to reinforce the deep emotions he had for her. He loved her aside from any promises he'd given to Adham Volcov and would never let her go. He had already decided that if Commander Kahir stooped to play stupid games and block her release he will implement Plan B and go undercover to rescue her from the governor's residence in Bagram. It would be an unfortunate development serving to prolong a mission which was something nobody wanted.

*

Commander Kahir arrived on time, perhaps indicating a desire to press on with discussions. Mike Harper escorted him into the visitors' room where Farez, Abdul, and Adham Volcov were already assembled and waiting to do business. The atmosphere turned tense the moment Kahir made his appearance, but Farez remained courteous as always.

"Welcome back commander, please take a seat. Bring tea for everyone please," Farez instructed Mike Harper. Farez's pleasant demeanour, all part of his earlier rehearsal before the mirror, belied the contempt he held for the odious creature sitting across from him. On cue Mike Harper stepped forward with a silver tray which he placed on the large mahogany coffee table at the centre of the room. Tea was served.

Commander Kahir, apparently comfortable in the same chair as before, took sips of his beverage while waiting for someone to make the opening remarks. Farez obliged. "I trust you have thoroughly examined my credentials and are satisfied," he said through clenched teeth.

"We have done so thoroughly, and I do not deny they are impressive. We find no reason why we shouldn't discuss business," he confirmed, uttering what sounded to Abdul as the closest thing to a congratulatory response. The big man was not known for his charm.

"I am pleased to hear that and I'm sure you discovered during your deliberations that in the sphere of operations we are discussing you either do business with me or you don't do business at all," Farez declared, hands held high with palms uppermost as if saying, "I told you so!" The village-head-turned-actor was portraying his role as a billionaire arms dealer (in nuclear weapons) in a manner fit for a Golden Globe award.

Abdul stifled a smile as Farez continued his spirited monologue. "As I made clear earlier, Adham Volcov is a dear friend and neighbour and that is the only incentive for doing business with you. That said, perhaps you have a list of your requirements to show me?" he said eagerly holding out his hand. Not for the first time, Farez was dictating the pace of the discussion leading Kahir like a goat. His bright red face registered the level of disdain he held for Farez. But he complied with the request. Fumbling around in a small valise he withdrew a sheaf of papers and handed them to Farez who scrutinised them as if he'd done it a thousand times before. "I see nothing listed here that I can't provide you with commander; it's just a matter of us coming to an amicable agreement," Farez pronounced with a smile reminiscent of a cobra hypnotising its prey before striking.

Sweating and fidgeting in his chair, Commander Kahir looked uncomfortable and eager to get on with matters. "Money is of no consequence Mr Alexopoulos," he said, mopping his sweaty brow. "Name your price!" he added, adding a measure of condescension.

"That is just as well commander," Farez declared, "because I don't come cheap! However, I am sure you will agree that life is not all about money, there are other things just as important. Let me assure you I can provide you with everything on your shopping list at what we might call market rates – black market of course – with one, important proviso. And this proviso is something you must agree to before we go any further. And keep in mind, that if you don't do business with me, you will not get the weapons on this list," he said, returning the papers.

"I think, Mr Alexopoulos, you need to explain yourself more clearly. I am not following you. Perhaps you can spell out your terms," he said, once again feeling he was being led by the nose.

"Very well commander. This is how we will proceed. I will supply everything you need, slightly below black-market rates in exchange for Mr Volcov's niece, Laura, delivered unharmed to my villa twenty-four hours from now. Please do not waste my time, and yours, by saying you don't know what I am talking about. I know that Miss Laura is being held as a bargaining chip to force Mr Volcov's hand. Deny that, and this meeting is over.

"I see from your facial expressions that we understand one another," Farez continued, putting in a superb performance and loving every minute of it. "As soon as the young lady is here and under my protection your arms order will be delivered to Villa Margalla at a mutually agreeable time. Those are our conditions to seal the deal, commander, which you may accept or decline. It's up to you." Farez was confident the need for a weapon of mass destruction would outweigh any other concerns after the terrorists had scrutinised his credentials and found them impeccable. Nevertheless, such bravado constituted a massive bluff and Farez knew it.

Apart from an audible bout of wheezing from the overweight, overstressed commander, the visitors' room fell silent.

"I am surprised at aspects of your proposal Mr Alexopoulos and I must request time to think it through." Kahir was not about to admit to Laura's abduction. Clearly he had not expected such a bombshell to be delivered by a friend of Adham Volcov. He would play for time.

"Take all the time you need. Discuss with your associates. Remember…twenty-four hours from now you must meet out terms, or we don't deal," Farez stated, satisfied he had Kahir's undivided attention. He felt confident of a successful outcome because he'd been assured that it was nigh impossible to find a black-market dealer in nuclear arms. His stick-and-carrot approach was a huge bluff, but it just might work.

Struggling to his feet, Commander Kahir nodded towards Farez and headed for his car escorted by Mike Harper who returned with a wide grin on his face. "I don't know about the commander," Harper commented, "but you certainly convinced me Mr Alexopoulos!"

Farez had winged it, relying on his acting ability to get his message over. Prior to that, no-one knew how he would connect the offer of weapons to the release of Laura.

"Well done Mr Kostas Alexopoulos," Abdul said emphasising Farez's *nom de guerre*, "I should have filmed that episode for posterity. At least we made a recording so we can impress and amuse the brass in Washington if nothing else," he added, laughing loudly as he placed a supporting hand on Farez's shoulder.

Smiling broadly, Adham Volcov also praised Farez for his acting prowess. "You were magnificent, and I can only thank you and hope that Laura will be released soon."

"We have a very slippery fish in on the hook," Farez assured Volcov, "and I think we will be reeling it in quite soon. I say this because time is of the essence for the terrorists and they will not wish to see their plans delayed. I don't know about you my friends," he said, addressing everyone in the room, "but that exchange with the commander has whetted my appetite!" he declared confidently as they headed for the dining room.

Kostas Alexopoulos, as head of Villa Magnolia, had excelled himself yet again by arranging a special lunch of Baluchi dishes. "Tell me Farez," Abdul said putting an arm around Farez's shoulders, "is there anything left of that delicious chicken sajji?"

"I am not sure. Why do you ask?"

"Commander Kahir was very impressed with the sajji you served him. It was a brilliant move my friend and I know for sure he will return tomorrow."

*

275

The next day, word came from Commander Kahir that the terms discussed had been agreed and Mr Volcov's niece would be released and returned to Villa Magnolia in twelve hours. Farez broke the news to the others, it sparked an impromptu bout of rejoicing.

Commander Zahir put it all down to Farez's handling of the situation. "I am sure Abdul's observations regarding your chicken sajji carries merit, but I feel I must say well done brother for your negotiating skills. I will inform Washington right away so they can prepare for the exchange as agreed. I do believe we are making progress and can only hope we are nearer to completing our assignment," he added, openly pleased with the day's exertions.

Abdul agreed but added a note of caution. "Until Laura is safe we can't relax our guard. But we can celebrate an uptick in proceedings. I suggest as a precaution we detail Noori to monitor the release and return of Laura. My guess is Darius Forsetti will be assigned the task of bringing her back to the villa. We will keep an eye on him because recent history tells us he can't be trusted. If he gets up to his old tricks, Noori will deal with him."

"I agree we need to remain alert," Farez said, "but, inshallah, we can look forward to the return of Laura to her father," he said slipping out of character for a moment to once again become the wise old malik of Marwah village.

***

Chapter Nineteen

In the early morning, seated all alone at the oval operations table in Villa Magnolia, Mike Harper was startled by the shrill ring of a phone. He stiffened as he recognised the caller but refrained from commenting other than for a brief acknowledgement. Immediately gathering up his notes he went in search of Commander Zahir who he'd last seen in the visitors room in deep conversation with Kostas Alexopoulos.

"My apologies for butting in gentlemen," Mike Harper said as both men looked up and smiled.

"Come in...what is it Master Sergeant?" the commander questioned, bidding Harper to take a seat. "What's on your mind?"

"Sir, a few moments ago I fielded a call from Noori. He reports movement at the governor's residence in Bagram. It seems they are preparing to move Miss Laura."

"If that's true, as we hope and expect," said Farez responding elatedly, "we may well see her back here very soon."

Tariq shared his optimism "Perhaps we should begin a review of our strategy," he quipped. "As soon as she's back safe and sound I will get in touch with the Pentagon. Then we can set about completing the deal with Madam Patcha and her cohorts. If we get this right, we can bag the entire nest of rats in one go!"

Both men were revelling in the thrill of the chase and word from Noori that Laura may soon be on the move educed an atmosphere of hope.

"I am concerned about Adham and how he might react to this news," Farez said pointedly. "I suggest we keep it among ourselves right up to the moment his daughter comes through the door." Intuitively, the old sage was thinking ahead imagining himself in Volcov's shoes, thus unwilling to prematurely build up anyone's hopes.

"I do agree brother," Tariq stated, supportively. "What Volcov doesn't know won't hurt him. So, for the time being, he added, looking directly at Mike Harper, only the three of us and Volcov's aide John Dwyer will be in the picture."

On cue, Abdul stepped into the visitors room bright and early as per his normal routine since establishing daily visits to Villa Magnolia from his temporary base in Volcov's villa. Mike Harper relayed the salient points of Noori's brief phone call.

"Ah...some movement at last," Abdul uttered, grinning at the others. "Mike, when Noori calls again – and I'm sure he will – I would like a word with him."

"Any particular reason?" Tariq asked out of curiosity.

"Yes, I anticipated this might happen, and it raises a few issues," Abdul said, sitting down to explain. "In the first place I believe it's likely that Darius Forsetti will be detailed to drive Laura from Bagram to Islamabad. As we all know that's a five-hour drive in daylight. If Patcha and her cohorts are to meet our agreed deadline Laura should already be on the road from Bagram if they plan to get here before nightfall. Second point is this: after Darius hands over Laura I expect him to make a dash for it. He's not the biggest fish we're hoping to land, but it would be a pity if he slipped through the net after all he's done. He may not have a price on his head but there are scores to be settled and some of us, myself included, would be sorry to see him get away scot free," Abdul added his eyes aglow at the prospect of dispensing justice to the man who kidnapped Laura from right under his nose.

"You make a valid point my friend," Tariq acknowledged before turning to Harper. "Mike, call Noori right away. Ask him to follow Laura back to Islamabad and keep Forsetti's vehicle in sight at all time. If he links up with Patcha and Commander Kahir then we know where he is. If he takes off on his own, Noori can follow and we will pick him up later. I know how you feel my friend," he added, reverting to Abdul. "Rest assured we won't allow Forsetti to escape."

Farez supported Tariq's assessment of Forsetti's likely behaviour. "Please accept Tariq's assurances my friend," he pleaded to Abdul. "Remember all three of us have personal scores to settle. But for now, and going forward, we must put our personal feelings on hold. There is much at stake and fulfilling our assignment overrides any other considerations," he added, placing a reassuring hand on Abdul's arm.

But Abdul had no intention of compromising the assignment, not when Laura's safe return looked to be within reach. "Please don't misconstrue my commitment; duty always comes before love - but only just," he said light-heartedly, intent on showing the team he was laser-focused on the task ahead.

"Let's talk about Adham Volcov. Has anyone informed him of Noori's message?" Abdul queried.

"We decided not to. If we raise the old man's hopes and she doesn't show up it will only add to his discomfort, perhaps even bring about a relapse," Tariq explained. "The best medicine for him will be when Laura walks through that door.

*

Abdul's restlessness grew apace; he suspected something was amiss. Accounting for the distance and time involved, they should have heard back from Noori. They attempted to call him by radiotelephone. No response. Maybe he had decided not to carry it with him, but why? They must be on their way if they are to meet the agreed timeframe for the handover. All manner of permutations swirled around in Abdul's head. Forsetti could never be relied upon to bring Laura to Villa Magnolia for fear of facing a frosty reception. Clearly, Darius was not the type to put his own life at risk. What was he likely to do? Abdul's mind was working overtime and he found it unnerving.

Perceptive as always, Tariq sensed Abdul's concern. "Stay calm brother. I know you are very worried about Miss Laura but until we hear from Noori we don't know what action to take."

"Be easy my friend," Farez said putting an arm around Abdul's shoulders. "We must wait to hear from Noori otherwise we are just blind men stumbling around in the dark!"

Wise words, thought Abdul, but just hanging around waiting for something to happen did not sit well with him. Recalling Laura's precious dog and thinking of Forsetti's penchant for violence was more than enough for a special ops marine to accept. Intuitively he knew he had to act.

"I am unable to sit here doing nothing," Abdul announced to the others. "I will pick up Jack Cummings from Villa Margalla and drive across the border to intercept their vehicle. If they have had a breakdown, or worse, we will intervene. We will carry radiotelephones in the Land Rover so you can contact us if Laura suddenly turns up here safe and sound."

Aware Abdul could not be dissuaded from any cause once he's made up his mind, Tariq and Farez had to accept the situation. Grudgingly, they settled down for what could be a long wait with their fully charged radiotelephones at hand.

*

The main road between Islamabad and Bagram is partly paved but heavily potholed. Volcov's Land Rover, borrowed by Abdul, was well suited for the semi-desert road conditions familiar to him after years of experience in the region.

Abdul figured Laura and her escorts should be little more than an hour away from Islamabad if his calculations were correct and assuming their vehicle had not suffered any serious delays en route.

The first few miles were covered in silence each man with his own thoughts. Abdul juggled with the notion that Forsetti had nothing to lose and that made the man a bit of an enigma. He glanced at Cummings grateful for his offer to do the driving. It gave Abdul time to filter a profusion of thoughts to come up with a plan.

Cummings broke the silence. "What's on your mind John? As I understand it Forsetti is someone who cannot be trusted. Are you wondering – as I am - if he's loyal to his masters or working for himself?"

Smiling at Jack's inciteful remarks, Abdul was blunt. "I guess Darius Forsetti will do whatever is best for Darius Forsetti. I always suspect any man who is willing to sell himself to the highest bidder! A man without scruples is a man lost at sea. At one stage, Jack," he continued, "Forsetti thought he was Madam Patcha's poster boy ideally suited for carrying out her crazy instructions. She could sweettalk him into believing anything was possible provided he did as he was told. He's a devious kinda guy and it wouldn't take long for him to realise Laura's worth as a pawn in their dirty game of chess. Perhaps he's confident he can enrich himself by going solo and playing each of us against one another," Abdul said, offering an honest assessment of the situation.

"I gotta say John, that entire scenario crossed my mind some time back."

Abdul did not respond. He knew Cummings was sincere as well as being a master of his craft in the intelligence community. They drove on in silence, watching as the sun set in the west in the direction of Bagram. Minutes later, darkness fell on the unlit road. Cummings adjusted his speed accordingly. A few miles later Abdul took over the driving.

Suddenly, the night was illuminated by intermittent flashes of light causing Abdul to pull over. The men watched as lights flashed again…three short bursts, three long, and three short again.

"Someone's using Morse code!" Cummings exclaimed, as Abdul stepped on the gas and moved forward at speed. "There it is again - S.O.S.," Abdul said, the lights much closer this time.

"Pull over John," Cummings cautioned, "we could be running into an ambush. I will circle around on foot and check it out. I suggest you creep forward slowly and pull up short of the flashing lights. I will signal you with my flashlight once I've assessed the situation," he added, now halfway out of the vehicle before Abdul could stop him.

"Take care Jack, it could be a trap…maybe Taliban fighters setting up an ambush. Stay alert and watch your back!"

Cummings disappeared into the night while Abdul remained stationary for five minutes before edging forward slowly. The emergency signal was repeated and getting closer. It was distracting him so much he hardly saw a figure emerge from the darkness and become framed in the car's headlights. He jammed on the brakes. To his amazement someone resembling Laura stepped into view, torch in hand. Abdul leapt from the vehicle, "Laura! Is that you? Stand still, I am coming over," he shouted, his heart beating wildly. The suddenness of her appearance caught him by surprise. He reached her in a few steps. She fell into his arms sobbing with relief. Holding her tightly he savoured the joy of finding her again. But in that blissful moment he failed to notice he had company.

A voice to his rear restored full awareness of his vulnerability. "Mister John Dwyer, how very touching," uttered a smug Darius Forsetti who had managed to sneak up unnoticed.

"This time John I seem to have the upper hand," drooled Forsetti. "I would say the ball is definitely in my court old buddy!"

Swinging around, and pulling Laura behind him, Abdul faced Forsetti who was standing several feet away with what looked like a .357 magnum in his hand – big enough to blow a man's head off at that distance.

"Listen Forsetti, if I find you've hurt Laura in any way, I will take you apart piece by piece," Abdul threatened, playing for time and hoping Cummings was alert to what was going down.

Forsetti savoured the moment, pleased to have the upper hand for once over his arch-rival John Dwyer. "And if you're concerned about your friend," he snarled, "I am afraid he's somewhat indisposed."

"Who are you talking about?" Abdul questioned, immediately concerned that Cummings had been taken down by Forsetti. Or was he talking about Noori who had been detailed to follow Laura?

"Miss Laura, why don't you tell Mr Dwyer everything that happened?" Forsetti suggested believing he was in full control of proceedings.

"Darius noticed a car following us It was getting closer, so he pulled over. He waved down the other car pretending we'd had a breakdown. A man came over to help and Darius shot him without saying a word," Laura recounted still trembling from the experience.

"Is he dead?" Abdul asked, certain now it was Noori.

"Not when I left a moment ago, but he will be if he doesn't get help soon," Laura replied sobbing uncontrollably.

"Okay, that's quite enough drama for now," Forsetti declared, pointing his gun at Abdul. Now it's your turn Dwyer," he said through clenched teeth. But before he could squeeze the trigger a shot rang out and Forsetti dropped to the ground with a head wound. The incomparable Jack Cummings emerged from the shadows, smoking gun in hand. He looked down at Forsetti to make sure he was no longer a threat.

"I will clear up this mess John while you take Laura and see what can be done for the injured man," Cummings urged, dragging Forsetti's body off the road towards some low bushes.

Dashing across to the other vehicle they found Noori lying semiconscious on the ground near the car. Laura established he'd been shot through the femoral artery. Tearing off a sleeve from Noori's *khet partug* she fashioned a tourniquet and wrapped it around his thigh. "We must get him to Villa Magnolia as quickly as possible. I can only do so much here and that may not be enough to save him," she pleaded as Abdul gently raised Noori in his arms and carried him across to the Land Rover, depositing him on the back seat to be joined by Laura who, by now, was covered in blood.

Cummings, who had stashed Forsetti's body under some desert scrub and small boulders, leapt into the front passenger seat as Abdul stepped on the accelerator. He drove as fast as night-time conditions would allow. Radioing ahead to the operations room, Cummings prepared the staff for an emergency "…and make sure you alert the doctor," he urged, after relaying Laura's diagnosis of Noori's injury.

They made good time on the return journey and were not stopped at the Afghan-Pakistan border which was something Abdul had expected. It was coming up to 2 a.m. and he figured the border guards would be tucked up in their bunks not expecting anyone to come in from the desert in the dead of night.

As the Land Rover screeched to a halt outside Villa Magnolia, Cummings jumped out to be joined by Mike Harper who was on hand to help carry Noori indoors. The doctor, who had everything prepared, asked Laura to assist him. Inspecting the gunshot wound, the doctor praised her efforts, "Your prompt action in applying the tourniquet helped stem the loss of blood...maybe saved his life. Now, Miss Laura, let's get him stabilised and then we'll get the lead out."

"John, it seems you were wise to go in search for them," Farez commented as Abdul and Jack Cummings stepped into the visitors room to be joined by Commander Zahir. "Once again your intuition was spot on," Farez added, offering the men glasses of *chai shireen* to help them relax after the excitement of their desperate drive through the desert.

"I must confess, Mr Alexopoulos, that we have our good friend Jack Cummings to thank for our safe return," Abdul commented, dryly. "If he hadn't taken out Forsetti none of us would be here today to talk about it. My only regret," he added, looking at Cummings, "is that your intervention robbed me of an opportunity to slit the bastard's throat. That said, please don't think I'm not grateful Jack - I am, and I owe you one!"

Laura stepped into the visitors room just as the men were exchanging pleasantries. "I have good news gentlemen to add to your obvious joy: Noori will recover. It will take time, but he will be back on his feet before too long." She was looking admiringly at Abdul as she spoke with an unmistakable glint in her eyes that radiated the love she felt for her rescuer. Before Abdul could react – and all he wanted to do was hold her tight - Farez stepped forward to greet Laura.

"Welcome to Villa Magnolia Miss Laura," he said, bowing slightly. "We were all very worried about your safe return. Now we can rejoice," he added, steering her towards a large settee. "We are all anxious to learn of your forced detention as soon as you feel well enough to talk about it," Farez continued. "Meanwhile, John wishes to speak to you privately before he takes you to Mr Volcov's room. Yes, he's staying here at the moment and the reasons for this will become clear, my child," he added, smiling warmly as Laura left with Abdul.

It was a foregone conclusion that Abdul would be the one to break the news to Laura about Volcov's change of heart – and allegiance. It not only made good sense, it was of paramount importance she should hear the complete story from Abdul to head off any wild rumours or careless whispers from villa staff. He led her into the garden, got her seated and, after taking a deep breath, set about relating all that had happened during her enforced absence.

"So, as you can see Laura, your faith in the man you thought was your uncle was well founded. Your father loves you for who you are and what you mean to him. And his heart aches to let you know his life has changed. Now he wishes to atone for his earlier misdeeds against you and society in general."

Laura sobbed quietly, her face quite pale from Abdul's astonishing revelations. "John, my tears are tears of relief and joy," she confessed, placing her small, elegant hand upon Abdul's hand. She looked at him and all the love she felt shone from her eyes.

"I thank you John for giving me the most precious gift I could wish for. Today I discovered that the uncle I have always loved as a father is my father," she whispered. "I care little about the past; as his daughter I just want to share with my father whatever time he has left. I know he will find it difficult to confess to me all that you have already told me. But, it will be alright…I promise you. You know how much I love you John and I know you love me. I hope we can talk about us later but, for now, it has to be all about my father. I know you understand," she added, squeezing his hand tightly.

"You are here safe and sound and that's all that matters," he said taking her in his arms and holding her close for a moment before heading back indoors.

It was Farez who shattered a romantic moment as they re-entered the villa. "I suggest you should pay a visit to your father, if you're ready," he said knowing that Abdul had brought her up to speed with recent events. "He is aware of your safe arrival and he's looking forward to seeing you."

Following behind Farez, Laura turned around on the staircase to blow a kiss to Abdul as if to say, "don't worry, I can handle this," before disappearing into Volcov's room.

After closing the door behind Laura, Farez joined Abdul. "I think it's time we reported events to brother Tariq so he can inform the Pentagon. And later, my friend, we must refine our plan to reel in the big fish!" he said, grinning. "Our prayers were answered today and for that I give thanks to Allah the Merciful," Farez announced slipping back into his more familiar role as malik of Marwah village.

"Please bear with me for a moment," Abdul pleaded. "I have something to attend to then you will have my undivided attention," he stated, picking up a small bundle before rushing up the staircase to Volcov's room. He could hear the sounds of laughter from within. He knocked and waited.

"Come in, come in," Volcov called out, his voice strong and his tone unmistakably joyful.

Abdul entered and approached Laura. "I have brought someone who is bursting to see you." Stooping, Abdul unleashed his small package more identifiable as Sykes, Laura's small dog – lively yet still recovering from injuries inflicted by Darius Forsetti. Pausing for a moment to get his bearings, Sykes took off at high speed and leapt into Laura's waiting arms squealing with delight.

"Sykes, my darling little friend. I thought you were lost to me forever," she exclaimed at the top of her voice as tears flowed down her cheeks. Sykes proceeded to inspect Volcov and then Abdul before returning to Laura.

Turning to Abdul, Volcov said, "John, I want to thank you from the bottom of my heart for bringing back my daughter. I always knew my trust in you was well founded," he added gripping Abdul by the hand. "Is there anything I can do for you my boy?"

"No sir, but I do have a question for Laura," he said, holding Laura in his arms.

"What is it John? What do you wish to ask me?"

"I want to know who taught you Morse code, little lady? he teased.

"I am afraid that's classified John," she replied, blushing. "I could tell you, but I'd have to kill you and I couldn't bring myself to do that to the man I love so dearly!"

***

Chapter Twenty

The occupants of Villa Magnolia uttered a collective sigh of relief upon Laura's safe return, willing it to have a positive effect on Adham Volcov's hitherto frail condition. It had been determined by the medical team, and acknowledged with joy by all present, that a full recovery was on the cards for Noori.

In due course he should be able to resume active duty alongside Commander Zahir his hero and mentor.

These relatively good tidings inspired a positive atmosphere and willingness to move to the next step of the operation to fulfil the promise to source nuclear component parts as previously bargained by Madam Patcha and Commander Kahir.

Viewing proceedings in his thespian role as Kostas Alexopoulos, a prominent dealer in nuclear armaments, Farez was overjoyed that Abdul was able to return Laura to her father. As a father himself, Farez had grown fond of Volcov considering him a principled individual with a good heart. He was convinced the old man had begun the transition from his dark past as a notorious arms trader dealing in death and destruction. And although Farez privately applauded Volcov's courage in agreeing to work with the Pentagon going forward, he was acutely aware of the cruel twist of fate that had robbed him of the time needed to enjoy a meaningful relationship with his daughter. That said, he knew that whatever time they had together would bring moments of great joy to make up for lost years.

Abdul savoured the moment with a sense of joy and welcome relief. Laura was out of harm's way and there was no longer any question in anyone's mind that the couple's love for one another had blossomed during their time apart. Many who knew the marine well knew that he always put duty first underpinned by a self-discipline refined over years of military service as a dedicated U.S. Marine. Now he was keen to focus on the next phase of this very important assignment to have it end well so all involved may return to their respective loved ones and get on with their lives.

Thoughts of America and home flooded into his mind as he pictured an end to the current operation. Smiling to himself he imagined how the children at his father's ranch would react when another four-legged friend appeared unannounced on the scene. Sykes, for his part, would surely be in his element from an abundance of attention courtesy of Sarah and the others.

No doubt Abdul's long-suffering father would extend a spirited welcome to Adham Volcov and his lovely daughter as the focus of love on the part of his son. He would delight in the moment because Abdul would become a family man and that was something Charles Sinclair had long hoped for. Likewise, Adham Volcov would be able to live out his final days at the Sinclair ranch that had become one of the securest locations in North America. America's military top brass would also find favour in such an arrangement not having to wonder where he was and what he was doing.

Over the years since Sarah's birth Abdul's family had swelled in numbers. Today, everyone at the ranch formed a part of one large family. All had experienced turbulent journeys from a war zone to the relative tranquillity of North Carolina. Now they were bound by familial bonds that would keep them united for the rest of their lives.

Sarah now had a brother in Khalil; Jamila and Ahktar were like cousins supplemented by adopted aunts and uncles all complementing the family circle. Moreover, Sarah could soon have a mother. Abdul couldn't be happier: "Now I know what is meant by my cup runneth over," he reminded himself occasionally. It was easy to see why he considered himself among the luckiest of men when he thought about all that had transpired since that incredible day when he was thrown clear of a Chinook helicopter as it crashed to earth near Bagram Air Base. The incident marked the start of an arduous and remarkable journey that was nearing its end.

*

"Good morning everyone," announced Commander Tariq Hasan Zahir preparing to address the occupants of Villa Magnolia. "I have an update from the Pentagon following the report we submitted concerning the safe return of Adham Volcov's daughter Laura. We are authorised to go to the next level to fulfil the promises made to Madam Patcha to source the nuclear weapon components yet to be specified. Full details of the plan will be given to those directly involved. What you all need to know, however, is that Madam Patcha and Commander Kahir will be invited to the villa to finalise arrangements for the transfer. We must get this right. We must be professional and remain courteous at all times. Our credibility - America's credibility - is at stake. Please take that to heart. Also understand that the success or failure of the next phase rests squarely on the shoulders of the brave and persistent Kostas Alexopoulos," he added prompting Farez to adopt a sheepish expression. "This next phase brings danger his way from being in the close proximity of unscrupulous people who trade in death and destruction. So, it is up to us to make sure we don't slip up by saying or doing the wrong thing. Think carefully before you make your every move. Start from today and get used to the idea of asking yourself "Am I making the right decision?"

Everyone turned to look at Farez Malikai, the esteemed nuclear arms dealer in the guise of Kostas Alexopoulos upon whose weathered shoulders rests the success or failure of the mission. It was an awesome responsibility, and everyone present knew so having listened to Commander Zahir's impassioned presentation. Everyone, that is, apart from Kostas Alexopoulos himself who sat quietly, a wry expression on his face.

Everything spoken by Commander Zahir was pertinent, serious and gave no cause for merriment. But Farez smiled anyway. "My dear Commander Zahir," he began somewhat condescendingly, "be assured I have the confidence necessary to uphold my part in this operation. I even look forward to playing…how shall I put it?...cat and mouse with two corrupt and dishonourable enemies." Farez's confidence was palpable and gave a morale boost to those within earshot which was the old malik's intention. They smiled at the comical expression on his face likening it to a wily old village cat that had been promised a giant bowl of camel's milk for catching lots of mice.

Commander Zahir saw it differently: he saw a good and loyal friend who had patiently waited a long time for revenge; a man determined to relish every minute going forward.

Anxious to move on, Commander Zahir brought the meeting back to its intended purpose as a staff briefing. "The Pentagon has sanctioned a meeting with Madam Patcha and Commander Kahir to take place here at the villa. I am working on that. As before I propose offering lunch with some of Kahir's favourite dishes to keep his mouth occupied. In fact, I fully expect Madam Patcha to lead from their side and set down terms for a deal. We will secretly record the proceedings for experts to study at the Pentagon. Also, it is important to have this formal meeting as evidence of their part in all of this. Particularly Patcha as she is the lynchpin. With luck she will say enough to implicate herself for deeds past and for what she and others are plotting prior to any exchange taking place."

What he didn't announce was that everyone by now should be aware that they are approaching a very delicate phase of the entire operation. That meant having Patcha and Kahir state clearly what they expected from their side of the deal. "This meeting will trigger action on our part," the commander went on, "to round-up sleeper cells in the States that have been protected so far by Americans, some in high places -- even Congress.

"It has to be said that information provided to the U.S. by Adam Volcov proved invaluable in identifying key players in this terrorist plot. All are currently under surveillance in the U.S. and the United Kingdom. Do you have any questions?"

Predictably, Mike Harper raised his hand. "Commander, do we have an approved procedure for delivering the goods?"

"That will be established after we assess the demands and can agree a delivery date. I think that's enough operational detail for now," he added, eager to get on, "but before I end this briefing session I want you to know that Noori is expected to make a full recovery. That said, he will not play a further part in this operation. Mister Alexopoulos has kindly offered to have Noori flown to the United States in his private jet. He will get the best medical treatment available. Let's all wish him a speedy recovery," he added to sustained applause.

The operations room emptied save for Farez, Abdul and Tariq. The malik, still projecting himself as a confident Kostas Alexopoulos, had something he wanted to share with his two good friends. "As we are in the last stage of this mission I want both of you to know that I intend to enjoy these final moments watching the former governor of Bagram being brought to justice," he declared. The malik's uncharacteristic bluntness prompted Abdul and Tariq to stare open-mouthed in mock surprise. While both men fully understood Farez's deeply held feelings where the former governor was concerned, they became concerned that Farez might allow his emotions to rule his head and compromise the entire operation.

It had been made clear on several occasions that Abdul and Tariq were uncomfortable with Farez playing such a danger-filled role. But that's how it was, and it prayed on their minds that they had almost lost him once and did not wish to face that prospect again. Understandably, Farez was in no rush to stare death in the face either. He sensed their concerns. "I wish to reassure you my good friends," he announced, touching hand to heart, "that I will never let you down. I have much to live for and will not put at risk an opportunity to return to the United States and my beloved wife and son." With a slight bow of the head, he added, "Let us be clear: if anything happened to me who would be left to keep you in order?" he quipped, masterfully wrongfooting Abdul and Tariq with his light-hearted remark.

Skilfully, Farez had made his point and the modicum of levity he employed circumvented further discussion about his commitment to the cause. A spontaneous outburst of laughter from all three men brushed away further concerns.

"Are we in agreement" queried Farez, "that Adham Volcov should invite Madam Patcha and Commander Kahir to a business meeting to lay down their requirements for nuclear weapons?"

"Of course," Tariq responded. "It is the next logical move. Volcov must let them both know that Kostas Alexopoulos is ready and able to do business. We will make it a business lunch," Tariq added, anxious to keep up the momentum. "Meanwhile," he continued, "I will report to the Pentagon that we are moving forward with caution."

Farez left the briefing to communicate with Adham Volcov.

Concerned about the delicately balanced role Farez was playing in this dangerous game of nuclear chess, Abdul and Tariq remained pensive. Both men were determined that no harm should befall Brother Farez.

"We must ensure Farez does not find himself alone with the enemy," Tariq cautioned, attempting to reassure himself as much as Abdul.

"I agree with you Tariq, but these two rogues are unlikely to bite the hand that feeds them at least up to the point of the handover," Abdul offered.

"But that is our only guarantee," countered Tariq. "However, if it goes the way we expect Madam Patcha and Commander Kahir will look upon Kostas Alexopoulos as someone they can do business with whenever they are in the market for nuclear weapons."

Abdul was more concerned that Farez might make it a personal vendetta if his emotions got the better of him despite Farez's assurances to the contrary. "My greatest worry is Farez may be tempted to avenge Naomi for all she's suffered at the hands of the wicked Kahir. So, we must be alert to his every move from now on. I believe Farez when he says he has too much to lose after being reunited with his family but what will he be like when these two depraved villains are sitting alongside him," he added, unaware that Farez had re-entered the operations room after a brief discussion with Volcov.

"What is all this talk about villains? I beseech you to not be concerned about my safety or my likely behaviour," Farez pleaded quietly but with emphasis. "I promise you, hand on heart, I will not do anything that puts this operation at risk. Please be assured I am not motivated by a need for personal revenge," he stressed, hand pressed against his heart. "Trust me please as I trust you," he added, moving forward to embrace his two stalwart friends.

"I came back to the ops room to inform you that Adham Volcov spoke to Madam Patcha about a formal meeting to discuss their requirements. They will be here the day after tomorrow for lunch," Farez confirmed, with a smile of satisfaction.

vehicle and manoeuvred his frame inside as a smiling Mike Harper held open the door.

"I am not sure if we have our fish on the hook," Abdul commented, as soon as the commander had left the room "but I suspect we will have confirmation quite soon."

"One thing we can take away from today," Farez commented, "is that my cook's recipe for chicken sajji is something we should have patented."

"I agree," Abdul commented. "So please ensure cook puts it on the menu for the next meeting." For the first time in months Adham Volcov laughed aloud.

*

Three days later, the atmosphere in Villa Magnolia was once again tense as the team awaited the arrival of Commander Kahir to continue discussions. Today's crucial meeting would decide whether or not a deal could be struck between the commander and Kostas Alexopoulos. If confirmed it could herald the beginning of the end of the mission – but only if negotiations produced an agreement to release Laura.

Since the last meeting, Volcov had tried hard to keep his emotions under control. It had been a challenge. He longed to be reunited with his daughter and to bare his soul to her. And he had an additional worry to carry around: concern for the safety of Kostas, now a kindred spirit and close friend who was prepared to risk everything to secure Laura's release. It all weighed heavily on his conscience.

This time, more than the last meeting, Farez knew he had to put in a convincing performance. He had revisited his video tutorials into the character Kostas Alexopoulos; checked his notes and practised earnestly in front of a mirror. He emerged confident he could provide Kahir and his cronies with the

"That is good news my friend," Tariq said, turning to leave. I will inform the Pentagon right away and make the necessary arrangements."

"Good work Farez, Abdul declared enthusiastically, an arm around Farez's shoulders. "If I am not mistaken my friend the next meeting could mark the beginning of the end."

***

Chapter Twenty-One

The forthcoming visit of Madam Patcha and New Taliban Commander Kahir had put Laura on edge. Although Abdul had gone to great lengths to explain how they had arrived at a critical stage in negotiations she was forced to accept she could not attend any meetings where Volcov was involved. The decision heightened her anxiety.

Laura's main concern was for her father. "I hoped I could be by his side today John," she announced resignedly, "if only to give him moral support."

In truth Laura did not relish the thought of meeting face to face with her dreaded nemesis Madam Patcha lest she lost control of her emotions. Her main concern was for her father's failing health and the need for him to remain as calm as possible. Now she was back by his side she saw it as her duty to stand by him and protect him to the best of her ability.

"Laura, darling, everyone here understands your concern," Abdul said quietly. "I promise you this: he will be alright because I will protect him," he added reassuringly. "Your father sincerely intends to make amends for his past indiscretions. He is serious about that. And we need his help to bring the evildoers to justice and help save lives. Please keep in mind that Kostas Alexopoulos is putting his life on the line to help your father. He sees good in his heart as I do.

Neither Commander Zahir nor I wish to see any harm come to either man. Laura, please believe me when I say we know what we are doing. I want you to trust me to do what's right," he added his facial expression a mixture of love and profound concern.

"I do trust you John, but I must ask you to understand my desire to help my father. We have much to share and, right now, time is not a reliable friend," Laura pleaded, tears filling her eyes. It prompted Abdul to place his arms around her. Oh, how he wanted to take away her pain.

"Please listen carefully Laura. You have given your father the greatest gift of his entire life: your love and complete acceptance that what occurred in his earlier life is now in the past. That alone has strengthened his resolve to live as long as he can to experience the magical moments of being a father to his daughter. When we all get back to the States, your father will have protection and every opportunity to make a fresh start. You may find it strange when I say I believe in miracles – some have already happened! I want you to trust in what I am saying because I know everything will turn out fine," he added, as they stood locked in one another's arms.

"So, why don't you go and find Sykes and keep a low profile until the meetings are over." They kissed and parted company.

*

The atmosphere in Villa Magnolia was tense as key members of the team awaited the arrival of their guests. Adham Volcov looked decidedly pale, which was understandable as he did not relish being face to face with the perpetrators of his daughter's abduction. Nevertheless, he resolved to play his part in the deal. He also saw his involvement as essential in bringing the bad guys to justice. In particular he salivated at the thought of the important part he was about to play towards having a noose placed around Patcha's neck.

297

Looking at Volcov, Farez smiled. He could read the man's thoughts. "Have courage my friend. Today we will take an important step to bring down the enemy. We all feel as you do: we all have scores to settle. With care and patience on everyone's part I believe justice will prevail."

Listening to the man he knew and respected as Kostas Alexopoulos, and looking at the man he knew as John Dwyer, Volcov began to relax for the first time in weeks. He felt he was in safe hands and was humbled by the depth of friendship coming his way.

Mike Harper knocked before entering the reception room. "They're here," he announced with a wide grin. As usual, the wily master sergeant relished the sense of drama and growing tension.

"Thank you, Mike, I'll be right with you," Abdul confirmed rising to his feet and walking with Harper to greet the visitors.

"Good morning Commander Kahir…Madam Patcha, follow me please. Mister Kostas Alexopoulos and Mr Adham Volcov are in the reception room," Abdul said respectfully, despite a frosty stare from Patcha. He glared back at her; the depth of hate between the two was mutual and absolute.

Inside the reception room, famed international arms dealer and billionaire Kostas Alexopoulos addressed his guests. "Welcome once again to Villa Magnolia. Please be seated and take some tea," he proposed, indicating the same large chair with which the commander was familiar. As he collapsed into it Patcha offered Volcov one of her trademark icy stares.

"So, my dear Adham, this is where you're hiding," she scolded. "I trust you are recovering from your ordeal. Can we be sure you aren't just overreacting? Laura is only your niece after all!" she added, her cruel words reigniting painful memories.

Abdul stepped in intending to admonish the Mamasan of Thailand. "Why don't you sit down and try to behave like a guest in this house?"

"And if I don't?"

"Try to show some decorum especially if you don't want to incur the displeasure of your host! Think about that. But, if you are incapable of behaving in an acceptable manner, I suggest you wait in your car," Abdul warned, speaking quietly but in a measured tone. She saw the menace in his eyes and knew he was serious though, for a split second, she thought about defying him. Sucking in her breath, she walked over to sit next to Adham Volcov.

"Not there!" Abdul cried out. "Your place is next to Commander Kahir. Now, please be good enough to sit down!"

Clearly affronted, she complied while staring daggers at Abdul as if to say this is not the last you'll hear of this. The arrival of *chai shireen* broke the tense atmosphere. Asad Jaheel, a.k.a. Mike Harper presented glasses of the sweet tea in a moment of relative calm.

"What time will lunch be served?" a wide-eyed, wide-bodied commander queried, the sight of refreshments whetting his appetite. Not that he ever needed an excuse.

"Quite soon, commander. I have prepared a truly magnificent feast for your pleasure. I trust you will agree we should tackle that after we get the business formalities out of the way," Farez suggested slipping into his thespian role of Kostas Alexopoulos. "So, let's begin with you informing me what you require. By now you must have had me thoroughly investigated and are aware that I am the man to deal with. There is no-one else in the sensitive nuclear space if I might put it that way."

Grabbing the arms of her chair, Patcha interrupted. "Why should we trust you?" she demanded of Farez.

"Madam, I was always advised never to trust anyone until verifying their credentials. So, as you're here today, you must have done your homework. Now, what can I do for you? For my part, let me assure you I can supply anything you want. So, the next move is yours," he said in a tone that made it clear that Farez was playing his role with authoritative poise. Even Adham Volcov was inclined to smile at the growing frustration on the face of a woman who was unable to control proceedings.

After receiving a curt nod of approval from Patcha, Commander Kahir handed over a large buff envelope. "This is what we need," he said. Listed were two pages of nuclear components that Farez studied in silence before handing it to Abdul.

"Set the wheels in motion John. When you've done that, come and join us for lunch," Farez instructed now fully immersed in his role as an internal arms dealer.

Tariq was waiting in the operations room when Abdul entered and delivered the list. "I will open up a channel to the Pentagon right away."

Meanwhile, back in the reception room, Farez invited Patcha and Commander Zahir to follow him into the dining room. "By the time we finish lunch," he informed them, "I will be able to fulfil your requirements assuming we can agree on the price."

At the mention of food, Commander Kahir began to extricate himself from his armchair, this time unaided. Wheezing his way towards the dining room his nostrils picked up the smell of freshly cooked chicken. In two steps he was at the table and picking at food like a starving beggar.

*

The items conveyed to the Pentagon by Commander Zahir also included conventional weapons presumably required by Commander Kahir and the New Taliban. It was clear from the list of sensitive nuclear components the terrorists intended to construct a nuclear bomb and several dirty bombs that could be used to take out numerous targets at the same time. This suggested a plot on a grand scale and was seen by the Pentagon as a probable threat to the United States and the UK. Following a hastily arranged meeting, the department of defense officials moved to get the requests sanctioned at presidential level. Time was of the essence. The next most important move was to bait the hook by agreeing to comply with the terrorists' requests. They had committed themselves in writing so all that was required now was a sting operation to deliver the goods and arrest the villains at the time of the money-for-goods handover. These two villains were key players that the Pentagon wanted to apprehend. Catching them red-handed in a venue like Villa Magnolia constituted the perfect setting. The White House immediately sanctioned the strategic plan with a deadline to have the goods delivered in one week. Commander Tariq wrote down the instruction, placed it in an envelope and instructed Mike Harper to deliver it to Farez.

"Good news," Farez announced addressing Madam Patcha as Commander Kahir tore into his third chicken. "I can source everything on your list and have the goods delivered in a week's time. If you have the financial resources to meet my price then the goods are yours for the taking," he added looking at Madam Patcha whom he took for lead negotiator.

"Tell me Mr Alexopoulos, how much is it going to cost?"

Returning the original list of requirements, Farez said, "I have written an inclusive price at the foot of the list. It is non-negotiable. Take it or leave it madam," he said bluntly, but with a smile.

Patcha's complexion paled as she scrutinised the figure. At first it looked as though she was about to lodge an objection but held back. Then, with a deep sigh, she nodded. "Let's talk delivery: Where and when?"

"How soon can you raise the money?"

"Within two or three days," she said with confidence looking at Farez as if trying to detect some weakness in him. But he remained the inscrutable Kostas Alexopoulos famed for driving hard bargains but also keeping his word.

"Good, in that case let's say one week from today. We will make the exchange right here in Villa Magnolia. I expect to see both of you along with the money," he added.

"Why here?" Patcha asked. "Why not Villa Margalla? Isn't that where you normally reside," she asked of Adham Volcov. "What do you have to say Adham?"

"I have this to say: you asked for my help and now you have it," Volcov stated in a measured tone. "You have been introduced to Kostas Alexopoulos a man known to keep his word- unlike you Patcha. Apparently he can satisfy your shopping requirements. Now it's up to you to have the good grace to accept and show some gratitude towards him and to me."

Such were the calculated comments of a liberated Adham Volcov. For the first time in months he was beginning to feel confident buoyed by the stirring performance of Kostas Alexopoulos. Patcha looked deflated as did Commander Kahir though all he cared about was getting the weapons he required whatever the cost.

"Very well. One week from today…here in Villa Magnolia!" Patcha confirmed after considering her position and realising she could not control proceedings. It was a matter of supply and demand but in this case there was only one supplier and that placed the buyer at a distinct disadvantage, and she knew it. It was useless to push back; her best position was to secure the deal while it was still on the table.

"Excellent!" Farez responded. "I expect both of you to be here for the exchange," he said as a reminder knowing that the Pentagon wanted these two villains to be netted at the same time. "Be sure to keep your end of the bargain," he warned. "If I suspect you may go back on your word or are unable to raise the funds, I will instruct my sources to cancel your order. Keep that in mind," he added as Patcha nodded curtly and turned on her heel.

"Asad, would you please escort our guests out of the villa?" Farez requested immediately noticing massive disappointment on the face of Commander Kahir who had looked forward to finishing off the rest of the food hardly touched by the others. Abdul offered his arm to the commander, without commenting, and along with Mike Harper, steered him towards the waiting vehicle. When they returned they found Farez and Adham Volcov in the reception room eyeing each other like jubilant matadors. Unable to hold back any longer, all four burst out laughing just as Commander Zahir entered the room smiling broadly.

"Well done everyone, especially you Mister Alexopoulos," Tariq said, associating their outburst of laughter with opening a spigot to release their pent-up emotions. "I enjoyed every moment of your performance. I believe we are all anxious to know more about Madam Patcha's written demands. Mister Alexopoulos, what do you think?" he asked.

"I would claim it is clear from the list of requirements that they intend making a nuclear device. I also believe they intend making a number of dirty bombs that could be used in a limited way over a wide area with great effect. I assume this could result in the spread of radiation which could do more damage over time than the initial blasts. Making a nuclear weapon of even more sinister proportions suggests they have the scientific resources and have very large and important targets in mind."

The seriousness of Farez's assessment, even as a layman, took a moment to sink in before Commander Zahir commented. "From what I recall from our Pentagon briefings, we are talking about fissile, fissionable and source materials as the key ingredients of nuclear devices. Let me find my notes," he said, reaching for his notepad and flipping through the pages. "Yes, fissile materials are those composed of atoms that can be split by neutrons in a self-sustaining chain-reaction to release energy," he read aloud to an avid audience. "Fissionable materials are those in which the atoms can be fused to release energy while the source materials are those which are used to boost nuclear weapons," he added, closing his notepad.

"As we can all see," continued Farez, "the materials requested cover every aspect of all three materials for making nuclear devices. It seems therefore they are planning a nuclear attack." Again, the room fell silent.

Abdul's mind was working overtime. "With one week to deliver the goods, I wonder if the Pentagon has formulated a plan. Or, are they expecting suggestions from us?" He was trying to be tactful. He knew the Pentagon would expect to be asked about their ideas for moving forward, and he was also aware they were likely to defer to local knowledge.

Commander Zahir could read Abdul's mind and smiled suspecting the marine was already formulating a plan in his mind. "Patience brother," Tariq cautioned. "As I see it the Pentagon will have their hands full meeting the terms of this deal. I am sure they'll see we are in the best position to put together a handover plan. We don't have to decide right away. We will meet again tomorrow after we hear back from the Pentagon which I will contact immediately. Tomorrow we can pool our ideas."

It made sense. Abdul went off the find Laura to bring her up to speed with developments. He knew she would be keen to find out how her father had held up to the anticipated exchange with Patcha and Commander Kahir - something she had cautioned him about. Abdul smiled recalling the satisfaction on Adham Volcov's face when he put Patcha in her place. It had been a good day for the old man and a form of therapy. Could it be that positive developments late in Volcov's life had given him newfound strength? Maybe he was gaining the confidence needed to be true to himself and his daughter. If so, that would be a moment of great joy.

"Well, I did impress upon Laura my belief in miracles," Abdul mumbled to himself as he went in search of the woman with whom he wished to spend the rest of his life.

＊

Chapter Twenty-Two

There was a heightened air of tension in Villa Magnolia with everyone on tenterhooks as the moment approached for the highly anticipated "nuclear weapons-for-dollars" meeting. It would feature billionaire arms dealer Kostas Alexopoulos, representing the sellers, with Madam Patcha and her cohort Commander Kahir representing the buyers. Previous encounters pointed to the redoubtable Mamasan of Thailand acting as lead negotiator for the buyers. Patcha's accompanying Taliban commander, meanwhile, would be expected to play a minor role as his main focus is more about filling his belly rather than haggling over the price of nuclear weapons. Not that it makes a lot of difference as the asking price, according to Kostas Alexopoulos, is non-negotiable.

Feeling better each day about his personal situation, Adham Volcov had adopted the habit of venturing further and further from his sick bed. He felt more at peace having decided to face up to his own mortality. And the new, joyful relationship struck up with daughter Laura served to bring into focus his many wasted years. The implications of his criminal activities during earlier years had brought him much shame, but now he was determined to put matters right for whatever time he had left.

Volcov was also comforted by the thought that the man he knows as John Dwyer, of whom he's quite fond, will look after Laura come hell or high water. He had promised as much. As for the implacable Kostas Alexopoulos, here was a man for whom he had enormous respect. Despite their differences, Volcov treasured the strong bond of friendship existing between them. It was something he would treasure to his dying day.

Reflecting on his newfound lease of life, Volcov had an opportunity to live a dream previously out of reach; all due to the friendship he had encountered among friends at Villa Magnolia – together with the lifeline thrown his way by Uncle Sam. He was now able to understand and accept that Americans preferrd to work on a quid pro quo basis.

Gazing out of a bay window across villa gardens bathed in warm sunshine he smiled as he watched Laura playing with Sykes. Seconds later he was startled when Abdul appeared alongside him.

"Ah, so there you are John. I was watching Laura and thinking of both of you. I don't believe I thanked you enough for bringing her back to me. You showed faith in me and for the first time in my life I feel at peace," he explained through tears of joy.

"I am also pleased. Sir, I want to assure you that I will love and cherish Laura for ever."

"Of that I have no doubt my boy. For my part I only hope I have enough time to enjoy the freedom that comes with being an honest man," he said, offering a wry smile. "In truth I feel liberated and I don't want it to end. That must sound selfish," he added, continuing to watch Laura and Sykes at play.

Placing a hand on the old man's arm, Abdul counselled Volcov. "Please try to concentrate on living one day at a time sir. Your strength is returning and when we all get back to the States you will have all the protection you need and more support than you can handle. I am sure Uncle Sam will assist you in keeping close to those you have come to know as friends and who are willing, like me, to support you when the time comes. You have much to look forward to as I see it," Abdul added, doing his best to keep Volcov cheerful and relaxed. Going forward, he was mindful that Volcov's services were essential to the success of the mission.

"When that moment arrives John," he responded, smiling at his PA, "I look forward to finding out just who you are my boy – apart from being my guardian angel of course!"

Suddenly serious, Volcov drew Abdul closer. "Listen carefully John – I have an important task I would like you to do for me." Kostov said, pulling an envelope out of his back pocket.

"Of course, sir, just name it."

"As my appointed representative, please take this envelope to my solicitor in Islamabad and wait until he carries out my written instructions. When you get back, I wish to hold a meeting with you, Kostas Alexopoulos and Commander Zahir to explain what this is all about. I would like Laura to attend also."

Pocketing the envelope Abdul went in search of Commander Zahir to inform him of his planned visit to Islamabad.

"Take Mike Harper with you for added security," Tariq suggested. "We should assume that outside the villa perimeter we are probably under surveillance. So, we should exercise caution."

"Good point. I will bring Laura along so it looks like a shopping expedition. Harper can assume the role of 'Asad the Porter' and lend a hand with Laura's shopping items. Isn't that the normal outcome when a woman is invited to go shopping?" Abdul asked a mischievous grin spreading across his face.

*

The mock shopping spree went off without a hitch and Abdul left the solicitor's office with a black leather briefcase in hand, the subject of Volcov's important letter. Reunited with Laura the trio headed back to the villa and a prepared lunch in the gazebo. Farez, Commander Zahir and Adham Volcov were already seated.

After patiently waiting until everyone had finished eating, Volcov got to his feet. "Laura…dear friends, I have something I wish to share with you."

"In which case Adham," Farez interjected, "I suggest you resume your seat and relax. "After all, you are among family and friends," he added more out of concern for the man's still fragile condition.

"Thank you Kostas, I will do as you suggest," he acknowledged reaching for the small briefcase that Abdul had planted next to his boss's chair. "This small case contains important information regarding the meeting we had with Patcha a few days ago," he explained, handing it to Commander Zahir. "Commander, open the case if you please and tell me what you see inside?" He smiled as he said it.

Holding high a weighty binder, a puzzled Commander Zahir looked askance at Volcov as if asking: "What am I supposed to do with this?"

"Commander, you are holding a dossier that the American authorities will probably consider to be almost as important as the Declaration of Independence," he proclaimed elevating to bursting point the inquisitiveness of those present. In your hands are coded account summaries of financial enterprises encompassing Madam Patcha's terrorism activities going back years. The dossier contains names of black-market consultants including some holding senior posts in the U.S. and U.K. governments. Expense details with authorising signatures are included along with P and L accounts going back to 9/11."

It was a stunning revelation that temporarily curbed any response.

Stirred by the questioning looks on the faces of everyone in the gazebo, Volcov continued, "I can see you are wondering how I came to have it in my possession. I will explain: Over a period of time, Patcha displayed overconfidence in our relationship forcing me to declare her persona non grata in my household. I was always aware she was tricky and could turn on me one day. So, as a precaution, I got hold of her briefcase one day when she was out of the villa. It was unlocked by the way. These documents were inside. I made a copy of everything. What she hasn't noticed until now, otherwise I would have heard about it, is that her briefcase has the photocopies. You, commander, are holding the originals," he added, a smug expression on his face. It was a subtle ruse and in a single moment he had earned the respect and admiration of all present.

"These records," he said, "will lead the American authorities to arrest the key players and effect a clean-up of sleeper cells in the States and the U.K."

For a moment Commander Zahir was stumped for words as he tried to process Volcov's assertions. "Excellent thinking Adham and I am inclined to agree with you with respect to sleeper cells. Regarding our next encounter, we should take appropriate action just as soon as the handover is concluded, and the two villains are in custody."

"Quite so, commander. Then I'll rejoice in the knowledge that I was the one who helped put a rope around each neck," Volcov said scornfully.

The data contained in the dossier was pure dynamite, earning Volcov everyone's approbation, especially from Laura who stepped over to kiss her father on the cheek. "You have been very clever and done the right thing papa," she declared tears in her eyes. "And I am sure this will be enough to give you safe passage to America."

"All that matters is that we are together my dear daughter!"

*

Days after the lunch meeting with Commander Kahir and the Mamasan of Thailand, Commander Zahir had received feedback from the Pentagon. It was time to update the team. "Listen up please. Washington has sanctioned the handover operation," he announced to Abdul, Farez, Volcov and Mike Harper who had been summoned to the ops room at short notice. It was the go-ahead for which they had been waiting and hoping.

"The component parts will be delivered here to the villa three days from today. Two vehicles will carry the goods from Islamabad airport, driven by U.S. Marines disguised as Afghan airport workers, with others riding on board with the goods. The marines will bolster our contingent at Villa Magnolia,' the commander explained, "so I look to you Master Sergeant Harper to see to the preparation of suitable quarters. The new men will give you an opportunity to brush up your Pashto," he added with a smile.

"Marines will be strategically positioned outside the perimeter of the villa ready to intercept and neutralise any Taliban fighters detailed to accompany Commander Kahir and Madam Patcha. We must be prepared for any eventuality. This is our one and only opportunity to catch these villains and we must seize it with both hands."

True to form, Mike Harper had a question. "Commander Zahir, sir, is it really our intention to hand over nuclear components to terrorists?"

It was a fair question given the volatile and untrustworthy behaviour of the villains involved. "I am sure you all have similar concerns," the commander said. "Be very clear that it is our job is to make them believe we intend to deal fairly. We must conduct a genuine sale and purchase meeting. So, to answer the question…yes, we are here to trade nuclear parts for cash. Having said that, they must never be allowed to get away with the goods after we make the exchange. Picking the right moment to act is what we must address."

Not surprisingly, Adham Volcov found the response unsatisfactory. "Commander, if I may interject," he said, clearing his throat to speak. "Forgive me if I am stating the obvious but we are dealing with an unstable and highly dangerous individual in Madam Patcha. From my experience dealing with this vindictive woman I would say her left hand rarely knows what her right hand is doing! But she never backs down from a challenge. She will walk on hot coals to succeed because she never knows when she's beaten. And, most importantly, she cannot ever be trusted – not ever!" he yelled aloud.

Abdul could see Volcov was becoming distressed bringing to mind his recent, highly charged altercation with the Mamasan of Thailand involving Laura. "What are you suggesting sir?" Abdul asked moving closer to Volcov who was now the centre of attention.

"What I am suggesting gentlemen," he said addressing everyone, "is that Patcha can be very deceptive. She knows how to appear weak when you are strong, and she knows how to act strong when you are weak!"

"It sounds like you're quoting Su Tzu and the art of war," Abdul declared thinking back to his special ops training in the States.

"I am! And I am cautioning you all that she will use every trick in her playbook to take possession of the weapons and hold onto them. Then, when she feels you are at your weakest…when your guard is down…she will renege on the payment. I have known it to happen before. She is as cunning as a fox and trickier than a boatload of monkeys. Be warned!" Volcov stressed, bringing a wry smile to the weather-beaten face of Commander Zahir.

Also smiling, Abdul was inclined to agree. "From the few dealings I have had with her sir, I fully support the need to be cautious. It is something we must bear in mind now, during the handover, and afterwards."

"We can be sure of one thing," Commander Zahir interjected. "She, along with others, is planning a mass attack using nuclear weapons and we are supplying a dangerous woman with the very means to carry out such an attack. Think about that because it should weigh heavily on all our shoulders."

"Darn right!" Abdul proclaimed. "The nuclear components must never be out of sight at any time. As the merchandise will be here in three days we must start strategising now to make sure we cover every angle."

Farez, who had kept his thoughts to himself thus far, had something to add: "It is clear my friends that we must guard against being caught unawares by any of Madam Patcha's cunning manoeuvres. As I see it we have two known facts to work with: firstly, the weapons will arrive in three days and secondly we will be reinforced by a contingent of U.S. Marines. "Looking ahead to the day of the handover all four of us must be prepared to deal with Patcha and Commander Kahir and whoever else they bring along."

Volcov jumped to his feet. "Forgive me Kostas but there are five of us in this room!"

"That is so my friend but Commander Zahir cannot attend the meeting," Farez responded.

"But why not?" questioned a puzzled Volcov.

"Because Kahir would recognise Tariq immediately and...how do you say...the game would be up!"

Volcov continued to look puzzled and Farez was reluctant to be pressed. "Adham, let me assure you that these two warring commanders have a longstanding history of mutual dislike for one another. But we don't have time to go into that now."

Commander Zahir attempted to lighten the mood. "I must take this opportunity to assure all my brothers here today that I will be there at the kill! Nobody will deprive me of that opportunity," he added, drawing expressions of surprise and looks of confusion from the others.

Abdul deftly steered the conversation back to the handover meeting. "We will all be present at the handover apart from Commander Zahir. It makes sense that billionaire Kostas Alexopoulos leads our side as he has been advertised as the only source for nuclear components on the black market. It's worth bearing in mind that Patcha will view Mister Alexopoulos as an important source for similar purchases – at least for the duration of the meeting. It follows therefore that our adversaries will not wish to harm him from the get-go. They will most likely see this eccentric billionaire as an indispensable contact and therefore a friend not an enemy."

"But also keep in mind," countered Farez, "that Madam Patcha was soundly humiliated at our last meeting."

"That's correct, she was as mad as a box of frogs," recalled Abdul.

"In which case," Farez continued, "she will demand revenge, especially if she's the sort of woman Adham described. So, we must be alert to that possibility and watch her like a desert hawk," he added before raising the question of foul play. "Adham Volcov has painted a vivid picture of Madam Patcha's vindictive nature and therefore she cannot be trusted. We have to accept that she will try to take the weapons without paying. But, consider this: if she takes that course of action she loses the opportunity to deal with us again," he cautioned.

Commander Zahir forwarded an alternative possibility: "The terrorists' planned attack or attacks could be so catastrophic that Madam Patcha would be motivated by her own success and crave more spectacular events using weapons of mass destruction."

"In which case, my dear Tariq," interposed Farez, "allowing her to live would be a grave mistake on our part."

"Which leads us to an obvious conclusion gentlemen," Commander Zahir responded. "I believe we now have a clear understanding of what we are up against and the parts each of us must play. The handover meeting will take place five days from today. New men will arrive soon and the nuclear components in three days, so we have work to do. We will meet again for a final briefing in four days from now on the eve of the handover meeting.

"Think through everything we have discussed and raise any issues with me. We cannot afford any missteps now that the hounds are closing in on the fox or should I say foxes?" he said, drawing muted chuckles from the team.

Commander Zahir wasn't the only one who knew that the next five days would be critical to their success or failure. But everyone felt that the determination and confidence that had been forged by principled men would see them through. "Along with a little help from Allah the Merciful," Tariq muttered under his breath as he left the meeting.

**

Chapter Twenty-three

Anxious to meet with Commander Zahir and Farez Malikzai, Abdul arrived early at Villa Magnolia. Fortuitously, the commander was on hand to greet Abdul and, from his friend's body language, could tell that he had something on his mind. "Good morning brother. Is something troubling you?"

During the night, Abdul had tossed and turned as an idea formed in his head. It was so simple he couldn't understand why he had not thought of it before. "I wouldn't describe it as troubling, but it is something I must discuss with you and

Farez whilst it's still fresh in my mind. So, Tariq, where is our wise old sage this morning?" There was a touch of edginess in his tone.

"The old sage is right behind you," Farez countered, grinning broadly as he entered the reception room catching Abdul completely off guard, something this marine was unused to.

"What is the urgency brother? You are behaving like a camel herder whose precious herd suddenly disappeared into the desert," lamented Farez concerned for his friend's uneasiness.

Before Abdul could open his mouth to speak, Commander Zahir took hold of his arm, steered him towards a chair and bid him sit. "Take your time and unburden yourself. You have our full attention."

"I have a plan and it does not concern camels," Abdul said testily. "But I want to know what you think," he explained as he sat down eager to convey as much detail as possible.

After listening intently to Abdul, Farez turned to Commander Zahir. "This plan is so simple, it may just work. How do you see it brother?"

Deep in thought, Commander Zahir had got to his feet and stared out of a window. "I agree it is simple, even daring I would say. But it could succeed. We should outline this plan to the others right away." All three headed for the ops room to assemble the team.

*

Prompted by Commander Zahir, M.Sgt Mike Harper summoned the main members of the team.

"Settle down please and listen up," the commander said. "I have something important that relates to the next and possibly the most significant part of our mission."

316

Looking around at a sea of faces – including a contingent of newly-arrived marines - Commander Zahir detected an air of eagerness for action.

Commander Zahir explained that vehicles transporting nuclear components and a variety of firearms and ammunition were expected to arrive at Villa Magnolia after dark. "The Pentagon informed us that they had selected Pakistan's air force base Chaklala as the entry point," he added.

Most of the men present either knew or suspected that Chaklala boasted a permanent US military presence – mainly logistics personnel – thus the arrival of a US military aircraft was unlikely to attract much attention. Yet the airfield is only a kilometre or so from Islamabad international airport.

"I was informed that the US military utilises Chaklala on an informal basis," the commander continued. "Vehicles with fake cargo identification will arrive under darkness to avoid attracting attention especially from occupants of Villa Margalla. Drivers and everyone else in the vehicles will become part of our guard contingent, so I look to you Master Sergeant Harper to coordinate and brief the new arrivals."

The commander briefed the team on handover plans. "Commander Kahir and Madam Patcha will arrive here the day after tomorrow. I expect they will bring a backup team in the form of Taliban fighters. I will now turn to John Dwyer to outline the main elements of a plan he has formulated. I believe it's operational strength rests in its simplicity. That said, we only handover the nuclear cargo after a wire transfer of cash is undertaken and verified and that may not be as easy as it sounds."

A few of those present stared at the ground as if confused while others shuffled their feet. Facial expressions, some a picture of incredulity, demonstrated mounting uneasiness at the thought of handing over weapons of mass destruction to terrorists – whether paid for or not.

"You must have questions," the commander said playing down their concern, "but hold them until John Dwyer has run through details of the plan."

"Thank you commander," Abdul said getting to his feet. "I anticipate Commander Kahir will post Taliban fighters outside the villa gates and at other places at the perimeter. Over at Villa Margalla we can expect another contingent of guards. The first order of the plan is to overpower any Taliban fighters amassed outside the gates of Villa Magnolia. Surprise is essential and that's why the marines will be dressed in khet partug similar to the style worn by Taliban fighters. Meanwhile, inside the villa our guests will be entertained to lunch – a sumptuous lunch. That much will be expected by Commander Kahir.

"Now…take note…because this is the crux of the plan: we will stage an attack on ourselves within the confines of the villa grounds," he announced, pausing to let it sink in. "During the attack two marksmen will receive a signal from me to open fire. One marine will pick off Mr Adham Volcov, the other Mr Kostas Alexopoulos. Both will fall to the ground and play dead. Upper torsos will be targeted. Both men will be stationary so it will be impossible to miss. In any event the marines will fire blanks and the targets will be wearing Kevlar vests. The point is that it must look and feel real to onlookers such as Madam Patcha and Commander Kahir."

More expressions of incredulity appeared on each man's face.

"While our men are staging the mock battle with the attackers," Abdul continued, "I will usher Madam Patcha and Commander Kahir into one of the trucks and send them on their way. They will think they are getting away with the goods while leaving us – the good guys - at the mercy of an attacking force from outside." He paused because M.Sgt Harper had his arm raised.

"Just one question John. Do you intend to let them get away with the nuclear WMD?" Harper had become de facto spokesman on numerous occasions and his questions never surprised Abdul.

"Not in a million years master sergeant. Once we have them in the vehicle I will bolt the door from outside sealing them inside with the WMD," he confirmed. "Having positioned earlier, Commander Zahir will drive the truck and you, Master Sergeant Harper, will ride shotgun with him. You will head for the airfield and drive straight onto the loading ramp of a transport aircraft that will ship Patcha and Kahir to the good old U S of A with an armed guard all the way.

The delighted expression on Harper's face foretold his endorsement of the plan.

"With luck," Abdul continued, "everything will go without a hitch and no-one will get hurt except for some folk will have their overblown egos dented. The last thing Patcha and the commander expect is for us to be attacked in our own villa grounds - an unlikelihood that I hope will prove convincing to the terrorists.

"Now I suggest we discuss combat details. The marine contingent will act as attackers after overpowering the Taliban fighters outside our gates. The contingent accompanying the incoming vehicles will be aggressors within the compound. Two of you in this room, selected later by me, will bring down Volcov and Alexopoulos using blanks as explained. Make it look real. The remainder will take on the mob from Villa Margalla. They will not put up much resistance in my opinion," he added bringing proceedings to a close for the time being.

As everyone left the ops room, save for Abdul, Commander Zahir, Mike Harper, Farez and Adham Volcov, Farez offered an opinion. "I think that went quite well," he conceded, looking at Abdul. "I must say I am looking forward to my role playing a dead man," he added tongue in cheek.

Volcov was more direct. "An ingenious plan John, if I may say so. It should catch the evil Patcha off guard," he added smiling at the thought of Patcha being wrongfooted and embarrassed.

"I hope you are right; at least long enough for me to bundle her into a truck with her weapons of mass destruction," Abdul commented. "What I'd give a month's pay for, sir, is to see the expression on Commander Kahir's face when he comes face-to-face with the driver in the shape of Commander Zahir."

Commander Zahir was unrestrained in his enthusiasm. "That will be a great moment. We have waited a long time for retribution," he added delighted at the prospect of the element of surprise. He had waited in the wings a long time for such an opportunity and he intended to enjoy every moment of it.

"Didn't you say commander that you intended to be in on the kill?" queried Mike Harper. "But I would never have guessed how you could do it. I have a question: will we all jump ship when we hand them over at the airport?" As usual, Harper was a stickler for details.

"No way Mike," Abdul stated firmly. "We go back to the States with our cargo. I want to be sure our packages arrive Stateside safely and are handed over to the authorities. You, Mike, and everyone else will be finished here.

"This is what will happen: Laura will not join the lunch. She, with Sykes, will position ahead to Islamabad airport and wait on board Volcov's jet for her father and Kostas Alexopoulos to join her. They will head to the States. Everyone else will leave the villa in a second truck for Chaklala airfield to be airlifted out on a USAF transport aircraft. Our job will be finished; everything in Villa Magnolia will be disabled or destroyed leaving the place devoid of anything important."

Farez had listened intently. "So, our D-Day is the day after tomorrow," he said stating the obvious. "Therefore we have no time to waste gentlemen. But I have something I want to raise now," he added looking at Abdul. "In case you weren't aware, the commander's stallions are already at Chaklala airfield waiting to be transported to America. I trust your father will not object to two more horses and a small dog joining Atuallah at the ranch?" he asked to a boisterous outburst of support from all present.

***

Chapter Twenty-four

An air of suspense hung over everything and everyone in Villa Magnolia. The day of reckoning had arrived, and everyone knew the role they must play, and the inherent risks involved. For brothers-in-arms Abdul, Farez, and Tariq it marked the culmination of months of effort to bring to justice at least two unscrupulous dealers in death and destruction. They were anxious to draw a line under the whole sordid business and get on with their lives.

Brimming with confidence, Commander Tariq entered the ops room at 1000 hours to deliver a final briefing to the team. He was met with a sea of anxious faces.

"I bid you all good morning. This is the day we have waited for, prepared for. With positive karma…and Allah's help…" he added with a smile, "…we will prevail and soon be home with those we love and cherish. That said, I want you to listen carefully to John Dwyer as he goes through the plan for one last time."

All eyes were on Abdul, who was also exuding confidence safe in the knowledge that the final plan was as good as he could make it. He paused briefly to reflect on Tariq's words: nobody was more anxious to go home than Abdul. He had much to catch up on and a new life ahead of him. But that had to wait.

"Thank you Commander Zahir. Make a note everyone that our guests will be here at 1230. A meal has been planned as soon as pleasantries are over. While everyone is eating, two trucks will be positioned to the front of the villa ready for inspection by our guests. One truck will have an assortment of armaments, the other nuclear material. Madam Patcha and Commander Kahir will be invited to inspect the merchandise and commit to paying the buyer's fee by bank transfer. After that is completed satisfactorily, Master Sergent Harper will take the laptop into the villa and undergo a wardrobe change to assume the appearance of a Taliban fighter. Then, Mike," Abdul said to Harper, "you should standby to board the truck carrying the nuclear components, but only after our two guests are persuaded to board the vehicle through the rear doors. Commander Zahir will drive that truck and you, Mike, will ride shotgun.

"I will drive the second truck with Jack Cummings alongside. We will pick up whoever is left standing from Villa Margalla and put them in the back of our truck. At Chaklala airfield we will hand them over to the military for processing.

"The marines who drove the trucks, along with marines that arrived earlier and who will be outside the gates of the villa, will follow us to the airfield in another vehicle that is parked at the back of this villa. The rest of you will join us and the prisoners on the transport plane back to the States. Until we touch down on American soil and discharge our obligations consider yourselves on active duty. Is that clear?"

Abdul did not wait for an answer. "Take nothing for granted. Madam Patcha is a wily adversary and a force to be reckoned with. Always take her seriously and keep in mind she would blow herself up, taking us with her, rather than face justice in the States." Nods and grunts of agreement assured Abdul that the message had been received and understood.

"Okay, now listen up: showtime kicks off the moment I hand the laptop to Master Sergeant Harper and he heads for the villa. That is when a shot will ring out and Adham Volcov will fall to the ground. A second shot will result in Mr Alexopoulos hitting the ground – dead. Both of you," Abdul emphasised looking at Volcov and Farez in turn, "must lay face down and play dead. Stay like that until we have Patcha and Kahir locked in the truck and the other contingent from Villa Margalla is rounded up and put into the second truck. Then both of you will be taken to Islamabad airport to board your private jet for the flight home. Clear? Good! Laura will already be there. The next time we meet will be on home ground. Any questions?"

To Abdul's surprise it was Farez and not Mike Harper who sought clarification, "What about Villa Magnolia…don't you think the Taliban will search it from top to bottom when they cotton on to what's going on?"

"Good question. We plan to destroy any evidence that would be of use to them. All sensitive equipment will be removed hours after our departure by a team from Bagram Air Base. They will return to Bagram right after they've finished. I think that's about it, Commander Zahir," Abdul concluded before sitting down and taking a sip of water.

There were no further questions. Everyone was deep in thought each assessing their role and calculating the odds of success. Commander Zahir had similar thoughts. "I suggest you prepare for what I anticipate will be a most successful final day at Villa Magnolia. Keep to the plan…stay safe, and good luck to all of us."

The briefing group disbanded apart from Farez, Adham Volcov, Commander Zahir, Abdul and Mike Harper.

Commander Zahir tapped the shoulders of Farez and Adham Volcov. "You must follow the plan to the letter. No heroics please."

Slightly irked, the old malik responded, "Please stop worrying. I intend to follow orders. Like my friend Adham Volcov I am anxious to return to my family. Both of us have much to live for." Farez smiled at Volcov. Abdul was certain that both men would play their roles with distinction.

Adham Volcov went a step further. "I intend to enjoy every moment I have with my daughter and with all of you, my dear friends."

"One final reminder; do not forget your Kevlar vests," Commander Zahir said. "We will be using rubber bullets, but you must be seen to be protecting yourself because the marines will join the fray in an attacking role against us as part of the action to convince Patcha and Kahir it is not a stunt. If we don't convince them we won't be able to get them into the back of the truck as planned." The ops room emptied; there was much to prepare.

Abdul ached to see Laura before she left for the airport. He found her in the garden with Sykes. His heart quickened as he approached her. "So, here's where you're hiding." She looked concerned.

"You seem to be deep in thought," he suggested as Sykes, uninhibited, threw himself at Abdul.

"I am very worried John. What if it doesn't go to plan. What if my father, you, or anyone for that matter gets hurt, or killed?" Her concern was real. Abdul felt the same but wanted to steer her towards a more positive scenario.

"What if the sun fails to rise tomorrow Laura," he said smiling. "I believe it will as I believe in our plan," he insisted as he gently took her in his arms and kissed her.

"I give you my solemn promise that everything will turn out well. I want you to put your trust in me."

They stood looking at one another for what seemed like an age. Laura knew she had to do what the man she loved directed and Abdul saw it in her eyes. Along with Sykes, she decided she'd wait patiently on board the jet and, if nothing else, would pray for a successful outcome. The thought made her smile. "John, I will set my prayer wheel to max revs until I see you and father at the airport."

"That's the spirit. And now you must say your farewells to your father. You and Sykes will be driven to the airport and Mike Harper will be with you. Imagine you're on a shopping trip to Islamabad, like before," he added. "Time to get a move on because Mike must be back before our guests arrive for lunch."

*

Right on time, the vehicle carrying Madame Patcha and Commander Kahir pulled up at the entrance to Villa Magnolia. Abdul checked his watch. It was 12.30 p.m. Can't fault them for punctuality, he thought.

Hastily pushing Abdul to one side, Patcha burst through the door where Adham Kostov and Kostas Alexopoulos - a.k.a. Farez Malikzai - were patiently waiting.

"Welcome to Villa Magnolia," Farez proclaimed, arms outstretched. Kindly follow me to the reception room for refreshments."

Commander Kahir became alarmed. "Refreshments!" he exclaimed mouth wide open. "Forget refreshments I am expecting to be served lunch," he declared, eyes glowing at the thought of tackling a chicken or two. The air was rich with the attractive odours of turmeric, cumin, and curry powder. He drooled at such a blissful thought.

Farez had anticipated the big man's reaction. "Please calm yourself commander. As we speak chef is preparing a magnificent Pakistani curry lunch for you and Madame Patcha. Meanwhile, please make yourself more comfortable," he suggested, guiding the stout figure towards an extra-large chair. The sarcasm was not missed by others in the room.

Patcha was less patient and not the slightest bit interested in Kahir's need for sustenance. "Tell me, Mr Alexopoulos, is the merchandise here and ready for inspection?"

"That I can confim. And you will be invited to inspect the merchandise once the financial arrangements are in place." It was said with a smile but in a manner Patcha would know she was dealing with a weathered businessman, someone who had cut his teeth on international deals. And someone whose acting prowess came to the fore though she would never know that. He just loved being the centre of attention.

"What are you suggesting?" Patcha asked impatiently.

"Insisting...not suggesting. Madam, I require a telegraphic transfer of funds from your account to mine. Much more preferable than dealing in notes I'm sure you agree." Again, it was said in a measured tone that exhibited his distrust in the Mamasan of Thailand.

"My man is waiting outside the villa gates. He will bring a laptop when you are ready, and we will complete the transaction to my satisfaction," Patcha confirmed, her demeanour far from friendly.

"That is quite understandable. I suggest you direct your colleagues to come inside the villa and wait in the courtyard. That will make the transfer more convenient."

It was unclear why Patcha had chosen to leave her escort party outside the gates, but Farez wanted them where everyone could see them. And bringing them inside would be a goodwill gesture on the part of Patcha. Without hesitation, she went outside and signalled for her contingent to enter the grounds.

Farez was satisfied. "Now that we understand one another, we can move to the dining room for lunch. Later, you may inspect the merchandise and, once satisfied, the transfer of funds can start."

With the prospect of food in the offing, Commander Kahir extricated himself from his chair and set course for the dining room. As the big man advanced purposefully across the floor, sniffing the spice-laden air, Farez mused that this could be the last meal the overweight Taliban chief might enjoy. It was a comforting thought for the village headman turned arms dealer.

*

True to form, Commander Kahir made an exhibition of himself sucking every morsel of food from his teeth. With a contented sigh, he leant back in his chair and flashed a grease-sodden smile at fellow diners. His infatuation with irresistible Pakistani curries, especially chicken, had not gone unnoticed. He capped off proceedings with a loud belch that resonated throughout the villa. Chef, alone, appreciated the candid gesture.

Accepting the commander's display of satisfaction to be an end marker for lunch, Farez turned to Patcha. "If you would like to inspect the merchandise, please follow me." Everyone followed.

Outside, in the bright sunshine, Farez surveyed the courtyard. Six men drafted in from Villa Margalla were at the far end of the courtyard along with six marines disguised as houseboys each one strategically positioned and ready for action.

With a discrete nod from Farez, Abdul approached the first truck loaded with an assortment of weapons. Both Patcha and Commander Kahir stepped into the rear of the vehicle for a short while. They nodded briefly at Abdul as they emerged, clearly satisfied.

Meanwhile, Farez and Adham Kostov had taken positions at the rear of the vehicles. They were ready for the final act.

By now Patcha and the commander had arrived at the second truck, the one with the nuclear WMD. Abdul opened the door. "Please take all the time you need," he said, standing aside.

Five minutes later Patcha emerged smiling broadly. Farez stood at the door. "I am impressed Mr Alexopoulos. It is all there as promised."

"Good, I always aim to please," he responded with a slight bow of the head as M. Sgt Mike Harper stepped forward to hand Abdul a laptop. Patcha beckoned to one of her men who stepped forward with another laptop. The telegraphic exchange was initiated.

With the transfer completed, Patcha handed her laptop to her man who left to join the others in Patcha's contingent. Mike Harper stepped forward and took the laptop from Abdul and started to walk back to the villa. Abdul moved closer to Patcha who had her back to the truck's rear doors as if guarding her merchandise. The commander was still on board the vehicle. "That will make life easier," Abdul said to himself.

Two shots rang out and, as planned, Farez and Adham Volcov dropped to the ground and lay still face down. Marines disguised as Taliban fighters staged their mock attack on the occupants of Villa Magnolia.

Initially, Madame Patcha was stunned, then enraged when Abdul accused her of staging the attack. Caught off guard she screamed her innocence but took his advice and boarded the vehicle to protect the precious merchandise which was now her property.

Abdul slammed shut and locked the truck's rear doors as Commander Kahir reached for his sidearm. Too late; Abdul had removed it earlier. Commander Zahir was already in the driver's seat when Mike Harper leapt in beside him. Amidst gunfire, the truck careered out of the villa at speed.

Abdul joined the other marines who had secured six of Patcha's men in the rear of the second truck. Jumping into the driver's seat he grinned at Jack Cummings already in the passenger seat. They tore off in hot pursuit of the first truck.

The plan was holding together. Helped by marines, Farez and Adham Volcov got to their feet and were guided towards other vehicles, engines running, to transport the villa's remaining staff. It was a moment that signalled victory and Farez and Volcov exchanged looks of relief, and joy, as they left Villa Magnolia at high speed for Islamabad airport.

The residue of marines boarded their vehicle and sped off in hot pursuit of the two trucks holding the cargo – human and nuclear! A well-planned manoeuvre had gone off without a hitch.

*

Laura could hardly contain her delight when her father and Farez stepped onto the plane. Not sure if Champagne was appropriate, or available, Laura celebrated the occasion with a glass of fruit punch. Minutes later their private jet was airborne and heading west.

Laura had one more question. "Tell me, Mr Alexopoulos, what about John. Is he all right?"

"He is fine and by now should be at Chaklala air base."

Adham Volcov seized the opportunity to voice his concern - sarcastically. "And, dear Laura, I hope one day soon to be introduced to the real man behind John Dwyer!" He gazed purposefully at Farez as he said it.

Allowing the comment to pass over his head, Farez simply answered with a smile before turning to clink glasses with his fellow passengers. It had been an interesting day. Sykes would agree; he was already asleep.

*

After a few kilometres, Patcha became suspicious. She began beating on the vehicle bulkhead and shouting angrily. Commander Zahir smiled. "Ignore the noise, master sergeant. I'm sure it's nothing more than frustration." In his wing mirrors he could see the second truck had fallen in behind. Everything was going according to plan. To Commander Zahir, it also confirmed that Adham Kostov and Farez would be on their way to the airport and safety.

"An excellent outcome, sir, if I may say so. No blood spilt and the rats held fast in the trap. Commander, I do believe I will remember this mission for the rest of my days."

Commander Zahir smiled. "I think my lingering memory, Mike, will be the look on the face of Commander Kahir when we come face to face again in a short while. I have waited a long time for that moment and, like you, it will be something to remember for the rest of my life."

Master Sgt Mike Harper stared at the weathered fighter sitting beside him. He could not help wondering what made the man so determined to take down Commander Kahir. It had to be personal. One day he might find out. Whether or not he did, he would always have the utmost respect for this battle-hardened warrior.

It was clear to anyone in the company of those Harper had come to know as John Dwyer, Kostas Alexopoulos and Commander Zahir, that they were joined by an unbreakable bond. Harper acknowledged and appreciated their professionalism and, if offered the opportunity, would work with them again in a heartbeat. Therefore, it was not hard for the master sergeant to accept that there could never be a finer, more qualified ambassador than Commander Tariq Hasan Zahir to represent Afghanistan in Washington D.C.

"Do you have something on your mind master sergeant?" the commander teased. "You are notably quiet. I thought you would have hundreds of questions for me." Commander Zahir regarded the marine as a formidable and trustworthy soldier. Someone he could depend on under battlefield conditions when the odds were not in your favour and time was of the essence. Such men were exceedingly rare.

Harper smiled. "I am beginning to regret that this mission will soon be over. We will all go our separate ways. It has been a pleasure working under you commander. Life for me will never be the same. Bitter-sweet outcome if you get my meaning sir."

"Permit me to respond this way: I will repeat to you what John Dwyer said to me when I expressed similar concerns. He said 'Brother Tariq, nothing is over until the fat lady sings.' I did not comment at the time, because I have absolutely no idea what a fat lady who sings has to do with this mission. But I assume you understand. I would just add that good men like you are hard to find. Therefore, I hope our parting is going to be one of farewell and not goodbye." It was a gesture that M. Sgt Mike Harper took to heart.

Inside the perimeter of Chaklala airfield, a convoy of vehicles surrounded their truck and escorted them to the transport aircraft. Tariq switched off the truck's engine. A glance at his wing mirror revealed armed marines gathering at the rear, waiting for Abdul's truck to arrive.

Disembarking, Abdul and Jack Cummings strode towards Commander Zahir's vehicle. Abdul gave a thumbs up to Tariq who was watching events through the truck's wing mirror. Abdul unbolted the rear door and stood back alongside Jack Cummings. A furious Patcha emerged, blinking in the strong sunlight. Confused and angry, she stared daggers at Abdul who held his ground, a wide grin on his face.

"What game are you playing. And who are you?" she demanded of Abdul. "I always knew you couldn't be trusted," she said, "but that old fool Adham Volcov thought otherwise. Never listened to me. He and you are both obsessed by Volcov's damn niece. Well, now he is dead – got what he deserved. And hopefully you will be next," she hissed through clenched teeth.

The Mamasan of Thailand was beside herself with grief; not only because she had lost control of the situation, but also because Commander Kahir was pushing her to one side to be heard. "I want to know who is responsible for this abduction," he shouted.

He didn't have long to wait as Commander Zahir joined Abdul and Jack Cummings. "Greetings Commander Kahir. It seems we are destined to meet yet again!"

Commander Kahir was dumbfounded. He froze, unable to comprehend what was happening.

"Abducting both of you was my idea," Commander Zahir said without hesitation. "And you can consider yourselves under military arrest for crimes not just in Afghanistan but also in America. Both of you will be tried in the United States for your crimes. And it will be my duty and pleasure to make sure you are incarcerated until you receive your just rewards. And that will be at the end of a rope if I have anything to do with it."

Patcha looked defiantly at Commander Zahir, while Commander Kahir's eyes glazed over. He became hysterical with a mix of anger and fear of what lay ahead. "You...how do you come to be here? I thought you were an ambassador!"

He was still jabbering away under a cloud of self-pity as he and Patcha were clasped in irons and frogmarched onto the plane where they were unceremoniously dumped into a double-celled cage. By now the contingent of marines had boarded and were seated around the cage which they would guard throughout the flight. Dejected, Patcha had slunk into a corner. Kahir was still talking to himself, trying to understand just what had taken place.

Commander Zahir placed a hand on Abdul's shoulder. "Well done brother. This was a well-conceived and well-executed mission. Everyone involved deserves recognition for their part and I intend to speak up in my role as an ambassador to the United States as soon as I get to Washington."

"In the marines we just call this a team effort Brother Tariq. But I do accept that it went as well as we could expect. Now, Mister Ambassador," he said with a slight bow of the head, "if you don't mind, we must get this crate airborne and head for the United States. It's time to go home!"

***

Printed in Poland
by Amazon Fulfillment
Poland Sp. z o.o., Wrocław

65939314R00188